ARCHANGEL'S KISS

Nalini Singh

BERKLEY SENSATION, NEW YORK

THE BERKLEY PUBLISHING GROUP
Published by the Penguin Group
Penguin Group (USA) Inc.
375 Hudson Street, New York, New York 10014, USA
Penguin Group (Canada), 90 Eglinton Avenue East, Suite 700, Toronto, Ontario M4P 2Y3, Canada
(a division of Pearson Penguin Canada Inc.)
Penguin Books Ltd., 80 Strand, London WC2R 0RL, England
Penguin Group Ireland, 25 St. Stephen's Green, Dublin 2, Ireland (a division of Penguin Books Ltd.)
Penguin Group (Australia), 250 Camberwell Road, Camberwell, Victoria 3124, Australia
(a division of Pearson Australia Group Pty. Ltd.)
Penguin Books India Pvt. Ltd., 11 Community Centre, Panchsheel Park, New Delhi—110 017, India
Penguin Group (NZ), 67 Apollo Drive, Rosedale, North Shore 0632, New Zealand
(a division of Pearson New Zealand Ltd.)
Penguin Books (South Africa) (Pty.) Ltd., 24 Sturdee Avenue, Rosebank, Johannesburg 2196,
South Africa

Penguin Books Ltd., Registered Offices: 80 Strand, London WC2R 0RL, England

This is a work of fiction. Names, characters, places, and incidents either are the product of the author's imagination or are used fictitiously, and any resemblance to actual persons, living or dead, business establishments, events, or locales is entirely coincidental. The publisher does not have any control over and does not assume any responsibility for author or third-party websites or their content.

ARCHANGEL'S KISS

A Berkley Sensation Book / published by arrangement with the author

PRINTING HISTORY
Berkley Sensation mass-market edition / February 2010

Copyright © 2010 by Nalini Singh.
Excerpt from *Bonds of Justice* by Nalini Singh copyright © by Nalini Singh.
Cover art by Tony Mauro.
Cover design by George Long.
Cover hand lettering by Ron Zinn.
Interior text design by Kristin del Rosario.

ISBN: 978-0-425-23336-8

BERKLEY® SENSATION
Berkley Sensation Books are published by The Berkley Publishing Group,
a division of Penguin Group (USA) Inc.,
375 Hudson Street, New York, New York 10014.
BERKLEY® SENSATION and the "B" design are trademarks of Penguin Group (USA) Inc.

PRINTED IN THE UNITED STATES OF AMERICA

10 9 8 7 6 5 4 3 2 1

PRAISE FOR THE NOVELS OF
NALINI SINGH

Angels' Blood

"It is amazing in every way!!!"
—*New York Times* bestselling author Gena Showalter

"This is probably one of the best stories I have ever read and will be one that I will rave about for quite a while. Not only was the world just completely awe-inspiring, but the characters and the story line are evocative and a pure pleasure to read."
—*Fallen Angel Reviews*

"Amazing. Fantastic. Darker than her Psy-Changelings, simmering with both violence and sexual tension, and with vivid world building that blew my socks off."
—National bestselling author Meljean Brook

"Incredibly original and beautiful." —*Errant Dreams Reviews*

"A refreshing twist on vampire and angel lore combined with sizzling sexual tension make this paranormal romance a winner."
—*Monsters and Critics*

"A fantastically, amazingly, good read and it gets the Guild Hunter series off to a great start . . . If you like paranormal romance, you want to read this book." —*Love Vampires*

"Wonderful . . . A great read with a very yummy archangel that you won't want to miss."
—*Night Owl Romance* (reviewer top pick)

"Nalini Singh's Guild Hunter series is a fabulous addition to the paranormal world . . . A definite must read." —*Fresh Fiction*

"A fully nuanced and startling story from start to finish . . . Nalini Singh should take a bow! *Angels' Blood* is going to leave you hungering for more instantly." —*Romance Junkies*

"Fans will relish Nalini Singh's excellent first Guild Hunter thriller." —*Midwest Book Review*

continued . . .

Branded by Fire

"An emotional masterpiece."   —*Romance Junkies*

"Another superb entry in what is easily my favorite paranormal series in romance."   —*Romance Novel TV*

"Singh has a rare talent for impressive world building, intricate plotting, and riveting characterization . . . Singh delivers excellence every single time!"   —*Romantic Times* (top pick)

"An amazingly talented writer . . . she grabs the reader and doesn't let go until the very end and leaves them begging for more . . . I give *Branded by Fire* and Nalini an enthusiastic 5 hearts."
—*Night Owl Romance*

Hostage to Pleasure

"Singh is on the fast track to becoming a genre giant!"
—*Romantic Times* (top pick)

"Nalini Singh has penned another keeper . . . If you want a thrilling read with action, danger, passion, and drama, don't miss Nalini Singh's *Hostage to Pleasure*."   —*Romance Junkies*

"An intriguing world that's sure to keep readers coming back for more."   —*Darque Reviews*

Mine to Possess

"Fierce . . . Paranormal romance at its best." —*Publishers Weekly*

"With its intense characters, story line, and scenery, *Mine to Possess* is quite a read. It showcases Singh's talent and shows her to be a writer that will no doubt shine for some time."
—*Romance Reader at Heart*

"If you've been looking for a book that will entice and entrance, look no further. The very talented Nalini Singh has yet again proven that her books are gems, true treasures that are intriguing, multifaceted creations that just get better and better . . . Don't miss *Mine to Possess*!"   —*Romance Reviews Today*

Caressed by Ice

"A fast-paced, edge-of-your-seat romantic paranormal that will pull you straight into the story and into the amazing Psy-Changeling world!"   —*Romance Reader at Heart*

"The paranormal romance of the year."   —*Romance Junkies*

"Craving the passionate and electrifying world created by the mega-talented Singh? Your next fix is here! . . . One of the most original and thrilling paranormal series on the market . . . Mind-blowing!"   —*Romantic Times* (4½ stars, top pick)

Visions of Heat

"Breathtaking blend of passion, adventure, and the paranormal. I wished I lived in the world Singh has created. This is a keeper!"
        —*New York Times* bestselling author Gena Showalter

"This author just moved to the top of my auto-buy list."
        —*All About Romance*

"Brace yourselves because the second installment of the Psy-Changeling series will set all your senses ablaze and leave your fingers singed with each turn of the page. *Visions of Heat* is that intense!"   —*Romance Junkies*

Slave to Sensation

"I LOVE this book! It's a must read for all of my fans. Nalini Singh is a major new talent."
        —*New York Times* bestselling author Christine Feehan

"An electrifying collision of logic and emotion . . . An incredible world where fire and ice mix to create an unforgettable sensual eruption. *Slave to Sensation* is a volcanic start to a new series that'll leave you craving more."   —*Romance Junkies*

"AWESOME! . . . A purely mesmerizing book that surely stands out among the other paranormal books out there. *Slave to Sensation* is captivating from beginning to end. It's a must read for any paranormal fan!"   —*Romance Reader at Heart*

Acknowledgments

This book was so much fun to write, not the least because of the wonderful response I received from readers for *Angels' Blood*. Thank you for taking a chance on this new series—and for the e-mails, the letters, and most of all, the smiles you bring into my life.

Special thanks to Tiazza for her help with the Moroccan Arabic; Helen and Pamela for the French pointers; and Travis for the tips (no pun intended) on different types of blades. They all know their stuff. Any mistakes are mine.

A huge, huge thank-you to my parents for being all-around amazing while I was on deadline, and to my sister for the insanity that keeps me sane. Same goes for my friends in RWNZ and online. You all rock. A deeply felt thanks to Hari Aja for your wonderful support of my work.

And last but never ever least, everyone at the Knight Agency and at Berkley Sensation, most especially my agent, Nephele Tempest, and my editor, Cindy Hwang, for all that you do, and all that you make it possible for me to do. You two aren't allowed to retire. Ever.

Genesis

Drip.

Drip.

Drip.

"Come here, little hunter. Taste."

Blood in the air, on the walls, under her feet. "Ari?"

"Ari's having a nice nap." A giggling laugh that made her want to run, run, RUN! "Mmm, I think I prefer Belle." A red-dipped finger lifted to her mouth, pressed against her lips.

Blood seeping onto her tongue.

Her sister's blood.

That was when she screamed.

1

Elena gripped the balcony railing and stared down at the gorge that fell away with jagged promise beneath. From here, the rocks looked like sharp teeth, ready to bite and tear and rip. She tightened her hold as the icy wind threatened to tumble her into the unforgiving jaws. "A year ago," she murmured, "I didn't know the Refuge existed, and today, here I stand."

A sprawling city of marble and glass spread out in every direction; its elegant lines exquisite under the razor-sharp burn of the sun. Dark-leafed trees provided soothing patches of green on both sides of the gorge that cut a massive divide through the city, while snow-capped mountains ruled the skyline. There were no roads, no high-rises, nothing to disturb the otherworldly grace of it.

Yet, for all its beauty, there was something alien about this place, a vague sense that darkness lurked beneath the gilded surface. Drawing in a breath laced with the biting freshness of the mountain winds, she looked up . . . at the angels. So many angels. Their wings filled the skies above this city that seemed to have grown out of the rock itself.

The angelstruck, those mortals who were literally enthralled by the sight of angelic wings, would weep to be in
this place filled with the beings they worshipped. But Elena
had seen an archangel laugh as he plucked the eyes out of a
vampire's skull, as he pretended to eat, then crush the pulpy
mass. This, she thought with a shiver, was not her idea of
heaven.

A rustle of wings from behind her, a squeeze from the powerful hands on her hips. "You're tiring, Elena. Come inside."

She held her position, though the feel of him—strong, dangerous, uncompromisingly masculine—against the sensitive
surface of her wings made her want to shudder in ecstasy. "Do
you think you have the right to give me orders now?"

The Archangel of New York, a creature so lethal that
part of her feared him even now, lifted the hair off her nape,
brushed his lips across her skin. "Of course. You are mine."
No hint of humor, nothing but stark possession.

"I don't think you've quite got the hang of this true love
thing." He'd fed ambrosia into her mouth, changed her from
mortal to immortal, given her wings—*wings!*—all because of
love. For her, a hunter, a mortal . . . no longer mortal.

"Be that as it may, it's time you return to bed."

And then she was in his arms, though she had no memory of having released the railing—but she must have,
because her hands were filling with blood again, her skin
tight. It hurt. Even as she tried to ride out the slow, hot burn,
Raphael carried her through the sliding doors and into the
magnificent glass room that sat atop a fortress of marble
and quartz, as solid and immoveable as the mountains
around them.

Fury arced through her bloodstream. "Out of my mind,
Raphael!"

Why?

"Because, as I've told you more than once, I'm not your
puppet." She grit her teeth as he laid her on the cloud-soft
bedding, the pillows lush. But the mattress held firm under
her palms when she pulled herself up into a sitting position.

"A lover"—God, she could still barely believe she'd gone and fallen for an archangel—"should be a partner, not a toy to manipulate."

Cobalt eyes in a face that turned humans into slaves, that sweep of night-dark hair framing a face of perfect grace . . . and more than a little cruelty. "You've been awake exactly three days after spending a year in a coma," he told her. "I've lived for more than a thousand years. You're no more my equal now than you were before I Made you immortal."

Anger was a wall of white noise in her ears. She wanted to shoot him as she'd done once before. Her mind cascaded with a waterfall of images on the heels of that thought—the wetly crimson spray of blood, a torn wing, Raphael's eyes glazed with shock. No . . . she wouldn't shoot him again, but he drove her to violence. "Then what am I?"

"Mine."

Was it wrong that sparks sizzled along her spine at hearing that, at seeing the utter possession in his voice, the dark passion on his face? Probably. But she didn't care. The only thing she cared about was the fact that she was now tied to an archangel who thought the ground rules had changed. "Yes," she agreed. "My heart is yours."

A flash of satisfaction in his eyes.

"But nothing else." She locked gazes with him, refusing to back down. "So, I'm a baby immortal. Fine—but I'm also still a hunter. One good enough that you hired me."

Annoyance replaced the passion. "You're an angel."

"With magic angel money?"

"Money is no object."

"Of course not—you're richer than Midas himself," she muttered. "But I'm not going to be your little chew-toy—"

"Chew-toy?" A gleam of amusement.

She ignored him. "Sara says I can walk back into the job anytime I want."

"Your loyalty to the angels now overwhelms your loyalty to the Hunters Guild."

"Michaela, Sara, Michaela, Sara," she murmured in a

mock-thoughtful voice. "Bitch Goddess angel versus my best friend, gee, which side do you think I'll choose?"

"It doesn't matter, does it?" He raised an eyebrow.

She had the feeling he knew something she didn't. "Why not?"

"You can't put any of your plans in action until you can fly."

That shut her up. Glaring at him, she slumped back against the pillows, her wings spread out on the sheets in a slow sweep of midnight shading to indigo and darkest blue before falling into dawn and finally, a brilliant white-gold. Her attempt at a sulk lasted approximately two seconds. Elena and sulking had never gone well together. Even Jeffrey Deveraux, who despised everything about his "abomination" of a daughter, had been unable to lay that sin at her feet.

"Then teach me," she said, straightening. "I'm ready." The ache to fly was a fist in her throat, a ravaging need in her soul.

Raphael's expression didn't change. "You can't even walk to the balcony without help. You're weaker than the fledglings."

She'd seen the smaller wings, smaller bodies, watched over by bigger ones. Not many, but enough.

"The Refuge," she asked, "is it a place of safety for your young?"

"It's everything we need it to be." Those eyes of purest sin shifted toward the door. "Dmitri comes."

She sucked in a breath as she felt the temptation of Dmitri's scent wrap around her in a glide of fur and sex and wanton indulgence. Unfortunately, she hadn't gained immunity to that particular vampiric trick with her transformation. The flip side was also true. "One thing you can't argue with—I can still track vampires by scent." And that made her hunter-born.

"You have the potential to be of real use to us, Elena."

She wondered if Raphael even knew how arrogant he sounded. She didn't think so. Being invincible for more years than she could imagine had made that arrogance part of his nature . . . But no, she thought. He could be hurt. When hell broke and an Angel of Blood tried to destroy New York, Raphael had chosen to die with Elena rather than abandon her broken body on that ledge high above Manhattan.

Her memories were cloudy, but she remembered shredded wings, a bleeding face, hands that had held her protectively as they descended to the adamantine hardness of the city streets below. Her heart clenched. "Tell me something, Raphael?"

He was already turning, heading to the door. "What is it you'd like to know, Guild Hunter?"

She hid her smile at his slip. "What do I call you? Husband? Mate? Boyfriend?"

Stopping with his hand on the doorknob, he shot her an inscrutable look. "You can call me 'Master.' "

Elena stared at the closed door, wondering if he'd been playing with her. She couldn't tell, didn't know him well enough to read his moods, his truths and lies. They'd come together in an agony of pain and fear, pushed by the specter of death into a union that might have been years in the making had Uram not decided to turn bloodborn and tear a murderous path through the world.

Raphael had told her that according to legend, only true love allowed ambrosia to bloom on an archangel's tongue, to turn human to angel, but perhaps her metamorphosis owed nothing to the deepest of emotions and everything to a very rare biological symbiosis? After all, vampires were Made by angels, and biological compatibility played an integral part in that transformation.

"Damn it." She rubbed the heel of one hand over her heart, trying to wipe away the sudden twist of pain.

"You intrigue me."

He'd said that at the start. So perhaps, there was a component of fascination. "Be honest, Elena," she whispered, running her fingers over the magnificent wings that were his gift to her, "you're the one who fell into fascination."

But she would not fall into slavery.

"Master, my ass." She stared at the foreign sky outside the balcony doors and felt her resolve turn iron-hard—no more waiting. Unlike if she'd still been human, the coma hadn't wasted away her muscles. But those muscles had gone through a transformation she couldn't imagine—everything felt weak, new. So while she didn't need rehab, she did need exercise. Especially when it came to her wings. "No time like the present." Lifting herself up into a proper sitting position, she took a deep, calming breath . . . and spread out her wings.

"Christ, that hurts!" Teeth gritted, tears leaking out of the corners of her eyes, she kept stretching the unused, unfamiliar muscles, folding her new-formed wings in slowly before expanding them outward. Three repetitions later and the tears had soaked into her lips until the salt of them was all she could taste, her skin covered by a layer of perspiration that shimmered in the sunlight streaming in through the glass.

That was when Raphael walked back in. She expected an explosion, but he just took a seat in a chair opposite the bed, his eyes never leaving her. As she watched, wary, he hooked one ankle over a knee, and began to tap a heavy white envelope bordered with gilt against the top of his boot.

She held his gaze, did another two stretches. Her back felt like jelly, her stomach muscles so tight they hurt. "What's"— a pause to draw breath—"in the envelope?"

Her wings snapped shut behind her, and she found herself leaning against the headboard. It took her several seconds to realize what he'd done. Something cold unfurled within the core of her soul even as he got up and dropped a towel on the bed, then retook his seat. No fucking way was this going to keep happening.

However, in spite of the turbulent fury of her anger, she wiped off her face and kept her mouth shut. Because he was right—she wasn't his equal, not by a long shot. And the coma had messed her up some. But as of now, she was going to work on those shields she'd started to develop back before becoming an angel. There was a chance that—given the changes in her—she could learn to hold them for longer.

Forcing her rigid shoulder muscles to loosen, she picked up a knife she'd left on the bedside table and began to clean the pristine blade with the edge of the towel. "Feeling better?"

"No." His mouth firmed. "You need to listen to me, Elena. I won't hurt you, but I can't have you acting in ways that bring my control over you in question."

What? "Exactly what kind of relationships do archangels have?" she asked, genuinely curious.

That made him pause for a minute. "I know of only one stable relationship now that Michaela and Uram's is broken."

"And the Bitch Goddess is another archangel, so they *were* equals."

A nod of his head that was more thought than movement. He was so damn beautiful that it made thinking difficult, even when she knew he possessed a vein of ruthlessness that was sewn into the fabric of his very soul. That ruthlessness translated into a furious kind of control in bed, the kind that made a woman scream, her skin too tight across a body that knew only hunger.

"Who are the other two?" she asked, swallowing the spike of gut-deep need. He'd held her since she woke, his embrace strong, powerful, and at times, heartbreakingly tender. But today, her body craved a far darker touch.

"Elijah and Hannah." His eyes glittered, turning to a shade she'd once seen in an artist's studio. *Prussian*. That's what it was called, Prussian blue. Rich. Exotic. Earthy in a way she'd never have believed an angel to be until she found herself taken by the Archangel of New York.

"You will heal, Elena. Then I will teach you how angels dance."

Her mouth dried up at the slumbering heat in that outwardly calm statement. "Elijah?" she prompted, her voice husky, an invitation.

He continued to hold her gaze, his lips at once sensual and without pity. "He and Hannah have been together centuries. Though she's grown in power over time, it is said that she's content to be his helpmeet."

She had to think for a while about that old-fashioned expression. "The wind beneath his wings?"

"If you like." His face was suddenly all hard lines and angles—male beauty in its purest, most merciless form. "You will not fade."

She didn't know if that was an accusation or an order. "No, I won't." Even as she spoke, she was vividly conscious that she'd have to use every ounce of her will to maintain her personality against the incredible strength of Raphael's.

He began tapping that envelope again, the action precise, deliberate. "As of today, you're on a deadline. You need to be on your feet and in the air in just over two months' time."

"Why?" she asked, even as delight bubbled through her bloodstream.

Prussian blue froze into black ice. "Lijuan is giving a ball in your honor."

"We're talking about Zhou Lijuan, the oldest of the archangels?" The bubbles went flat, lifeless. "She's . . . different."

"Yes. She has evolved." A hint of midnight whispered through his tone; shadows so thick they were almost corporeal. "She's no longer wholly of this world."

Her skin prickled, because for an immortal to say that . . . "Why would she hold a ball for me? She doesn't know me from Adam."

"On the contrary, Elena. The entire Cadre of Ten knows who you are—we hired you after all."

The idea of the most powerful body in the world being interested in her made her break out in a cold sweat. It didn't help that Raphael was one of them. She knew what he was capable of, the power he wielded, how easy it would be for him to cross the line into true evil. "Only nine now," she said. "Uram's dead. Unless you found a replacement while I was in a coma?"

"No. Human time means little to us." The casual indifference of an immortal. "As for Lijuan, it's about power—she wants to see my little pet, see my weakness."

2

His pet. His weakness.

"Her words or yours?"

"Does it matter?" A negligent shrug. "It's true."

She threw the knife with deadly accuracy. Raphael caught it in midair—by the blade. His blood flowed scarlet against the gold of his skin. "Was it not you who bled the last time?" he asked conversationally as he dropped the knife to the formerly pristine white carpet and tightened his hand into a fist. The blood flow halted within a single second.

"You made me close my hand over a blade." Her heart was still racing from witnessing the sheer speed of him. Dear God. And she'd taken this man to her bed. Craved him even now.

"Hmm." He rose to his feet, walked to her.

At that moment, though he'd said he'd never hurt her, she wasn't so sure. Her fingers clenched on the sheets as he came to sit in front of her, one of his wings lying over her legs. It was a warm, surprisingly heavy weight. Angel wings weren't for show—as she was beginning to learn, they were pure muscle and tendon over bone, and like any other muscle, they had to be strengthened prior to use. Before, she'd only had to worry about tripping if she overtired herself. Now, she had to worry about falling out of the sky.

But that wasn't the danger that danced in front of her eyes right then.

No, all she saw was blue.

Never before Raphael had blue meant the color of sin, of seduction. Of pain.

He leaned in, brushed her hair from her neck with fingers that could bring pleasure so excruciating it hurt . . . and pressed a kiss to the ragged beat of her pulse. It made her shiver, and she found she'd tangled her hands in his hair. He kissed her again, causing the warmth in her stomach to uncoil with lazy grace through her body, demand in every slow pulse.

When something glittered at the edge of her vision, she realized he was covering her in angel dust, a decadent, delicious substance that mortals paid enormous amounts to possess. But Raphael had a special blend just for her. As she breathed in the motes, the seduction intensified, until all she could think of was sex, the ache in her wings, even her anger, forgotten.

"Yes," he whispered against her mouth. "I think you'll intrigue me through eternity."

It should've shattered the moment, but it didn't. Not when there was such erotic promise in his eyes, in the tone of his voice. She found herself trying to draw him closer, but his jaw tightened. "No, Elena. I'll break you." A blunt statement. A truth. "Read this." Dropping the envelope onto the sheet, he rose, those magnificent wings of white—every filament tipped with luminous gold—flaring out to dust her in ecstasy.

"Stop that." Her voice was breathy, her mouth filled with the hotly masculine taste of him. "When will I be able to do that?"

"It's an ability that develops over time, and not every angel gains it." He folded back his wings. "Perhaps in four hundred years' time, you'll know."

She stared. "Four hundred? Years?"

"You're immortal now."

"How immortal?" It wasn't a stupid question. As she'd learned too well, even archangels could die.

"Immortality takes time to grow—to set—and you're barely formed. Even a strong vampire could kill you right now." Tilting his head slightly to the side, he turned his attention to the sky beyond the glass he'd told her was reflective, affording her privacy to study the Refuge without worrying about being watched in turn.

"It seems the Refuge is a popular place today." With that, he strode to the balcony doors. "We must go to this ball, Elena. To do any less would be a sign of fatal weakness." Closing the doors behind himself, he spread his wings and took off in a straight vertical flight.

Elena gasped at the unintentional show of strength. Now that she'd felt the weight of the wings at her back, she'd realized the extraordinary nature of Raphael's vertical takeoffs. As she watched, he swept in front of the balcony and away. Her heart was still pounding from the combination of his kiss and the display of aerial brilliance when she finally glanced down at the envelope.

The fine hairs on her arms stood up the instant she grazed the thick white paper with her fingertips. The sensation was eerie—as if the envelope had been somewhere so cold, it wouldn't warm up, no matter what. Some would call it the chill of the grave.

Goose bumps broke out over her skin.

Shaking them off, she turned the envelope over. The seal had been broken, but she could see the image once she lined up the edges. An angel. Of course, she thought, unable to stop staring at it. It was inked in black but why that should disturb her, she didn't know. Frowning, she brought it closer to her face.

"Oh Jesus." The whisper rippled out of her as she glimpsed the secret hidden within the image. It was an illusion, a trick. Looked at one way, the seal was a kneeling angel, his head bowed. But change your focus and that angel stared directly at you, his eye sockets empty, his bones bleached white.

She's no longer wholly of this world.

All at once, Raphael's words took on an entirely new meaning.

Shuddering, she lifted the flap and removed the card inside. It was heavy cream-colored stuff, reminding her of the expensive note cards her father used in his personal correspondence. The writing scrolled across in antique gold. She rubbed her finger over it—why, she didn't know—it wasn't as if she could sense whether it was real gold or not. "Wouldn't surprise me though." Lijuan was old, so old. And an ancient being of power could amass a great deal of wealth over a lifetime.

Funny, but though she thought of Raphael as powerful, she'd never thought of him as ancient. There was a sense of life about Raphael that denied that. A sense of . . . humanity? *No.* Raphael wasn't human, wasn't anything close to human.

But he wasn't like Lijuan.

Her eyes went to the card again.

I invite you to the Forbidden City, Raphael. Come, let us welcome this human you have embraced. Let us see the beauty of this connection between immortal and what was once mortal. I find myself fascinated for the first time in millennia.
~ Zhou Lijuan

Elena didn't want to fascinate Lijuan. In fact, she wanted nowhere near the rest of the Cadre of Ten. She was pretty sure most of the time that Raphael wouldn't kill her. But as for the others . . . "Oh, hell."

My little pet.

My weakness.

She might despise the words, but that made them no less accurate. If the Archangel of New York really did love her, then she might as well be wearing a target on her back.

Again she saw him, face bloodied and torn, wings shredded, an archangel choosing death over eternal life. It was a
truth she'd never forget, a truth that anchored her even as everything else in her world shifted and changed.

"Not everything," she murmured, reaching for the phone.
Because while this place might look as if it existed in some
long-ago age of chivalry and grace, the amenities were cutting-
edge. Unsurprising when you thought about it—angels didn't
survive eons by clinging to the past. New York's Archangel
Tower, with its cloud-piercing form, was the perfect example.

As the phone rang on the other end, she found herself staring out through the balcony doors, searching for the magnificent being who ruled that Tower, the one she dared call her
lover.

The ringing stopped. "Hello, Ellie." A raspy voice, followed by an audible yawn.

"Crap, I woke you." She'd forgotten the time difference
between wherever the hell she was and New York.

"It's okay—we crashed early. Hold on." Rustling sounds,
a click, and then Sara was back on the line. "I've never seen
Deacon go back to sleep that fast—though he did mutter
something that sounded vaguely like 'Hi, Ellie.' I think our
baby girl wore him out today."

Elena smiled at the thought of Sara's "scary son-of-a-
bitch" of a husband being run ragged by little Zoe. "Did I
wake her?"

"Nah, she's wiped out, too." A whisper. "I just peeked. Going into the living room."

Elena could easily visualize Sara's surroundings, from the
elegant sofas in a caramel shade that brought warmth inside,
to the large black-and-white portrait of Zoe on the wall, her
giggling face covered with bath foam. The gorgeous brown-
stone was more home to Elena than any other place except her
own apartment. "Sara, my apartment?" She hadn't thought to
ask during Sara's visit to the Refuge two days ago, her mind
too full of the chaos of dying . . . and waking up with wings
of midnight and dawn.

"Sorry, babe." Sara's voice held the painful echoes of memory. "After . . . everything, Dmitri blocked off access. I was more interested in finding out where they'd put you, so I didn't push too hard."

The last time Elena had seen her apartment, it had had a huge hole torn out of one wall, blood and water everywhere. "I don't blame you," she said, burying the hurt that stabbed into her at the thought of her haven being shut up, her treasures broken and lost. "Hell, you probably had more than enough on your plate." New York had gone pitch-dark during the archangel-to-archangel battle, power lines destroyed and pylons overloading as Uram and Raphael both pulled power from the city below.

It hadn't only been the electrical grid that had become collateral damage in the cataclysmic battle between two immortals. Her mind showed her a snapshot of crumbled buildings, crushed cars, and the twisted blades that meant at least one heliport had suffered severe damage.

"It was bad," Sara admitted, "but the majority of the damage has been repaired. Raphael's people organized it all. We even had angels doing construction work—that's not a sight you see every day."

"Guess they didn't need the cranes."

"Nope. I never knew how strong angels were until I saw them lift up some of those blocks." A pause filled with an unspoken depth of emotion that gripped Elena by the throat. "I'll go by your apartment tomorrow morning," Sara finally said, her voice rigidly controlled, "let you know what's what."

Elena swallowed, wishing Sara was here again so she could reach out and hug her best friend. "Thanks, I'll tell Dmitri to make sure his hench-people know you're coming." In spite of her attempt to not let it matter, she couldn't help but wonder if any of her keepsakes, the little things she'd collected on her trips as a hunter, had survived.

"Hah! I can take on hench-people with one hand tied behind my back." A thready laugh. "God, Ellie, I get this wave of relief every time I hear your voice."

"You'll be hearing it for a lot longer now—I'm immortal," she joked, not yet able to truly comprehend the enormity of the change in her life. Hunters in the field died young. They didn't live forever.

"Yeah. You'll be around to watch over my baby and her babies long after I'm gone."

"I don't want to talk about that." It made her heart ache to imagine a future without Sara, without Ransom, without Deacon.

"Silly girl. I think it's wonderful—a gift."

"I'm not so sure." She told Sara what she'd been thinking in regard to her value as a hostage. "Am I being paranoid?"

"No." Now, the other woman sounded like the hard-assed Guild Director she was. "That's why I packed Vivek's special gun in the bag of weapons on its way to you."

Elena's fingers curled into her palm.

The last time she'd used that weapon, Raphael had bled endless red on her carpet, and Dmitri had almost slit her throat. But none of that, she thought, uncurling her fingers one by one, diminished the value of a weapon meant to disable wings, not when—her gaze went to the skies beyond the window—she was surrounded by immortals in a place that whispered of things no human was supposed to know. "Thanks. Even if you did get me into this in the first place."

"Hey, I made you filthy rich, too."

Elena blinked, tried to find her voice.

"You forgot didn't you?" Sara laughed.

"I was too busy being in a coma," Elena managed to choke out. "Raphael paid me?"

"Every last penny."

It took her a second to realize what that meant. "Wow." The deposit had been more money than she could've hoped to make in a lifetime. And it had been a mere twenty-five percent of the total. "I think 'filthy rich' might be an understatement."

"Yeah. But you did complete the job he hired you to do, which I'm guessing had something to do with that fight with Uram?"

Elena bit her lip. Raphael had been explicit in his warning about all information connected to the sadistic monster who'd killed and tortured so many—any mortal she told would die. No exceptions. Perhaps that had changed now, but she wasn't going to chance her best friend's life on the faith of a relationship she barely understood. "I can't tell you, Sara."

"You'll tell me all these other secrets but not this one?" Sara didn't sound pissed, she sounded intrigued. "Interesting."

"Don't go digging that way." Elena's stomach pitched as her mind put on a nausea-inducing slideshow of the horror that had been Uram. That last room . . . the stench of rotting flesh, the gleam of blood-soaked bone, the slimy pulp of the eyes he'd dug out of a dying vampire's skull.

Steeling her spine against the bile burning the back of her throat, she tried to imbue her voice with the depth of her worry. "It's bad news."

"I don't have a death wis—ah, Zoe's awake." Maternal love filled every syllable. "And look at that, so is Deacon. Zoe's daddy wakes to her slightest cry, doesn't he, sweetie pie?"

Elena drew in a cleansing breath, the loving images created by Sara's words banishing those of Uram's depravity. "I think you guys are getting more sickening with each day."

"My baby's almost one and a half now, Ellie," Sara whispered. "I want you to see her."

"I will." It was a promise. "I'm going to learn to use these wings if it kills me." Her eye fell on Lijuan's invitation as the words left her mouth, death closing a skeletal hand around her throat.

3

However, a week after her conversation with Sara, Elena found herself thinking not of death but of vengeance. "I knew you were into pain, but I didn't know you were a sadist," she said to Dmitri's back, her bones melting into the luscious heat of the isolated hot spring the damn vampire had all but carried her to—after pounding her ass to dust in a training session meant to toughen her muscles.

Turning, he focused the full power of those dark eyes on her, eyes that could tempt an innocent into sin, a sinner into hell itself. "When," he murmured in a voice that spoke of closed doors and broken taboos, "have I ever given you reason to doubt me?"

Fur stroked over her lips, between her legs, along her back.

Her skin tightened in response to the potency of his scent, a scent that was an aphrodisiac to one of the hunter-born, but she didn't back down, well aware he was enjoying having her at such a complete disadvantage. "Why are you here? Shouldn't you be in New York?" He was the leader of Ra-

phael's Seven, a tight-knit group of vampires and angels who
protected Raphael—even against threats he might not yet
see.

Elena was deathly certain that Dmitri would execute her
with ice-cold precision should he come to consider her too big
a chink in Raphael's armor. Raphael might kill the vampire
for it, but as Dmitri had once said to her—she'd still be dead.
"Surely some little groupie's crying her heart out over you."
She couldn't help but think of that night in the vampire wing
of the Tower—Dmitri's head bending over the supple neck of
a ripely curved blonde whose pleasure had scented the air in
a sensual perfume.

"You break my heart." An insincere smile, the amusement
of a vampire so old, his age was a heavy weight on her bones.
"If you're not careful, I'm going to start thinking you don't
like me." Stripping off his thin linen shirt without blinking—
and there was snow on the ground up here for crissakes—he
went to the top button of his pants.

"You planning to die today?" she asked conversationally.
Because Raphael would rip out Dmitri's heart if the vampire
touched her. Of course, it'd be hard for the archangel to do
that—she'd have already cut it out. Dmitri might be able to
taunt her body to keening need with that scent of his, but
Elena wasn't about to be compelled. Not by this vampire. And
not by the man he called sire.

"It's a big pool." He pulled off his pants.

She caught a glimpse of one sleekly muscled flank before
she closed her eyes. Well, she thought, conscious of the heat
blazing across her cheeks, at least that cleared up all doubts
as to his coloring—Dmitri wasn't tanned. The exotic honey of
his skin was inborn . . . and flawless.

A wash of water that announced his entry into the pool.
"You can look now, hunter." Pure mockery.

"Why would I want to?" Opening her eyes, she turned
her gaze toward the breathtaking mountain vista instead.
Hunters weren't prudes, but Elena chose her friends with
care. And when it came to people she was comfortable

being naked with—being vulnerable with—that list was even shorter. Dmitri was in no way, shape, or form in that group.

As she focused on the snow-capped peaks in the distance, she kept an eye on him with her peripheral vision. Not that she'd survive him if he came after her, not given her current physical state, but that was no reason to make herself an easy target. *Fur and diamonds, sex and pleasure.* The scents wrapped around her, a thousand silken ropes, but they were muted. It was his gaze that worried her right then—that of a predator sizing up prey.

It took almost a minute before he shrugged and dropped back his head, his arms braced on the rocky edge of the natural pool. He was, she was forced to admit as she glanced back, sexy as the most wicked of indulgences. Dark eyes, dark hair, a mouth that promised pain and pleasure in equal measures. But she felt nothing beyond a reluctant female appreciation. Blue was her addiction and her salvation.

A tendril of darkest chocolate wrapped around her.

Rich. Compelling. In no way muted.

She hissed through her teeth. "Turn it off." Her body grew tight, her breasts swelling with a need as raw as it was unwanted.

"I'm relaxing." Irritation coated in masculine arrogance—not exactly surprising given who Dmitri called sire. "I can't do that if I have to control an integral part of my body."

Before Elena could reply to an assertion she wasn't sure she believed, a feather of heavenly blue edged in silver floated into the water in front of her. It reminded her of another day, another feather, Raphael's hand opening to drop silver blue dust to the ground as possession glittered in his eyes. Using the memory to fight the sensual impact of Dmitri's scent, she focused on the distinctive sound of wings settling behind her. "Hello, Illium."

The angel walked around to sit on the snow-dusted rim to her right, dipping his legs into the water, jeans and all. In fact, like many of the angelic males in the Refuge, that was all he wore, his muscular chest naked to the sun's rays. "Elena." He looked from her to Dmitri with those breathtaking eyes of inhuman gold. "Something I should know?"

"I've threatened to kill him for the ten thousandth time," Elena shared, closing her hand hard around a rock on the rim. Its edges dug into her palm as she fought the compulsion to go to Dmitri, to lick up his scent until it was all she was, all she knew. The vampire mocked her with his gaze, a silent challenge. No matter the sexual pull, this wasn't about sex. It was about her right to be at Raphael's side. "And he beat me to a pulp by proxy," she completed, her voice steady though her body was screaming with arousal.

"In some circles," Illium murmured, black hair tipped with blue lifting in the breeze, "that would be considered foreplay."

Dmitri smiled. "Elena doesn't care for my brand of fore-play." Memories of blood and steel in his eyes. "Though she did—"

The scent of the sea, a wild turbulent storm, crashing into her mind. *Elena, why is Dmitri naked?*

The surface of the pool began to ice over.

"Raphael, no!" she said out loud. "I am not going to give him the pleasure of watching me freeze to death!"

That, I would never allow. The ice retreated. *It seems I must have a discussion with Dmitri.*

She forced herself to think to him, though it was far more instinctive to speak; her heart, her soul, were still unalterably human. *No need. I can deal with him.*

Can you? Never forget that he's had centuries to hone his power. A soft warning. *Push him too far and one of you will die.*

She didn't misunderstand. *Like I said, Archangel, don't kill anyone on my account.*

The response was a cool breeze, the stamp of an immor-tal's possession. *He is the leader of my Seven. He is loyal.*

She'd already guessed what he didn't say—that Dmitri's loyalty might equal her death. *I'll fight my own battles.* It was who she was, her sense of self tied intrinsically to her ability to stand on her own two feet.

Even if you have no hope of winning?

I told you once, I would rather die as Elena, than live as a shadow. Leaving him with that truth—a truth that would never change, no matter her immortality, Elena returned her attention to Dmitri. "You forget to tell Raphael something?"

Shrugging, the vampire shot a speaking glance to her right. "If I was you, I'd worry more about his blue hide."

"I think Illium can take care of himself."

"Not if he keeps flirting with you." A fine, almost elegant tendril of heat, champagne and sunshine, decadence in the light. "Raphael's not the sharing kind."

She pinned him with her eyes, attempting to ignore the twisting warmth in her stomach, a warmth he was fanning very deliberately. "Maybe you're just jealous."

Illium snorted with laughter as Dmitri's own eyes narrowed. "I prefer to fuck women who aren't covered in prickles."

"I'm so brokenhearted about that that I can't put it into words."

The force of Illium's laughter almost tumbled him into the water. "Nazarach's arrived," he finally managed to say to Dmitri—even as he ran a strand of Elena's hair through his fingertips. "He wants to talk to you about the extension of a Contract as punishment for an escape attempt."

Dmitri's face betrayed nothing as he rose from the water with an inherently sensual grace. This time, Elena kept her eyes open, refusing to lose the silent battle of wills. His body was a sweep of smooth sun-kissed skin over pure muscle, muscle that flexed with power as he began to pull on his pants.

His eyes met hers as he zipped them up, diamonds and fur and the unmistakable musk of raw sex wrapping around her throat like a necklace . . . or a noose. "Until next we meet." The scent faded. "Let's go." It was directed at Illium, the tone one of command.

Elena wasn't the least surprised when Illium rose to his feet and left with a simple good-bye. The blue-winged angel might mess with Dmitri, but it was clear that he—like the rest of the Seven, the members she'd met at least—would follow him without question. And for Raphael, each and every one would lay down his life in the blink of an eye.

The water rippled away from her in the wash of wind caused by an angel's landing.

The scent of the sea, the rain, clean and wild on her tongue.

She felt her skin go taut, as if it was suddenly too small to contain the fever within. "Come to tease me, Archangel?" His scent had always spoken to her hunter senses, even before they became lovers. Now . . .

"Of course."

But when she turned her head to meet his gaze as he came to crouch on the rim, what she saw made her breath catch in her throat. "What?"

Reaching forward, he pulled out the plain silver hoops in her ears. "These are now a lie." He closed his hand and when it opened it again, silver dust fell to sparkle on the steaming water.

"Oh." Unadorned silver was for the unattached—male or female. "I hope you have replacements," she said, turning—her wings wonderfully waterlogged—so she could brace her arms on the ledge and face him. "Those were from a market in Marrakesh."

He opened his other hand and a different pair of hoops shimmered back at her. Still as small, still as practical for a hunter, but a beautiful, wild amber. "You are now," he said, putting them in her ears, "well and truly entangled."

She stared at the ring finger of his hand, possessiveness a raging storm inside of her. "Where's your amber?"

"You haven't made a gift of it yet."

"Find a piece to wear until I can get you something." Because he wasn't free, wasn't open to invitation from those who would sleep with an archangel. He belonged to her, to a hunter. "I wouldn't want to get blood on the carpet killing all those simpering vampire floozies."

"So very romantic, Elena." His tone was clear, his expression unchanged, but she knew he was laughing at her.

So she splashed him. Or tried to. The water froze between them, a sculpture of iridescent droplets. It was an unexpected gift, a glimpse into the heart of the boy Raphael must've once been. Reaching out, she touched the frozen water . . . only to find it wasn't frozen. Wonder bloomed. "How're you keeping it like this?"

"It's a child's trick." The breeze flirted with his hair as the water settled. "You'll be able to control such small things when you're a little older."

"Precisely how old am I in angel-speak?"

"Well, our twenty-nine-year-olds tend to be considered infants."

Lifting her hand, she ran her fingers down the rigid line of his thigh, her stomach tight with expectation. "I don't think you see me as an infant."

"Correct." His voice had dropped, his cock brutally hard against the tough black material of his pants. "But I do think you're still recovering."

She looked up, her body slick with welcome. "Sex is relaxing."

"Not the kind of sex I want." Calm words, white lightning in those eyes, a reminder that this was the Archangel of New York she was trying to tempt into wickedness.

But she hadn't survived him the first time by giving in. "Come in with me."

He rose to his feet and circled around until he was at her back. "If you watch me, Elena, I might break my promises to both of us."

She would've turned anyway, unable to resist the temptation that was the gut-wrenching masculine beauty of him, but then he said, "It would be so easy for me to hurt you."

For the first time, she realized she wasn't the only one who was dealing with something new, something unexpected. Staying in place, she listened to the dull thud of his boots hitting the snow, the intimate whisper of his clothes sliding off his body. She could see the corded strength of his arms and shoulders in her mind, her fingers aching to stroke the ridged plane of his abdomen, the muscular length of his thighs.

Her own thighs clenched as the water lapped around her, disturbed by a body far bigger and stronger than her own. She held her breath as he came closer, until he braced his hands against the rock on either side of her. Spreading out her wings so he could press against her back, she sucked in a breath. "Raphael, that's not helping matters."

The heat of his cock pulsed against her skin, a living brand, even as her wings arrowed sensation straight to the liquid-soft core of her body. An instant later, his lips touched her ear. "You torture me, Elena." Teeth closing over her flesh, a none too gentle bite.

She yelped, the sound high, startled. "What was that for?"

"I've been celibate for over a year, Guild Hunter." One big hand boldly cupped her breast, his fingers strong, unmistakably male against her flesh. "Need is rubbing on my temper."

"What, you didn't sink your cock into a vampire honey while I was out?"

Raphael pinched her nipple just hard enough to let her know she'd crossed a line. "You think so little of my honor?" Ice hung in the air.

"I'm jealous and frustrated," she said, reaching back to press her palm against his cheek. "And I know I look like shit." While vampires past their first few decades of life were beyond stunning, their skin unblemished, their bodies sleek. Very few humans ever came close to sleeping with an angel— they were simply outclassed.

Raphael skimmed his hand down her side. "It's true you've lost a little weight, but I still want to fuck you mindless."

4

Her brain blanked for several seconds. When she could speak, it came out a breathy moan. "You're trying to kill me."

A squeeze of her breast, the skin so tight the pleasure was almost pain. "It's a much better form of punishment than tearing you limb from limb."

"Can't have sex with a dead woman, huh?"

"Precisely."

Flames licked along her spine as he stroked both hands downward, sweeping his thumbs over the taut flesh of her buttocks. "Half the time, I'm not certain if you're being serious or not."

His fingers paused in their sensual torment. "Are you sure you wish me to know that? It's a weakness."

"Someone's got to take the first step." Lifting her foot, she ran it up behind his calf.

A kiss pressed to the beat of the pulse in her neck. "Such honesty will not serve you well among angelkind."

"What about with you?"

"I'm used to utilizing what I know to maintain power."

Elena leaned her chin on her hands, letting him ease the knots along the edges where her wings grew out of her back. It felt exquisite—so good she knew she'd never let another man touch her there, even in friendship. It would be a betrayal. "You're being pretty honest yourself."

"Perhaps between us," he said slowly, as if considering the matter, "it may not be a weakness but a strength."

Surprised, she turned her head. "Really? Then tell me something about yourself."

He pressed his thumb into a particularly tight spot and she moaned, dropping her head onto her hands. "Lord have mercy."

"It's not the Lord you should be asking for mercy." His tone held a possessive undercurrent that was becoming intimately familiar. "What would you like to know?"

She picked the first thing that came into her mind. "Are your parents still alive?"

Everything froze. The temperature of the water dipped so fast, she gasped for breath, her heart kicking out in panic. "Raphael!"

"Again, I must apologize." A breath of heat against her neck, the water warming until her skin was no longer in danger of turning corpse-blue. "Who have you been talking to?"

The water might've warmed, but his voice remained an Arctic breeze. "No one. Asking about parents is a fairly normal activity."

"Not when it's my parents you're asking about." He pressed his body flush against hers, his arms coming around her waist.

She had the strangest feeling he was seeking comfort. It was such an odd thought to have about a being who held within him a power so vast, she could scarcely comprehend it, but she didn't hesitate to put her arms around his, trusting him to hold her upright in the water. "I'm sorry if I opened old wounds."

Old wounds.

Yes, Raphael thought, breathing in the scent of his hunter, the wildness barely contained beneath her skin. He'd wondered what Elena would do to a race of immortals—this mortal who'd made him a little bit human even as she became immortal. But he'd never stopped to wonder what she'd do to him.

"My father," he said, surprising himself with the words, "died a long time ago."

Flames everywhere, his father's scream of rage, his mother's tears. Salt on his lips. His own tears. He'd watched his mother kill his father and he'd cried. He'd been a boy, a true child, even among angelkind.

"I'm sorry."

"It was an eternity ago." And it was only in those rare moments when his shields fell that he remembered. Today, Elena had caught him unawares. His mind had flooded with the last images he had, not of his father but of his mother, her delicate feet walking lightly over grass stained with her own son's lifeblood. She'd been so beautiful, so gifted that angels had fought and died for her. Even at the end, as she crooned over Raphael's fallen, broken body, her beauty had outshone the sun itself.

"Shh, my darling. Shh."

"Raphael?"

Two feminine voices, one pulling him into the past, the other into the present.

If there had been a choice, he'd made it a year ago in the skies above New York, as the city lay in ruins around him. Now, he pressed his lips to the curve of Elena's shoulder and soaked in her warmth, warmth that was distinctly mortal, melting the ice of memory. "You've been in this water long enough I think."

"I don't ever want to move."

"I'll fly you back."

Her protest was weak as he lifted her out of the water, her body still so breakable.

"Don't move, hunter." Drying her wings with care, he pulled on his pants, then watched her dress, his heart overflowing with a mix of possession, satisfaction, and a terror unlike any he'd ever known before. If Elena fell from the sky, if she was thrown onto the unyielding earth, she wouldn't survive. She was too young, an immortal just born.

When she came into his embrace, her arms going around his neck, her lips pressing to his pectorals, he shuddered and, closing his own arms around her, rose into the orange red glow of a sky skillfully painted by the rays of the slowly setting sun. Instead of going high, above the cloud layer, he stayed low, mindful that she felt the cold. If he'd known what they'd find, he'd have made a far different choice, but as it was, Elena saw the nightmare first.

"Raphael! Stop!"

He halted at the urgency in her tone, hovering just over the border that delineated where his territory ended and Elijah's began. Even in the Refuge, there were lines—unmarked, unspoken, but existent all the same. One power could not stand too close to another. Not without destruction of a magnitude that would savage their kind. "What is it?"

"Look."

Following the line of her arm, he saw a body colored in a hundred shades of copper by the sun. It lay in a small, silent square on his side of the border. His vision was acute, better than a raptor's, yet he could see no movement, nothing that spoke of life. But he did see what had been done to the male. Fury ignited.

"Take me down, Raphael." Distracted words, her eyes on the body that had curved in on itself as if in a desperate attempt to lessen the brutality of its injuries. "Even if there isn't a vampiric trail to follow, I know how to track."

He stayed in place. "You're still recovering."

Her head snapped up, those silver eyes liquid mercury. "Don't you dare stop me from being what I am. Don't you dare." There was something very old in those words, in that anger, as if it had aged within her.

He'd taken her mind twice since she'd woken, both times to protect her from hurting herself. Today, those same primal drives urged him to disregard her orders—she might've been hunter-born, but she wasn't yet anywhere near strong enough to handle this.

"I know what you're thinking," Elena said, taut pain in

every word, "but if you take my mind, if you force me to go against my instincts, I'll never forgive you."

"I won't watch you die again, Elena." The Cadre had chosen her because she was the best, relentless in her pursuit of her prey. But then, she'd been disposable. Now, she was integral to his existence.

"For eighteen years"—somber words, a haunted expression—"I tried to be what my father wanted. I tried not to be hunter-born. It killed me a little more each day."

He knew what he was. He knew what he was capable of. He also knew that if he broke her, he'd despise himself for all eternity. "You'll do exactly as I say."

An immediate nod. "This is unfamiliar territory—I'm not going to go off half-cocked."

Descending in a gentle dive, he came to an easy landing a few feet from the body—in the shadow of a dual-level home that bore the soft patina of age. Elena held onto him for a couple of seconds, as if getting her muscles under control before turning to kneel beside the badly beaten vampire. He crouched beside her, reaching out to place his fingers on the vampire's temple. A pulse wasn't always a good indicator of life when it came to the Made.

It took him several seconds to sense the dull echo of the vampire's mind, a sign of how close the male was to true death. "He lives."

Elena blew out a breath. "Dear God, someone really wanted to hurt him." The vampire had been beaten so severely he was nothing much more than ground meat over bone. He might've been handsome, probably had been from the sense of age pressing against Elena's skin, but there wasn't enough left of his face to tell.

One eye was swollen shut. The other . . . the eye socket had been shattered with such vicious thoroughness that if you didn't know he was meant to have an eye there, you'd never guess where his cheek ended and his eye began. Oddly, his lips had been left untouched. Below the neck, his clothing was driven into his flesh, evidence of a sustained and repeated kicking. And his bones . . . they stuck out—bloody, broken branches through what had once been a pair of jeans.

It hurt to see him, to know what he must've suffered. Vampires didn't lose consciousness easily—and, given the savagery of the attack, she'd bet his attackers had kicked his head last. That way, he would've been conscious for almost the entirety of the ordeal. "Do you know who he is?"

"No. His brain is too bruised." Raphael slid his arms under the vampire, a carefulness to his movements that made her heart squeeze. "I need to get him to a physician."

"I'll wait and—" She froze as he shifted the body to get a better hold. "Raphael."

The air was suddenly kissed by frost. "I see it."

There was a square of jarringly unbruised skin on the vampire's breastbone, as if it had been left specifically unharmed. The cold-blooded nature of the beating made her stomach curdle. These people *would* have attacked his brain last. "What is that?" Because while the vampire's skin wasn't bruised, it wasn't unmarked. A symbol had been burned into his flesh. An elongated rectangle, slightly flared at the bottom, sat atop an inverted curve, which in turn covered a small bowl. Holding it all up was a long, thin line.

"It's a *sekhem*, a symbol of power from a time when archangels ruled as pharaohs and were called the scions of the gods."

Elena felt her face flush hot and cold. "Someone wants to take Uram's place."

Raphael didn't tell her not to jump to conclusions. "Do your track. Illium will watch over you until I return."

She looked up as Raphael rose but couldn't isolate Illium's blue wings even against the light show of the approaching sunset. Thankfully, her legs waited to tremble until after Raphael had left. Her archangel had finally seemed to hear her today—she had a feeling he'd think long and hard before ever again forcing her to act against her will.

But there was nothing to stop him from picking her up bodily and dumping her in bed if he realized the extent of her exhaustion. Her wings felt like hundred-pound weights on her back, her calf muscles so much jelly. Blowing out a breath, she dug up a fraction more stamina from somewhere and started circling out from the spot where they'd found the body, glad that this area, while not abandoned, appeared shut up.

As a result, there weren't a lot of scents to muddy the trail. The tree in the corner, some kind of a cedar, its branches bowed with the weight of its foliage, didn't trump the smell of pine trees in autumn, their needles littering the earth. And that scent belonged to the vampire who'd been beaten into an unrecognizable pulp. No matter how hard she tried, she couldn't find a single other new scent.

There was also no evidence of activity on the ground, the paving stones clean, but for a few stray leaves and some clearly delineated spots of blood near the dark smudge where they'd discovered the body. Examining the scene with extreme care so as not to compromise any trace evidence, she confirmed the splatter was contained within a radius of about one foot.

"Dumped from a low height," she said to Raphael when he landed beside her. "And since this place is rife with wings . . ." Her body swayed.

Raphael had her in the iron of his embrace before she could even register the lapse. "Then you can do nothing. We'll speak to the vampire when he wakes."

"The site? Needs to be processed, just in case."

"Dmitri's on the way with a team."

It went against the grain to give up without a fight, but her body was shutting down on her, her wings threatening to drag their way through the blood. "I want to know what the victim says." The words came out slurred, her last thought that anyone cold-blooded enough to brand a living being as a message was probably not going to be an improvement on Uram.

Sire.

Easing quietly from bed less than an hour after he'd placed Elena on the sheets, her wings spread out in a caress of midnight and dawn as she lay on her stomach, Raphael pulled on a pair of pants and met Dmitri in the hallway outside. The vampire's face was expressionless, but Raphael had known him for hundreds of years. "What did you discover?"

"Illium recognized him."

"How?"

"Apparently the male was wearing a ring he won from Illium in a game of poker."

Raphael had seen the vampire's fingers. Most had been shattered so badly they'd been nothing more than crushed pebbles in a sack of skin. And yet, that skin hadn't been broken. That level of brutality took both time and an emotionless kind of focus. "Who?"

"His name is Noel. He's one of ours."

Raphael felt his anger turn granite-hard. He'd allow no one to butcher his people. Before he could speak, Dmitri said, "Why didn't you tell me he'd been branded?" The words fell like mines between them, a scab hiding still raw wounds.

5

"The burn will fade." Raphael held the vampire's gaze. "It will fade."

Dmitri said nothing for several moments before drawing in a long breath. "The healers found something stuffed in Noel's chest cavity. The ones who took him broke him open, then allowed him to heal enough to conceal it."

It was another example of the methodical nature of the beating. "What was it?"

Dmitri withdrew a dagger from his pocket. It had a small but distinctive *G* on the pommel, the symbol of the Hunters Guild. A cold blade, rage unsheathed, sliced through Raphael's veins. "He plans to become Cadre by destroying what another archangel created."

The old ones saw Elena as exactly that—Raphael's creation, his possession. They didn't understand that she held his heart, held it so utterly that there was nothing he wouldn't do, no line he wouldn't cross to keep her safe. "Did you find anything at the scene that could lead to the identity of the one behind this?"

"No, but there aren't many who'd dare taunt you," Dmitri said, putting the dagger back into his pocket. "Even fewer who'd think they could get away with it."

"Nazarach is in the Refuge," he said, knowing the other angel was more than old enough to be dangerous. "Find out who else might consider themselves a contender."

"There's only one on the verge of becoming an archangel."

The Cadre alone was supposed to be privy to that truth, but Raphael trusted Dmitri far more than he trusted his fellow archangels. "He also has no need to play these kinds of games." To be an archangel was to be Cadre. It was as simple—and as inevitable—as that.

"It's one of the old ones." Angelic history told of a few rare instances of those who were not archangels becoming Cadre. They never lived long. But the fact of their existence gave dark hope to those who craved the drug of power without understanding the price it inevitably demanded. "Someone strong enough to seduce others."

"There's something else," Dmitri said as Raphael was turning to go back to Elena. "Michaela"—he named another member of the Cadre of Ten—"has sent a message to say she's about to arrive at the Refuge."

"She waited longer than I expected." Michaela and Elena were like oil and fire. The female archangel couldn't stand to be anything but the center of attention. And yet when Elena, with her rough hunter clothing and pale hair, walked into a room, the balance of power shifted in the most subtle of fashions. Raphael didn't think Elena was even aware of it—but it was why Michaela had despised her from their very first meeting.

"Whether it's against Michaela or this pretender, she"— Dmitri glanced at the closed door at Raphael's back— "isn't strong enough to defend herself. It would take very little effort to end her life."

"Illium and Jason are here. Naasir?" He'd trust only his Seven to watch over her.

"On his way back." Dmitri, as the head of Raphael's security, knew exactly where each of his men was at any given time. "I'll make sure she's never alone."

Raphael heard the unspoken words. "And will she be safe with you?"

The vampire's expression altered. "She weakens you."

"She is my heart. Protect her as you did once before."

"If I'd known the consequences of that decision . . . But it is done." When Dmitri gave a curt nod, Raphael knew his Seven wouldn't move against her. Some archangels might have killed Dmitri for daring to stand against him, but the vampire had earned that right.

More, Raphael understood the value of what Dmitri and the rest of his Seven had given him. Without them, he may well have become another Uram, another Lijuan, long before Elena was even born. "Give Illium the majority of the shifts. Elena's less likely to object to him."

Dmitri snorted. "Her precious Bluebell's going to fall in love with her, and then you'll have to kill him."

"What better guard for Elena than one who loves her?" As long as that guard never forgot it was an archangel's mate he watched over. Betrayal would not be tolerated. "When's Michaela scheduled to arrive?"

"Within the hour. She's extended an invitation to dinner."

"Accept it." It was always better to know your enemy.

Elena woke from a mercifully dreamless sleep to the knowledge that she wasn't alone. And it wasn't the clean scent of rain, of the wind, that filled her senses. Her shields, however, remained down. Shifting on the bed, she glanced through the open balcony doors to see Illium's distinctive blue wings spread out as he sat nonchalantly on the railing, his legs hanging over the steep plunge of the gorge.

Silhouetted against the starlit sky, he appeared a being out of myth and legend. But as she'd seen this afternoon, if this place was a fairy tale, it was the dark and blood-soaked original. "You'll fall off if you're not careful."

He turned to glance at her. "Come sit with me."

"No thanks. I just finished healing all my broken bones." She'd shattered so many when she'd fallen in New York. But strange as it was, there'd been no pain in those final moments. All she remembered was a sense of peace.

And then Raphael had kissed her.

Golden and exquisite, erotic beyond compare, the taste of ambrosia had filled her mouth as Raphael's arms held her safe, as her archangel seized her from death itself.

"The look on your face," Illium murmured. "I once had a woman look at me that way."

Elena knew Illium had lost his feathers, lost his ability to fly, for speaking angelic secrets to a mortal . . . a mortal he'd loved. "Did you look at her that way, too?"

Those eyes of beaten gold were compelling even with the distance between them. "Only she'd know. And she went to earth long before the world grew cities of steel and glass." He returned his attention to the vista before him.

Sitting up in bed, she stared at the curving beauty of his wings, shimmering silver blue in the dark, and wondered if Illium still mourned for his human lover. But that was a question she had no right to ask. "The vampire?"

"His name is Noel. He hasn't regained consciousness." His voice was a naked edge. "He's one of ours."

And she knew they wouldn't stop until they tracked down the assailant. The hunter in her approved. "What about this angel's attempt to become Cadre?" The world didn't need another archangel with a penchant for the most malicious kind of pleasure.

"Secondary." A flat statement. "It'll be taken care of when we execute him for the insult to Noel, to Raphael."

Elena understood about cutting off evil at the root, but she wasn't used to the swift justice of immortals. "I'm guessing angels don't have a judge and jury system."

A snort. "You saw Uram—would you have wanted him to have a day in court?"

No. Mind turbulent with the memories of Uram's atrocities, she said, "Tell me about Erotique."

Illium raised an eyebrow at her mention of the exclusive Manhattan club patronized by vampires. "Thinking about a career change?"

"Geraldine worked as a dancer there." Elena would never forget the plea in the other woman's eyes as she lay dying after Uram slit her throat. "She wanted so badly to be Made."

"I don't know that she would've enjoyed immortality." Swinging his legs off the railing and down onto the balcony, Illium walked over to lean his shoulder against the doorway. "Geraldine struck me as a natural victim."

Elena remembered that pale, pale skin overlaced with the scent of vampire. The world would have called her a vamp-whore, and once, Elena would have agreed with them—that was before she'd stood in a room full of vampires and their lovers, before she'd understood that while seduction could be a drug, it could also be the most adult of exchanges, a game in which the victor would spend the night seeing to the loser's pleasure.

But Geraldine hadn't been like the men and women Elena had seen in the Tower, full of an easy sensual confidence. Illium was right. She'd been a victim. "And she'd have been that for eternity."

"Yes." Wings a delicate arc over his back, Illium met her gaze. "Trust me on this, Ellie. It's not a good thing to be."

"Why do you sound as if you know?" she asked, aware she'd never forget the mute desperation of Geraldine's dying plea. "You're no victim."

"I Made a human once," he murmured, his lashes shading the expression in his eyes. "He was biologically compatible, and he passed all the personality tests. But he had no . . . core, no sense of self. I only discovered that later, when it was too late. He'd tied himself to another angel by then, one who enjoyed having a victim."

"He's dead?"

"Of course. Victims never last long."

It was a stark glimpse into one of the darker sides of immortality. "The longer you live, the more mistakes you make."

"And the more sorrows you carry."

Perhaps she should have been startled by the solemn comment, but Illium, she was beginning to learn, was an angel who rarely showed his true face to the world. Much like the man he called sire. "Do you remember everything?"

"Yes."

A gift. A curse.

Bruisingly aware that memories could make you bleed as effectively as any razor, she took a step back from the past. It would return to haunt them both soon enough. "Are your eyelashes like your hair?"

He followed her lead without skipping a beat. "Yes. They're very beautiful—want to see?"

Her lips twitched. "Vanity is a sin, Bluebell."

"When you have it, flaunt it, I say." Grinning, he wandered over to perch on the side of the bed. "Look."

Curious, she did. He'd told the absolute truth—his eyelashes were inky and black tipped with the same bright blue as his hair, a startling contrast against the gold of his eyes. "They're okay," she said offhandedly.

He scowled. "And here I was about to offer to brush your hair."

"I'll brush my own hair, thank you." Pushing at his shoulder, she nudged him off the bed. "Grab me the brush."

He threw it to her before returning to the balcony. "Why haven't you asked why I'm here?"

"I'm not at full strength, Raphael is overprotective, it's not difficult to do the math." Her frustration at her current physical state did nothing to negate the cold, hard truth—her head *would* make a mighty fine trophy for more than one immortal. Especially the most beautiful and most vicious one of them all.

"Apparently, this aspirant," Illium said over his shoulder, "plans to make his mark by stabbing a Guild dagger through your heart. Or maybe by using it to hack off your head one piece at a time."

The echo of her own thoughts startled her—but it shouldn't have. Because like it or not, she was hot news in the angelic world, the first angel Made in living memory. "I think I need some food before I start thinking about all the horribly painful ways I could conceivably die."

"There's some in the living area."

"Where's Raphael?"

"At a meeting."

Elena had been saved by her instincts more than once. Now, her hand clenched on the carved wooden handle of the brush. "With who?"

"It'll only make you mad."

"I thought you were my friend."

"Who's currently trying to save you from unnecessary fretting."

Fretting? "Stop stalling and tell me."

Turning with a huge sigh, Illium said, "Michaela."

A flash of memory, bronze angel dust on Raphael's wings. Elena ground her teeth together. "I'd think the Refuge would be too quiet for Her Royal Bitchiness." New York, Milan, Paris, that was more Michaela's milieu.

"You'd be right." His eyes gleamed. "But seems she's developed a sudden interest in the place."

Yanking the brush through her hair, she found the hair-tie she'd left on the bedside table and put the unmanageable mass up in a high ponytail. As she swung her legs over the side of the bed, Illium gave a pointed cough. "I wouldn't suggest going to them in your present condition."

"I'm not an idiot," Elena muttered. "I want to do some exercise."

"You're supposed to rest 'til morning."

"Trust me, I know my body." She stood with a groan. "If I don't loosen these muscles now, it'll be worse tomorrow."

Illium didn't say anything, simply watched as she walked to the bathroom. Closing the door, she splashed water over her

face and willed herself to stop thinking about what might be
happening between Raphael and Michaela. She wasn't worried that Raphael would sleep with Michaela—quite bluntly,
Raphael wasn't the cheating kind. If he tired of her—and
yeah, it hurt to even consider that—he'd tell her to her face.
More, she had a feeling he saw through Michaela's beauty to
the venom inside.

But it was impossible to forget the female archangel's stunning face, that body that had seduced kings and destroyed
empires. By contrast, Elena's own face—reflected in the
mirror—was too thin, her skin carrying the pallor of a year
spent in sleep. Confidence wasn't exactly easy. "Enough."
Putting down the face-towel, she walked back out.

The bedroom proved empty, but she was in no doubt that
Illium was nearby. Heading out onto the wide space of the balcony, she began to go through a stretching routine she'd been
taught at Guild Academy. Most of the moves still worked,
though she had to get creative with a few, given that she now
had wings to consider. She tripped a couple of times—until
she forced herself to remember to keep the trailing edges
raised. It had the same effect as if she'd been trying to keep
her arms straight while typing—the ache was a slow burn that
got progressively more painful.

Stubborn determination made her want to push through it,
but remembering the state she'd been in this afternoon, she
took a break. Dragging herself back into the bedroom and
out to the large living area, she found some juice and threw it
back. The taste was fresh and tart on her tongue, an indication
that this medieval-looking city of mountain and rock had an
orange grove hidden somewhere deep within.

"You have a phone call."

Turning on her heel, she found Illium holding up a sleek
silver portable handset. So much for the medieval imagery. "I
didn't hear it ring."

"I turned off the ringer while you were napping." Passing it
over, he took an apple from the fruit bowl. "It's Ransom."

Surprised at Illium's familiar tone, she lifted the receiver to her ear. "Hey, handsome."

She could hear the smile in the other hunter's voice when he replied. "You flying yet?"

"Soon."

"You sure are keeping some interesting company lately."

Glancing at Illium as the blue-winged angel walked out onto the separate balcony that flowed off this room, she said, "Where did you meet Illium?"

"Erotique."

"You know some of the dancers?" Ransom had grown up on the streets, retained most of his contacts even now.

"A couple. I get a lot of good intel there—even the most powerful of vamps gets talky when a woman's got her mouth near his cock."

Elena wasn't surprised—vampires had once been human after all. It took a long time for the echoes to fade completely. "So what did they blab?"

A crackle through the lines. ". . . want to know."

"What?" She pressed the receiver closer.

"Word's out that you're alive. Everyone thinks you're a bloodsucker—far as I can tell, none of the ones in the know have let the truth slip."

"Good." She needed time to get her own head around her new reality before explaining it to anyone else. "Was that what you wanted to tell me?"

"No. One of the dancers heard the vamps are placing bets on you surviving a year."

"What're the odds?"

"Ninety-nine to one."

Elena didn't have to ask which was the winning side. "What do they know that I don't?"

"Rumor is, Lijuan has a habit of feeding her guests to her pets."

6

Raphael watched Michaela lift the crystal wineglass to her lips with the effortless grace of a woman who'd had centuries to perfect her elegant facade. Impartially speaking, she was beautiful, perhaps the most beautiful woman in the world, her skin a flawless shade akin to the most exotic coffee swirled with cream, her eyes a green that put gemstones to shame, her hair a tumble of black threaded with bronze, brown, a hundred shades in between.

Stunning—and she used her looks as effectively and as unemotionally as others might a gun. If men, mortal and immortal, had died because they'd fallen prey to that beauty, that was their mistake.

"So," she now purred, venom coated in honey, "your hunter survived." When he didn't say anything, she made a moue of disappointment. "Why keep it a secret?"

"I didn't think you were that interested in Elena's survival." *Only her death.*

To her credit, Michaela didn't pretend not to understand. "Touché." Raising her wineglass in a toast, she took a small sip of the golden liquid. "Will you be very angry if I kill her?"

Raphael met those poisonous eyes of vibrant green, wondering if Uram had ever seen through to the vicious heart of the woman he'd called his consort. "You seem to have a fascination with my hunter." It was a deliberate statement. Elena was *his*, and he would protect her.

Michaela waved off the words. "She made interesting prey, but now that she's lost her abilities, the sport will be far too easy. I suppose I should just let her be."

It was a very smooth, very calculated offer. "I think," he said, not correcting her erroneous assumption, "Elena is more than capable of looking after herself."

Michaela's cheekbones cut sharply against skin men had died to touch. "Surely you don't think her my equal?"

"No." He waited, watched her face suffuse with pleasure, with satisfaction. "She's something utterly unique."

For a single icy instant the mask slipped. "Be careful, Raphael." A predator looked back at him, one who'd clean blood off her fingers with chilly fastidiousness, even as she watched her victim writhe in agony at her feet. "I won't sheathe my claws because she's your pet."

"Then I'll ask Elena not to sheathe hers." Taking a sip of his own wine, he leaned back in his chair. "Will you be at the ball?"

A blink and the mask returned, pristine and perfect. "Of course." She ran a hand through her hair, the move pushing her breasts against the olive-colored fabric of a dress that bared just enough to tempt most men to madness. "Have you ever been to Lijuan's fortress?"

"No." The oldest of the archangels lived in a mountain stronghold secreted within China's extensive borders. "I don't think any of the Cadre have." Though Raphael had managed to get several of his men inside over the centuries. At present, that task was Jason's, and each time he returned, Raphael's spymaster brought more and more disturbing news of Lijuan's court.

Michaela swirled the liquid in her glass. "Uram was invited there once when he was much younger," she told him. "Lijuan took a shine to him."

"I'm not sure whether Uram should've been flattered or not."

A soft, intimate laugh. "She is rather . . . inhuman, isn't she?" This, coming from a member of the Cadre, spoke to the extent of Lijuan's "evolution."

"What did Uram tell you of her stronghold?"

"That it was impenetrable and filled with countless treasures." Her eyes sparkled, whether in contemplation of those treasures or from the memory of her lover, Raphael couldn't say. "He said he'd never seen such artwork, such tapestries and jewels. I don't know that I believed him—have you ever seen Lijuan wearing even a diamond?"

"She has no need to." With hair of purest white and eyes of a strange pearlescent gray that he'd seen nowhere else on this earth, Lijuan was unforgettable without ornamentation. And these days, Raphael thought, the other archangel's attention was fixed on a world the rest of them couldn't even begin to fathom. She hadn't left her stronghold at all this past half year, not even to meet with her fellow archangels. Which made the ball all the more extraordinary. "Has she invited the entire Cadre?"

"Chari has received an invitation," Michaela said of another of her former lovers, "and he says Neha has as well, so I assume she's invited the others. You should ask Favashi to accompany you. I think our Persian princess would like you for a consort."

Raphael met Michaela's gaze. "If you could kill every single beautiful woman in the world, would you?"

Her smile never faded. "In an instant."

Elena hung up the phone with a frown and stepped out onto the balcony. "Illium, do you know anything about Lijuan's pets?"

The other angel shot her a wide-eyed glance. "Ransom has very good sources."

Yes, Elena thought, he did. But even he hadn't been able to discover the identity of these creatures that had the vampires so certain of her death. "What are they?" Her spine locked as her mind offered an explanation. "Not vampires who've given in to bloodlust?" Locked in a constant loop of violence, feeding and hunger, those vampires made the most sociopathic of killers.

"Come here, little hunter. Taste."

Illium shook his head as she slammed the door on a memory that refused to stay buried, his hair tumbled by the stiff breeze coming off the mountains. He was a jewel against the night, his beauty so intense that it forced the eye to him rather than the stars. She took the lifeline, hung onto the present. "Why hasn't Michaela killed you yet?"

"I'm male. She'd rather fuck me."

The blunt answer threw her off balance for a second. "Have you?"

"Do I look like I want to be eaten alive after sex?"

Startled into a grin, she turned her face into the wind, enjoying the biting freshness. "So, Lijuan's pets?"

"Ask Raphael."

Her smile disappeared at the thought of where Raphael was at that moment. Searching for a distraction, she nodded at the lights she could see dotting the sides of the gorge that fell away beneath them, a massive split in the earth's crust. "Don't tell me people live down there?" Water ran far, far below the lights, but even so, she could feel the raging thunder of its passage.

"Why not? The caves make the most perfect of aeries." His grin was a slash of white across his face. "I have one. When you can fly, you can come see it."

"At the rate I'm going, I'll be eighty by the time I can actually fly."

"It'll only take once," Illium said softly, his face lifted up to the moonlight. The beams played over him as if entranced, turning his skin translucent, his hair a thousand strands of liquid ebony dipped in sapphires. "That first flight is something you never forget—the rush of air as your wings spread, the intoxicating freedom, the sheer joy that dances in the soul from being all that you're meant to be."

Caught by the unexpected poetry of his words, she almost didn't see Raphael sweeping in to land. Almost. Because nothing and no one else could ever hold her attention when her archangel was in the vicinity. Barely aware of Illium going quiet beside her, she watched the devastating grace of Raphael's descent. Illium was as beautiful as a gleaming blade, but Raphael . . . Raphael was magnificent.

"Time for me to go, I think."

She felt Illium leave, but it was a distant knowledge, her eyes drawn inextricably to the archangel who'd landed before her. "How was dinner?" she asked, staring into those cobalt eyes full of secrets it would take her an eternity to unravel.

"I survived."

It should've made her smile, but all she felt was a violent possessiveness—honed to the most lethal of edges by the knowledge that right now, the green-eyed female archangel could kill her without even a modicum of effort. "Did Michaela mark you?"

"Why don't you check?" He flared out his wings.

Feeling stupidly vulnerable all of a sudden, she turned to grip the balcony railing. "It's none of my business if you choose to spend time with a woman who'd eat your heart and dance gleefully on your grave if it would mean she gained power."

"Oh, but I disagree, Elena." Strong arms on either side of hers, big hands closing over the railing. "Tighten your wings."

It took her a minute to figure out how to do that neat tucking into the body thing she'd seen other angels do with their wings. "That's harder than it looks."

"Takes muscle control." Words spoken against her neck as he pressed closer, her wings trapped between them.

It hurt . . . with a pain that made her skin shimmer in hunger, in need. Every shift of his body, every brush of his lips, it went straight to her core. But she'd been fighting her attraction to Raphael since the moment she met him—it had never made her an easy target. "What do you disagree about?" she asked, her gaze drawn to the wings she could see sweeping through the lush black of the night, heading for those isolated aeries.

Angels going home.

A strange thought, a strange sensation, to stand here in their most secret place when they'd always been shadows in the darkness to her.

"I consider it very much your business if I choose to spend time with Michaela."

She heard a dangerous undertone in his words, one that curled her toes even as it pricked at her hunter instincts. "Do you?"

"As I consider it very much my business that your wings are dusted with blue."

Eyes widening, she pushed away from the railing. Or tried to. "Raphael, let me go so I can see."

"No."

She blew out a breath. "Stop it. Illium didn't mean anything by it."

"Angel dust is not an instinctive act . . . unless one is in the throes of sex." His fingers plucked at the tight peak of her nipple, a shockingly sensual reminder that the Archangel of New York had once lost control in bed. "It's very much premeditated."

"If he wasn't down there," she said, fighting to speak through the slamming rush of need, "I'd smack him. He's jerking your chain."

Lips on her ear, his hand moving to cup her breast with devastating intimacy. "Illium has always had a wild disregard for his life."

She couldn't help it. She curved her neck to give him better access. "And yet he's one of your Seven."

"I think in this case, he knows he's your favorite." Kisses

along her neck, hot and sexual in a way that told her he had only one thing in mind.

Giving a laugh husky with need, she reached back to run the fingers of one hand over his cheek. "Do I have that much influence over you?"

The graze of teeth. "If your Bluebell is alive tomorrow, you'll have your answer." His body pressed into her, hot, hard, and demanding, as his hands slid under her clothing to close over her bare breasts.

"Raphael."

Finally allowing her to turn, he crowded her against the railing. Instinct drove her to spread her wings over the metal that was all that kept her from falling to the rocks below. No, she thought, on the heels of that thought. Raphael would never let her fall. And if she fell, he'd fall with her. "Kiss me, Archangel."

"As you wish, Guild Hunter." His lips met hers, harshly masculine and earthy in a way that paid lie to any myths about angels being too "evolved" to indulge in such physical pleasures.

Moaning in the back of her throat, she wrapped her arms around his neck, rising on tiptoe to meet him kiss for tangled kiss. When his hand brushed the side of her breast, she shivered from the pleasure of it. Biting at his lower lip, she opened her eyes. "Now."

"No." Another hotly sexual kiss.

Breaking it, she ran her hand down the muscled plane of his chest, lower. He gripped it before she could close her fingers over the rigid length of him. "I'm not that weak," she protested.

"You're not that strong either." Power ringed his irises. "Not for what I want."

She stilled. "And what is that?"

Everything. The sea and the wind. Clean and wild . . . and inside her mind.

"I'll give you my hunger, my heart," she said, fighting to retain her independence, and more—to build a foundation for their relationship that would last an eternity. "But my mind is my own. Accept that."

"Or?" The cool question of a being used to getting exactly what he wanted.

"I guess you'll have to wait and see." Leaning back against the balcony, her body aching, unfulfilled, she simply looked at him, at the exquisite balance of beauty and cruelty, perfection and darkness. His own hunger had turned his face acetic, that flawless bone structure dramatic against his skin. But he made no move to kiss her again.

"I'll break you."

The words he'd spoken earlier came back to her, an invisible wall between them. Knowing he was right, she blew out a breath. "I have a question."

He waited without impatience—as if he had forever and she was the only woman in the universe. It threatened to take her breath away. How had she, Elena Deveraux, a common hunter according to her father, ended up with the right to ask questions of an archangel?

"What do you know about Lijuan's pets?"

A slow blink was all the indication he gave that she'd surprised him. "Dare I inquire how you knew to ask that question?"

She smiled.

His expression changed, holding an intensity that seared her through and through. "As I said"—eyes turning to chrome—"you'll make eternity far more interesting."

That was when she noticed the light coming off his wings. Bright, lethal, just enough to make him seem precisely what he was—an immortal who held enough power in his body to level a city. Instinct had her muscles tensing in preparation for flight, the adrenaline rush so strong, it was difficult to form words. "You're glowing."

"Am I?" Fingers undoing her hair, threading through the strands. "Lijuan's pets are the reborn."

Startled at getting a straight answer, she sucked in air through lungs that protested the effort—struggling past the pressure of Raphael's presence, his power. She didn't call him on it, intensely conscious that he wasn't doing it to intimidate her. He was simply *being*. And if she planned to dance with an archangel, she had to learn to deal. "Something to do with vampires?"

"No. As archangels age," he said, the glow beginning to fade, though his eyes stayed that metallic shade no human would ever possess, "we gain power."

"Like your mental abilities," she murmured, her heart still racing. "And the glamour." Paranoia would run rampant if it got out that some archangels could walk among the populace unknown, unseen.

"Yes. Lijuan is the oldest among us, and as such, has the greatest store of abilities."

"So these reborn are something only she can create?"

A nod that sent the coal black strands of his hair sliding over his forehead.

Reaching up to push them back, she lingered, playing with the heavy silk. "What are they?"

"Lijuan," he said in a voice touched with midnight, "can make the dead walk."

Her heart stopped for a second as she read the truth in his eyes, processed the awfulness of what he was saying. "You don't mean that she can somehow bring people truly back to life, do you?"

"I would not call it life." He bent his head, pressing his forehead against hers.

Sliding her hand around to the back of his neck, she held him close as he told her things no mortal knew.

"They walk, but they do not talk. Jason tells me that for the first few months of their existence, they seem to have some semblance of sentience, that it's possible they know what they are—but with no power over their reborn bodies. They are Lijuan's puppets."

"Dear God." To be trapped in your own body, knowing you were a nightmare . . . "How does she keep them alive?"

"She awakens them with her power, but they then feed on

blood." Raphael's voice twined around her, filling her cells with horror. "The old ones, the ones who went to the earth long ago, feed on the flesh of the recently dead to keep their own bones clothed in flesh."

Her soul grew cold, so cold. "Will you gain that ability?"

7

Raphael threaded his hands through her hair once more. "Our abilities are tied to who we are. I would hope I never become capable of creating the reborn."

Shivering, she slid her arms around his torso. "Have you gained any new abilities in recent years?" Because she knew him, knew how thin the line he'd skated. Not that long ago, he'd broken every bone in a vampire's body while the pitiful creature remained conscious. It had been a punishment Manhattan would never forget. "Raphael?"

"Come." He rose into the air.

Yelping, she shifted her hold to around his neck. "You could've warned me."

"I have faith in your reflexes, Elena." *After all, if you hadn't shot Uram, New York might yet be drowning in blood.*

She snorted. "That wasn't all me. I seem to remember you throwing fireballs at him."

"Angelfire," he murmured. "One touch and it would've killed you."

Rubbing her face against his chest as he flew them over the

lethal beauty of the massive mountain range that surrounded the lights of the Refuge, she said, "I'm hard to kill."

"Take care, hunter." Dipping, he swept down toward the edge of a crashing waterfall. "You can still be hurt."

They were so close she could skim her fingers along the glittering beauty of the water, the droplets diamonds trapped under moonlight. Wonder burst to life inside of her. "Raphael!"

Rising, he flew them back up into the icily clear night sky, each star cut in crystal.

"You said a strong vampire could kill me," she said, feeling the cold color her cheeks as the wind ripped through her hair. "Angelfire, I can guess. What else am I vulnerable to?"

"Angelfire is the easiest method, but those archangels who can't create the fire have other means."

"I wasn't planning on hanging out with the Cadre, so that's good."

Lips against her ear, a touch that seared her to the toes, but his words . . . "Disease is no longer your enemy, but fellow angels can also kill you. You're so young that if you were partially dismembered, you'd die."

She swallowed her gorge at that violent image. "That happen often?"

"No. Usually, the head is cut off and burned. Very few survive that."

"How could *anyone* survive?"

"Angels are resilient," he murmured, twisting to glide them back down.

"This place is huge," she said, glimpsing lights far in the distance. "How can no one know it exists?"

Raphael didn't answer until he'd landed on the balcony outside their bedroom. "Immortals may disagree on many things, but on this we are united—our Refuge must never be known to mortals."

"Sara?" She clenched her fingers on his upper arms. "Did you do something to her mind?"

"No." Eyes of endless, merciless blue stared down at her,

eclipsing everything else. "But if she speaks of it, I must silence her and all those she tells."

A cold knot formed in her stomach. "Even if that would break my heart?"

"Make sure she doesn't speak." He cupped her cheek, his fingers cool from the night air. "And that will not come to pass."

She pushed away from him. This time, he let her go, let her walk to the end of the balcony and stare down into that ragged tear in the flesh of the earth. There were fewer lights now, as if the angels were bedding down for the night. "I'm not part of your world, Raphael. I'm still human inside—I won't sit back and let my friends be slaughtered."

"I would expect no less." He opened the doors. "Come, sleep."

"How can you expect me to sleep after saying something like that?" Swiveling on her heel, she stared at him.

He glanced back, a being of such power that she still couldn't accept he loved her. But was an archangel's love like a human's? Or did it cut deeper? Draw heart's-blood?

"I forget," he said, "that you are so very young." Moving to her, he stroked his fingers down her temple, over her jaw. "Mortals fade, Elena. It is a simple truth."

"So I should forget my friends, my family?"

"Remember them," Raphael said, "but also remember that one day, they won't be there."

Grief was a wild-eyed beast inside of her. She couldn't imagine a world without Sara, without Beth. The ties she had with her younger sister might've been eroded by the choices they'd both made, but that didn't mean Elena loved her any less. "I don't know if I have the courage to survive that kind of loss."

"You'll find it when the time comes."

The pain in his voice slid a dagger hilt deep into her own heart. "Who?"

She didn't really expect an answer. Raphael might be her lover, but he was also an archangel. And archangels had made an art form out of keeping secrets. So when he ran his knuckles down her face and said, "Dmitri," it took her several seconds to respond.

"He was Made against his will," she guessed, remembering the conversation she'd once had with Dmitri about children. Had the vampire watched his children grow old? Had he lost a wife he loved?

Raphael didn't respond this time, nudging her into the bedroom. "You must rest or you won't be fit for flight by the time of the ball."

She followed, shaken by the truth he'd forced her to face.

Raphael placed his hands on her shoulders. "Undo the straps." The heat of his body was a lush stroke against her, invisible, inescapable.

And that quickly, her wings were afire with sensation, with a need that obliterated all else. It took effort to breathe, to speak. "Raphael, are you inside my mind?" She was pulling out and undoing the straps that held the piece of fabric crisscrossed over her breasts even as she spoke.

"No." Long, strong fingers playing over her collarbones, the dip of her breastbone. "Such soft skin, Guild Hunter."

Every inch of her seemed to burn with a thirst that couldn't be quenched. "Then what's happening to me?"

"You are still becoming."

He slipped off her top, and she felt the rasp of every fine thread, shuddered against the fleeting brush of his fingertips.

"Do you know what I taste at the curve of your neck?" He pressed his lips over that very spot. "Fire and earth, spring windstorms cut by a hint of steel."

She shivered, reaching back to tangle her hand in the heavy silk of his hair. "Is that how you see me?"

"It's who you are." He moved his hand up the slope of her hip, a slow seduction that made her suck in her stomach in anticipation.

But nothing could've prepared her for the shock of lightning that was his hand on her breast, his intent explicit. She couldn't help but watch, her entire being attuned to the merest shift of his.

Then he kissed her neck again and her senses splintered. Clenching the hand she'd thrust into his hair, she spun around, cupping his face between her hands, taking that beautiful, cruel mouth with her own. The kiss was wild, full of the fury of her need, the savage possession of his. One male hand fell to her hip as the other gripped her neck, refusing to let her draw back.

Her breasts were crushed against the linen of his shirt, the texture deliciously—almost painfully—abrasive against her sensitized nipples. She bit his lip in revenge for what he'd done to her. He bit her back, but he held the bite, releasing her flesh with a slow concentration that had her thighs pressing together in a burst of damp heat.

She went to slip her hand underneath his shirt. He caught her wrist. "No, Elena."

"I'm not that fragile," she said, frustrated. "Don't worry."

His hand tightened on her wrist for a second before he dropped it and took a step back, breaking their connection. Ready to fight him for what she needed, she looked up . . . and froze. "Raphael." Azure flames surged in those eyes, deadly as the angelfire he'd thrown at Uram in that final, cataclysmic fight.

"Go to bed," he said in a tone of voice so calm it was a sheet of ice.

But the fire continued to burn. Feeling her heart spasm at the lethal edge of it, she wrapped her arms around her body, covering her breasts. She didn't know if she was protecting herself or him. "Will you come back?"

"Are you sure you want me to?" He'd turned and was through the balcony doors before she could answer.

She watched him take off into the infinite darkness of a mountain night, before closing the doors with fingers that had dug dark red crescents into her own skin and crawling into bed. But though she pulled every single one of the blankets over her, it took her a long time to stop shivering.

She'd thought she'd known, had thought she'd understood. But she hadn't. Ever since she'd woken, she'd been treating Raphael as if he was "safe." Tonight, she'd had a rude awakening. Raphael would never be safe. All it would take was one slip and he could kill her.

Was she strong enough to take that risk, that chance?

"You've made me a little mortal."

He'd said that to her the night she'd shot him, the night he'd bled so much that she'd cried, her hands trembling as she attempted to stop the crimson flow of blood. Had he been afraid then? Did Raphael even understand fear? She didn't know, wasn't sure he'd answer her if she asked.

Elena knew fear far too intimately. But, she thought, her muscles relaxing, she hadn't been afraid at the end. When her body lay shattered in Raphael's arms, she hadn't been afraid. And that was her answer.

Yes, she said speaking to Raphael, not knowing the strength of their mental connection, not sure how far it'd reach. *Yes, I want you to come back.*

He didn't answer, and she didn't know if he'd even heard her. But deep in the night, she felt the caress of lips against the curve of her neck, sensed the dark heat of a big male body curving around hers, her wings trapped in between . . . an indescribable intimacy between two angels.

8

Elena woke alone, but there was a cup of coffee waiting for her on the nightstand—right next to Destiny's Rose. Raphael had given her the priceless treasure—a sculpture carved impossibly from a single diamond—not long after they first met. She kept trying to return it, only to find it back on her bedside table the next morning.

Eyes on the gift, one that was undeniably romantic, she struggled up into a sitting position and drew in the intoxicating scent of fresh coffee. However, she'd hardly taken a sip when she felt it—the cool stroke of satin blended with the promise of a pain that would hurt oh-so-good.

"Dmitri." Throat husky, she put down the cup and tugged the sheet above her breasts.

Just in time.

The vampire walked in with the most perfunctory of knocks. "You're late for training."

Her eye went to the envelope in his hand. "What's that?"

"It's from your father." He handed it over. "Be down in half an hour."

She barely heard him, her eyes fixated on that envelope. What did Jeffrey Deveraux want now? "I'll be there." Words forced out past the rocks in her throat.

Dmitri left her with a kiss of diamonds and cream, a sensual taunt that trapped the air in her throat, made her thighs press together in involuntary reaction. But the distraction was momentary. All too soon, she was alone, staring at the envelope as if it might grow fangs and strike. "Don't be a coward, Ellie," she told herself and reached out to slit it open. It was, she saw, addressed to her care of the Guild.

Her lips twisted. How he must've hated that, having to go through his daughter's filthy, inhuman occupation to get to her. *Abomination.* That's what he'd called her the final night she'd spent under his roof. She'd never forgotten, would never forget.

Her fingers clenched on the enclosed letter as she almost ripped it from the envelope. For an instant, she didn't understand what she was seeing, then she did and her emotions crashed in a violent wave.

It wasn't from her father. The letter had come from the Deveraux family solicitors—a note advising her that they'd paid the fees for her storage unit out of courtesy for her father's business, though the items in that unit now belonged solely to her.

The paper crumpled in her fist. She'd almost forgotten . . . no, that was a lie. She'd deliberately put the memory out of her mind. Her inheritance from her mother, she understood. Marguerite Deveraux had left Elena half her small personal estate, the other half going to Beth.

But the things in that storage unit . . . they were from Elena's childhood.

Drip.

Drip.

Drip.

"Come here, little hunter. Taste."

Shoving aside the blankets with hands that wouldn't work right, she got out of bed, the letter lying abandoned on the sheets as she stumbled into the bathroom and turned on the shower. Her fingers slipped off the knob. Biting her lip hard enough to draw blood, she tried again. Finally, thankfully, the water came down in a soft, warm rain. It washed away the sleep, but nothing could erase the memories now that they'd awakened.

Ariel had been the best big sister any girl could want. She'd never once told Elena to go away, though Elena knew she must have been a pest with her constant need to know what was going on in her teenage sister's life. Mirabelle, the oldest of them all, had been more apt to snarl, but Belle had also taught Elena to play baseball, spending long, patient hours teaching her how to throw, how to catch.

Yin and Yang, her mother had called her two oldest. Ari was the sweetness, Belle the spice.

"Belle, where do you think you're going dressed like that?"

"Aw, come on, Mom. It's all the rage."

"It might be all the rage, mon ange, *but you'll be grounded for a month if your father sees your butt hanging out of those shorts."*

"Mom!"

Elena remembered sitting at the kitchen table, giggling, as her long-legged fifteen-year-old sister stomped upstairs to change. Across the table, Beth, too little at five to really understand, had giggled with her.

"And you two little monsters, eat your fruit."

Her heart twisted at the memory of her mother's uniquely accented voice; her fingers rose to her cheek, searching for the faded echo of Marguerite's kiss. "Mama." It came out a broken whisper, a child's plea.

There'd been so much blood later. Elena had slipped, fallen hard. And heard Belle's dying breaths as she met Ari's horror-filled eyes. Even then, her sister had been trying to protect her, trying to tell her to run, her voice a gurgle as blood filled her throat. But Slater Patalis hadn't been interested in killing Elena. He'd other plans for her.

"Sweet little hunter."

Jerking off the water, Elena stepped out and dried herself off with a concentrated kind of focus. She snapped out her wings like she'd seen Raphael do, then gasped at the pain that radiated down her back. Embracing the pulses of hurt because they broke the endless loop of memory, she dressed in workout gear—loose black exercise pants with a white stripe down the sides, and a severe black tank with a built-in bra.

As with all the clothing she'd found in the wardrobe that was hers, it had clearly been designed with wings in mind, the tank pulled tight at the halter neck, and having three panels—one on each side of her wings, the other down the middle of her back—that looped into a wide strap she wrapped around her waist then locked at the sides using adjustable clasps. Extra support was provided by boning around the breast area. Satisfied her body wouldn't distract her from what she needed to learn, she plaited the damp mass of her pale hair into a braid close to her skull.

Then, unused to leaving things a mess, she made the bed—stuffing the letter in a drawer—and walked out. The bedroom, with its walls of glass, was connected to the large living area she'd already used. Across the hallway outside the living area lay what appeared to be an office and a small but well-appointed library, both with clear walls that brought the mountains inside. Books filled the low shelves, some old, some new, but she'd also glimpsed a sophisticated computer station. It all sat at the very top of the stronghold, above the soaring central core. More living quarters spread out below, rooms for the Seven, other angels and vampires. But the top wing was private, Raphael's.

The hallway—which led eventually to stairs cut into the side of the central core—was a symphony of clean lines broken up by the unexpected. A scimitar, ancient runes burned into the blade itself, was mounted on the left wall, the steel gleaming wicked sharp. She could see Dmitri holding that blade, wondered if it had been his once upon a time. Because Dmitri was old, one of the oldest vampires she'd ever met.

A few feet down, a handwoven tapestry covered most of the right wall. She'd spent almost half an hour staring at it yesterday, compelled by something she didn't understand. Now, in spite of her need to get out, to combat the churning in her gut with raw physicality, her feet hesitated, then stopped. There was a story woven within those precise threads, a story she desperately wanted to understand.

The panel showed an angel silhouetted golden against the sun, his face obscured by shadow as he headed downward to a forest village engulfed in flames. Another angel rose up toward him, her hair a rippling fall of black down her back, her wings the purest white Elena had ever seen. The flying strands of her hair hid her face, until she, too, was a shadow. But the faces of the villagers as they writhed in agony . . . each had been woven in exquisite detail, down to the screaming horror in the eyes of a woman who stood trapped as flames licked at her skirts, began to blister the skin of her arm.

Who were the two angels? Were they trying to help the burning? Or were they the reason for the massacre? Most important of all, Elena thought, shivers trailing over her skin, why did Raphael have this disturbing image in a place where he couldn't help but see it almost every single day?

Raphael looked down at the injured vampire, even more sharply conscious of the calculated nature of the insult, the care that had been taken to beat Noel so that his face was so much ground meat—but one eye remained undamaged, a dull blue visible around the swelling caused by his other injuries. His remaining eye was nothing but pulp. His nose was gone, but his lips untouched, perfect in their form.

Below the neck, he'd been all but crushed, his bones in so many pieces that some were dust. Raphael had broken a vampire not long ago—punishment for disloyalty. He'd snapped Germaine's bones, each with a single move of his hands. It had been a brutal penalty, one Germaine would remember for the rest of his existence, but Raphael had taken no pleasure in it.

Noel's attackers had most assuredly taken pleasure in what they'd done, continuing to savage him far beyond the point of sending a message. The brand lay a malignant cancer over the flesh of his breastbone, but their healer, Keir, had also found boot imprints on his back, his face. The dagger hadn't been the sole thing they'd left inside the vampire, either. Shards of glass had been shoved deep into his wounds, where his flesh would grow over them. He'd been battered in other ways, too, his body assaulted by something that had cut and torn. The only mercy was it appeared to have been done after he lost consciousness.

Raphael would've liked to be absolutely certain that he wasn't capable of such meaningless viciousness, but part of him wasn't so sure. Nadiel, too, had once been considered the greatest of archangels.

However, one thing *was* certain—Raphael would not countenance the slaughter and torture of his people. "Who did this to you?" he asked.

The vampire's good eye remained dull. He'd survive, but whether his mind would be the same . . . "I don't know." The answer was surprisingly clear, so clear that Raphael revised his opinion of Noel's chances of a true recovery. "Was jumped."

"You're not young," Raphael said, having gotten Noel's history from Dmitri. It seemed the vampire was a trusted member of the team that operated below the Seven, a man Dmitri had been planning to bring to Raphael's attention for his intelligence and loyalty. "You shouldn't have been so easily taken."

"More than one. Wings. Heard wings."

Raphael had executed an archangel. He felt no compunction in taking out an angel who sought to make his name by brutalizing those who looked to Raphael. "Markings?"

"I couldn't see." His good eye shifted toward Raphael. "They took my eyes when the beating started."

The dullness of the vampire's gaze suddenly made sense. The eye hadn't been left undamaged after all—it had simply begun to regenerate before its mate. "Did you sense anything about your attackers?"

"They said I was a message from Elijah." A cough rasping out of his chest.

Raphael called no archangel friend, but he didn't call Elijah an enemy either. "Male or female?"

"I was half insane by then." Flat words. "To me it sounded like pure evil. But at least one of them got off on the pain. While they were branding me . . . someone laughed and laughed and laughed."

Elena was on her way back to shower and change from the training session with Dmitri when something cut through the air with a chilling whistle. She hit the ground hard, smashing one elbow on the stone paving and scraping the palm of her other hand. Her wings escaped damage, but only because she'd remembered to fall to her side. The payoff would be a giant bruise on her left flank, a bone-deep pain in her arm.

She lifted her head with hunter cautiousness the instant after she hit the earth, knowing she'd be a sitting duck if she didn't move. Sensing nothing, she made the decision to rise to her feet. Even then, all she heard was silence; this part of Raphael's territory was filled with trees that seemed to thrive on the crisp mountain air, no angelic residences within a hundred feet.

Wondering if she'd just given herself a good hard whack for no reason, she began to turn in a slow circle. That whistling noise, it had sounded so much like— Her eye fell on the hilt of a throwing knife still quivering as it lay embedded in the trunk of a tree directly in line with where she'd been standing. Limping over on a slightly twisted ankle, she took a sniff of the knife before touching it.

Fur and diamonds and all things good girls shouldn't want.

"Goddamn vampire." She was so annoyed at herself for having missed him shadowing her that it took her two attempts to pull off the piece of paper wrapped around the hilt and secured with a rubber band.

The message was written in a strong masculine hand, flowing bold and dark.

This is not a Refuge for you. You're prey. Don't forget.

9

Raphael watched Elena walk in, her hand shredded, her foot dragging, and wondered if he'd have to kill the leader of his Seven after all.

"I get to kill him," she said, collapsing on a sofa in their living area. "And I plan to enjoy every minute of it."

Assessing the bloodthirsty expression on her face, he decided he'd leave Dmitri to her. "Does your foot need looking at?"

"It seems to be fixing itself up real fast." A questioning glance. "My ability to heal has been accelerated?"

"To an extent. Simple scratches and sprains will fade within the day, but, given your recent transition, breaks will still take weeks."

"Better than months." She ran her uninjured hand over her face. "I figured you were busy doing archangel stuff."

Looking at her, bedraggled and beaten, some might have seen weakness. He saw strength, determination, and a will no one could crush. "I've spoken to Noel."

"What did he say?" Her expression was grim by the time he finished. "No solid trail for us to follow."

"No. He was ambushed while alone in one of the less populated sections of Elijah's Refuge territory." Cross traffic was permitted throughout the city, so long as certain courtesies were observed. "I've had Jason checking, but he's been unable to find any witnesses."

"The ambush site?"

"Exposed to the elements. Any trace of their passage is long gone." Which spoke to some very careful planning. "And Noel was so badly injured, it was impossible to tell whether the ones who took him left anything of their own blood or sweat behind."

Elena shook her head. "I don't think they did—I would've picked up the most minute trace when we first saw him, that area was so clean of scent. What about the shoe prints on his back?"

"Not enough detail—his flesh had already begun to heal." Raphael was certain that had been deliberate. Not to hide the boot marks, but to ensure the shards of glass were buried deep enough that they'd cause excruciating pain when Noel rose to consciousness.

"How bad is it for him?" A quiet question.

"Brutal."

She closed her injured hand over her knee, the tendons turning white against the dark gold of her skin. "You give any credence to the Elijah angle?"

"Nothing but an attempt to play me." If Elijah decided to kill Raphael, he wouldn't waste time on petty games. "Elijah has no desire for conquest."

Elena met his gaze, her frustration at the dead ends clear. "Can I do anything?"

"The stronger you get, the more difficult it becomes to hurt you."

Her expression grew intent, as if she'd heard something he hadn't been aware of saying. "It's personal for you, just like it is for Illium and the others."

"I won't allow my people to be treated as disposable pawns." And he'd cold-bloodedly end the life of anyone who dared come after Elena.

"That's how hunters work. Attack one, attack us all." A quick nod. "I have a feeling you suspect someone."

"Nazarach is over seven centuries old and as with many of the old ones, pain has become his pleasure." Nazarach was also bound to Raphael. If he'd turned traitor, his punishment would send a scream through the world.

Elena played her fingers along the hilt of a knife he hadn't seen her draw. "That's when you know you've stepped over the line." She looked up, her eyes haunted. "When it starts to feel good."

"You'll never cross that line," he said, moving to pull her to a standing position. He might not be certain of himself, but he had no doubts when it came to Elena.

"How do you know?" Her face was a mask hiding a thousand nightmares. "I was glad when Uram died. I was so damn *happy* the bastard was dead."

"Did you delight in his pain?" he murmured in her ear. "Did you smile when he bled, when his flesh burned? Did you laugh when I ended his life?"

He felt her rejection of the idea even before she shook her head, wrapping her arms tight around him. "Do you ever worry?"

"Yes. Cruelty seems to be a symptom of age and power." He thought of Lijuan, raising the dead, playing with them as a child would with toys. "I look into my heart and see the abyss looking back at me."

"I won't let you fall." A fierce promise.

He held her close, his immortal with a mortal heart.

An hour later, and still able to feel Raphael's arms around her, Elena walked into a classroom. Ten pairs of shiny eyes stared at her in mute fascination as she took a seat in the semicircle. Elena was doing some staring of her own. This was the closest she'd ever been to the youngest of immortals—they appeared significantly frailer than she would've guessed, their wings so delicate she could've torn apart each with her bare hands.

Finally, one little girl, her tawny hair in pigtails, wings of autumn and sunset at her back, dared to speak. "Are you a kid?"

Elena bit the inside of her lip and shifted on the big, firm cushion—to her eternal gratitude there'd been one in her size in the corner—that seemed to function as a chair. "No," she answered, feeling her spirits lighten in a way she'd never have expected after her conversation with Raphael. "But I haven't been an angel very long." Of course, when Dmitri had told her she'd be attending lessons to bring her up to speed on angelic culture—to save her from her own ignorance—she hadn't quite expected this.

Whispers behind raised hands, passed angel to angel. Until one almond-eyed girl said, "You were mortal."

"Yep." She leaned forward, resting her elbows on her knees.

"You're not supposed to do that," a boy with loose black curls whispered urgently from her left. "If Jessamy sees you, you'll be in trouble."

"Thanks." Elena sat back up as the boy—who looked about four—nodded in approval. "Why am I not allowed to do that?"

"Because it's bad for your posture."

"Excellent, Sam," an adult voice said from behind Elena. An instant later, a tall, painfully thin angel dressed in a long blue gown swept around Elena's right, heading to the top of the semicircle. This, Elena though, must be the dreaded Jessamy.

"I see you've all met our newest student," the teacher said.

Sam raised his hand.

"Yes, Sam?"

"I can show her around."

"That's very kind of you." A twinkle in those stern brown eyes, hidden within a blink.

But Elena had seen it, and it made her like this woman.

"Now," Jessamy said, "because it's Elena's first day, I'd like to review some of the material we've already covered, particularly that which relates to our physiology."

Elena glanced at Sam. "You're not four, are you?"

"I'm *not* a baby," was the indignant response, before they were both hushed by their neighbors.

Then, as Elena listened and learned, the other students taught her the names and functions of every muscle, every bone, and every feather, from the ones that controlled direction to the ones that reduced drag and increased thrust.

By the time class was over, Elena had a head full of information and a keen awareness of just how much more she still needed to learn.

"You may go," Jessamy said to the class as she rose. "Elena, I'd like a word with you."

Sam's disappointment was all huge brown eyes. "Shall I wait for you?"

"Yes," Elena said. "I haven't been to this part of the Refuge before." It lay in the dead center of the sprawling city—neutral territory according to Illium.

A sunny smile, so innocent it made her suddenly afraid for him. "I'll wait in the play area." Inclining his head toward the teacher, he made his way out the door, his black-tipped brown wings trailing on the floor.

"Sameon," Jessamy said gently.

"Oops." Another smile. "Sorry." The wings lifted up.

"They'll be back down the instant he's out of sight," Jessamy waved to two adult-sized cushions beside a desk piled with books. "Who told you to join the class?"

Suspicion licked up Elena's spine as they took their seats. "Dmitri."

"Ah." The teacher's eyes sparkled. "You weren't supposed to be with the little ones. I'm meant to tutor you separately."

"I'd threaten to skin him," Elena muttered, "but I enjoyed the lesson. Do you mind if I sit in on more? They teach me by simply being."

"You're welcome at any time." Jessamy's thin face grew solemn. "But you must learn far faster than they if you're to survive Zhou Lijuan."

Elena hesitated.

"I know about the reborn," Jessamy said in a voice thick with horror. "I'm the depository of angelic knowledge. It's my duty to keep the histories—but this history, I wish I didn't have to write."

Nodding in silent agreement, Elena put her hand on the books piled on the desk. "Are these for me to read?"

"Yes. They contain a concise glimpse into our recent past." She stood. "Read as much as you can, come to me with any questions, no matter how small or impolitic. Knowledge is very much power when it comes to dancing with the oldest among us."

Elena rose to her feet, her eyes going to Jessamy's wings as the angel turned to retrieve something from behind her. The left one was twisted in a way that made Elena's stomach clench.

"I can't fly," the angel said without rancor though Elena hadn't spoken. "I was born this way."

"I—" Elena shook her head. "That's why you are who you are."

"I don't understand."

"You're kind," Elena said. "I think you're the kindest angel I've ever met." There was no sense of malice in this thin angel with her eyes of burnt sienna and hair that shone a rich chestnut. "You understand pain."

"So do you, Guild Hunter." A perceptive glance as they exited into the sunshine, one that was replaced almost immediately by a quiet but intense happiness. "Galen."

Following Jessamy's gaze led Elena to an angel who'd just landed on the raised platform in front of the school. There was something familiar about the muscular, red-haired male, though she could've sworn she'd never seen him before. Then those eyes of palest green met hers and the cold warning in them opened the floodgates of memory.

Raphael bleeding on the floor. Two angels flying in with a stretcher. This one looking at her as if he'd like to pitch her into the blackness beyond the shattered remains of her plate-glass window . . . and watch as her body fell to hit the ground at terminal velocity, her spine breaking through her skin, her skull nothing but a crushed eggshell leaking gray matter.

Clearly, he hadn't changed his mind.

"Galen." It held censure this time.

The male angel finally looked away from Elena, but didn't speak. Taking the hint, she said good-bye to Jessamy and walked down the steps, her nape prickling in primitive awareness.

"Here I am!"

Startled, she looked up to find Sam flying over to her on wings that looked far too big for his small body. "You can fly already?"

"Can't you?" He hovered beside her.

"No."

"Oh." A wobbly left turn and he was landing at her side. "Then I'll walk, too."

She had to fight a smile as she saw his wings drag along the scrupulously clean pathway. "Is it easier for you to stay airborne?"

"Sometimes, if there's a good wind." He tugged at her hand, pointing to someone on the other side of the courtyard. Looking up, she saw a wide-shouldered angel with wings patterned like an eagle's coming to land. "That's Dahariel. He's one of the old ones."

Dahariel's eyes locked with hers.

Age. Violence. The whiplash of strength.

It was all in that single glance before he gave a curt nod and walked away in the direction of what she'd learned was the archangel Astaad's territory. She shivered in spite of the sunlight. That one, she thought as Dahariel disappeared from sight, might just be capable of beating a man with such heartless precision that nothing whole remained.

Sam pulled at her hand again. "Come on."

As her tiny tour guide took her through the small campus, the sky agonizingly clear overhead, Elena allowed her mind to go quiet. These children were immortal-born, many of them likely older than she was, in spite of their appearance.

But age was a relative thing. In their faces, she saw the same innocence she'd seen in the face of Sara's baby, Zoe. They hadn't yet tasted the bitter tears the world had to offer them.

It seemed the older, more powerful angels, for all their cruelty, made an effort to keep this part of the Refuge free of the stain of violence. It was an oasis of peace in a city that whispered with a thousand dark secrets.

Air over her head, the wash of an adult angel's wings.

Glancing up, she saw a flash of wild blue and then Illium was landing. Shrieks and giggles abounded as the children, Sam included, swarmed him like so many little butterflies. "Save me, Elena," Illium said as he took off into the air . . . but not so high, not so far that the little ones couldn't follow.

Smiling, she sat down on a piece of playground equipment and watched them swoop and dive. Belle would've loved this, she found herself thinking. Her brash older sister had had a secret—she'd loved butterflies. Elena had given her a coin purse in the shape of a monarch once, a pretty thing she'd found at a yard sale for a dime. She'd used her own pocket money to buy it. And Belle had had it in her jeans the day Slater Patalis broke her legs into so many pieces, she'd looked like a child's forgotten doll.

Elena could still see the bright orange sequins glittering in the sea of blood, Belle's lifeless fingers dipped in red.

10

Raphael landed on the outer balcony of Elijah's base in the Refuge, knowing Elena would have liked to meet Hannah. But she was still an immortal barely born—Raphael would never trust her life to the mercurial moods of his fellow archangels and angels. And it wasn't coincidence that both Elijah and Michaela had chosen to come to the Refuge at this time.

The scent of magnolias preceded Hannah's entrance onto the balcony. "Raphael." She held out both hands. "It has been too long."

He took those hands and bent his lips to her cheek. "Over five decades." Hannah didn't often leave her South American home. "You are well?"

Hannah's ebony skin shimmered under the afternoon sunlight as she nodded, her hair a mass of black curls shot with embers that caught the sunlight. "I've come to meet your hunter."

"You surprise me, Hannah." He dropped her hands as she turned to lead him inside.

She laughed, and it was a warm, gentle sound. "I have my flaws. Curiosity is one of them."

"Elena will be flattered to know she has drawn you from your home."

Hannah went to a small, beautifully carved table and picked up a bottle shaped from the most delicate glass. "Wine?"

"Thank you." He looked around the room, saw the touch of Hannah's artistic hand in every painting, every piece of furniture. "You travel more than people know."

A small, secret smile. "Elijah will be through soon. We arrived not long ago."

"Thank you." He took the golden liquid she held out, and the glow of it reminded him of another time, another place. A dying hunter in his arms, her hair a sheet of white. And a heart he'd thought long dead breaking open in anguish.

"What does it taste like?" Hannah asked.

Raphael shook his head. Ambrosia . . . that moment—it was indescribable . . . and utterly private.

After a second, Hannah bent her own head in silent acquiescence. "I'm happy for you, Raphael."

He met her gaze, waited.

"I've always thought of you as a friend," she said quietly. "I know that if the others decided to come after Elijah behind his back, you wouldn't join in."

"Where does your faith come from?"

"From the heart, of course."

Elijah walked out at that moment, his hair damp. "Raphael. You didn't bring your Elena?"

My Elena.

He wondered what his hunter would think of the way immortals spoke of her. "Not this time." Perhaps one day, Elijah was the one archangel he might trust. But that day wasn't today.

"Come," Hannah said, "let us sit." As he watched, she turned to Elijah, and Raphael knew some silent communication passed between them, for Hannah's lips curved before she took her seat.

"So," Elijah said as his mate poured him wine with a poise that held an elegant maturity, "I hear Michaela graces us with her presence."

"It seems she finds the Refuge to her taste these days."

A small smile from the other archangel. "Has Hannah told you about her newest painting? It's extraordinary."

"I've scarcely begun," Hannah demurred. "But, it's almost painting itself."

The next half hour passed in such easy conversation, and though Raphael had guessed the shape the meeting would take, he found himself impatient. It wasn't a feeling he was familiar with—after having lived so long, he'd learned the art of patience. But then he'd met a hunter, and everything had changed.

Finally, he stood with Elijah on the balcony, Hannah having discreetly excused herself. "Do you tell her everything?" Raphael asked.

"Such a personal question. Not what I'm used to from you."

"Elena asked me about angelic relationships. I find I know very little."

Elijah looked down at the river that rushed so far below, twisting in and out of crevices that had grown ever deeper with the passing centuries. "Hannah knows what I know," he said at last.

"Then why does she not stand with us?"

"She knows because she is my mate. She has no desire to be caught up in the workings of the Cadre." A pause. "You don't understand because your hunter has always been entangled with the Cadre."

"How can someone of Hannah's power"—and she'd strengthened a great deal since he'd last seen her—"be content to remain in the wings?"

"Hannah has no taste for politics." Elijah turned to glance at Raphael, his jaw granite. "Such as that which has another angel daring to use my name."

"It displays an arrogance that'll lead to a mistake," Raphael answered, echoing something Elena had said to him after those taut moments when she'd held him so tight—as if she'd physically keep him from falling into the abyss. "He seeks glory. For that, he must be known."

"I understand your anger, Raphael"—Elijah's own fury was a violent heat—"but we can't allow this to distract us from the true problem."

"You've heard something." It was there in the other archangel's eyes, his voice.

Elijah nodded. "There are rumors Lijuan plans to openly show off her reborn at the ball."

Raphael had guessed as much. Jason's last report, delivered after Lijuan's reborn managed to corner him long enough to claw off part of his face, had spoken of an ever-strengthening army of the reawakened dead. "We must prepare for the consequences should the extent of Lijuan's evolution become known."

"The world will shudder," Elijah said, his voice soft in the dusk. "And they'll learn to fear us a little bit more."

"That isn't always a disadvantage." Fear stopped mortals from taking foolish chances, from forgetting that an immortal would always win any battle.

Elijah's face was an aristocratic silhouette against the orange red glow of the setting sun, his golden hair aflame. "Do you think that applies in this case?"

"Mortals are unpredictable—they may brand Lijuan a monster, or they may call her a goddess."

Elijah glanced behind him as Hannah stepped out to ask if they'd like more wine. "Raphael?"

Raphael shook his head. "I thank you, Hannah."

"It's my pleasure."

"What Lijuan is becoming," Elijah said after his mate left, "part of me fears that that's what awaits us all in the end."

"You know as well as I do that our abilities are tied to who we are." Raphael still couldn't understand his own unexpected new talent—where had it grown from, what seed, what act? "And you've never taken the firstborn child of every family in a village just to show your power."

Elijah was visibly shocked. "I've never heard that of Lijuan."

"She was ancient when I was born, when you were born." And Elijah was over three thousand years older than Raphael. "She's done many things which have been hidden in the mists of time."

"Then how do you know?"

Raphael simply looked at the other angel.

After a while, Elijah nodded. "It says little about our intelligence that we do not. What did she do with the children she took?"

"Some, she apparently raised as her mortal pets—kept alive so long as they amused her. Others, she gave to her vampires as a source of food."

"That," Elijah said, "I cannot believe." His face was a mask of revulsion. "Children are not to be touched. It is our most sacred law."

Angelic births were rare, so rare. Each child was considered a gift, but—"Some among us believe it's only angelic children who matter."

Elijah's bones pushed up white against his skin. "Do you?"

"No." A pause, brutal honesty. "I've threatened mortal children to leash their parents." But no matter the parents' transgressions, not once had he touched their young.

"I did the same in the first half of my existence," Elijah said. "Until I understood that the threat is only a step distant from the act."

"Yes." A year ago, while in the grip of the Quiet—a cold, inhumanly emotionless state caused by a specific use of his power—the darkness in Raphael had weighed up the life of a mortal child like so much grain. It was a stain on his soul, a crime for which he'd never seek forgiveness—because it was unforgiveable. But never again would he hold a child's life as ransom. "The one who discovered the atrocity committed by Lijuan," he said, wondering once more what he'd have become without Elena, "witnessed things that make a mockery of any doubt."

"I saw the bodies." Jason's voice strained to the breaking point, his tribal tattoo standing out vivid black against skin that was normally a healthy brown. "Tiny, shriveled things. She keeps them as souvenirs."

"How are they still preserved?"

"After her vampires took their blood, killing them, she had them dried." Jason's dark eyes met his. "There are babies in that room, sire."

Even now, Raphael couldn't think of it without a feeling of profound abhorrence. There were some things you simply did not do. "Had Uram lived," he said, speaking of the archangel he'd killed the night he tasted ambrosia, the night he made a mortal his own, "he may have been well on the road to Lijuan's evolution. He butchered an entire town, even the young in their cribs, for giving offense to one of his vampires."

"The angel who tried to break Noel"—Elijah's rage a thousand steel blades—"he's already on that road. We don't need another on the Cadre."

"No." Because once an angel held that position, the Cadre wouldn't step in—not so long as the angel in question limited his atrocities to his own territory, causing no problems on a global scale. No archangel would countenance interference within his or her sphere of power.

"Have you seen some of the girls Charisemnon's taken to his bed?"

"Too young." It was Venom who'd brought him that information, the vampire—with his skin that spoke of the Indian subcontinent—sliding smoothly into the desert heat of Charisemnon's territory. "But he straddles the line just enough that it remains an internal matter."

Charisemnon was careful not to take any girl under fifteen, his excuse being that he'd grown up in times where fifteen was considered more than old enough for marriage. Except the girls he chose were always the ones who looked far, far younger than their chronological ages. There were enough immortals—and mortals—who agreed with Charisemnon that the archangel could indulge his perversions unchecked.

Elijah looked to Raphael. "Titus is saying Charisemnon took and abused a girl from his side of the border."

"I've been keeping an eye on the situation—it looks to develop into a border war."

"Titus might have his flaws, but on this I agree with him. If Charisemnon broke the territorial boundaries, he must pay—he'll not account for his crimes in any other court."

Raphael agreed. But even Charisemnon, for all his repellent ways, wasn't the threat coming inexorably closer. "I'm not certain Lijuan can be stopped."

"No." Elijah's mouth was a grim line. "Even if we combined our strength, I don't think we could end her life." He took a deep breath. "But we're getting ahead of ourselves. Perhaps she'll remain content to play with her reborn inside her court."

"Perhaps." And perhaps Lijuan would decide to unleash her armies, become the literal embodiment of the demigoddess she already was in her homeland. But this goddess would bring only death, her reborn feasting on the flesh of the living as she watched with smiling indulgence.

It was, Elena later thought, inevitable that she'd dream that night. She could feel the past pulling at her with hands dipped in blood. She fought, kicked out, but still they dragged her down that black corridor, down the curving path her father had laid stone by stone one hazy summer, and into the bright white kitchen her mother had kept spotless.

Marguerite was at the counter. "*Bébé*, why are you standing there? Come, I will make you *chocolat*."

Elena felt her lower lip tremble, her feet hesitate. "Mama?"

"Of course, who else would it be?" A laugh, so familiar, so generous. "Shut the door before the cold gets in."

It was impossible not to reach behind herself, not to close the door. Her hand, she was startled to see, was that of a child, small, marked with the nicks and cuts of a girl who'd rather climb trees than play with dolls. She turned back, terrified the miracle would fade, so scared that it'd be the monster looking back at her.

But it was Marguerite's face she met, her mother's eyes quizzical as she knelt before Elena. "Why so sad, *azeeztee*? Hmm?" Long, gifted fingers tucking Elena's hair behind her ears.

Marguerite knew only a few words in Moroccan Arabic, faint remembrances of the mother she'd lost in childhood. The sound of one of those precious memories made Elena believe. "Mama, I missed you so much."

Hands stroking down her back, holding her close until the tears passed and Elena could force herself to shift back a tiny step, to look down into that beloved face. It was Marguerite who looked sad now, her silver eyes wet with sorrow. "I'm sorry, *bébé*. So sorry."

The dream fractured, bleeding at the edges. "Mama, no."

"You were always the strong one." A kiss pressed to her forehead. "I wish I could save you from what's coming."

Elena stared frantically as the room began to collapse, trails of dark red liquid creeping down the walls. "We have to go outside!" She grabbed her mother's hand, tried to pull her through the doorway.

But Marguerite wouldn't come, her face fierce with warning even as the blood dripped to touch her bare feet. "Be ready, Ellie. It's not over."

"Mama, outside! Come outside!"

"Ah, *chérie*, you know I never left this room."

Raphael rocked his hunter as she cried into his chest, her vulnerability a knife in his heart. He had no words with which to assuage her grief, but he murmured her name until she seemed to see him, until she seemed to know him.

"Kiss me, Archangel." It was a ragged whisper.

"As you wish, Guild Hunter." He thrust his hand into her hair, pressed his lips to hers, and took her over. She still wasn't strong enough to bear the savage depths of his hunger, but he could give her the oblivion she sought—even if the control required meant a violent amplification of the sexual agony already threatening to drive him to madness. He would not hurt her, would not take what she wasn't ready to give.

Shifting on the bed, he pressed his body along hers, letting her feel the heavy weight of his possession. *The nightmares have no claim on you, Elena. You belong to me.*

Eyes of liquid mercury glittered back at him, filled with a roiling storm of emotion. "Then take me."

"Or I could simply tease you." And he did, driving her to a fever pitch with his kiss, with his fingers, with the unrelenting demand of his need to vanquish her nightmares.

Her body was slick on his fingers, her skin damp with perspiration, her eyes blind with arousal when he finally pushed her over. "Raphael!" Her spine went taut as pleasure rushed through her in an overwhelming wave, a pleasure all the more vicious for being denied so long.

He felt his own skin begin to burn with power, his cock pulsing with the need to drive into her until he was all she knew, all she saw. Gritting his teeth, he buried his face in her neck, fighting for control . . . and realized the brutal satisfaction of her body had shoved her into unconsciousness.

11

Five days after Raphael had loved her into merciful oblivion, Elena found herself sitting in a quiet, sunlit garden. The dreams hadn't returned since that night, but she could feel them heavy on the horizon, a storm she wasn't ready to face. If she hadn't had the pitiless discipline of Dmitri's brand of training to keep her occupied, her mind might have beaten itself into insanity in an effort to escape the constant pressure. Because oddly, the Refuge had gone quiet, too, the assault on Noel a seeming aberration.

However, Raphael's anger hadn't abated a fraction. "Nazarach denies involvement," he'd said to her last night as he played his fingers down the plane of her stomach. "I could break his mind, but if he's telling the truth, I'd have to kill him, losing one of the strongest angels in my territory."

Elena had swallowed at the ease with which he spoke of tearing open the other angel's mind, an angel another hunter had once described to Elena as a "monster who'd probably smile as he fucked you to death." "Nazarach would turn against you?"

"As you would if I did the same to you, Elena." His hand played with the top edge of her panties. "I must have proof—or I stand to lose not only his loyalty, but also that of the other strong angels who look to me."

She gripped his wrist, squeezed. Always he gave. Her body wanted him to take. But there was a warning in his gaze, a passion so dark she knew she wasn't ready, wasn't strong enough. Not yet. "Do you need him to hold power?"

He flattened his hand on her abdomen, dipping his head to take her lips in a lazy kiss that made her toes curl into the sheets. Easing them both down from the razor-sharp edge of hunger. "No."

It took her two long seconds to find the breath to reply. "Then?"

"Humans need him, Elena." An almost gentle reminder.

She saw the nightmare he was trying to spare her. "The only reason more vampires don't give in to bloodlust is because an angel has them on a leash."

"And even an archangel can't control every single vampire within his borders. I'd have to slaughter them all if they turned to blood." A raised eyebrow. "Such shadows in your eyes. What do you know of Nazarach?"

"Another hunter did a track for him a while back." Ashwini had refused point-blank to return to Atlanta when an unrelated job came up. "She said his house was full of screams, full of a pain that could drive the sane into hell itself. He apparently took two female vampires to his bed for no reason but to punish their men."

"Vampires choose their eternity when they choose to be Made." A silky answer.

And one she couldn't argue with. Even her sister, Beth, had attempted to be accepted as a Candidate, though she'd witnessed her husband's barbaric punishment at the hands of the angel he called master. "Do you believe Nazarach?"

"He lies with ease, but he's not the only one arrogant enough to believe he can become an archangel."

"Who else is in the Refuge, or was at the time?" They'd

both agreed that the instigator would've been close enough to witness—to revel in—the results of his actions. "Dahariel?" That emotionless gaze, akin to that of the bird of prey whose wings he bore, had spoken of an icily rational mind, able to justify any act if it led to a successful outcome.

A nod. "Also Anoushka, Neha's daughter, has been here for several weeks."

Neha, the Queen of Poisons, of Snakes.

Shivering to think of what her offspring might be capable of, Elena picked up one of the volumes Jessamy had given her and turned her mind to the present, to the prettiness of her surroundings. She'd never have found this secret garden without the blue-winged angel sprawled by her side.

Wildflowers bloomed in bold abandonment, gleefully surrounding the marble pavilion where they'd chosen to sit. The pavilion itself was simple yet elegant in design—four columns holding up a roof that had been carved in faithful imitation of a silk tent from the Arabian lands. "It's way too cold for these flowers." She touched the cheerful pumpkin-colored petals of one that brushed against her thigh as she sat with her feet hanging over the edge.

"The flowers began blooming without warning a month ago." Illium shrugged. "We enjoy them—why question such a gift?"

"I see your point." Opening the book, she spread her wings on the cool marble. With her muscle strength increasing day by day, they no longer seemed a burden but a natural extension of her self. "It says here that the Archangel Wars began because of a dispute over territory."

Illium sat up from his lazy sprawl, his hair tumbling messily over one eye. "That's the whitewashed version for our children," he said, pushing it back. "The truth, as always, is far more human. It all began with a woman."

"Oh yeah?" She made no effort to hide her skepticism.

His smile was a wicked tease. "I'm going to fly. Call if you need me."

She watched him walk to the edge of a rocky cliff, sweep

off in a wave of exquisite silver blue. Then, frowning, she thought, *Raphael.*

The answer came in a split second. *Yes,* he said, *it did begin over a woman.*

Elena almost ripped the page in her hand. *How long have you been listening in?* He hadn't once forced her to act against her will since their silent understanding high above the Refuge, but this—the violation of her thoughts, her secrets—it was as bad. Maybe worse. Because she'd trusted him with her pain, chosen to expose a part of herself she kept tightly held.

We are one, Elena.

"I don't think so." If it had gone both ways, she might've been able to accept it. But it didn't. And she'd fought too hard for her right to be who she was to resign herself to the situation. Taking a deep breath, she shoved mentally outward with all her willpower.

Elena, what are you—

Sudden silence. *Raphael?*

Nothing. No scent of rain inside her head. A scent she hadn't realized she'd been smelling until it was gone. There was no headache, not immediately, but she began to feel the strain after an hour of reading about the wars. It said that Titus had sided with Neha and Nadiel, while Charisemnon had fought beside Antonicus. Lijuan had remained impartial. "Nadiel, Antonicus," she said under her breath, having never before heard those names.

Reaching up to rub at her throbbing temple, she turned the page. The lovingly detailed image took her breath away. The woman's face was a study in purity, her eyes an impossible blue Elena had seen on only one other being, her hair dark as the night . . . dark as Raphael's. "Caliane," she read. "Archangel of Sumeria."

A shooting pain down her neck, and she knew it was time to drop the shield. She'd held it far longer than she'd been able to as a mortal, but not long enough—so she'd have to save it for those secrets she couldn't bear to expose to the world, couldn't even bear to expose to herself.

The scent of wind, of the rain, didn't immediately reappear. But another scent did.

A sensual exotic musk layered with the delicate touch of the rarest of orchids.

It wasn't in her head, she realized at almost the same instant. It was in the air.

Adrenaline spiking, she dropped the book and rose to her feet as Michaela landed in front of her. The visual impact was stunning. Much as Elena disliked her, there was no escaping the truth. Michaela's wings were a gorgeous bronze, her body a landscape of curves and hollows balanced to perfection. And her face . . . there wasn't another as striking in the world.

"So"—lush lips shaping into a smile that made Elena very happy she had her gun with her—"I've unearthed the little mouse Raphael has been hiding." The archangel stepped into the pavilion, her wings caressed to amber by the rays of a sun just beginning to set. She was dressed in sleek camel-colored pants today, her "top" consisting of a single strip of soft white fabric that had been wound around her neck to create a halter before being crisscrossed over her breasts to tie in a knot below her wings. Clean, sexy, inviting.

Elena knew exactly who the invitation was aimed at. Her fingers curled into her palms, common sense crashing and burning in the face of the possessive anger that gripped her by the throat. "I didn't know you found me that fascinating."

Michaela's eyes narrowed. "You're an angel now, hunter. And I'm your superior."

"I don't think so."

The archangel glanced at the book. "That's the company you should be keeping. The half-angel is more your status."

To hear Jessamy—wise, kind, intelligent—described in such a denigrating way made Elena see red. "She's ten times the woman you'll ever be."

Michaela flicked a hand, as if the idea was so ridiculous, it didn't even bear consideration. "She's three thousand years old, and she spends her days shut up with dusty tomes no one but a cripple would consider enticing."

"Galen apparently finds her far more than enticing." It was a shot in the dark.

But it hit home. "Galen's a pup who hasn't yet learned to choose his enemies."

"He didn't want you, either?" Elena said, and even she knew it was a provocation. "But of course, he must've taken his cue from his sire." The breath slammed out of her as she flew through the air to smash up against the marble column on the other side of the pavilion. It hurt like hell, but nothing seemed broken.

That was when it hit her. The cold fist of fear. "Where's Illium?"

"Otherwise engaged." A mocking smile as the archangel walked closer, her every move inherently sensual. "You're bleeding, hunter. How very clumsy of me."

Elena tasted iron from the cut on her lip, but her eyes stayed locked on Michaela. She was well aware the bitch was playing with her, that she'd come here for that specific reason. "If you've harmed him, Raphael will hunt you down."

"And if I harm you?"

"*I'll* hunt you down." Kicking out, she slammed her right foot against Michaela's knee.

To her shock, the archangel went down. But it was, Elena thought, more surprise than anything else, because she was up again a second later, her eyes glowing from within. "I think," the archangel said in a tone that reminded Elena eerily of Uram's sadistic brand of evil, "I'm willing to find out what Raphael will do to someone who dares hurt his little pet."

Elena pressed the trigger on the gun she'd managed to draw the instant after Michaela fell. Nothing happened. Then her fingers unclasped, digit by stiff digit, to drop the weapon to the marble. She felt something hit her chest at the same instant, but when she looked down, there was nothing there. Her heart began to thump in panic. An instant later, it felt as if bone-thin fingers—hard, tipped with nails filed to malicious points—were closing around that panicked organ, squeezing until blood filled her mouth, dripped down her chin.

Michaela looked almost amused. "Good-bye, hunter."

Elena saw a flash of blue to her right, glimpsed Illium surrounded by wings, covered in blood. Feeling returned to her fingers at the same instant. "Bitch." It was a soundless whisper meant to distract as her hand closed on the knife hidden in the side pocket of her pants. Gripping it with all the stubborn determination she had in her, she ignored the pain, ignored the blood welling up in her mouth, and threw.

Michaela shrieked, her hand dropping to the side as the blade embedded itself in her eye. A white-hot fire scorched the pavilion in the next breath, but it was Michaela who ended up smashed unconscious against the back column, not Elena. Trying to see through eyes that watered against the haze of power, Elena glimpsed Raphael, his hands ringed with the deadly glow of angelfire.

She spit out the blood. "No." A croak no one would be able to hear. *Raphael, no, she's not worth it.* He'd killed Uram because it had had to be done, but it had taken something from him to end the life of another archangel. She'd felt the scar, though how, she couldn't say. *I provoked her.*

It doesn't matter. She came here to kill you. He raised his hand, the blue flames licking up his arms, and she knew Michaela was going to die. Sliding to the ground as her legs went out from beneath her, she said something she'd never said to any other man. *I need you.*

Raphael's head snapped to her, his eyes alien in their luminescence. Time froze. And then he was kneeling by her side, the blue fire sucked back inside his body in a violent backdraft. "Elena." He touched her cheek, and she felt an odd warmth invade her body, touch her bruised heart. An instant later, the beat smoothed out.

Raising arms that trembled in reaction, she drew him to her, holding his head as she whispered in his ear. "Don't let her turn you into what she is. Don't let her win."

"She came to harm that which is mine. I can't let that go unpunished."

Possession was a wall of black flame in his eyes, but she knew it was about more than that. "It's about power, right?"

A nod that sent midnight silk sliding over her hands, her archangel willing to listen to reason. For now.

"She's out, unconscious, with my blade in her eye. Leave her somewhere where everyone can see that."

"That's bloodthirsty of you." Lips against hers, his rage held in check. "The humiliation will be worse than any physical torment."

"The bitch not only came after me, she hurt Illium. Is he—"

"He's one of my Seven," Raphael said. "He'll live—though I wouldn't say the same for Michaela's men."

"Poor Bluebell," she said, looking out to see Illium bring down the last angel who'd been fighting with him. "It seems he's always being wounded for—" Her throat closed up as Illium sliced the wings off the fallen male with a sword he'd pulled out of literally nowhere. "Raphael . . ."

"It's a fitting punishment." Rising to his feet, he went to Michaela's body. The other archangel made a moaning sound as he lifted her, but didn't regain consciousness. "Stay, Elena. I will return for you."

She watched him take off, not entirely sure the female archangel would survive the cold rage that had turned Raphael's expression remote in a way she hadn't seen since they became lovers. Bracing her hand on the column behind her, she struggled to her feet just as Illium walked into the pavilion. Blood streaked his face, his hair, his sword.

"Where did the sword come from?" she asked as he took up a sentinel position in front of her. His back was bare, his shirt ripped off him. Spreading his wings, he hid her from sight, until her world was a wall of blood-streaked male muscle and feathers of silver blue drenched with fluid turning to rust.

"I failed you again." It was a tight response.

She took several deep breaths, touched her hand over her heart, still able to feel those phantom fingers clawing at her. "Illium, you took down five other angels. And sliced their wings off." With cold, calm efficiency.

He turned his head to meet her gaze, the faintest trace of a British accent in his frigid tone as he said, "You feel sorry for them?"

"I just—" Shaking her head, she tried to find the words. "When I sat in my apartment watching the angels land on the Tower roof, I used to envy them their ability to fly. Wings are something special."

"They'll grow back," Illium said. "Eventually."

The callous coolness of his voice was a shock. It must've showed, because he gave her a smile formed of ice. "Your pet has fangs, Elena. It disgusts you."

It was the slap she needed to clear the remaining mental fog. "I think of you as my friend. And most of my friends can out-tough a prissy angel any day of the week."

He blinked. Once. Twice. That familiar wicked smile slashed its way across his face. "Ransom has very long, very pretty hair. Maybe I should introduce it to Lightning?"

Of course Illium would name his sword. "Try it and I bet you, you'll be missing some feathers when you get back."

The blue-winged angel lifted the long, double-edged blade as if to sheathe it at his back. She was about to warn him that his harness was gone . . . when the sword disappeared. "We all have our talents, Ellie." A sheepish smile. "Mine is a useful one. I have no personal glamour, but I can make small objects close to my body disappear."

Elena wondered if that meant he'd one day become an archangel. "Have you been wearing a sword the entire time I've known you?"

A shrug. "A sword, a gun, occasionally a scimitar. It's excellent for beheadings."

Elena shook her head at the bloodthirsty recital, then froze when that head began to spin. "Go wash off the blood, Bluebell."

"After Raphael returns."

Elena took a few steps around the pavilion after pushing at Illium to move. "I can walk home." She could feel the bruises blooming, but it wasn't as bad as it could've been—especially when it came to her heart. She rubbed the heel of her hand over it. A little sore, but otherwise okay. "And since I'm not suicidal, you can escort me there."

"The sire asked you to stay."

Actually, Elena thought, it had been more of an order—with no expectation that she'd choose to do anything else. "Illium, you should know something about me if this friendship's going to have a hope in hell of working. I'm unlikely to obey Raphael's every order."

Illium's face filled with censure. "He's right, Ellie. You're not safe here."

"I'm hunter-born," she told him, the words husky. "I've never been safe."

"Oh, my little hunter, my sweet, sweet hunter."

Jerking off the memory like an unwanted coat, but knowing it would return to claim her again and again and again, she began to walk. Illium tried to get in her way, but she had the advantage—she knew he wouldn't lay a finger on her.

She'd forgotten about the angels he'd left in the gardens.

They looked like broken birds, their blood staining the ground, turning the field of flowers into an abattoir.

12

Blood and pain scented the air in a rich perfume that seeped into her very pores. Suddenly, she missed her apartment, the bathroom she'd turned into a personal haven, with a strength that made her tremble inside, her stomach tight enough to hurt.

"How long will they lie there?" she forced herself to ask.

"Until they can move themselves," Illium said, each word a razor. "Or until Michaela sends someone to retrieve them."

That, Elena knew, would never happen. Turning away from the mass of bodies, severed wings, and crushed flowers, she walked slowly up the path. "Wait. My book."

"I'll retrieve it for you after Raphael returns."

Elena hesitated, but knew she didn't have it in her to turn back and walk past the bodies again. "Thank you." She'd only taken a few more steps when the scent of rain, of the wind, infiltrated her every sense.

Illium melted away in silence, and it was Raphael who walked beside her. She expected a reprimand for deviating from his orders, but he said nothing until they were inside the walls of their private wing. Even then, he simply watched her strip off her clothes and enter the shower.

He was waiting with a huge towel when she stepped out, and as he wrapped it around her, the tenderness of the gesture threatened to break her. She looked up, met his eyes as he pushed damp strands of hair off her face. His words were quiet as he said, "The violence of our life shocks you."

Under her palm, his heart beat strong and sure. It was such a human sound, so honest, so real. "It's not the violence." She'd killed her own mentor when he went mad, butchering young boys like they were so much meat. "It's the inhumanity of it all."

Raphael stroked his hand over her hair, his wings unfolding to surround her. "Michaela came after you for a very human motive—she's jealous. You're now the center of attention, and she cannot stand it."

"But the cruelty in her eyes." Elena shivered at the memory. "She enjoyed hurting me, enjoyed it in a way that reminded me of Uram." The bloodborn angel had kicked at her broken ankle, sent her screaming. And then he'd smiled.

"They were mates for a reason." Another stroke, his heart so warm and vibrant under the cheek she'd pressed to his chest. But he was also the man who'd punished a vampire with such icy practicality that New Yorkers avoided that once bloodstained patch of Times Square even now.

"What did you do to Michaela?" she asked, her skin going cold with the realization that humiliation alone would have never been enough for Raphael. He didn't act capriciously, but when he did act, the world shivered.

A midnight breeze in her mind. *I told you once, Elena. Never feel sorry for Michaela. She'll use that to rip out your heart while it is still beating.*

The heart he'd referred to gave a panicked beat of memory, the muscle bruised, painful. "How was she able to do that, reach inside me that way?"

"It seems Michaela has been hiding a new power." His

voice dropped. "It's no coincidence that she gained it so soon after coming close to death with Uram."

"He had her alone for long enough," Elena said, remembering the raw fear in Michaela's eyes when they'd rescued her. It had been the first time she'd seen an archangel afraid, and it had rocked her. "Do you think he changed her somehow?"

"His blood changed the woman, Holly Chang. She's neither vampire nor mortal now. It remains to be seen what becomes of Michaela."

Elena was ashamed to realize she'd forgotten about the only surviving victim of Uram's attacks. "Holly? How is she?" The last glimpse Elena had had of her, she'd been naked, her skin caked with blood, her mind half broken.

"Alive."

"Her mind?"

"Dmitri tells me she'll never again be who she was, but she isn't lost to madness."

It was far more than Elena had expected, but she caught the things he didn't say. "Dmitri's still got people watching her, hasn't he?"

"Uram's poison altered her on a fundamental level—we must know what she's become."

And, Elena understood without asking, if Holly proved too much Uram's creature, Dmitri would slit her throat without hesitation. Instinct warred with harsh reality—Uram's evil could not be allowed to spread. "You never answered my question," she said, hoping Holly Chang would spit in her attacker's face, that she'd save herself. "What did you do to Michaela?"

"I left her in a public place with your dagger in her eye. The eye had already healed around it."

"What does that mean?"

"Pain for Michaela when she pulls it back out, when she reheals." There was no mercy in him. "It's why Noel's attackers drove shards of glass into his flesh."

She knew he'd linked the vicious beating and his own actions on purpose. Another reminder of who he was, what he was capable of. Did he expect her to run? If he did, he had a lot to learn about his hunter. "You did something else."

You think you know me so well, Guild Hunter.

At that moment, he sounded like the archangel she'd first met, the one who'd made her close her hand over a knife blade, his eyes devoid of mercy. "I know you well enough to figure out you'd never let an insult pass unanswered." She'd seen that in his relentless search for Noel's attackers—his resolute determination likely the reason the angel behind it had gone to ground.

"In your travels around the Refuge, did you ever see a rock that reaches toward the sky on the other side of the gorge?"

"I think so. It's very thin, sharp . . ." Her mind made the connection with sickening ease. "You dropped her on that rock, didn't you?"

She would've ripped out your heart. I simply returned the favor.

Goose bumps crawled over her skin at the ice in his tone. Crushing the fabric of his shirt under her hand, she took a deep breath. "What would you do to me if I ever did something to make you that angry?"

"The only thing you could do to make me that angry would be to lie with another man." A quiet statement against her ear. "And you would not do that to me, Elena."

Her heart clenched. Not at the darkness in his words. At the vulnerability. Again, she was shaken by the power she had over this magnificent being, this archangel. "No," she agreed. "I would never betray you."

A kiss pressed to her cheek. "Your hair is damp. Let me dry it."

She stood motionless as he stepped back and picked up another towel, drying her hair with the careful gentleness of a man who knew his own strength far too well. "You closed your mind to me."

"I might not be human any longer, but I'm still the woman who stood against you on the Tower roof that first day." Now that terrifying male she'd met was her lover, and she knew if she gave in to his demands, the relationship between them would be irrevocably, unalterably damaged. "I can't accept your right to invade my mind as you please."

"It is said Hannah and Elijah share a mental bond," he told her, putting the towel down and tugging her hand to lead her into the bedroom. "They are always with each other."

"But I'm betting their link goes both ways." She stroked the arched line of his right wing—rising gracefully from his back. His shirt draped easily over his muscular frame, the back designed to accommodate wings. "Doesn't it?"

"In time," Raphael said, his voice changing, becoming deeper, "we will have that."

She stroked the ridge again, dropped a kiss to the center of his back. "Why do you sound so certain when so many things about angelic power seem to depend on the angel?"

You speak to me with the ease of a two-hundred-year-old already. You'll gain the power.

"That's good to know." She walked around to face him. "But until I do, I won't allow one-way traffic."

His eyes were arctic, so very, very blue she knew the color would follow her into her dreams. "If your mind had been open," he said, "I would've known of Michaela's arrival the moment you did."

Okay, he had her there. But— "If you let me have my privacy, then I won't mind calling out to you when I need you."

His hand on her cheek, a protective, possessive touch. "You didn't call today."

"I was taken by surprise." She shook her head, took a deep breath. "No, I'll be honest. I haven't yet learned to rely on you. I'm used to dealing with things alone."

"That's a lie, Elena." He brushed her cheekbone with his thumb. "You'd call Sara for help in a heartbeat."

"Sara's been my friend since I was eighteen. She's more my sister than my friend." Reaching up, she put her hand over his. "I don't know you like I know Sara."

"Then ask, Guild Hunter." An order from the Archangel of New York. "Ask what you would know."

13

Raphael was angry. But, Elena thought, this clean, bright anger, she could deal with. When he became as he had earlier with Michaela, then she was fearful for his very soul. "Tell me about your childhood," she said. "Tell me what it's like to grow up a child in an angelic world."

"I will, but first, you'll get into bed, and I'll bring you something to eat."

Realizing that was one battle she didn't particularly want to fight, she shucked off the towel as he went to the other room to get the food, and shimmied into one of Raphael's shirts. The slots in the back flowed around her wings, but she could find nothing with which to secure them at the bottom. Deciding she couldn't really be bothered searching for the illusive closures, she was sitting quietly in bed when he returned.

He halted for a second. "I'm surprised to find that you obeyed an order."

"I'm not unreasonable . . . so long as the order is reasonable."

A gleam of amusement lit the arctic blue as he placed the

plate of bite-sized treats on the mattress between them, the glasses of water on the bedside table, and came to sit on the bed diagonally opposite her. They'd taken this position before, but that time, he'd been on her side of the bed.

Very conscious of the subtle distance, she picked up a tiny sandwich filled with what looked like thin slices of cucumber. "So?"

A long, long moment passed before he spoke. "Being a child among angels is a joy. Children are petted and generally spoiled. Even Michaela wouldn't harm a child's heart."

Elena found that hard to believe. But then again, Michaela had once gotten out of bed to let what she'd believed was a trapped bird out of her room. The archangel wasn't pure Wicked Witch of the West, for all that Elena would've liked to typecast her in that role.

"My childhood was ordinary, except that my father was Nadiel, my mother, Caliane."

The breath rushed out of her. "You're the son of two archangels?"

"Yes." He turned, looking toward the mountains, but she knew it wasn't the snow-capped peaks, the starlit sky, that he saw. "It's not the gift it seems."

Elena stayed silent, waiting.

"Nadiel was a contemporary of Lijuan's. Older by only a thousand years."

A thousand years. And Raphael spoke of it so very easily. How old did that make Lijuan? "He was one of your ancients."

"Yes." Raphael turned back to her. "I remember listening to him talk of sieges and battles long past, but mostly, I remember watching him die."

"Raphael."

"And now you feel sorrow for me." Raphael shook his head. "It was at the dawn of my existence."

"But he was your father."

"Yes."

Tracing her eyes over that harshly masculine, impossibly

beautiful face, she moved the tray of food to the floor. He watched, silent, as she pushed aside the blankets and came to sit in front of him, her hand braced on his thigh. "Fathers and mothers," she found herself saying, "leave their mark, no matter if we've known them a lifetime or only a day."

He raised his hand to her wings, stroking one hand down the sweep of black and indigo. "Raphael." It came out husky, a censure.

"I haven't spoken of my parents in centuries." Another lingering stroke along her wings. "My mother executed my father."

The words cut through the haze of pleasure with ruthless precision. "Executed?" Images of broken, decaying bodies filled her mind as she was catapulted back into Uram's depraved playground.

"No," Raphael said, "he didn't turn bloodborn."

There was no scent of the wind, of the rain, in her mind. "How did you know?"

"The horror is painted across your face." His eyes shifted to a color that had no name, it was so heavy with memory. "Uram revered what my father was."

"Why?"

"Can you not guess, Elena?"

It wasn't hard, not when she thought back to what she knew about Uram. "Your father thought angels should be worshipped as gods," she said slowly. "That mortals and vampires should bow down before you."

"Yes."

There was a knock on the balcony doors before she could formulate a reply. Glancing over, she saw only darkness. "Is it Jason?"

"Yes," Raphael said, rising off the bed, his expression grim. "And Naasir awaits below."

She watched him step out onto the balcony, and though she knew Jason was there, she still couldn't make out anything of the black-winged angel's form.

Elena, get dressed.

Caught by the urgency of the command, she got out of bed and pulled on a pair of cotton panties, ignoring the bruises that had already begun to turn a nice putrid purple on her back and thighs. Over the panties, she donned a pair of black pants made of some kind of tough, leatherlike material, and—after shedding the shirt—a top that wrapped around her in a complicated pattern of straps, but ended up covering her chest while leaving her arms and most of her back bare. The fit was snug, leaving her free to move without worrying about extraneous material getting in her way.

Having felt the approaching cold front, she slipped on long, tight sleeves that fit securely just below her shoulders—they'd provide warmth while ensuring her arms remained unrestricted. As she grabbed her boots, she arrowed her thoughts to Raphael, aware he was no longer on the balcony. *Where?*

Dmitri will escort you.

The vampire was waiting for her in the hallway, and for once, there was no hint of sex about him—unless you liked your sex lethal. Wearing black leather pants, a black T-shirt that hugged his leanly muscled frame, and a long black coat that swept around his ankles, he was death honed to a gleaming edge. Straps crisscrossed his chest and she recognized them as a dual holster.

"Weapons?" he asked.

"Gun and knives." The knives sat on either side of her thighs, but the gun she'd tucked into her boot after debating whether to put it in the curve of her lower back and deciding she wasn't yet confident enough in terms of getting her wings out of the way fast enough.

"Let's go." Dmitri was already walking.

The sky was a brilliant, exotic black when they exited, the stars so clear it felt as if she could reach out and touch them. The first snow to hit the Refuge glittered underfoot, having fallen with stealthy silence in the interval since she'd gone inside.

"How bad are your injuries?" A cool glance, his eyes assessing her as nothing but another tool.

"I'm functional," she said, knowing she could work through the muscle stiffness, the dull ache in her chest. "Nothing's broken."

"You may need to track."

"That part of me never stopped working. As you know very well."

"Wouldn't want you to get out of practice." Casual words, but his eyes were those of a predator on the hunt, his strides eating up the ground as they walked toward a section of the Refuge that seemed made up of midsized family dwellings.

Lights blazed in every window they passed, but the world was eerily hushed.

"Here." Dmitri headed down a narrow pathway lit with lamps that appeared as if they'd been transported from mid-nineteenth-century England. Mind swirling with possibilities, she kept her eyes firmly on the path as it twisted this way and that, leading finally to a small home on the very edge of a cliff.

A perfect location.

The cliff would provide for easy takeoffs, and there was plenty of space in front when it came to landings. But, given the terrain, there appeared to be only one way out for those on foot—the path they'd just traversed. A stupidly easy trail. So why would Raphael need a scent-tracker?

Elena.

Following Raphael's mental voice, she headed to the house . . . to the smell of iron turning to rust. Her body froze on the doorstep, her foot refusing to step over the threshold.

Drip.

Drip.

Drip.

"Come here, little hunter. Taste."

It was a shock of memory, shoving her into the past with such brutal swiftness that she couldn't fight the descent.

Belle, still alive when she walked in. But only for a fragment of a moment, her eyes filming over with death even as Elena reached out—

Waves of scent, the most decadent chocolate and cham-pagne, promises of pleasure and pain. Arousal uncurled, and it was so wrong for this moment that it snapped the loop of nightmare. Taking a shallow breath, she stepped over the threshold, forcing herself to walk into another home stained with the kiss of malice.

Dmitri's scent began to fade almost immediately and at rapid speed. He was leaving, she realized, aware she couldn't track effectively with his intense scent bleeding into the air. But he'd remained long enough to give her that mental slap when she hesitated on the doorstep.

It put her in his debt.

Scowling at the idea, she concentrated on her surround-ings. This was clearly the main living area, with a vaulted ceiling and an overall impression of space. Books filled the shelves that lined the walls, and there was a handwoven rug in Persian blue beneath her feet. On her left she saw a cup sitting atop a small, intricately carved table, while underneath it lay what appeared to be a stuffed toy of some kind. The sight of the raggedy thing made her heart chill. Angels, as she now knew, did have children.

Setting her shoulders against the horror she might find, she ignored the doors on either side and walked straight down the hallway to the room at the very back.

White walls splashed with red.

The sound of a woman's sobs.

A tumbled glass, the scarlet of an apple on the counter.

Fragments of thought, images coming in like splinters of glass. Her throat locked, her spine went rigid, but she forced herself to stay, to *see*. The first thing she registered was Raphael kneeling before another angel, a tiny woman with tumbling curls of glossy blue black, her wings a dusty brown streaked with white. Raphael's own wings spread on the floor, uncaring of the fluid that turned the gold to mottled umber.

Find him. A command laced with a violence of emotion.

Nodding, she took a deep breath . . . and was hit by an avalanche of scents.

Fresh apples.

Melting snow.

A whisper of oranges dipped in chocolate.

Unsurprised at what vampires smelled like to her hunter senses by now, she drew in that last scent, stripping it down to its very basics—until she could isolate that particular combination of notes even in the midst of a crowd of thousands.

However, the other scent, the fresh apples and the snow, that wasn't a vampire. The composition of it was unique, unlike anything she'd ever before tasted. She did a double check. No, categorically not a vamp. And not, as she'd first thought, merely a magnification of the scents floating in the atmosphere. It was another person.

The fresh, exhilarating bite of the sea. Wind scouring her cheeks.

A taste of spring, sunlight, and freshly mown grass.

And beneath it all, the flickering, familiar taste of fur against her tongue.

But it wasn't Dmitri playing with her this time. "Who lives here?" she managed to ask through the chaos of impressions. "Snow and apples and fur and spring." It made no sense, but Raphael was in her mind almost before she finished speaking. She fought her instinctive attempt to repel him, realizing he needed to know what she'd picked up.

Sam is the snow and the apples, his father the fur, his mother the spring.

Her heart froze in her chest as she met the excruciating blue of his eyes. "Where's Sam?"

"Taken."

The tiny female angel lifted a fist to her mouth, her hand so small it could've been that of a child's. "Find my son, Guild Hunter." The same words, said by Raphael, would've been an order. From this woman, they were a plea.

"I will." It was a promise and a vow. Hunkering down, she drew in the scents again, then stood, angling her head like the bloodhound she was.

The faintest trace of oranges.

Following the tug, she walked past Raphael and Sam's mother to place her hand on the back doorknob. The scent rocked through her. "Yes," she whispered, her hunter senses singing in recognition. Pulling open the door, she stepped out . . . into nothing.

14

She'd fallen before. But then, she'd been held in the arms of an archangel. This time, there was nothing between her and the unyielding embrace of the rocks below. Panic threatened but was beaten into submission by her will to live. Elena P. Deveraux had never given up yet.

Gritting her teeth, she spread out her wings. They faltered, still weaker than necessary for flight, but managed to slow her descent. Not enough, she thought, her eyes tearing against the wind, her back muscles starting to spasm. Even an immortal—especially a young immortal—couldn't survive such a crippling fall.

Her body would be shredded by the velocity of the impact, her head separated from her body. That killed vampires. And Raphael had said—"Oh!" A wash of powerful air that sent her spiraling, terror a shock through her bloodstream. Then arms grabbing hold of her with a steely strength she'd never mistake for anyone but Raphael's.

They fell several more feet, their velocity accelerated by the impact, before Raphael steadied and they began to rise in a storm of speed. She wrapped her arms around his neck, shaking with relief. "Seems like you're always catching me when I fall."

His answer was a hard squeeze.

They landed on an empty section of the cliff, the nearest angelic home hidden from sight by the jutting teeth of the craggy rock face. "Okay, lesson number one," she said, trying to relearn to breathe as Raphael put her down, "never assume there's going to be earth beneath my feet."

"You must stop thinking like a human." Raphael's voice was a whip. "It could've gotten you killed today."

She jerked up her head. "I can't simply stop. It's all I've ever known."

"Then learn." He gripped her chin between his fingers. "Or you'll die."

Her first instinct was to strike back, but something stopped her. Perhaps it was the more important life at stake, or perhaps it was the way his wings came around her, sheltering her from the snow-laced wind even as he spoke to her in such anger. "I need to get back inside," she said, "see if I made a mistake in the track."

Raphael held onto her chin for another second before placing his lips over hers. They were still locked in the angry relief of the kiss as he rose into the air, flying her to the front entrance of Sam's home. Shaken but determined, she walked through the house, every sense on alert . . . and came to the same conclusion.

"He went out through there," Elena said, glad Sam's mother was no longer in the room. It was impossible for Elena to look at her and not remember another mother's anguish in a small suburban home almost two decades ago.

"That means he had an angelic accomplice." Raphael's voice was toneless—and all the more terrifying for it. In this mood, the Archangel of New York might kill without remorse, torture without compassion. "You picked up the members of Sameon's family—can you separate out the angel's scent?"

"Raphael," she asked, needed to ask, "are you going

Quiet?" He'd become someone she didn't know in those terrifying hours before she'd shot him, an archangel who'd stalked
her across New York, relentless in his menace.

No.

Her heart still erratic with fear—for him, for what the
Quiet might take from him if he fell into it again—she returned to the now open doorway, attempting to intentionally
trigger what appeared to be an extension of her abilities.

Spring and fur.

Apples dusted with fresh sno—

A crackle of white noise.

Disappointment stabbed her, harsh, final. "If my Making
altered my hunter senses, the change isn't complete. It seems
to be cutting in and out." She shoved a hand through her hair,
falling back on her training and experience. "He likely didn't
touch the door in any case—the vampire's scent was too rich,
too strong to have been diluted." Looking down into the inky
depths of the ravine, she felt her cheeks turn to ice. "How
strong would an angel have to be to catch someone if they
knew that individual was about to jump?"

"No one younger than three hundred." His wing brushed
hers as they stood side by side, staring at the dense blackness. "I'll begin sweeps of the area." And then he said what
she hadn't been able to articulate. "There's a chance the fall
wasn't successfully executed."

Elena's whole being rebelled against the idea of Sam's
small body lying irrevocably broken in the cold dark. "If
those bastards have hurt him, I'll gut them myself."

That is why you're mine, Elena.

Watching as he stepped out into the night air, she closed
the door and walked back to the front. All the angels were
gone, but a vampire moved out of the shadows as she exited
the house. His skin was a shade that drew the eye, inviting
tactile contact—a dark, dark brown with an undertone of true
gold. The color was so rich, so warm that it shimmered even
as the moon slid behind a cloud, enveloping the Refuge in purest night. But his eyes, a brilliant, impossible silver, pierced

the darkness as if it didn't exist. Hair of the same shade as his eyes fell around his face, sleek and cut in jagged lines that accentuated the angle of his jaw.

"A tiger," she whispered, watching him walk to her, though to call it a walk was a gross disservice. His stride was the fluid, silent prowl of the animal she sensed around him. "You have the scent of a tiger on the hunt." Rich, vibrant, deadly.

"I am Naasir." His voice was cultured, his words gracious, but those metallic eyes watched her with unblinking focus. "Dmitri asked me to assist you."

"You're one of the Seven." There was power in Naasir, not like Dmitri's—sensual and lethal—but sharply feral, as if that exquisite, strokable skin was nothing but a mask for the predator within.

"Yes."

The clouds parted, throwing a beam of moonlight onto his face. And she realized the vampire's eyes reflected as brilliantly as a cat's. *Impossible*. But Naasir wasn't the mystery she had to solve tonight. "I'm going to start canvassing the area," she said, "see if I can find a landing point." It'd be a crapshoot given how far angels could fly, but she needed to do something.

"Dmitri's organizing the vampires and younger angels into a similar search."

And, Elena thought, they'd cover ground far faster than she could—especially when she had no starting point for a scent-track. But she needed to do *something*. Looking away from Naasir's unblinking stare, she found her eye caught by a needlelike formation in the distance. Her heart ricocheted off her ribs. "How well do you know the Refuge?"

"Very."

"Show me to Michaela's section." Raphael had been ruthless with the other archangel's humiliation. Maybe the angel who'd brutalized Noel had crawled back out of his hole . . . or maybe Michaela had decided on payback, striking at the heart of those who looked to Raphael for protection.

"This way." Naasir began to move with the preternatural grace of a being at home in the night.

She could only just keep up with what she guessed was a crawl for him.

Stepping out into an open area a few minutes later, he raised his arm in some kind of a signal before turning to her. "Michaela's home is far on foot."

Elena felt her spine lock as Illium landed less than three feet from them. She trusted no one but Raphael to carry her. Not only did she have a problem with trust, the act seemed too intimate, too close. Especially given the near painful sensitivity of her wings. However, tonight, there was a far more pragmatic reason for her reluctance. "I go up," she said, "I might miss the vampire's scent on the ground if he wasn't flown straight to Michaela's."

Illium held out a hand. "It'll be much quicker for you to fly to Michaela's, check the grounds, then return."

Knowing he was right, she squelched her personal reluctance and went to him, aware of Naasir vanishing into the dark. "Is it me or is Naasir about as tame as your average mountain lion?"

"Compared to him, the lions are tabby cats." Illium closed his arms around her waist as she wrapped hers around his neck, her wings held tight to her spine. It made her easier to carry—and it hid the incredibly sensitive inner curve where her wings grew out of her back.

"Your bruises."

"Don't drop me because you're worried about holding on too hard."

"I won't let you fall." It was an intimate whisper against her ear as he rose into the air.

"Famous last words," she muttered, the wind whipping the hair off her face, threatening to steal her breath, her words.

"You're spoiled, Ellie. You're used to being carried by an archangel." He skimmed under several other angels, heading toward an elegant group of buildings on a relatively smooth piece of ground. The land around the buildings was lit with delicately shaped metal lanterns, the paths a lilting melody of form and function.

"Are there gardens down there?" she asked, Illium's breath warm against her cheek as he bent his head to catch her question.

"She rarely visits, but Michaela's gardens are famed in the Refuge. Even in the cold, she finds things that will grow, sometimes even bloom."

Bloom.

Her mind cascaded with images from the garden of wildflowers—blood-soaked petals littering the ground, maimed bodies crushing the flowers, and most powerful of all, the setting sun glinting off Illium's sword as he amputated wings with merciless efficiency. She wondered if those angels were still there, lying forsaken in the dark.

"She may be many things—cruel, malicious, selfish," Illium murmured as he brought them to a smooth landing on the outer terrace of Michaela's home, "but I don't think the Queen of Constantinople would harm a child."

"You didn't see the look in her eyes at the pavilion." Stepping out of Illium's arms, she wasn't surprised to see Riker appear in front of the closed doorway. She'd picked up his scent—cedar painted with ice, evocative and unexpected—the instant they landed. "Hello, Riker." It took effort to keep her voice civil—the last time she'd seen Michaela's favorite guard, he'd been pinned to a wall, his heart skewered by the torn-off leg of a table, but the time before that, he'd tried to play a very nasty game with her.

Riker stared at her in that way he had—cold-blooded as any reptile. "You're in my mistress's territory. You have no protection here."

"I'm looking for Sam," Elena said. "Illium tells me Michaela wouldn't hurt a child, so I'm hoping she'll give us permission to search the grounds—in case the vampire passed through here."

"My mistress has no need of your approval."

Elena shoved her hand through her hair, attempting to keep her tone temperate though a helpless urgency pumped through her blood. "Look," she said, "I'm not here to pick a fight. And if your mistress truly cares about the young, she won't be happy to find that you blocked us."

Riker didn't move, those reptilian eyes never shifting off her.

Feeling time slipping through her fingers, she was about to ask Illium if he could simply fly her over the grounds so she could see if the scent lingered in the air, when Riker reached for the doorknob. "The mistress will allow you to walk through the house."

Surprised, Elena made no delay in following Riker, with Illium at her back. Michaela's home took her breath away—the entranceway alone was worthy of the term "work of art"; the tiles beneath her feet were ebony veined with quartz, the walls on either side painted with scenes that sent the mind soaring. Elena was no sophisticate, but even she recognized the artist. "Michelangelo?"

"If he did," Illium murmured, "he'd have forgotten it the moment he left. No mortal must know of the Refuge."

And yet, Elena thought, Sara did. Her heart squeezed. She knew Raphael had allowed it because of—and *for*—her, taking a far bigger step than she'd ever have expected of the archangel she'd met on that windswept roof in New York. "He remembered somewhere deep in his soul," she said, checking out a room that flowed off the entranceway.

It proved clean. She picked up the scents of several other vampires as they continued to walk, but not even a flicker of the one she'd sensed in that small kitchen drowning in the salt of a mother's tears. But they'd barely scratched the surface. Looking up at the soaring central core, she put her hand on the banister. "I need to go upstairs."

"You will keep your distance from the mistress's quarters."

"Fine." If Michaela was protecting the vampire, it wouldn't do any good for Elena to go barging in and get both herself and Illium killed before they'd gotten Sam out of danger. All she had to do was find the merest trace of scent.

But the second floor proved as pristine and as elegant as

the first, each sculpture placed in exactly the right position to enhance the overall grace of the house, the rugs beneath her feet drenched with color. It was as she was crossing the ruby and cream one near the second set of stairs that it hit her.

Oranges dipped in chocolate.

Her entire body stiffened. Spinning on her heel, she sprinted down a hallway that Riker had specifically warned her not to enter, instinct overriding common sense. This was what she'd been born to do, her senses honed to—

An arm around her waist, pulling her back against a firm, muscled chest, her wings screaming against the overload of sensation. "Riker would like nothing better than to have a legitimate excuse to kill you." Illium's voice, that faint British accent laced with a steely thread of warning.

"Right." She shook her head to clear it, suddenly aware of Michaela's favorite vampire standing only inches from her side. And she'd let him get that close, she'd been so blinded by the compulsion to follow the scent, to bring back the child. "Right."

Illium continued to hold her until she pushed at his hands and took a step to the left, creating more distance between her and Riker. "Raphael?"

"It's done." Eyes the rich, unique color of Venetian gold looked into hers. "He won't be long."

Elena had to fist her hands, grit her teeth, to fight the thundering need to run after that fading scent. Riker stood on Illium's other side. But his eyes, they never moved off her. The hairs on the back of her neck rose. Michaela had obviously never rescinded the order she'd once given Riker—to kill Elena.

"You run to your master," the vampire said without warning. "Like a child."

"Raphael is my lover, not my master." She cursed herself for responding to the barb the instant the words left her mouth.

"Is that what you think?" he said, and it was a croon, soft and mocking in its sweetness. "They call you his pet."

Her spine went rigid, the words too close to the ones Raphael had said to her when she'd woken. "How's that purse your mistress had made?" she asked, reminding him that Michaela had once flayed the skin off his back, then cured it. "She still taking good care of it?"

"The best." His tone didn't change, and that was the creepiest thing of all. Riker was so far in the abyss that he liked it. "Your master comes."

Refusing to respond to the taunt, she waited until Raphael walked up to stand beside her. "Michaela is not pleased," were his first words.

"Do you care?"

We're in her home, Elena. The rules of Guesthood apply.

She tried to temper her tone, but it was difficult, her hunter senses shoving at her with escalating force. "I can smell the vampire who took Sam. The scent leads that way."

"Follow it." *Michaela is furious, but she wishes to see you humiliated more.*

Then she's going to be disappointed. But it niggled at her, that the other archangel would be so sure of Elena's failure, because the vampire who'd abducted Sam had been here, no ifs, no buts. The tart bite of orange, the sweetness of chocolate—she could all but taste it.

It was so pungent, so rich, she almost missed the scent hidden beneath.

Snow falling on apples.

15

"Sam." It was less than a whisper as she began running, far more interested in that gentle scent than the one that had drawn her here. The hallway ended at a door, a heavily carved slab that had been varnished until it glowed darkest amber.

Her palms slammed up against it as she came to a halt. "He's behind here."

"No, he's not." Michaela's voice lashed the air as she appeared from their left, her face and body pristine once more. A silent testament to the power of an archangel. "I shall enjoy delivering your punishment for violating my home without cause."

"There'll be no punishment," Raphael said. "She falls under my protection."

Michaela smiled, small, satisfied, vicious. "But she doesn't accept you as her master. You cannot stand as her shield."

And Elena knew Michaela was really, really looking forward to making her scream. It didn't matter. "Open this door."

Michaela waved a languid hand at Riker. "Do as the hunter says."

Elena shifted away to avoid physical contact with the vampire as he moved to do his mistress's bidding. The door swung inward to reveal a room swathed in shadow, but for the faint snow-reflected silver of the moon. Elena didn't need light to find her target. Walking inside, she headed unerringly to what proved to be a large chest when Riker threw on the wall-mounted lights, their glow a muted honey.

"Can a baby immortal survive without air?" she whispered desperately as she struggled to lift the heavy lid.

"For a time," was the chilling answer as Raphael took over the task, while Illium stood watch.

For the first time in her life, Elena hoped she was wrong, that Sam wasn't in that trunk. But the Cadre had hired her because she was the best—she didn't make mistakes. "Oh God!" Instinct had her reaching inside, but she hesitated an inch away from that tiny curled-up body. "I'll hurt him." He was so bloody, so very broken.

"We must take him to the healers."

Nodding, she brought out that crumpled body in her arms. Sam's wings had been crushed, the fine bones likely shattered. The majority of the blood had come from what looked like a head wound, as well as a cut on his chest. A chest that wasn't moving. *God, please.* "Is he alive?"

Raphael, his face a stone mask, touched the boy's cheek, and it was only then that Elena saw the *sekhem* branded into that delicate skin.

"Yes, he lives."

Rage a hurricane inside of her, she held Sam as close as she dared and went to walk past Michaela, but the archangel was staring at Sam, such a stricken expression on her face that Elena felt her throat lock, her feet root to the floor.

"He's alive?" the archangel asked, as if she hadn't heard a single word that had passed 'til then.

"Yes," Raphael answered. "He lives."

"I can't heal him," Michaela said, looking at her hands as if they belonged to a stranger. "Raphael, I can't *heal* him."

Raphael walked forward to place one hand on the female

archangel's shoulder. "He'll be fine, Michaela. Now we must go."

Elena, already at the door with Illium, waited only until Raphael was in the hallway before handing over her precious burden. "You're faster. Go."

Raphael left without further words. Elena was about to follow when she heard Michaela say, "I didn't do this." It was a broken sound.

Shaken, she looked back to glimpse Riker kneeling beside his mistress, her glorious wings dragging on the floor as she collapsed to the ground. "I didn't do this," she repeated.

Riker stroked Michaela's hair back from her face, the devotion in his eyes a brilliant, blinding thing. "You did not do this," he said, as if in reassurance. "You could not."

"Elena"—Illium's lips brushing her ear—"we must go."

Snapping her head back around, she followed his lead, not speaking until they were out in the ice-cold air. "I had her all figured out," Elena said in a low whisper, conscious of the large number of vampires who surrounded the house. "She was the Bitch Queen and that was that."

"A big part of her is exactly that."

"But what we saw today . . . where did that come from?"

She felt Illium hesitate. His words when they came, were quiet. "Angels don't have many young. It is our worst pain to lose a child."

Michaela had lost a child.

The realization shook her, skewing her view of Michaela in a wholly unexpected direction. "Then this bastard wasn't out to hurt Sam, not really." That somehow made it worse. "He was out to hurt Michaela."

"Or," Illium said, "his aims were higher. Titus and Charisemnon are already warring over a girl-child Charisemnon swears he didn't take, and Titus swears he did. Whether this angel had anything to do with that, or simply took inspiration from it, they're locked in their own world, indifferent to outside concerns."

The pieces fell into place. "He failed to pit Elijah against

Raphael, but if you hadn't grabbed me when you did, if Riker had managed to touch me—"

"Raphael would've gone for blood."

"Sam was *bait*?" Her stomach roiled.

"If the trap had been successful, it would've taken two more archangels out of the equation."

Weakening the Cadre, leaving room for a power play that would turn a sociopath into an archangel. "I need to check the grounds," she said, forcing herself to think past the abhorrent nature of this act, to ignore the gut-wrenching sight of Sam's blood on her hands, her clothes. "There's a chance the vampire left here on foot."

Illium pulled out his sword. "Go."

Michaela's vampires smelled like many things—cloves and eucalyptus, burgundy and agar, with base notes as far apart as sandalwood and the darkest cherry-flavored kiss. But there wasn't even a hint of citrus, of oranges dipped in chocolate. "Nothing," she said more than thirty minutes later, having checked in an almost hundred foot radius around the house, vividly conscious of their silent audience.

A few vamps had moved out into the open, their eyes gleaming as they trailed her. One had even smiled. It made her beyond glad that she was armed to the teeth.

"Do you want to do a sweep from the air?"

"Yeah." But she wasn't hopeful, not given how much time had passed.

Illium flew her over the estate several times, but she had to shake her head in the end. "No." They didn't speak again until he brought them to an easy landing in front of a low white building that blended harmoniously into the fine coating of snow. "Hospital?"

A small nod. "This is the Medica."

She strode inside . . . and almost stepped off a ledge and into thin air. Illium caught her as she backpedaled. "Damn it," she muttered, her heart racing. "I will remember this!"

"It'll become second nature after a while."

Rubbing her face, she looked down. Wings filled her vision,

a hundred different shades, a thousand unique patterns. And still she couldn't see to the bottom of the cavernous space—which meant the building was more than three-quarters underground. "Is this the waiting room?"

"They're here because of Sam," Illium said, sliding his arms—muscular, familiar now—around her in a caress of warmth. "Come, I'll take you to him."

That won't be necessary. Elena found herself being plucked off the ledge by an archangel, her palms pressed against his chest as he took them down through the cascade of wings and to the wide open space at the very bottom. "Were you able to track the vampire any further from Michaela's?"

"No. Looks like his angelic accomplice brought him in, took him out." She kept her mind on the mechanics, not sure she could handle thinking about the assault on Sam. The poor baby had to have been so afraid. "The question is—how did they get into the house in the first place? Her security is impressive."

"But are her men loyal?" Words potent with the coldest of rages as they entered an area of pristine quiet. *Riker might be her creature, but she hasn't yet broken them all.* "Come, you must meet Keir."

She went to reply, but the words stuck in her throat. "Sam." The glass enclosure in front of her was drenched in soft white light. Sam's fragile body lay unconscious on a large bed in the middle, his wings attached to some kind of thin metal frame that spread them out on the sheets. His mother sat beside him, leaning into the embrace of a shaggy-haired male angel with solid shoulders. Sam was badly injured, but he looked better than when she'd first taken him into her arms. "Am I imagining it?"

"No." The taste of the wind, of the sea, clean and fresh, an unspoken assurance. "He recovered a little of his spirit during the flight to the Medica."

Slipping her hand into his, she squeezed it in silent relief just as an angel rounded the corner from the opposite end. The male was maybe five feet six and as slender as an eighteen-year-old boy, his uptilted eyes a warm brown, his black hair framing a dusky face that was pretty in an almost feminine way, his jaw pointed, his mouth lush. What saved him was the confidence with which he carried himself, the sense of maleness that was just *there*.

"I feel as if I know you," Elena murmured, staring at that face that defied categorization. He could've been born in Egypt, in Indonesia, in a hundred different places.

Raphael's hand released hers to curve around her neck. "Keir watched over you as you slept."

"And sometimes"—a smile on that perfect mouth—"I sang to you, though Illium begged me to stop."

Light words, but that smile . . . old, so *old*. Elena's bones sighed with the knowledge that notwithstanding the fact that he looked like a teenage boy on the cusp of adulthood, Keir had seen more dawns than she could imagine.

"Are you keeping Sam asleep?" Elena asked.

"Yes. He's too young to remember not to move his wings, so we won't bring him back to full consciousness until the bones have knit back together."

Raphael's fingers tightened on her skin. "Are any of his injuries likely to cause long-term harm?"

Elena stared through the glass in dismay. "Angels can be hurt that way?"

"When we are very young," Keir said, "yes. Some injuries take centuries to heal fully." Brown eyes lingered on Raphael's face. "It takes a ruthless kind of will to survive that much pain, but Sam won't need it. He has no hurts that won't heal within the next month."

Elena pressed her palm to the glass. "I can't understand the malice that could lead someone to do this."

Fingers brushing the pulse in her neck, her archangel's rage so fiercely contained, she wondered what it cost him. "You've seen innocents drown in blood, and yet you ask?"

"Bill," she said, naming the hunter who'd butchered a string of young boys before Elena had ended his life, "did what he did because of a mental illness that eroded the soul of the man he was. But this was a calculated act." The brand on Sam's cheek, the ugliest of abuses, had been covered by a bandage. "Will that fade before he wakes?"

"I'll make certain of it." Keir's tone turned so cold it was as if he was another man, a man who'd never known a healer's mercy and never would. "This is a deed that threatens to taint the Refuge forever."

Raphael stared through the glass. "His mind?"

"He's young." A long glance up at Raphael. "The young are resilient."

"But scars remain."

"Sometimes, the scars are what make us who we are."

Elena wondered at the scars that marked the son of two archangels, whether he'd one day share them with her. She wouldn't push, knew exactly how bad old wounds could hurt. A year. A century. It had little bearing when it came to the heart. The scars formed in that suburban kitchen when she'd been barely ten had indelibly marked her. They'd marked her father, too, but in a different way. Jeffrey Deveraux had chosen to deal with it by wiping his first wife and two eldest daughters from his memory.

Her nails dug into the palm of her hand. "I'm going to go see if I can find any trace of the vampire." The city was huge, but she might get lucky—and it was better than doing nothing.

"I'll return with you," Raphael said. "Keep well, Keir."

The other angel lifted his hand in a small wave as they left.

"Do your healers have special abilities?" Elena asked.

"Some do. Some are more akin to human physicians."

"They'd have seen things go from leeches to transfusions to organ transplants." Arriving at the waiting area, she wrapped her arms around Raphael and let him take her up to the ledge.

Illium's wings were shadowed blue against the snow when they walked out, his face turned up to the flakes falling soundlessly from the night sky "The water, Ellie," he said, "it'll wipe away the scents."

"Damn." Water was the one thing that ended any hope of a scent trail. Melting a few flakes in the palm of her hand, she tried to think positive. "Sometimes, snow isn't so bad—I once successfully tracked a vamp because the snow trapped his scent instead of washing it away."

"Then you need to hurry." Raphael spanned her waist with his hands. "Illium, Naasir thinks he may have found something in the north quadrant."

Illium's eyes almost glowed against the clean lines of his face. "I'll go and help him check it out."

Pressing her lips to Raphael's ear as they rose into the air, Elena asked a question that had been simmering at the back of her mind. "Is Illium getting stronger?"

He was badly injured by Uram, went into a deep healing sleep known as anshara. *It was the first time he'd done so— sometimes, there's a change in a man after* anshara.

"How strong will he get?"

Unpredictable. He swept down, the wind frigid across her cheeks. *We're in the area around Sam's home.*

"Nothing in the air. Put me down—I'll see if I can track him through the snow."

But that, too, proved futile. "It's not a total loss." She blinked away a flake caught on her lashes. "It's so cold, the snow won't melt anytime soon. That gives me time to search across the Refuge."

"How far through snow can you pick up a scent?"

"A couple of feet at most."

Raphael looked up. "The skies will open tonight."

"Then I guess we'll be staying up." Elena met the midnight storm of his eyes, felt compelled to reach up, cup his cheek. "We'll find the bastards."

He didn't soften under her touch, didn't become any less distant. "The fact that they dared take a child, it speaks of a deep rot, a rot that must be excised before it infects our entire race."

"Nazarach and the others?"

"They were all in open sight."

"Of course they were."

"It doesn't matter if the angel driving this didn't participate in the physical act—their corruption is the root. What was done to Noel merited death. What was done to Sam . . . death would be a mercy."

Light edged her fingertips where they touched Raphael's skin. She feared his power, would've been a fool not to. But she couldn't let him cross that line, couldn't let the hunt drag him into the abyss. "Raphael."

"There is," Raphael murmured, his eyelids lowering to hood the ice of his gaze, "a dark music in the screams of your enemies."

"Don't," she whispered, trying to reach him. Cruelty, as he'd once told her, seemed to be a symptom of age and power. But she refused to surrender to that, to let him be consumed by the violence of his own strength. "Don't."

But he wasn't listening. "Would you not like to stroke a stiletto across his throat, Elena?" His own hand closed around her neck, sensual, gentle, lethal. "Would you not like to watch him beg for his life?"

16

"Part of me," Elena whispered, admitting to the angry need within, "wants to do exactly that, wants to torture the bastard until he whimpers, until he crawls."

"But you will pity him when the time comes."

"My heart is human." And that heart was his. Ignoring the hand he still had around her throat, she pulled his head down to hers. As their lips met, she felt the slow burn of his power grow until it pulsed against every inch of her flesh. It was a reminder that no matter if she now had wings, she was very much mortal in comparison to this archangel.

His energy surrounded her, soaked into her very pores, his lips taking hers with a terrible, beautiful cruelty. There was no attempt to harm, no pain. No, Raphael kissed her like the immortal he was—with the heartless skill of a man who'd kissed so many women across the ages, their faces had to be a blur by now. It was a direct, unmistakable display of the ruthless heart that beat within his chest.

You can't scare me, she thought to him.

A lie, Guild Hunter. I can feel your heart thudding like a trapped rabbit's.

I'd be stupid not to be afraid. But I'm not going to back away from us just because you're feeling a little extra snarly.

A split second when his lips stopped, then she felt them curve, his hand rising from her throat to cup her cheek. The white-hot burn of his power faded, was replaced by the erotic touch of his skin. *Only you would ever dare say that to me.*

Needing to breathe, she broke the kiss, her entire body a humming flame. Man, but the archangel knew how to kiss. "We have to go."

A small nod, his hair sliding across his forehead before the wind pushed it back. "Where do you want to start?"

"How about the school—he might've been watching Sam or the other kids to decide which one to take."

Raphael's face went quiet, but though his eyes turned a deep indigo lit from within, he didn't flame with power again. "I'll fly you to the school grounds."

However, though Elena searched until the early hours of morning, when the snow began to come down in white sheets, she didn't find even the faintest trace of the vampire who'd laid brutal hands on a child in a place meant to be the safest of havens. More angry than anything else, she walked into their bedroom and began to strip off snow-wet clothes, her bruises stiff with cold.

"Let me." Raphael placed his hands on her shoulders. "Your wings are dragging on the floor."

"I'm tired," she admitted, allowing him to peel off her sleeves, undo the straps of her top, and pull it from her body. "I'm used to being stronger than the people around me. Here, I'm pathetically weak."

A kiss on the bare skin of her shoulder, warm hands on her stomach. "Strength comes in many forms, hunter. Yours is deeper than you know."

Leaning back into him, she let her body relax, trusting him to keep her upright. "This is nice. Having someone to hold me when I'm tired." It was an intimacy, a gift she'd never expected.

A long pause. Another kiss on her shoulder, those hands quietly possessive. "Yes."

It had been a leap in the dark to admit that much, that she was coming to rely on him—she, a woman who hadn't relied on a man since the day her father threw her out on the street—but she'd never expected that he'd honor her trust with his own. Closing her hands over his, she dropped her head to one side, exposing her neck.

He took the hint, kissing a line up the curve of it. "Shower?"

"Bath." She didn't think she could stand unaided.

"You'll fall asleep." His lips pressed to the quickening beat of her pulse, the possessive strength of his body reaching through her exhaustion to awaken the most primal of needs. *But I'll hold you up.*

It was another kiss, that offer. "Promise?"

"Promise."

Upper body naked, she stayed in place as he remained behind her.

"So many bruises." His hands were gentle over them, his voice holding a thrum of anger.

"Get used to it," she said with a laugh. "I seem to have a knack for getting myself in trouble."

A slow smile against her cheek, his hands on the button of her pants. "As you did the first time we met."

When she was bared to the very skin, her pants kicked away, she reached back to wrap her arms around his neck, arching her body in a sinuous stretch.

"Elena." A husky warning even as his hands stroked up her rib cage to close over her breasts.

Breath shaky with want, she pushed into him, her nipples aching for a rougher touch. "More." A brazen demand.

"As you command, hunter."

Her thoughts splintered as he pinched her nipples, sending a sudden, sharp ache straight through to the heat between her thighs. She moved, restless, wanting something only he could give her. "Raphael." His lips met hers as she angled her head to reach him, his hands soothing the ache he'd aroused with slow, easy movements. He was intensity contained, passion leashed. Breaking the kiss, she met the blazing cobalt of his eyes. "I think I've got my second wind."

The slightest of smiles, one hand leaving her breast to slide down her body and over the sensitive plane of her stomach to circle her belly button. She wiggled. "Tickles." Her bottom rubbed over the jutting hardness of his arousal, turning the heat between her legs liquid.

When he moved his hand farther down, she didn't resist, letting him part her with stark intimacy. He toyed with her, flicking his thumb over the ultrasensitive bundle of nerve endings at the top, but not giving her the hard pressure that she needed. Shuddering, she moved her body against him, tempting, arousing . . . teasing.

He grazed his teeth along her neck. "Doing that will get you punished."

"Oooh, I'm scared."

He pinched her clit. Pleasure short-circuited her system, her body tightening into a bow, ready, so ready . . . but the pressure eased a moment too soon. "Raphael." A sensual complaint, her skin shimmering with a fine layer of sweat.

"I warned you." It was an intimate reminder as he thrust two fingers inside her, pumping hard and deep. She rode him, rode those wicked fingers, her breath coming in harsh little pants, her body moving with a will of its own. On her breast, his other hand was a possessive brand, molding and shaping. His mouth touched her neck, her shoulder, his lips marking her without hesitation, without any attempt to hide that that was exactly what he was doing.

So tight and slick and mine.

Blatantly possessive, hotly male.

Her bottom rubbed against him with every undulation of her body, driving her to a fever pitch. "I need more."

You can't have my cock, Elena.

She trembled, tried to find her mind. "Why not? I'm rather fond of it."

That got her another teasing brush across her clit. Sparks flared behind her eyelids, and she barely heard him through the buzz in her head.

You're not strong enough to take what I want to do to you.

Half insane with need, she rode him harder, faster. "Give me more."

Are you sure? An explicit sexual question.

"Yes."

She cried out as he spread his fingers inside her, making room for a third. The extreme fullness threw her to the edge. Then he pressed down on her clit with his thumb and she fell. The orgasm rocked through her, a hard, almost violent release that left her limp in his arms.

Raphael drew in the scent of Elena's satisfaction, holding back the dark passion within him by the narrowest of margins, passion that wrenched at the restraints, hungering to take her with a fury he wasn't certain she'd survive even at full strength.

A year he'd waited for her. A year he'd heard only silence when he spoke to her. He didn't have much patience left in him. "Soon," he murmured, speaking to the voracious need within him.

When he began to withdraw his fingers from the tight slickness of her body, that need kicked him hard, making his cock throb. He wanted to throw her onto the bed, splay her legs wide, and thrust. *I'll bite your breasts,* he told her, taking his time removing his fingers, enjoying the way she clenched on him as he spoke. *But mostly, I plan to fuck you until you can't walk.*

Her body spasmed, and he realized his hunter was ready once more. Taking advantage, he slid a single finger back into her body, the second no longer able to inch in now that she was so lushly swollen with pleasure. *After I sate myself, I'll spread your legs, make you hold them open for me.*

A slow, lingering thrust.

"Raphael." Her voice was husky.

Then I'll take my time tasting the sweet, plump flesh between your thighs.

Another thrust, another stab of pleasure-pain as her buttocks rubbed over his cock.

Mine, Elena, you are mine.

Moving up a hand, he pulled her back with his fingers on her jaw and took her mouth as he gave her a final, exquisitely intimate caress that pushed her over into orgasm once more. Her sexuality was earthy, wild, honest. It sang a siren song to him that hazed his brain, threatened to make him lose all control.

Holding her up when she finally tumbled down from the peak, he removed his finger and maneuvered her around until he could pick her up in his arms, her wings as limp as her limbs. But this time the limpness had come from passion well sated. Even if he hadn't felt the damp evidence of it on his fingers, her sloe-eyed gaze as she looked at him from beneath her lashes was all the proof he needed.

You don't play fair, Archangel.

She so rarely initiated mental contact that he savored it. *Neither do you. My cock is about to burst.*

"I promise to make it better."

Blowing out a breath between clenched teeth, he put her on her feet in the shower, then reached over and turned on the cold water. She shrieked as the water hit her, slapping her hands on his still-clothed chest. "Get me out of here!"

"You're an angel," he said, soaked to the skin. "You aren't that sensitive to the cold." But he turned up the heat.

She glared at him. "What was that for?"

He waited in silence.

"Good," she said after a few seconds, "I'm glad you're suffering."

He was a being who'd lived over a thousand years, thought

he'd long ago lost the ability to truly laugh. Tonight he felt humor tug at his lips, despite the fact that his body remained painfully hard with need, his blood a fever. "That wasn't very nice of you, Elena."

A suspicious look as she pushed her hair off her face.

"After all, I brought you to your pleasure twice."

"We're keeping track now?" Her eyes glittered.

"Of course."

Her nose crinkled up, and then she couldn't hold it in any longer, her laughter bubbling out of her in a wave of pure delight. It hit him right in the heart he hadn't been certain he still had before he met Elena. Holding her under the water, he buried his face in the dampness of her hair and smiled. *When you're back up to full strength, you're going to be very busy catching up.*

Her arms came around his neck, her body pressed to his in an open kind of affection that he knew was rare for his hunter. Trust, he thought, she was beginning to trust him. Fear was an emotion he hadn't felt for centuries—not until the night Elena lay broken in his arms, in a Manhattan that had become a war zone—but now, it whispered through his veins.

Elena's trust was not easily given.

But it could so easily be lost.

"Are you planning on taking off your clothes?" Her fingers were already on the buttons of his shirt.

Shifting back, he let her strip him, let her tease him, let her make him a fraction more human.

Half an hour later, Raphael watched Elena give in to sleep, her lashes pale against gold-touched skin that spoke of a land of orange sunsets and thriving markets, snake charmers and veiled women with kohl-rimmed eyes, her wings spread out in a sweep of midnight and dawn as she lay on her front. Those wings, the wings of a warrior-born, were a fitting accent to her strength. But it was the woman, he thought, kneeling down beside the bed for an instant, who was the true treasure.

Brushing her hair off her face, he ran the back of his hand down her cheek. *Mine.* The possessiveness had grown ever stronger since she'd agreed to be his lover. He knew it would only increase. Because in all his centuries of existence, he'd never before taken a lover he considered his on every level. He'd kill for her, destroy for her, savage anyone who dared attempt to take her from him.

And he would never let her go . . . even if she begged for her freedom.

Rising to his feet, he walked out of the room through the balcony doors, closing them gently behind himself. The snow had stopped falling, leaving the Refuge clothed in the shade of innocence. *Watch over her*, he said to the angel circling above.

Galen's response was swift. *I'll let nothing reach her.*

Raphael knew Galen wasn't convinced about Elena, but the angel had given his word—and none of the Seven would ever betray Raphael. Taking off in a steep dive, he touched his mind to Elena's resting one—the act had become habit after the year she'd spent locked in a sleep he hadn't been able to penetrate.

The silence had been endless. Relentless.

Today he felt her exhaustion, her mind at peace, free of the dreams that so often stalked her. Withdrawing, leaving her to her slumber, he cut through the icy air toward the Medica. It was as he was about to dive from his position high above Keir's domain that he felt another mind touch his.

Michaela.

17

The other archangel came into sight seconds later, her wings copper in a sky slowly turning from gray to light. He waited as she brought herself to a standing hover in front of him. "The boy?" she asked, her expression haunted by an agony he knew would've made Elena's heart fill with pity, with sympathy.

He was older, harder. He'd seen Michaela end lives on a whim, play with men and angels as one would with chess pieces. But in this . . . she'd earned the right to know. "He will heal."

A shudder rippled through her body, a body so beautiful that it had made fools of kings and led to the death of at least one archangel. Neha might be the Queen of Snakes, but Raphael was certain it was Michaela who'd helped push Uram to the point of no return, goading him with the most poisonous of whispers.

"Your hunter," Michaela said, making no effort to hide her dislike, "was she able to pick up the trail?"

"Not beneath the snow. Indications are that the vampire

was helped by an angel." And if that knowledge leaked to the general populace, it would devastate what remained of the Refuge's equilibrium. "You need to check your people."

Her face turned to a stone mask, her bones blades against her skin. "Oh, I will." A pause, her eyes piercing even in the dark. "You don't think my people are loyal to me."

"It matters little what I think." What he believed was that fear alone, shaped by capricious whim, would never foster loyalty. "I must go. Elena will try to trace the scent again when she wakes."

"She remains as weak as a mortal."

"Good-bye, Michaela." If she believed Elena weak, that was her mistake.

He landed beside the Medica with a silence born of a million such landings, the snow hardly lifting around him. The building was serene, empty, but he knew angels and vampires both would return with the rising of the sun, to reassure themselves that Sam lived, that his heart still beat.

Until then, Raphael would watch over him.

Elena woke to the knowledge that she was in an archangel's arms, the sun streaking its way into the room on gilded fingers. "What time is it?"

"You've only slept a few hours," Raphael told her, his breath an intimate caress against her neck. "Do you feel strong enough to continue the track?"

"Oh, the track's happening," she said, stealing a single moment to savor the wild heat of him. "It's just a matter of how fast I'll be able to go." A deep breath and she dragged herself out of bed, her wings held close to her back until she was standing beside it. She turned to find Raphael watching her with those eyes of unearthly blue, his chest naked enticement bathed in sunlight.

"Elena." A subtle reprimand.

Blushing, she went through a quick but comprehensive warm-up. "Nothing's too stiff." Her eyes returned to that magnificent body he wouldn't let her touch. "I might need a massage at the end of the day, though."

"That might be a temptation too far."

Memories stroked into her mind, of his fingers teasing her to ecstasy as that deep voice told her every wicked thing he planned to do. Feeling her body flush, she turned away from a face that could make even a hunter fall into sin, and made her way to the bathroom. A quick shower later, she was feeling a bit more human.

Human.

No, she wasn't that anymore. But she wasn't a vampire either. She wondered if her father would find her more acceptable now, or would this make her even more of an abomination in his eyes?

"Go then, go and roll around in the muck. Don't bother coming back."

It still hurt, that rejection, the way he'd looked at her from behind the thin metal frames of his spectacles. After her mother's death she'd tried so hard to be what Jeffrey Deveraux wanted in a daughter, in his oldest surviving heir. Her existence had been a tightrope, one that wobbled constantly beneath her terrified feet. Never had she been comfortable in the Big House, the house her father had bought after the blood, the death, the screams. But she'd tried. Until one day, the tightrope snapped.

Drip.

Drip.

Drip.

"Your hunger makes mine sing, hunter."

She stiffened in rejection. "No."

Turning off the water, she got out and stood with the towel pressed to her face. Was it real, that whisper? It had to be. She'd never forget that low, sinuous voice, that handsome face that hid the soul of a murderer. But she'd forgotten those words, had buried them. The words . . . and what came after.

Elena.

Clean, fresh, the sea and the wind. She clung to it. *Hey, I'll be out soon.*

I can sense your fear.

She didn't know how to answer that, so she didn't. The scent of the sea, the fresh bite of wind, didn't disappear. Part of her wondered if he was stealing her secrets, but another part of her was glad he hadn't left her alone in that home turned butcher's shop. *Raphael?*

He appeared in the doorway, a being she'd once shot in terror. A being who now held her very soul in his hands. "You have need of me?"

"How much do you know?" she asked him. "About my family?"

"The facts. I had you fully investigated before the Cadre decided to hire you."

She'd known that, but now she met his gaze, walling up her suddenly vulnerable heart. He could hurt her so much. "Have you taken more than the facts from me?"

"What do you think?"

"I think you're used to taking what you want."

"Yes." A slow nod.

Her heart threatened to break.

"But," he said, "I'm beginning to learn the value of that which is freely given." Walking across, he ran one hand over the acutely sensitive arch of her wing.

She shivered, caught by the magnetism of an archangel who'd never be anything close to mortal. And then he spoke, his eyes the infinite blue at the deepest part of the ocean, endless and pure beyond description. "I haven't taken your secrets, Elena."

Everything crashed open, emotion threatening to tow her under. "That's not the answer I expected."

Picking up a towel, he moved behind her and began to dry her wings with slow, soft strokes. Too late she realized that with her holding the towel to her front, her entire back was bare to his eyes.

"The color sweeps up your back." He slid her hair over one shoulder, pressing a kiss to the delicate skin of her nape.

She shivered, tried to lift her wings so she could slide the towel around her body.

"No." Stroking his hand down the curve of her spine and over her buttocks, he trailed his fingers back up.

She found herself rising on tiptoe to escape the delicious torment. "Raphael."

"Will you tell me your secrets?"

Her feet lowered to the ground on a ripple of pain and fear. Leaning back into him, she let her head fall against his chest. "Some secrets hurt too much."

He ran his hand down her wing again, but this time, the sensation felt more like comfort. "We have eternity," he said, one arm coming around her neck from the front.

She felt her heart skip a beat at the certainty in his tone. "In that eternity, will you tell me your secrets?"

"I haven't shared my secrets for more sunrises than you can imagine." He tugged her even closer. "But until I met you, I'd never claimed a hunter, either."

There was something strange about scent-tracking through the Refuge. It wasn't only that she seemed to be developing the ability to track angels—that came and went, the new scents static in the back of her mind—it was that she could feel eyes on her every step of the way. "You'd think they'd never seen a hunter before," she muttered under her breath.

Illium, walking beside her, vivid interest in his own eyes, took her words for a question. "Many of them haven't."

"I guess." She frowned as she caught a hint of a scent that tugged at her instincts, but it whispered away so fast, she couldn't pinpoint the elements that made up the whole. "Maybe they're just checking you out." Bare-chested and with the lithe muscle of a man who knew how to use his body, he was, as Sara would put it, "deliciously bitable."

A wicked smile. "Your wings are trailing in the snow."

Glancing behind her, she saw the white tips encrusted with ice. "No wonder they feel numb." She pulled the wings back up, realizing they'd entered one of the main thoroughfares. It bustled with activity, but beneath it all was a hum of lethal anger. "Do all vampires know about this place?"

"No, only the most trusted."

Which made the assault on Sam all the more egregious. But of course, everyone knew the vampire had been nothing but a tool. It was the angel who mattered, the angel who'd be put to death in the most painful way known to immortals—and they'd had a long time to come up with methods of torture. Catching a minute hint of citrus, she angled left, to a section almost free of angelic eyes. "Any orange groves in this direction?"

"No. They're in Astaad's and Favashi's parts of the Refuge."

Chocolate. Oranges. Faint, so faint.

Going down on one knee, she brushed aside the snow with her bare hand, having learned that while she felt the cold, she was in no danger of frostbite.

"I could dig for you," Illium offered, crouching across from her, his forehead almost touching hers as he leaned in. One of his feathers floated to the ground, an exotic accent against the pristine white. "Should I?"

She shook her head. "I need to go down layer by layer, in case the snow trapped his—" Her fingers scraped against something hard, colder than the snow. "Feels like a pendant or a coin." Brushing off the white flecks that melted at contact with her skin, she angled it to catch the light.

Her breath turned to ice in her chest.

"That's Lijuan's symbol." Illium's voice was low, hard, her laid-back escort replaced by the man who'd amputated his enemies' wings with clean efficiency.

"Yes." She'd never forget that kneeling angel with a deaths-head face as long as she lived. "What kind of an archangel uses that as her personal symbol?"

Illium didn't answer, and she hadn't really expected him to. Fighting her instinctive urge to throw the disturbing thing into the deepest crevice she could find, she brought the medallion to her nose, and drew in a long breath.

Bronze.

Iron.

Ice.

Oranges glazed in chocolate.

"The vampire touched this." Wanting no further contact with the artifact, she placed it in Illium's outstretched hand. "Let's go."

"Have you got the scent?"

"I might have." She could feel it tugging at her, buried beneath all the snow, in constant danger of being melted away if the winter sun turned blazing in one of the rapid transitions she'd come to expect up here.

Pulling on that faint thread, she began to walk. "What's down there?" Her target was a covered passageway between two neatly shut-up buildings. It appeared a black hole into nowhere.

"A small internal garden." Illium's sword made a *shush*ing sound as he slid it out of its scabbard. "The angels who reside here are currently in Montreal, but there should be a lamp burning on the wall."

"Let's go." It got very, very dark less than a meter into the passage, but light appeared at the other end not long afterward. She sped up her pace, exiting into the bright white scene that awaited with a silent sigh of relief.

It was, as Illium had said, an enclosed garden, a private retreat from the world beyond. In summer, it likely overflowed with blooms, but it had a unique kind of charm even in the arms of winter. The fountain in the middle lay still, its two upper basins and pool filled with snow. More snow covered the statues that ringed the pool, some inside, some outside, all caught in motion.

Walking closer, she felt an unexpected delight spark to life inside her—the statues were all of children, each face drawn with a loving hand. "There's Sam!" she said, seeing a smaller version of the child angel, one foot in the fountain, hands on the rim, pure mischief in his expression. "And there's Issi."

"Aodhan used them as models." At her questioning look, he added, "One of the Seven."

"He's gifted." Each statue was meticulously detailed, down to the torn button on a shirt or the hanging lace of an abandoned shoe. As she circled the artwork, her smile faded, her gut raw with the knowledge that someone had defiled this place.

Oranges dipped in chocolate.

And below that . . . *the putrid ugliness of rot just begun.*

18

Fury arcing through her in a cold wave, she brushed off enough snow from the rim that she could perch on it. She didn't have to clear much in the fountain itself before her fingers bumped against flesh gone blue with cold. Withdrawing her hand, she jerked her head at Illium. "I think we just found the vamp who took Sam."

"Another desecration." The bones of his hand cut white against skin as his fingers clenched on the grip of his sword. "I've told Raphael."

"Not Dmitri?" Raphael's second-in-command ran any number of things, and with Raphael having scheduled an early-morning "discussion" with Dahariel, she'd figured the vampire would be the one to deal with this.

"He left for New York soon after Sam was found," Illium told her, sheathing Lightning in a fluid motion. "Venom's the youngest among us. With Galen having been recalled from the Tower, there are some who may get ideas."

She thought of how much time Raphael was spending away from his Tower because of her, to give her time to become strong enough to deal with the world, wondered what it was costing him. "But, if necessary, Venom could hold off a challenge long enough for help to arrive?"

"Of course. He's one of the Seven." Illium's tone said everything about the requirements for membership in that very exclusive club. "The Tower is also built to be defensible. There are over a hundred angels and the same number of high-level vampires either in or around the Tower at any time."

Quite an army, she thought. But archangels didn't rule because they were benevolent beings. They ruled because they had power and weren't afraid of using it to enforce their decrees. At that very instant, an example of that power landed in the garden—a full wing of angels led by Galen.

The red-haired angel walked directly to the fountain, and it was the first time she'd really had a chance to examine him. He looked, she was surprised to note, like a bruiser. Well over six feet tall, his shoulders were wide, his thighs thick with muscle, his biceps—one ringed by a thin metal band—that of a man who'd earned his body, and not through a workout in any gym. And his face—square jaw, sensual lips, the kind of mouth that made women think hot, sweaty, distinctly unangelic thoughts.

His eyes cut to the body. "You believe this is the vampire who took Sam?"

Shaking off her startlement at this angel who looked so very earthy, so very human, she nodded. "He has the right scent and as far as I know, no one's ever been able to mimic that well enough to fool a hunter-born."

A curt nod, red hair aflame in the sunlight. "Give us room to dig him out."

Shifting back, she watched as they uncovered then removed the body, taking care to ensure they overlooked nothing. As she'd expected, the head was missing—beheading was the most efficient way of killing a vampire, followed closely by burning. Leaving Galen and his troops to check the fountain and the surrounding area for the head, she began to crisscross the garden. "No trail," she finally muttered, staring at the now empty fountain. "Vamp was dropped from above."

"Either the leader or one of his angelic followers." Illium's familiar voice, his wings the most vivid point of color in all the white as the angels who'd come with Galen left, taking the body with them.

Galen's own wings reminded her of a northern harrier's—a dark gray with white striations that only became visible when he spread them in preparation for flight. "The head isn't here," the red-haired angel began when there was a gust of wind, the powerful backlash of wings raking up the snow.

Elena felt her heart catch all over again as Raphael landed. "We found the head," he said, his tone freezing the air around them. "It was left on Anoushka's pillow, the *sekhem* branded on its forehead."

Elena was quite certain the vampire must have been alive for that humiliation. His fear when he realized the jackal he worshipped had turned on him would have been agonizing— because he knew exactly what was coming.

"A jeer," Galen said. "Aimed at Neha through her daughter."

"Or a very clever double play," Elena murmured, recalling the notes she'd read on Anoushka. Intelligent, ambitious, and with several powerful vampires and angels in her court, she could have pulled it all off. But then, so could Nazarach and Dahariel.

"If she is a true victim," Illium said, "how did anyone get that close? Anoushka's guards are deadly."

"No security is absolute. And it's beginning to appear as if this angel laid his plans months in advance."

"Jason?" Elena guessed.

A hard nod, Raphael's hair blue black under the winter sun. "One of his men managed to get out a message from Charisemnon's court—there's no evidence of the girl-child ever crossing the border. Yet Titus is adamant he has proof in the form of a recording that was sent to him."

It was Galen who spoke next. "Are we certain the one behind this is still in the Refuge?"

"The political games may well have been run from a distance, but these are too personal. He's close, eager to see the results of his acts." Raphael's voice held a remoteness that scared her. The last time he'd sounded that distant, he'd ended up holding her above a spiraling fall, a being who might have dropped her just so he could listen to her scream.

Her blood a rush of thunder in her ears, she had to focus to hear his next words.

"Ignore the distractions. He may have begun this with the intent of proving his power, his entitlement to become Cadre, may have convinced himself these acts will lead to that goal—"

"—but really, the bastard just enjoys his sick little games," Elena completed, her gut churning. Because that kind of a sociopath? He wouldn't stop until he was forced to stop. And he'd already shown he had a taste for children.

Chrome blue eyes met her own. "Our aim hasn't changed. We hunt for the blood insult to Noel, to Sam. And for the renewed threat on Elena's life."

She blinked, feeling the sun's increasing heat against her skin. "What?"

"A Guild dagger was jammed into the mouth of the head left in Anoushka's bed."

Angry at the vicious acts, at the continued mockery of a Guild that had given her a family when her own had thrown her out like so much trash, she felt her mind calm, her brain chill. "Forensics lab?" Even if she hadn't had that conversation with Raphael about possible trace evidence on Noel's battered body, she'd have intuited the Refuge had such a lab. Because while angels might look like beings out of myth and legend, they were, for the most part, ruthlessly practical. She wouldn't be surprised if they had a central DNA bank.

"The body's being processed," Galen said, "and I'll have people go over the scene one more time, but I predict we'll find nothing of value, just as with Noel and Sam."

"The only clue was the dead vamp's scent," Elena said, knowing that that was why he'd died. It was disturbing to know her talent had signed his death warrant, but then, hadn't he done that himself the night he decided to help brutalize a child? Her jaw tightened. "Do we know who he was?"

"He looked to Charisemnon," Raphael said. "A midlevel vampire seduced by the promise of more."

It was such a human motive that she knew he was right. Because vampires had once been human after all. "Are there still only three possibles?"

"Nazarach, Dahariel, and the Princess herself," Illium confirmed.

"Any of the three like to live in the past?"

"No." Illium again. "Anoushka keeps a court like her mother, but she also owns a chemical plant that manufactures poisons. They're all aware of modern forensic techniques."

"Then we go back to basics, watch them until they make a mistake."

"Nazarach," Raphael said, "has been under constant surveillance since the attack on Noel, but that doesn't prove his innocence. Dahariel is Astaad's, and will require more care."

"Even with what was done to Sam?"

The answer was that of an archangel. "Dahariel is as integral to the smooth running of Astaad's territory as Nazarach is to mine."

And Anoushka was Neha's daughter. "You can't go after them without risking war."

"Dahariel appeared disgusted by the attack on Sam," Raphael said, his expression impenetrable, "but his home is filled with vampires who all but whimper at the sound of an angel's wings."

Elena's mind shot to the last—and only—time she'd seen Holly Chang. The woman had turned hysterical at the sight of Raphael's wings after the trauma of having been forced to witness Uram's atrocities. What was Dahariel doing to elicit the same reaction from almost-immortals who'd lived hundreds of years?

Illium extended his hand as a stiff breeze lifted the snow

into the air. But it couldn't erase the lingering spoor of murderous violence. "The medallion that led us here."

Taking it, Raphael traced the lines of the metal sphere as if searching for something. She knew he'd found it when his fingers went still. "This could've only been acquired through the death of one of Lijuan's men."

"Do you think she's involved?" Elena asked.

"No. She's too busy playing with her reborn." He closed his fingers around the medallion even as the hairs on the back of her neck rose at the reminder of Lijuan's preferred form of amusement. "Elena—the trail?"

"Snow's melting," she said, frustrated. "Trail's history."

"Patience, hunter," Raphael said with the confidence of a being who'd seen centuries pass. "He made a mistake in killing one of his own men—fear will loosen tongues."

"Then I guess we hope that he—or she," she added, remembering Anoushka, "continues to strike out at his own people." She stared at the fountain. "At least they'll die a cleaner death than if we catch them."

The scent of the wind, clean and harsh. *I'd say you were losing your innocence, but your nightmares tell me you lost that a long time ago.*

Yes, she admitted, giving him a glimpse of the most secret corner of her heart. *There was so much blood that day. I could see it on my skin even at the funeral.*

19

The next day brought an unwelcome surprise. With the scent trail having grown cold, and Raphael's people working the other facets of the hunt, she'd returned to getting her body back in fighting shape—the angel who'd already harmed two of Raphael's own wouldn't find her the easy target he seemed to assume she was. She had every intention of thrusting a Guild dagger right between his ribs when he came after her.

Unfortunately, she'd forgotten that Dmitri had returned to the Tower.

"You'll be dead two seconds after you run out of bullets if that's your sole means of defense." Galen swallowed up her gun in his hand, his pale green gaze about as friendly as your local grizzly bear's. "Secondary weapon?"

"Knives." She'd never admit it in a million years, but she was already starting to miss Dmitri's wicked brand of humor.

"If you're going to be using knives," Galen said as she entered the training ring, a simple circle of beaten earth in front of a large wooden structure without windows, "then you need to learn to draw them without nicking your wings." He picked up what looked like a rapier from the table, though the guard was far simpler than the intricate ones she'd seen in another hunter's collection. Handing it to her, he said, "I need to see what you've got."

"I said knives," she told him, dropping her wrist as she tested the weight of the blade. "This is much longer than anything I've used."

"Knives take you too close to the target." He was suddenly in her face, a short, lethally sharp blade nicking her throat, her breasts crushed against the male heat of his bare chest. "And you aren't fast enough to win against another angel."

She hissed out a breath but didn't back off. "I could still gut you."

"Not as fast as I could cut your throat. But that isn't the point of this exercise."

Feeling blood begin to trickle down her throat, she shut out the anger and ran through her options with cold-blooded focus. Her sword hand was effectively useless—he was too close. Given the lack of leverage, her other hand wouldn't do much damage, either.

Except angelic wings were extremely sensitive.

Grabbing his wing with her free hand, she brought up the sword with the other. Galen danced out of reach, the knife disappearing so fast she barely caught the movement. "Wings," she said, realizing the bastard had taught her something critically important, "give me an advantage in terms of surprising an opponent, but get too close and they become a weakness."

"At this stage, yes." Galen swiveled the rapier he'd picked up. The slender dueling sword looked far too delicate for his big hand. She'd bet her newfound fortune that his personal weapon of choice was something closer to a broadsword. Heavy, solid, effective.

"Guess I'll be using the crossbow to chip vamps from now on," she said, thinking wistfully of the necklets that had been her favorite method of immobilizing her targets.

Embedded with a chip that neutralized a vampire by temporarily rewiring the brain, the special weapons were a hunter's sole advantage against stronger, faster opponents. She'd debated getting some very illegal copies for personal use now that she was surrounded by vamps, but had realized all too quickly that the first time she used one, she'd not only create a shit storm that might bury the Guild, she'd cost Raphael the loyalty of the vampires under his command. The chips were closely regulated for a reason—vampires didn't want to spend their lives looking over their shoulders.

Elena understood exactly how they felt—it was a bitch to lose control over your body, to become a puppet. And the fact of the matter was that most of the ones around her these days were too strong to be affected by the chips. That was a secret she'd take to her grave. Because sometimes, all a hunter had was the element of surprise, of the vampire's *belief* that he'd been neutralized.

"You plan to return to your position within the Guild?" Galen's tone was the embodiment of disapproval.

"What else am I going to do? Sit around looking pretty?"

"You're a liability." Cool, hard words. "Out in the field, you'd be a sitting duck for anyone wanting to get to Raphael by taking you hostage."

"That's why I'm out here adding to my bruises." She would not back down. "Raphael doesn't want a princess. He wants a warrior."

My lovers have always been warrior women.

Her archangel had said that to her. And now that they'd set the boundaries, he was using her skills, her talents. She wasn't about to let a grim-faced martinet change the very bedrock of their relationship.

"He almost died because of you." A slash of the blade, so close that she reacted instinctively to block the blow.

Twisting away, she raised her rapier. "He chose to fall with me."

"Sometimes, even an archangel makes mistakes." A blur of movement.

But she'd read his feet, was already sliding out of reach. When she turned, it was to see several strands of her hair lying on the beaten earth of the ring, sliced clean through by Galen's blade. He might have looked like a bruiser, but he could *move*. "I guess the gloves are off."

"If they were, you'd be dead." Snapping back to a waiting stance, he glanced critically at her hand. "You need to change your grip. The way you're holding it now, I could break your wrist with a single hit."

"Show me."

He did, adding, "The rapier is, at heart, a thrusting weapon. Use it."

The rest of the morning passed in an increasingly grueling manner.

Three hours later, she was dripping sweat, and they'd drawn a crowd of curious onlookers. Galen didn't let up, ordering her into another sparring session. She could feel her wings dragging, her leg muscles quivering.

Bastard. Refusing to let him drive her into the ground, she avoided his blows with deliberately sluggish movements . . . until he dropped his guard for the barest fraction of an instant. Then she lunged. The rapier hit his shoulder, sinking in several inches.

Red dripped down the tanned skin of his chest.

A horrified gasp from the onlookers. But Galen just wrenched his body away from the blade, lowered his own weapon, and held out his hand for hers. "Good. You should've done that an hour ago."

Wanting to stab him with it, she handed over the rapier. "I've got the basics, but it'll take me time to become effective with this." Time she didn't have.

"We'll focus on throwing knives later, but you need some skill with a longer blade in case you have to fight in close quarters." Pale green eyes locked with hers. "If you plan on surviving Lijuan's idea of a ball, you need to stop acting human and go directly for the jugular." He left the training ring without another word.

All she wanted to do was collapse in a puddle of jelly, but pride kept her upright.

No one got in her way as she left the ring, though she felt eyes on her the entire distance to Raphael's stronghold. Guns and knives, she thought as she entered, were the lightest, most versatile weapons for everyday use. The rapier was a bit too long, but a shorter sword . . . yeah, that might work.

Too bad about the miniature flamethrower in her stash. It wouldn't exactly be easy to carry around on a day-to-day basis—and while it'd be effective against vampires, it'd only enrage an angel. The best she could hope for with an angel was to disable him—or her—long enough to get a head start.

She was so busy going over her options that it took her several minutes to realize she'd turned right instead of left after entering the main hallway. Might as well keep going, she thought, too damn exhausted to turn back—the passage would eventually spit her out into the central core. Rubbing the back of her neck, she saw the walls here were hung with lush jewel-toned silks that shifted in the breeze coming in through the windows high above. The carpet underneath her feet echoed the theme, being a deep rose accented with the faintest hint of amethyst.

A giggle carried on the air currents.

She froze, realizing the import of her surroundings. Rich and exotic and almost too vibrant, the colors stroking over her with velvet fingers. The last time she'd been in a place this soaked with sensuality, it had been the vampire wing of the Tower. And Dmitri had all but fucked a woman in front of her. It didn't matter that they'd both been clothed; that curvy little blonde had been a whisper's breath away from orgasm.

It was too late to turn back. Steeling her spine . . . and sensing the familiar, primal scent of a tiger on the hunt, she began hauling ass. But her head insisted on turning toward an open doorway, insisted on glimpsing that sleek, muscled back of flawless brown touched with gold, insisted on watching that silver-maned head bend over the neck of a woman who sighed in unmistakable sexual submission.

A woman with wings.

Her feet bolted themselves to the floor. Naasir was feeding from an angel, and from her breathy moans, the way her hands clutched at his biceps, it was obvious who held the reins. Unable to look away, she watched Naasir close his fingers over the flesh of one plump breast. The angel's head fell back, exposing her neck—begging for another blood kiss—as he lifted his head. As he turned. As those eyes of liquid platinum locked with Elena's.

Shivering, she wrenched her own head back around and continued on her way as fast as her legs would carry her. It was a relief to exit into the central core of the house with its vaulted ceiling and abundance of light. *Dear God.* There'd been sex in those eyes, on that face, but there'd also been a darker need, a darker hunger . . . as if he'd as easily tear open his lover's chest and drink straight from her still-pumping heart as fuck her.

Goose bumps broke out over her spine. She pitied the hunter who ever had to track that silver-eyed beast of prey through the night.

Twenty minutes later, she was clean, a towel wrapped around her body as she sat on the bed rubbing her calves, and contemplating the walk to Jessamy's classroom. But her mind insisted on returning to the disturbing tableau she'd glimpsed in the vampire wing, the foreignness of it all suddenly overwhelming.

This place, with its piercing beauty and secrets, its violence wrapped in peace, it wasn't home. She was mortal in her heart—and there were no mortals here. Cranky taxi drivers zipping by in the rain, snappily dressed investment bankers with cell phones surgically attached to their ears, bruised and bloody hunters cracking jokes after a difficult track—that was her life. And she missed it all until she couldn't breathe.

Sara would understand.

Holding the towel more firmly around herself—wings and all—she picked up the phone. Hoping desperately that her best friend was awake, she listened to it ring on the other end.

"Hello." A deep, masculine tone, as welcome as Sara's would've been.

"Deacon, it's me."

"Ellie, it's good to hear your voice."

"You, too." Fisting her hand on the towel, she blinked away unexpected tears. "Is it late there?"

"No. I was watching *Sesame Street* with Zoe. She's just gone to sleep."

"How is she?" Elena hated that she'd missed out on a year of her goddaughter's life.

"Caught a little cold," Deacon said. "But Slayer's got her back."

Elena smiled at the reference to the slobbering hellhound of a dog who thought Zoe was *his*. "Sara?"

"You two must have a psychic hotline going." Quiet humor, very Deacon. "She was about to call you but she went out like a light right after dinner. Had a tough few days at the Guild—almost lost one of her hunters."

Elena's heart crashed into her ribs. "Who?"

"Ashwini." He named the hunter who'd first told Elena about Nazarach. "She got cornered by a pack of vamps in some back alley in Boston—apparently they were out to settle a score because she tracked one of them after he went rogue. They cut her up pretty bad."

"Are they dead?" An ice-cold question.

"Ash killed two, wounded the others. Ink wasn't even dry on the execution orders when their heads were delivered to the Guild, express delivery."

"Probably their angel." For the most part, angels did *not* like vampires acting out. It was bad for business. "Is Ash okay?"

"Doctors say no lasting damage. A month recovery tops."

Relief made her entire body tremble. "Thank God."

"What about you, Ellie?"

The care in those words had her swallowing. "I'm okay. Getting used to this new body. Things don't work the same, you know?"

"I have an idea for a special crossbow for you."

"Yeah?"

"I'm going to design it so you can strap it over one arm comfortably, instead of over your back. That way, you won't have to worry about your wings."

"Sounds good."

"What do you think of lightweight bolts? They'll do the job without weighing you down in flight."

"Can you make it so it loads automatically?" Galen could go eat his sword, she thought. Childish, yeah, but it made her feel better. "I need speed."

"Something with small spinning sawblades might be better—let me work on it. You can use the bolts for chipping and the blades for serious defense." A pause. "You are coming back to the Guild?"

"Of course." She was hunter-born. Wings didn't change that.

Raphael met Neha's eyes on the wide screen mounted on the wall. The Queen of Snakes, of Poisons, sat in a chair carved out of a light-colored wood that gleamed. The sheen did nothing to hide the fact that the carvings were of a thousand writhing snakes, their scales catching the light as Neha leaned back, the bindi on her forehead a tiny golden cobra.

"Raphael." Her lips—red, lush, poisonous—parted. "I hear there is trouble in the Refuge."

"An angel who seeks to become an archangel."

"Yes, so my daughter tells me." She waved an elegantly shaped hand, the bangles on her wrists making a delicate clinking sound. "There's always one who seeks to rise above his station." Reaching forward, she picked up something, the silk of her emerald-colored sari a quiet rustle. "But I agree, this one must be punished in a way that'll never be forgotten. Our children are too rare to be used as pawns."

Raphael knew that in spite of the way she'd phrased that, Neha was one of the few members of the Cadre who treated human children as precious. That didn't stop her from ending adult lives—but any resulting orphans grew up in the lap of poisonous luxury, the memories of their parents' agonizing deaths wiped from their minds.

"Anoushka," she now said, stroking the python she'd placed in her lap, "says you know of the distasteful object that was left in her bed."

"You have many enemies." And Anoushka, he thought, was beginning to grow a phalanx of her own.

Her hand moved over the snake's viridian skin, sleek, sensuous, as if she were petting a lover. "Yes."

"Have you heard anything from the others that may help in the hunt?" The one they sought may well have made mistakes in any acts predating the assaults within the Refuge.

"Titus and Charisemnon have closed their borders—none of my people can get in or out." An irritated light filled those dark eyes. "Favashi mentioned something about losing a few of her older vampires two months ago. She hasn't yet tracked down the perpetrator." This time, Raphael saw open disbelief.

Neha, he knew, would have killed and kept killing until someone confessed. It wasn't the best way to get to the truth—but then, the Queen of Poisons had never had a rebellion in her lands. "How is Eris?" It was only as the words left his mouth that he realized he'd lied to Elena. There *was* another long-term archangelic pairing. But it hadn't been a lie with intent—he'd simply forgotten about Eris, as most people did.

"He lives." Neha's words were chilling in their very preciseness. "Anoushka is going through her people to find the traitor who defiled her bed. I'll let you know if she unearths anything of value."

As he terminated the connection, Raphael thought of the last time he'd seen Eris.

Three hundred years ago.

20

Elena was reading a dossier of current events in a corner of the classroom while the kids created presents for Sam using arts and crafts when the sea crashed into her mind.

Something's happened, she thought before Raphael could speak, scanning the classroom with frantic eyes to ensure everyone was present. *Not another child?*

Lijuan has sent you a gift.

Her soul iced over at the thought of what an angel who used death as her symbol would consider a suitable gift. *Do you know what it is?*

It's keyed to your blood.

She couldn't help her shiver. *We're going to visit Sam. I'll be by after.* She had a feeling the gift wouldn't exactly put her in the right frame of mind to be seeing a hurt child.

Come to my office. I'll send someone to guide you.

Anyone but Galen. She had nothing against his skills as a weapons master—bastard was good. But his dislike of her was as solid as rock. And even on such short acquaintance, she understood that he wasn't the kind of man who'd easily change his mind. Better to save them both the aggravation and avoid unnecessary contact.

The sea began to retreat. *I must go.*

She wanted to ask him what else was going on, but decided to keep her questions 'til their meeting over the "gift." For now, she was going to focus on the children, their excitement infectious as they readied themselves to visit their friend . . . not an archangel who found pleasure only in the dead.

Raphael flew to a distant corner of the Refuge, the echo of Elena's mental touch still resonant in his mind. Elijah was waiting for him on a rocky outcropping far from prying eyes, his golden hair whipped by the mountain winds. Landing, Raphael joined him on the cliff edge. "What have you found?"

"They haven't just closed their borders," the other archangel replied. "Titus is readying himself to move against Charisemnon."

Archangels didn't meddle in each other's affairs, even when those affairs led to mass bloodshed, but they needed to be prepared. "Titus refuses to accept that his evidence might be false?"

"He will not believe that a *mere* angel could've played them so very easily," Elijah said, "sparking a war that keeps them entangled in their own lands while this pretender desecrates the Refuge."

Raphael stared out at the white-capped peaks beyond the gorge, thinking about their policy of noninterference. "Even in a border war, thousands will die. And yet we consider that an acceptable toll to maintain the balance of power within the Cadre."

Elijah took a long time to reply. "That's a very human statement, Raphael."

"Then she will kill you. She will make you mortal."

Lijuan had said that to him, after advising him to kill Elena.

The older archangel had been right—Elena had changed

something in him. He bled faster, healed slower. But he'd also been given the most unexpected of gifts. "Perhaps it'll keep me sane when I reach Lijuan's age."

"So one of us is brave enough to say it." Elijah nodded. "She is not insane in the accepted sense."

"Her mind isn't broken," Raphael agreed, "but the things she's using that mind for—they're not what she would've done had she been truly thinking." Lijuan was no longer anything close to what was known, but she'd always played the political game with a clear head.

"Are you sure?" Elijah bent down to pick up a pebble that had somehow ended up on the otherwise barren ridge. "None of us witnessed her youth, but there are whispers that she was fascinated with death even then. Some say . . . no, I cannot lay that slander on her without proof."

Raphael said what the other archangel wouldn't. "That she took the dead to her bed."

A sharp glance. "You've heard the rumor?"

"You forget, Elijah, both my parents were archangels."

"Caliane and Nadiel knew Lijuan in her youth?"

"No. But they knew those who had." And what they'd told his parents had been whispered behind the thickest veil of secrecy. Because by then, Lijuan had already become a being to be feared.

"Now she's the only ancient," Elijah said, his voice contemplative. "They call us immortals, but we, too, eventually end up dust on the sands of time."

"After millennia," Raphael pointed out. "As Elena would say—are you not curious about what awaits us on the other side?"

"According to many humans, we are the messengers of their gods."

Raphael glanced at Elijah. "After Lijuan, you're the oldest among us. She's a demigoddess in her territory. Did you ever consider setting yourself up as one?"

"I've seen what happens to those who take that path." Elijah didn't look at Raphael, but his meaning was clear. "Even had I not, I have Hannah. What I feel for her is far too real, far too much of this world."

Raphael thought of the way his parents had loved each other, that powerful, almost exalting love, compared it to what he felt for Elena. There was nothing exalted about the hard ache of his cock when he touched her, the pulsing lust of his need. "Titus and Charisemnon will slaughter hundreds," he said at last, "but it's Lijuan who remains the true threat.

"My men tell me her army of the reborn has doubled in number over the past six months." And there were disturbing rumors that some of her soldiers were the very newly dead—as if they'd been sacrificed to feed the cold embrace of Lijuan's power. "If she unleashes them on the world, it will augur the start of another Dark Age."

The last Dark Age had devastated civilizations that had grown up over thousands of years, destroying buildings and works of art so magnificent, the world would never again know their like. Millions upon millions of humans had fallen—collateral damage in a war between angels.

But then, they hadn't been fighting armies of the dead, nightmares given flesh.

Elena watched child after child accompany Jessamy into Sam's room. Keir had brought the boy up into a half-awake state where he was aware of what was happening but felt no pain. A chaotic mix of happiness and rage tore through her as she watched him beam at the gifts his classmates had brought him.

How could anyone be immoral enough to hurt such innocence?

Drip.

Drip.

Drip.

"She likes it, you see."

Pain shot through her jaw as she wrenched herself back to

the present, but it wasn't enough; her daylight hours were no longer safe from the long hand of nightmare. She could see Ari's eyes staring into hers, that bright turquoise gaze going slowly dull as Slater fulfilled his monstrous thirst. Ari had whispered at Elena to run, but her older sister hadn't been able to run herself, her legs not just broken like Belle's, but torn off altogether, a barbaric amputation.

Kindling.

That's what the broken bones sticking out of her thighs had looked like, the blood drying as it came into contact with the air.

"She won't run." A giggle. *"She likes it, you see."*

"Would you like to see him?"

Swiveling on her heel, Elena stared unseeing at Jessamy's startled face, her mind locked in that kitchen awash with a suffering that would stalk her for eternity.

Jessamy touched her with a hesitant hand. "Elena?"

"Yes," she said, forcing the words out past the brutal hammer of memory. "Yeah, I'd like to see Sam."

"Go on in." Jessamy's eyes held a quiet concern, but she didn't pry. "I'm herding the other children back to the classroom."

Digging up a smile from somewhere, Elena shut up everything else and walked inside Sam's room. "So," she said, "this is how you get out of writing Jessamy's essays."

A sparkle in that gaze she'd worried would go forever dull. According to Keir, Sam remembered nothing of his abduction—likely as a result of the head wound. There was a good chance he'd remember later on, but the healers and his parents planned to prepare him for that eventuality. By then, he'd be stronger, hopefully more able to process the events of that terrible night.

"No," Sam said, his voice husky. "She said I have to catch up."

"Sounds like her," Elena whispered, then gestured at the gifts. "You got a good haul."

"Did you bring me a present?"

Elena grinned. "Did I ever? I even asked your parents if I could give it to you."

Excitement had him straining forward. "What is it?"

"Hey, careful." Settling him back on the bed, she reached into her pocket to bring out a small dagger tucked into an intricately designed metal sheath.

Sam's eyes went huge as Elena put it into his hands. "I was given this after I completed a hunt for an angel in Shikoku, Japan. He told me it was a thousand years old." She touched the ruby at the bottom of the hilt. "The legend is that this ruby was once part of the eye of a dragon."

Small fingers ran reverently over the jewel. "What happened to the dragon?"

"He was such an ancient being that one day, he simply decided to sleep. After a while, he turned to stone, becoming the biggest mountain the world had ever seen." As she spoke, she couldn't help but remember the times her mother had told her and her sisters stories as they lay tumbled in their parents' bed.

Even Belle, far too cool for everything, had sprawled on the floor, painting her toenails or reading magazines. But she'd never turned a page while Mama told her stories. Blinking away the bittersweet images, Elena continued to tell the tale she'd originally heard from an old Buddhist monk as they sat drinking green tea beside an immaculate sand garden. "His eyes turned to rubies, his scales to diamonds, sapphires, and emeralds. Only one warrior was brave enough to venture near the sleeping dragon."

"Did the dragon wake?"

"Yes." She leaned close, her voice a conspiratorial whisper. "And because the warrior had been so brave, the dragon gave him a piece of his eye."

"The rest?"

"They say the dragon still sleeps, and that if anyone is ever smart enough and brave enough to find it again, the dragon will give him the world's riches."

"I'm going to find the dragon." Sam's eyes turned as bright

as those mythical jewels. "And I'll take good care of your present."

"I know you will." Reaching out, she brushed tumbling black curls off that sweet face, keeping a tight hold on the rage that had her hunter senses humming for blood. "Sleep now. We'll talk again later."

Keir came in as Elena rose. She watched him soothe his pianist's hands over Sam to lull the boy into a deep sleep. "He'll treasure it, you know," the healer said, placing the dagger carefully on the bedside table. "It's the kind of thing a child takes into adulthood."

Elena gave a small nod, barely keeping her feet under a sudden avalanche of memory—as if her subconscious had just been waiting for Sam's eyes to close. Why here? Why now? Neither Ari nor Belle, nor her mother, had ever made it to a hospital. Only to the morgue.

"Why did you bring her here?" A strident feminine voice. "She's a child."

A big hand around hers, giving her the courage to stand firm. "She deserves to see her sisters one last time."

"Not like this!"

"Beth's too young," the man said, "but Ellie isn't. She knows what happened. Dear God, she saw it all."

"Her mother—"

"Screams every time the drugs wear off, screams until the doctors medicate her again." Jagged words. "I can't help Marguerite, but I can help Ellie. It's all jumbled up in her mind. She keeps asking me if the monster made Arielle and Mirabelle like him."

"I won't let you do this."

"Try standing in my way."

"Elena?"

Mumbling a hurried good-bye when Keir looked at her with a too-perceptive gaze, she made her way out and into the corridor. Her mind couldn't stop circling around the truth her subconscious had just disgorged—Jeffrey had taken her to see her sisters. He'd fought her aunt, fought the hospital staff, fought everyone . . . because she'd needed to see that Arielle and Mirabelle truly were gone, that they hadn't been dragged into Slater's foul world.

"It's okay, Ellie." A big hand stroking over her head. Tears in that deep voice. "There's no more pain where they are now."

Ari and Belle *had* appeared at peace in spite of the way their lives had ended, their eyes closed in rest, their bodies looking whole beneath the white sheets. Elena had pressed her lips to each cold cheek, patted their hair, and said good-bye. They'd stayed beside the bodies for over an hour until . . .

"Okay, Daddy." She slipped her hand into his, looking up at the man who'd always been the strongest pillar in her universe. "We can go now."

Moisture glittered in that pale grey gaze that had always been so firm, so strong. "Yeah?"

"Don't cry." Reaching up as he bent down, she wiped away those tears. "They're not hurting anymore."

Elena staggered into a side corridor, her hand shaking as she braced herself. She'd always believed she'd lost her father the day it all ended in blood, but she'd been wrong. He'd still been her father that afternoon at the hospital, still been a man willing to fight for his daughter's right to say good-bye.

When had it all gone wrong? When had her father begun to treat her as an abhorrence he couldn't stand to look at? And how many more memories had she buried?

"Elena?"

Turning, she found herself face-to-face with Keir, his expression careful. "Would you—"

But Elena was already shaking her head. "I'm sorry, but I have to go." She almost ran to the waiting room, taking the hidden stairs to the top level. Her wings dragged on the steps designed for vampires, but she made it up and out into the icy air without being stopped by anyone else.

The wind was a cold slap against her overheated cheeks, the fresh air a welcome balm. "I don't want to remember." A cowardly thought, but she wasn't strong enough to bear the knowledge hanging heavy on the edge of her horizon. Because it was bad. Worse than anything else. And she was already struggling to survive the memories.

A cough from her left. "I'd ask if you were stargazing, but it's only five."

Her back went stiff. What had she said? Anyone but Galen. "Venom."

21

The vampire was wearing his signature black sunglasses, his lips holding a familiar mocking edge. "At your service."

She realized he had to have left New York as soon as Dmitri arrived. "Do vampires suffer from jet lag?"

Venom removed his sunglasses, giving her the full impact of those eyes slitted like a snake's. It didn't matter that she'd seen them before—her skin still crawled in visceral shock, a gut-deep response to the alien intelligence in those eyes. Part of her wondered if it was only his eyes that had been changed when he was Made—did Venom think like a human, or was his intellect a far more cold-blooded thing?

"Offering to soothe my aches, hunter?" the vampire said, flicking his tongue over one long incisor and coming away with a golden droplet full of poison. "I'm touched."

"Just being friendly," she said, matching snark for snark.

Venom's pupils contracted the instant before he slid his sunglasses back on.

She couldn't help it. "Why isn't your tongue forked?"

"Why can't you fly?" A smirk. "Those things on your back aren't accessories you know."

She gave him the finger, but part of her was glad for his annoying presence. He'd pulled her firmly into the present, the past locked in that cupboard where she preferred to keep it the majority of the time. "Aren't you supposed to act as my guide?"

He waved a hand. "Follow me, milady."

Despite his words, they walked side by side as he led her to Raphael's main office, something she hadn't even known existed until then. "What's the mood like in Manhattan?" She'd spoken to both Sara and Ransom about it, but a vampire's take on things, especially a vampire as strong as Venom, was likely to be different from a human's.

Of course, Venom didn't give her any kind of a straight answer. "People are starting to believe the rumors of your resurrection were greatly exaggerated. Most think you're dead and buried somewhere. So sad."

She ignored the deliberate provocation. "The truth still hasn't gotten out? I know Raphael's people wouldn't tell, but the others? Michaela?"

"All jealous. Raphael's the first archangel in living memory to have Made an angel." A glance at her from those mirrored frames that showed her nothing but her own face floating in darkness. "You're a unique prize. Be careful you don't get bagged and put up on some wall."

Raphael was sitting behind a huge black desk when she walked in, Venom having left her at the door. Déjà vu hit her with relentless force. He had a desk like that in his Tower, too.

"If I were to splay you out on my desk and thrust my fingers into you right now, I think I'd find different."

Raphael looked up at that instant, his eyes smoldering with an unequivocally sexual heat that said he knew exactly what she was thinking. Holding that gaze, she closed the door and walked to him with slow, intent steps. Instead of stopping when she reached the granite, she jumped up and, sweeping the papers out of her way, swung her legs over the other side, spreading them to bracket him in between.

The archangel put his hands on her thighs. "Again you come to me with nightmares in your eyes."

"Yes," she said, pushing her hands through his hair. "I come to you." It was a trust she'd given no one else.

He squeezed her thighs, pulling her closer with an effortless strength that made her heart race. The Archangel of New York was in a dangerous mood today. Bending down as he lifted up his head, she kissed him. Her dominant position lasted a bare second. A subtle shift in his hold and he had her in his lap, her legs on either side of his, the damp heat between her thighs pressed to the rigid line of his cock.

Gasping at the sudden, electric contact, it took her a second to realize she'd spread her wings over his desk. "I'm messing up your papers," she whispered against lips that had tempted her into the most erotic of sins.

He moved up his hand to close over her breast.

A shock of sensation. Her spine arched.

"I'll take recompense for your misdemeanor in flesh. Are you ready to pay?" A question full of a sensual cruelty that made her survival instincts ripple in fear.

But instead of fighting she relaxed. Raphael, she thought, was more than terrifying enough to banish even the worst nightmare. When his teeth closed over the pulse in her neck, when his hands ripped away her top to leave her upper body bare, she gripped his shoulders and hung on.

Then those strong white teeth moved lower.

Her stomach swirled with an addictive mix of fear and desire. "Raphael."

He flicked out his tongue, one hand on her back, the other plumping up her breast so he could lave the nipple with a slow focus that had her entire body going taut in expectation. "Are you planning to bite?" It was a husky question.

Perhaps.

Hearing the chill in that, she found herself hesitating, even as her body craved his touch. Was she anywhere near strong enough to take on the Archangel of New York in this kind of a mood?

You're my mate, Elena. You have no choice but to learn.

He was in her mind, slipping in as desire short-circuited her defenses. "Will you ever understand the need for boundaries?" She nipped at his lip, frustrated enough to act on instinct.

His eyes turned to midnight as he lifted his head, his thumb brushing over the peak he'd aroused to throbbing readiness. "No."

"Sorry"—she wrapped her arms around his neck—"you don't get away with autocratic answers with me." And she wasn't going to let her anger drive a wedge between them. This thing that tied them together—this raw, painful emotion— was worth fighting for. "And I'm never going to accept being made a puppet. Not by Lijuan, and certainly not by the man I consider mine."

He didn't answer, just watched her with that aloof focus. He'd watched her like that the first time they'd met. Then, she'd been afraid he'd kill her. Now, she knew he wouldn't. But . . . he might hurt her in ways only an immortal could. She should've backed down—but she'd never been one to do that.

"What," she said, touching her nose to his in unspoken affection, in a trust that was a fragile thread he could snap with a single careless act, "has you in such a bad mood?"

The scent of the sea swelled, until she could almost touch the foam. The pause, it was full of things unspoken, a gleaming blade hanging over their heads. Sweat broke out along her spine but she continued to hold him, continued to fight for a relationship that had come out of nowhere and become the most important thing in her universe.

Elena. A caress across her mind as he dropped his head to the curve of her neck.

Heart thudding at the knowledge that the danger had passed, she stroked her hands through his hair, nuzzled her face against him. "You have your own nightmares," she said, understanding coming to her in the clarity after the storm. "They were bad today."

Both arms around her, he tugged her even closer. She went, needing the warmth of him as much as he needed her. And wasn't that a kicker? The Archangel of New York needed her? Her, Elena Deveraux, Guild Hunter and unwanted daughter. Squeezing him with a fierce tenderness, she pressed her lips to his temple, his cheek, any part of him she could reach.

"Must be something in the air," she found herself saying in a voice so quiet, it was almost not sound. "I can't seem to stop thinking of my mother, my sisters." It was the first time she'd ever spoken of her nightmares aloud. Even her best friend didn't know the truth of her childhood, of the evil that haunted her until some days she could hardly breathe.

"Tell me their names." Warm breath against her neck, his arms so strong around her.

"You know."

"It's only fact."

"My mother," she said, holding on, holding tight, "her name was Marguerite."

Elena. A mental kiss, his scent enfolding her as protectively as his arms.

Her lip quivered until she caught it between her teeth. "She'd been in the States since she married my father, but she still spoke with a Parisian accent. She was this fascinating, lovely butterfly with her laughter and her quick hands. I used to just love sitting in the kitchen, or in her work room, watching my mother talk as she worked."

Marguerite had made quilts, beautiful one-of-a-kind pieces that had sold for enough money that she'd built up a small nest egg. Nothing in comparison to her husband's fortune, but hers had been passed on to her daughters with love, while Jeffrey . . . "She'd never have let my father do what he did."

"He lives only because I know you love him."

"I shouldn't, but I can't stop myself." That love was rooted too deep, so deep that even years of neglect hadn't snuffed it out completely. "I used to wish he'd died instead of my mother, but I know my mom would've hated me for thinking that."

"Your mother would've forgiven you."

Elena wanted to believe that so much it hurt. "She was the heart of our family. After her death, *everything* died."

"Tell me of your lost sisters."

"If Mama was the heart, then Ari and Belle were the peace and the storm." They'd left a gaping hole in the Deveraux family when their blood slicked across the floor.

Slater's handsome face, his lips painted a glistening red.

She clung to Raphael, shoving away the hated image with desperate hands. "I was the middle child and I liked it. Beth was the baby, but Ari and Belle let me do things with them sometimes." No more words would come, her chest tight with lack of air.

"I didn't have siblings."

The words were unexpected enough that they broke through her anguish. Staying in place, wrapped around Raphael like ivy, she listened.

"Angelic births are rare, and my parents were both thousands of years old when I was born." Each birth was a celebration but his had been particularly feted. "I was the first child born of two archangels in several millennia."

Elena, his hunter trusting him to hold her safe, lay quiet against him, but he could feel her attention, her palm warm through the linen of his shirt. Sliding one of his own hands down her naked back, slow and easy, he continued to talk, to share things he'd not spoken of in an eternity. "But there were some who said I shouldn't have been born."

"Why?" She raised her head, clearing her eyes with hard swipes of her knuckles. "Why would they say that?"

"Because Nadiel and Caliane were *too* old." Holding her close enough that her breasts brushed his chest with every breath, he moved his hands up over the curve of her waist, her rib cage, savoring the feel of her skin against his own. "There was concern that they'd begun to degenerate."

Elena frowned. "I don't understand. Immortality is immortality."

"But we evolve," he said. "Some of us devolve."

"Lijuan," she whispered. "Has she evolved?"

"That's what we say, but even the Cadre wonders what it is she's evolving into." A nightmare, that was certain. But a private one, or one that would lay waste to the world?

Elena was in no way stupid. She understood in bare seconds. "That's why your mother executed your father."

"Yes. He was the first."

"Both?" Pain—for *him*—arced through those expressive eyes.

"Not at the start." He saw the last moments of his father's existence as clearly as if the scenes were painted across his irises. "My father's life ended in fire."

"That mural," she said, "on the hallway in our wing—it's his death."

"A reminder of what might await me."

She shook her head. "Never. I won't let it happen."

His human, he thought, his hunter. She was so very young, and yet there was a core of strength in her that fascinated him, would continue to fascinate him through the ages. She'd already changed him in ways he didn't understand—perhaps, he thought slowly, there was a chance she might save him from Nadiel's madness. "Even if you fail," he said, "I have every confidence that you'll find a way to end my life before I stain the world with evil."

Rebellion in those eyes. "We die," she said, "we die together. That's the deal."

He thought about his final thoughts as he'd fallen with her in New York, her body broken in his arms, her voice less than a whisper in his mind. He hadn't considered holding onto his eternity for a second, had chosen to die with her, with his hunter. That she would choose to do the same . . . His hands clenched. "We die," he repeated, "we die together."

A moment of utter silence, the sense of something being locked into place.

Releasing the pain of memory, he pressed a kiss to the pulse in her neck. "We must see what Lijuan has sent you."

She shivered. "Can I have your shirt?"

He let her scramble off his lap, her body beautiful and lithe . . . and strong. Gauging her muscle tone with a critical eye as she turned to look at something on his desk, he made a decision. "Flying lessons begin tomorrow."

She spun around so fast, she almost tripped on her wings. "Really?" A huge grin bisected her face. "Are you going to teach me?"

"Of course." He'd trust her life to no one else. Sliding off his shirt, he gave it to her.

She pulled it on and rolled up the sleeves. It was much too big for her, of course, but she left the ends hanging. When he commented on that, a touch of color streaked across her cheeks. "It's comforting, okay. Now where's this stupid gift?"

22

Elena saw Raphael's lips shape into the barest hint of a smile at her bad-tempered words, but he didn't comment. Instead, he walked to a cabinet in the corner, the muscles of his back shifting with a fluid strength that made every female hormone in her sit up in begging attention.

Staving off the lingering echoes of the past with the sensual pleasure of watching her archangel move, she walked to stand beside him as he opened the cabinet to reveal a small black box about the right size and shape for jewelry. She recoiled, taking a physical step backward, her words coming in a hard rush. "Throw that thing into the deepest pit you can find."

Raphael glanced at her. "What do you feel?"

"It gives me the creeps." Hugging herself, she rubbed her hands up and down her arms, ice forming in the hollow of her stomach. "I don't want it anywhere near me."

"Interesting." Reaching in, he picked up the box. "I sense nothing, and yet even without blood, it sings to you."

"Don't touch it," she ordered between gritted teeth. "I told you to throw it away."

"We can't, Elena. You know that."

She didn't want to know it. "Power games. So what? We tell her thanks and send back a bauble or something. You must have a few lying around."

"That will not do." Eyes that had shifted to the shadowed color found in the deepest, darkest part of dawn, before the sun rose to the horizon. "This is a very specific gift. It's a test."

"So what?" she said again. "Archangels play power games. Who the fuck says I have to?"

Raphael put the box on a corner of his desk, his wings whispering against hers. "Like it or not, by becoming my lover, you've accepted an invitation to those games."

Her skin felt as if it was being touched by a thousand spidery fingers. "Can we throw it away after I open it?"

"Yes."

"That won't be bad politics?"

"It'll be a statement." He held out his hand. "Come, hunter. I need a drop of your blood."

"See? Creepy?" Shuddering, she took out one of her knives and pricked her left index finger. "Anyone who gives gifts locked by blood isn't ever going to give you a bath set."

Taking her hand, Raphael held it over the box, squeezing her finger just hard enough to release a single, luminous drop of blood. She watched it hang on her skin for a frozen moment, as if loathe to touch the velvet box, before it fell in a slow, soft splash. The box seemed to consume it, a voracious blackness that hungered for the taste of life. Her hand clenched around the knife. "I really don't want to go to this ball."

Raphael kissed her fingertip before releasing her hand. "Do you want me to open it?"

"Yes." She wasn't going to touch that thing if she could help it.

He flipped it open. She couldn't see what was inside at first, her view blocked by his hand, but then he moved . . .

Her gorge rose. Dropping the knife, she spun and headed for the door she hoped led to the bathroom. Her relief was overpowered by the retching that ripped through her as she stumbled into the tiled enclosure. Dropping her head above the toilet, she brought up her lunch in a hard, rough pulse that felt like it was peeling off the lining of her stomach itself.

Sometime in the middle, she became aware that she was on her knees, Raphael beside her, his hand holding her hair away from her face, his wings spread to enclose her in white-gold. Trembling as the muscle spasms quieted, she pushed the flush button and sat back.

Raphael got up, bringing her a cold cloth. She wiped it over her face, very aware of him hunkering in front of her, his anger a blistering flame. "What," he said in that frigid tone she'd heard him use with Michaela once, "does that necklace mean?"

"It has to be a copy," she choked out. "We buried the real one. I *saw*." The lid of the coffin closing, her last glimpse of Belle's face.

Hands cupping her cheeks, beautiful wings spread wide. "Don't let her win. Don't let her use your memories against you."

"God, the *bitch*." Anger rose in a blinding wave. "She did it on purpose, didn't she?" It wasn't truly a question, because she knew the answer. "I'm no threat to her, she's just doing this because it's *fun*. She wants to break me." For no reason than that it would give her a few moments amusement.

"She obviously doesn't know you." He tugged her to her feet.

Walking to the washbasin, she put the cloth on the counter and rinsed out her mouth with near-scalding water. "Belle," she said after she felt clean at last, "would've ripped out Li-juan's throat for daring to use her against me." The memory of her sister's sweet, wild nature had her straightening her spine. "Let's go."

This time, though she continued to refuse to touch it, she looked very carefully at the necklace Lijuan had sent her. "It's a copy." Relief rocked through her, her legs threatening to collapse until she braced her hand on the desk. The Chinese archangel hadn't desecrated Belle's final resting place. "We decided to engrave Belle's name on the back one year with a heated metal wire. We only got a wobbly *B* on there before Mama caught us." The memory made her smile, wiping out the ugliness. "She was so mad—that pendant was nine carat gold."

Putting the necklace back in the box, Raphael closed it. "I'll make sure it's disposed of."

"Do it . . . but make me a copy first." She bared her teeth in a savage smile. "Bitch wants to play games, let's play games."

"Her spies will report it," Raphael said. "It's a good move, but I won't allow it."

She jerked up her head. "What?"

"This was meant to hurt you. Wearing that pendant will only remind you of the past."

"Yeah," she said. "It'll remind me of how Belle punched out the neighborhood bully even though he was three years older and fifty pounds heavier. It'll remind me of her strength, her will."

Raphael looked at her for a long moment. "But those memories come wrapped in darkness."

She couldn't disagree. "Maybe it's time I embraced the darkness instead of running from it."

"No." Raphael's jaw was a brutal line. "I won't let Lijuan pull you into a waking nightmare."

"Then you're letting her win."

A hard, unexpected kiss. "No, we're letting her believe she has won."

Raphael disposed of Lijuan's gift and flew back to the Refuge cloaked in the black shadows of night. What he'd said to Elena had been the truth—but it had hidden other, deeper truths.

He'd done it to protect her.

And she'd known. But she'd let him convince her. Which

told him more about the depth of her scars than anything else. Once, when Uram had been sane, when he'd still remembered a little of the youth he'd been, he and Raphael had had a conversation.

"Humans," the other archangel had said, "they live such flickering lives."

Raphael, not yet three hundred years old, had nodded. "I have human friends. They speak of love and hate, but I wonder, how much do they truly know of such emotions?"

To this day, he could recall the look Uram had given him—that of an older male amused with the pretensions of youth. "It's not quantity that matters, Raphael. We flitter away our lives because they're endless. Humans must live a thousand lifetimes in one. Every hurt is keener, every joy more incandescent."

Raphael had been surprised—even then, Uram had been dissolute, careless in his pleasures, open in his cruelty. "You sound as if you envy them."

"Sometimes, I do." Those vivid green eyes had stared down at the human village that sheltered below the ancient castle they'd called home at the time. "I wonder what I would've been had I known I only had five or six paltry decades to make my mark on the world."

In the end, Uram had made a huge mark on the world, but it hadn't been what that younger self would've wished for. Now, he'd be forever remembered among most as the archangel who'd lost his life in a battle for territory, for power. Only a rare few, even among the angels, knew the truth—that Uram had turned bloodborn, bloated by a toxin that had turned his blood to poison. Raphael's father had never fallen into that kind of bloodlust. But Nadiel's lust for power had been, in many ways, worse.

Seeing Elena standing on the balcony of their home still clothed in his shirt, her magnificent wings spread as if in hunger for flight, he dived hard and fast.

Raphael! It was a cry filled with equal amounts of wonder and fear.

Feeling something long asleep awaken within him, an echo of the cocky boy who'd amused Uram, he rose up in a hard vertical climb, before twisting into a spiraling plummet that could send the inexperienced smashing onto the rocks below.

It was at the midpoint that he felt it—Elena's mind locking with his, her mental gasp as she experienced the dangerous ecstasy of the fall. Then he was sweeping out and upward. She stayed with him until he coasted down on a luxurious air current to land on the balcony.

She stared at him for a moment, her own wings closing. "What"—a shake of her head—"just happened?"

"You linked to me." It should have been impossible—he was an archangel, his shields impenetrable. But, he remembered, she'd done it once before—as a mortal. He'd lost himself in her that day, sunk so deep into the wild perfume of her hunger that he'd ceased to think. Later, he'd suffered her rage at what she'd believed had been an attempt at coercion on his part. His hunter hadn't understood what she'd done.

"There are some humans—one among half a billion perhaps—who make us something other than what we are. The barriers fall, the fires ignite, and the minds merge."

Lijuan had killed the mortal who'd touched her that deeply.

Raphael had chosen to love, instead.

"I could feel what you felt." Exhilaration still sparked in Elena's eyes. "Is that what it's like when you're inside my mind?"

"Yes."

A pause, her expression intent. "You don't like it, do you? That I can slip beneath your shields."

"I've had over a thousand years to get used to being alone inside my head." He ran the back of his hand down her cheek. "It is . . . disconcerting to have another presence there."

"Now you know how I feel." A raised eyebrow. "It's not nice to know that nothing inside me is private."

"I've never taken your deepest thoughts."

"How do I know that?" she asked. "When you're so cavalier about your ability to enter whenever you want? How can I ever be certain that what I choose to share with you is truly a choice?"

For the first time, he felt a glimmer of understanding. "It'll be a much slower way of learning each other."

"Speed isn't everything." Her hands clenched on the railing.

He thought of her trust when she'd spoken of her mother, her compassion as she accepted the burden of his own memories. "I will try, Elena."

"I guess that's the best I'm going to get from an archangel." The words were softened by the amusement in her eyes. "The mind-talking doesn't bother me. That goes both ways. This other thing—I have a feeling it's not something I'm going to be able to control for a long time yet."

"Did you catch any of my thoughts while we were linked?"

"Not really. I was too caught up by the flight—God but you can fly, Raphael." She whistled. "I know that's not easy, what you did."

Pride unfurled inside him, born from the heart of the youth he'd been before Caliane. Before Isis. Before Dmitri.

"I did catch one name." Hesitant words. "Were you thinking about your father?"

"Yes." He watched the wind blow a few rebellious white blonde strands across her face, her body silhouetted against the diamond-studded night sky, and made a choice of his own. "I was thinking that in many ways, my father's madness was worse than Uram's."

Elena didn't interrupt, simply shifted forward so that she could tangle one hand with his. He curled his fingers around hers, wondering at the tectonic shift in his life since the day he first met Elena Deveraux, Guild Hunter. So quickly she'd twined around his heart, becoming the most vital part of his existence.

"With Uram, though there was a little hesitation, in the end, the Cadre all agreed he needed to die." It was Lijuan who'd worried him the most—still worried him. "Lijuan wondered if perhaps the power that came with becoming blood-born was worth it."

Elena shivered. "You should've showed her that room where Uram kept the remains of his victims." Her stomach lurched at the memory even now. "It was a slaughterhouse. The smell alone would send most people screaming."

"You forget, Elena," Raphael said, his gaze almost black, "Lijuan plays with the dead."

"Hold the pendant still, Ellie."

"I'm trying."

"Shh, Mama will hear."

Breathing in the fresh bite of Raphael's scent, she swallowed the poignant whisper of memory and focused on the present. "Why was your father worse?"

Raphael's hair lifted in the night breeze, darker than the blackness that surrounded it. "He didn't kill indiscriminately. For the longest time, they were all convinced he was simply driven by a hunger for power, for territory."

"Others joined him," she guessed.

A slow nod. "He was an emperor, but he wanted to be a god. When the murders began, they were stealthy, even political."

Elena reached up to push his hair off his face, needing to touch him, he'd become so suddenly remote. "What made people change their minds?"

He leaned into the touch, but his expression remained acetic, distant. "When he began incinerating entire villages in territories not his own."

The reading she'd done under Jessamy's guidance came to her aid. "A declaration of war."

"My father didn't see it that way. He expected the others in the Cadre to fall under his command—he'd come to believe he *was* a god by then."

"How old were you when he died?"

"Mere decades into my existence."

A child, she thought, he'd been nothing but a child. "That means . . ." She stopped, couldn't continue.

"That he was well on the way to madness before I was born."

She slid her arms around his waist, laying her ear over his heart. "That's why the worry over your birth."

His own arms were steel bands around her. *Sometimes, I wonder what he passed on to me. What my mother passed on.*

23

In that moment, Elena understood that the Archangel of New York had shared something with her he'd shared with no one else. How she knew, she couldn't say. But she knew. As she knew there were no words to answer Raphael's question. Only time could do that, but . . . "The course of your life has taken a direction I bet not even Lijuan could've foreseen. Nothing is predestined."

Raphael didn't speak for several long minutes, and they stood there while the night winds played dark music across their bodies, stroked over their wings. Her archangel hadn't bothered with a replacement shirt, and his skin felt wonderful under her hands, her cheek. She was, she realized, oddly content in spite of the unsettling events of the day.

"The night is quiet," Raphael said at last, "the winds fairly calm. Visibility is clear in every direction."

"A good night to fly," she whispered.

"Yes."

She held on as he lifted off, shifting her hold to around his neck. The wind of takeoff whipped her hair off her face, then snapped it back to tangle around them both. "I need to cut this," she muttered, pulling strands out of her mouth with one hand, the other locked around Raphael.

Why did you not, even as a hunter? I would've thought it a vulnerability.

The wound was too close to the surface today, but she answered anyway. *My hair's like my mother's. I was the only one of her four children to retain the color as I grew.* Ari and Belle had both gone a golden blonde like Jeffrey, while Beth was a throwback to their paternal grandmother, her hair a gorgeous strawberry blonde.

So, we are both our mother's shadows.

Knowing that what she cherished might be to him a curse, she brushed her lips over his jaw in silent comfort. "Go faster."

Raphael swooped up and down without warning, making her laugh in sheer joy as she locked her legs around his. She didn't realize she'd expanded her own wings until they began to catch air. "Raphael!"

"Pull them in," he said. "Otherwise our landing will be rough."

Thinking it through step by step, she contracted her wings—her muscles gave a mild twinge at going against the wind, but nothing to worry about. "They want to open again."

"Instinct." Angling them lower, he flared out his own wings to their greatest width and brought them to a gentle, precise landing on a small mountain plateau overlooking a shallow valley filled with snow.

"This place looks different from the land close to the Refuge." Its edges softened by time, the valley appeared as if it would cradle rather than crush.

"The snow here tends to be soft," Raphael said. "That's why it's a good place for flight training."

Her heart skipped a beat. "Now?" She'd thought he planned only to take her flying in his arms.

"Now."

Excitement a tattoo against her ribs, she stepped to the lip of the plateau, and glanced down.

And down.

Vertigo had never been a problem, but— "It suddenly looks a lot farther away now that I know I'll be falling toward it."

"You, afraid?" The touch of his wings against her own, a shimmer of gold that she caught with the corner of her eye.

Her lips twitched. "Are you dusting me, Archangel?"

"Angel dust looks beautiful coming off wings in the dark." A kiss pressed to her jaw as he shifted to stand behind her, the aphrodisiac dust a taste of unadulterated sex. "As you fly, it'll sink into your skin, readying your body for me."

"You're all talk," she murmured, feeling him settle his hands firmly about her waist. "So, what do I do now?"

"The only way to learn to fly, is to fly." He pushed her off the edge of the cliff.

Fear obliterated everything but the need to survive. Her wings spread, catching air, slowing her descent as her muscles screamed at the sudden strain. Raphael's shirt twisted around her, baring her stomach to the elements. She didn't care, more concerned about getting her wings to work. But it was too late, the ground rushing up at terminal velocity.

No snow was that soft—she was still going to hit hard enough to splinter bones.

Hands gripping her under her arms, lifting her up with effortless strength. *Close your wings.*

She obeyed, though the adrenaline pumping through her body made her want to do the exact opposite. The instant her feet touched the ground, she swiveled around to push him in the chest, her palms sizzling at the contact with his bare skin. "That's your idea of teaching? I could've been splattered from here to Manhattan!"

"You were never in any danger." His eyes gleamed with laughter and that just made her madder. "That's how young angels learn to fly—they're pushed out of the aeries before they have a chance to develop a fear of it."

Her fury came to a screeching halt, though her heart continued to ricochet violently in her chest. "You push babies out into thin air?"

"How do you think birds learn to fly?"

"Huh." She folded her arms, the shirt clammy against her sweat-soaked skin. "You know, I'm an adult—I already know fear."

"That's why I didn't give you any warning. Instinct did what it was supposed to."

Wiping her hands across her cheeks in an effort to cool them down, she took a deep breath, tied the tails of the shirt at her side and walked back. "Okay, push me again."

"You can step off yourself."

Elena had long ago learned to keep her fears to herself, seeing them only as weaknesses that could be used against her, but this time, there was nothing to do but admit it. "I'm too chickenshit."

Raphael pressed a kiss to her nape, put his hands on her waist again. "This time, snap your wings out as soon as possible."

Nodding, she was barely in position when he pushed. It took her at least three seconds to snap out her wings. Too slow. Raphael brought her up again. And again. And again.

"Once more," she said, her muscles crying with exhaustion. "I need to get it."

Raphael's face was all austere lines, but he nodded. "Once more."

Knowing her body would give out even if her will wouldn't, Elena took a few steps back from the edge. "It won't be as bad if I run."

"Remember, you must unfold your wings the instant you become airborne, or the downward momentum will be too strong to stop."

She nodded, pushing sweat-soaked strands of hair off her face. Then, filling her mind with the image of her body in flight, she began to race over the plateau. She went airborne seconds later, and it was only when she felt the hard pull of muscle in her shoulders that she realized her wings were out.

There was even, for a single moment, a slight upward drive before she began to fall again. Except this time, she felt a sense of control.

Her landing was nowhere even remotely close to Raphael's grace. She came down bruisingly hard on her knees, her momentum throwing her face forward, but she was grinning when she lifted that face from the powder. "I did it!"

The archangel crouching in front of her had eyes filled with a fierce kind of pride. "I had no doubts you would." He watched her dust off her face. "You'll hurt as if you've been beaten tomorrow, but you must continue to train."

"I know. Same principle as applies to normal training."

"However, if you feel true pain, let me know." Fingers on her chin. "It's better to wait for minor injuries to heal than turn them into major ones."

"Especially since we're on a deadline." She met his gaze, so brilliant even in the snowy dark. "You think Lijuan will use my inexperience in handling my new body against me."

A curt nod as he released her chin. "She'll use every weapon she can."

"Why?"

"A break from ennui." His lips flattened into a thin line. "If asked, she'll say it's about power, about politics, but in the end, it's about nothing but her own amusement. You're a new toy, one that's caught her interest."

"And we must play." Aching in every muscle, she got to her feet.

Raphael rose with her, seeming not to feel the cold at all, in spite of the fact that he was magnificently shirtless. "At another time, I may have declined the offer of the ball"—an unspoken reminder that he, too, was an archangel—"but we must attend this one."

She nodded. "You need to see how far Lijuan's devolved." According to what she'd heard, the oldest of the archangels was no longer willing to leave her homeland, even to meet with the Cadre.

"If she unleashes her reborn on the world, there'll be no going back."

The idea of the dead walking, their souls trapped in those horrific shells made Elena shiver. As she did, fine traces of gold glittered in the air. "Will you fly for me, Raphael?" she asked, deciding to hold on to the wonder tonight. "I want to see the angel dust coming off your wings."

Raphael flared out his wings, making her breath catch. The patterns that marked his wings as unique were indistinct in the dark, but she knew the bright sunburst on his left wing down to the last streak, the last line. It was a scar, made by a weapon she'd shot. He'd been so very cold that night. "Will you ever go Quiet again?" she found herself asking.

His answer was potent with memory, with the knowledge of how close he'd come to the precipice of evil. "The need would have to be very great." And then he lifted off in a tempest of the finest snow and wind, his power making her dig her feet into the powder to keep herself upright. Ecstasy soaked into her tongue a moment later, and she realized he'd flickered the aphrodisiac dust on her as he rose.

The special blend.

Her entire body beginning to hum with need, she watched as he rose ever higher, becoming a silhouette in the night sky. When he started to descend, it was in a series of slow, almost lazy dives, as if he was riding the air currents. Streamers of gold tracked his every movement, a wondrous light show against the velvet black sky.

It hit her again, right in the heart—how could this amazing, powerful being be hers? And yet he was. Perhaps he wasn't hers, would never be hers, in the way a mortal man might have been, but then, she'd never really fit well with those mortal men. They'd found her hunter strength off-putting, had called her unfeminine to her face. *You're amazing*, she thought up to her archangel.

He heard her, because his next dive was steep, the climb up even steeper.

Show-off.

Another steep dive, so hard and fast that her breath caught. She reached out as if to catch him as he plummeted, her heart racing a hundred miles an hour. He pulled up with less than a meter to spare between him and the unyielding earth, the wind of his ascent hitting her as he lifted back up.

She knew before she tasted it that he'd showered her with more of the dust. Every exposed part of her body tingled . . . including the entire span of her wings, which she'd spread out in preparation for flight, though she was far too inexperienced to execute a vertical takeoff like Raphael. *I hope all this dust isn't just a tease, because that might put me in a killing frame of mind.* She could already feel the erotic impact, the pulse between her thighs lush with need.

The scent of the sea swept over her as he answered. *Your muscles will feel much better after a bath and a massage.*

It was all her mind needed to mount a sensual assault filled with images of the last time they'd been in a bath together. His fingers driving into her, his gorgeous body bare for her perusal, his arousal heavy and demanding. She drew in a trembling breath as her breasts pushed against the damp fabric of his shirt, the tips aching at even that fleeting contact. Lifting her hand, she dropped it before she could touch herself. Everything felt too sensitive, too needy. *I think it's time to go home.* She imbued her mental words with the raw sexual craving that had her skin so tight, so exquisitely tender.

Raphael's response was to land behind her, his arms coming around her in a steely hold as he swiveled her to face him. Starving for the taste of him, she wrapped her arms around his neck, snapped her wings tight to her back and held on for the ride.

They rose through lingering traces of angel dust, each fine mote kicking her further into a kind of heat she wasn't sure she could survive. Groaning, she pressed her mouth to the uncompromising angle of his jaw, licking at his skin, sucking and tasting as he flew them home. Against her belly, he was hard, deliciously tempting. She wanted to close her hand

around that heavy heat, but had to satisfy herself with biting
kisses along his jaw.

He didn't stop her, but his body grew increasingly more
taut, his muscles electric with strain by the time they landed
on the balcony outside their bedroom. She felt him slide open
the doors, shut them after they entered. And then the archangel lost control. She was being turned with a hard move
that left no room for argument, the shirt ripped off her like
so much mist.

A fragment of thought before his hands closed over her
breasts from behind, his teeth sinking into the sensitive flesh
of her neck. The scream of pleasure was torn out of her, a
short, sharp burst. The hands curved so possessively around
her breasts squeezed, sending another bolt of lightning
straight through to the heat between her thighs, her body slick
with welcome, with *need*.

Releasing the grip he had on her neck, Raphael sucked on
the mark he'd made, his body a furnace that burned her from
the inside out. When she twisted, trying to turn, he slipped one
hand down to her abdomen, holding her in place with effortless strength, his other hand continuing to torment the sensitive flesh of her breasts, her nipples almost painfully aroused.

"Your mouth," she whispered, her voice husky. "I need
your mouth."

Not yet.

She shivered at the implacability of that comment, the dark
sexual tone of it. Raphael was not only out of control, he wasn't
going to allow her any either. She could have fought, but she'd
hungered for him since the instant she woke from the coma.
The archangel could have her any and every way he wanted.

Raising her arms, she went to twist them behind her and
around his neck, but he was already nudging her forward,
onto the bed. She flowed with the movement, ending up on
her knees on the sheets. Raphael pressed his hand to her lower
back. Understanding the silent message, she went down onto
her hands, too.

It was a starkly submissive position. However, she was

feeling anything but submissive. Using one hand to shift her hair to the side, she glanced back over her shoulder, wanting to tease him in the way a woman could tease a man in bed. "Oh God."

The archangel was glowing. A visceral terror in her gut, born of eons-old instinct.

I can feel your fear, Elena.

Blowing out a breath, she sucked in another, the action shaky. "It'll add spice to the proceedings."

A slow blink, his eyes lingering over the sweep of her back as he unfolded his wings with a careless grace that left her mouth watering. Then, eyes hooded, he stroked one hand down the curve of her bottom. *Spread your thighs.*

She resisted.

A glance of savage, wild blue.

Smiling just enough to let him know she was teasing, she widened her stance the merest fraction. He responded by running a single finger across the seam of her pants, stroking right over the hottest, most hungry part of her.

"Raphael!"

You wanted to play.

Still as dark, still as full of sexual intent . . . but holding an undertone of sensual amusement. Shuddering under the intimacy of the caress, she blew out a breath. "Yeah, I did." She went to flip over onto her back, but he read the tension in her muscles faster than she could move, holding her in place with a single hand on her hip.

"No fair," she murmured, dropping her head. "I'm not as strong."

Who said anything about playing fair?

She laughed, feeling as if her skin was stretching to accommodate the sexual energy within. "Are you planning to take off my pants anytime soon? I'm burning up."

Another lushly intimate caress. "I can feel your dampness through your clothing." His voice dropped, became impossibly more sensual as his fingers pushed upward. "I'll lick you here."

The stark statement of intent had fire burning across her cheeks.

"A blush?" A tug at the back of her pants, and suddenly, the material was gone, her skin bared to his gaze. "A blush all over." He traced the scalloped edges of her panties high on her thighs. "Pink," he murmured, "with blue ribbon. Your favorite pair."

Her blush felt like it would eat up her whole body. "I didn't realize you paid so much attention to my clothing."

"Certain pieces hold my interest." That sensual amusement was back, his finger tracing the ribbon across her buttock and along her hip. "Such heat under your skin. Surely you're not shy now?"

She couldn't speak, too focused on the mouthwateringly masculine strength of his body, on the way he was touching her, as if he had all the time in the world, as if there was no impatience in him. "Raphael."

"I like the sound of my name on your lips." His hand closed about her thigh as he widened her stance even more. This time, she didn't resist, even in play, wanting to entice him to go faster. When he cupped her, it was all she could do to suck in a few gasping breaths. The sheets blurred in front of her eyes as he shaped the fabric of her panties to her, parting her through the soaked material as if it didn't exist. "Hurry." It was a whisper.

But he heard. *No.*

Her flesh dampened even more for him, a rush of liquid flowing to the juncture of her thighs. She went to squeeze them instinctively tight, but he stopped her with one knee on the bed, his leg pushing against her thigh. She felt the bed dip as he shifted fully onto it, mirroring her position—except he kept that thigh between hers, his left hand palm down beside hers, while his right reached beneath to mold her breasts, her wings caught in between.

She expected it to hurt, but her wings fell into graceful lines, as if the knowledge of carnal pleasure was imprinted on her very muscles. And the sensation . . . Every feather, every fine filament was attuned to the powerful male heat of his body. "It's too much," she said, trying to pull away.

He held her in place. "You'll get used to it."

Frustrated, needy, she rubbed against the ridge of his arousal. *Behave, hunter.* Raphael pinched her nipple just enough to spark a wildfire inside of her.

Crying out, she bucked against him. When that didn't work, she followed instinct and dropped to her front, twisting over and onto her back before he could stop her. Legs tangled awkwardly with his, she looked up at an immortal who had a very human possessiveness burning in his gaze. "Enough," she whispered.

He shifted so that she could free her legs, but shook his head. "No."

24

He spread his wings above her, his entire frame burning white-hot. It dazzled, overwhelming her senses. But she couldn't, wouldn't, close her eyes, fascinated by the unearthly beauty of him. Dangerous, he was so very dangerous. But he was hers. Raising her hands, she pressed them against his chest.

An unadulterated adrenaline rush.

His eyes met hers, the whites eclipsed by blue. She should have been afraid, but she was in too much need to feel anything close to fear. "Raphael." It was a plea and a demand in one, her body moving in sinuous welcome.

Leaning down, he pressed his lips to hers at last, kissing her with a slow, almost primal intensity that had her stroking her hands up to his shoulders, trying to pull him down. But he continued to hold himself above her, closing his teeth over her lip when she insisted.

The contained power behind that steely frame was magnificent, a storm she could taste in the intensity of his kiss. Need twisted inside her, a clawing, voracious hunger. Gripping his shoulders, she threw her leg over his . . . and moved one hand in a slow glide over the arch of his wing.

The power of him blazed so bright, she couldn't keep her eyes open any longer. His lips met hers again a moment later and this time, there was nothing contained about him. The archangel had well and truly let go of the reins. His body came over hers, his erection pressing demandingly into her abdomen.

She twisted, trying to get him between her thighs. But Raphael had other ideas. Tearing his lips from hers, he pinned her down and began to kiss his way down her body. Her heart stilled, then restarted at frenetic speed.

I promised to lick you there.

"No!" She kicked out in an attempt to get away from a pleasure she knew would smash through her, a thousand glittering shards.

Yes. You're strong enough now.

Reaching out, she tried to hold him to her, but his hair slid out of her hands like black water, silky and cool across her flesh. She gripped the sheets, dug her heels into the bed. But nothing could have prepared her for the way he tasted her through the by-now transparent fabric of her panties, his hands keeping her spread for his delectation. It was agony and ecstasy, liquid lightning contained within a body that seemed suddenly too small, too fragile, for what it was being asked to bear.

As if he knew he'd pushed her too far, Raphael rose to press a kiss to her navel. *Hunter mine.*

Heart catching at the affection laced with the sexual heat, she reached down to run her fingers across his lips. There was no smile—the force of the emotions between them was too strong, too much to allow for laughter—but he didn't halt her exploration. When his hand moved against her hip, she shivered.

A single tug and the last barrier between his kiss and her most intimate flesh was gone. Then those lips were on her, firm, determined, unrelenting in their demands.

Mine, you are mine.

Raphael's kiss was as earthy as his words, full of masculine possession and a wild, inexorable hunger. Pleasure filled her body, rose through her veins, suffused her pores as he caressed her on every level, as he pushed her to *feel* as she'd never before felt, as he took her over.

The peak was a slow climb, a shattering descent. Color exploded in a wild wave but she didn't break, floating with the tide to come home in Raphael's arms.

Raphael held his hunter as her heart slowed, her skin sheened with a fine layer of perspiration. The primal heart of him, the part that urged him to possess her to the core, purred in silent satisfaction.

She was his, would never be anyone else's.

Stroking his hand down her body, he savored the jagged rise and fall of her chest, the low moans that caught in her throat as she reacted to his touch. When her hand rose to cup his cheek, he rubbed against her palm, his fingers tracing the passion-flushed curve of her mouth.

Heavy-lidded eyes looked up at him, silver with desire sated. "I think you've done me in, Archangel."

"I've only begun, hunter." Rising off her, he swung his legs over the side of the bed. "It's time for our bath."

Elena groaned. "You're torturing me." Her eyes went to the engorged push of his cock against the tough leather-like material of his pants as he stood, turned to face her. "And yourself."

The sight of her lying so deliciously rumpled in their bed made his body harden impossibly further. "I've learned to savor my pleasures, as I intend to savor you . . . again and again."

Her breasts flushed as a shiver rippled through her. "I love the way you talk in bed." Throaty words as she pushed herself up into a sitting position, then shifted until she was on her knees near the edge of the bed. "Come here." A sensual demand.

He'd lived well over a millennium, developed iron control over the primal side of his nature, but he could have no more resisted the lush invitation in his hunter's eyes than he could've given up the ability to fly. "What would you do with me, Elena?"

Reaching out, she unsnapped the top button on his pants, her fingers strikingly feminine against the black fabric. "Wicked, wicked things." A single slow stroke along the outline of his cock.

He hissed out a breath, thrust his hands into her hair. But he didn't stop her, this woman who played with him—who trusted him. "Be gentle."

She shot him a startled silver glance. Then a slow, delighted smile. "I won't bite . . . unlike some people." A fraction more pressure on his aroused flesh as she shaped him with her hand.

His abdomen went tight. "You're giving me ideas." He could still taste the wild musk of her on his tongue, sumptuous and earthy. "Next time, I might use my teeth on far more delicate flesh."

Shuddering, she unsnapped the next two buttons . . . before leaning forward to press a wetly sensual kiss on the lowest part of his navel. His hips jerked, his hand fisting in her hair. "I," he ground out, "do not have that much control." Releasing her, he stepped back.

"That's no—" Her words trailed away as he stripped off what remained of his clothing, wanting nothing between his flesh and her touch.

Elena's breath whispered out of her. The impact of him was . . . indescribable.

Then he was walking back to her, his erection pure unadulterated temptation. She curved her fingers around him, aware of his hand going to her hair again, of him wrapping the strands around his fist. "Enough teasing." A gentle nudge. "Fulfill your promise."

Her skin went hot, tight at the rough sexual tone of that demand, but she shot him a teasing smile. "Giving orders even in bed?"

Elena.

Hearing the edge in that, suddenly violently aware of how long her archangel had waited for her—and it was still a kick to the heart, that she was loved by him—she dipped her head and ran her tongue over the vein that pulsed along the thick line of his arousal. He made an inarticulate sound of mingled pain and pleasure, his hand tugging slightly at her hair. Unable to resist now that she'd had a taste of him, her thighs clenching, she retraced her journey and took him into her mouth.

Elena!

She couldn't take all of him. He was too big, too thick. *But I'll have eternity to refine my technique.* The sensual thought blazed out on an inferno of need as she loved her archangel, licking and tasting and sucking.

Brilliant white fire against her skin and she knew he was glowing, this lethal being she dared tease in the most intimate of ways. His response when it came, was starkly sensual. *Your mouth*—his voice sandpaper in her mind—*is a little piece of heaven and hell.*

Moaning low in her throat, she stroked up, swirled her tongue around the head before sliding her mouth back down the enticement that was his body. She loved the taste of him, the contrast of steel and silk, the way he murmured hot little promises of retribution.

Under her hands, his muscles grew granite-hard, his skin sheened with heat. "Enough, Elena." A command.

She let him feel her teeth.

A crash of waves inside her mind, a wild storm. *I am,* he said, no trace of the civilized male in him now, *tying you to the bed next time.*

Knowing he was so close to the edge that another caress would tip him over, Raphael stroked his hand down the sensitive arch of Elena's left wing, sliding out of the sweet, hot prison of her mouth while she was distracted by the shock of sensation. But though her eyes glittered with the fever of their combined hunger, she didn't give in. Lifting a single taunting finger, she sucked it between the kiss-swollen beauty of her lips.

That was all the encouragement the voracious hunger inside him needed. Spreading through his veins, it took him over, a rippling black fire. He returned to the bed in a dark wave of heat, flipping Elena onto her front, pulling her legs up and spreading them wide.

It was the rawest, most primitive way to possess a woman, but his hunter pushed up on her elbows, gave him a challenging look, and said, "I'm waiting."

He slid into her in a single hard thrust. Her scream echoed off the walls, but it was a scream that held equal parts demand and need. Gripping her hips tight, he pulled out almost fully, then slammed back in. There was no mercy in him any longer, but Elena didn't ask it from him.

Learn to fly fast, Elena, he said as he pushed them both to a final, blinding peak. *Then we will dance in the sky.*

They did have that bath—much later, Raphael stroking the washcloth over her wings with lazy movements as she leaned on the rim. "That feels so intimate."

"It is." A kiss pressed to the ultra-sensitive edge where her right wing grew out of her back. "Allowing someone to care for your wings is considered an act that takes a relationship well beyond the sexual."

Limbs heavy with desire sated, she thought about that. "Can I wash your wings?" It would be the most delicious of indulgences, the most exquisite of pleasures.

"You've had that right since our first bath."

The unadorned truth of his words made her heart ache.

"But," he continued, placing the washcloth on the rim as he fit himself to her back, "right now, you're in no shape to do anything but relax."

She heard the thread of male pride in that, felt the ache translate into sensual affection. "You give good sex, Archangel."

A squeeze of her breasts, his free hand reaching between them to stroke two fingers into her. Sucking in a breath, she found her voice. "Again?" Heat uncurled in her abdomen.

"Again." Withdrawing his fingers, he dropped a kiss to the curve of her neck, his erection nudging at her.

"Be gentle."

She felt him smile at her echo of his earlier words. *For you, Elena, anything.* He slid into her in a smooth thrust, her body stretching to accommodate him in sharp ecstasy. And when he moved this time, it was slow and deep, a claiming so tender, he would've stolen her heart if she hadn't already given it to him high above a ruined Manhattan.

Elena was fairly certain her muscles were jelly the next day, but she crawled to the training session with Galen regardless. Raphael had given her the massage he'd promised her before they fell asleep, and nothing was actually torn or broken, so it was going to be all about working through the muscle pain.

Galen took one look at her and threw her what felt like a ten-ton metal brick. She stared at the claymore—and it sure looked like the heavy Scottish weapon—for a second, then set her feet and lifted. Her biceps quivered, but the damn blade ended up vertical, the tip pointed to the cloudy blue sky.

Galen scanned her shoulders, her arms. "You're stronger than a normal mortal."

"I'm no longer mortal," she pointed out, only just keeping the claymore upright.

"No one has records on an angel Made, but if the same principles apply as with vampires, then your strength won't increase to immortal levels for a significant period."

Shrugging, she left it at that. The fact that the hunter-born were slightly stronger than ordinary humans wasn't exactly a secret, but neither was it advertised. And while she might now be an immortal, she was still hunter-born, still a member of the Guild. Those were loyalties she'd never betray.

"Throw it to me."

She narrowed her eyes and walked across the snow-sprinkled ground to hand him the blade. "What? Do you want to prove to me how weak I am? You can do that with one punch."

"But then Raphael would kill me." An imminently practical response as he took the claymore and turned to retrieve something from a small table in the corner of the training area. He was shirtless once again, but still wore that thin metal band around his left arm, the metal a solid gray with the slightest sheen. A small amulet of some kind hung from the center, but she couldn't put a handle on its origins.

Norse? Maybe.

She had no trouble seeing him as part of a bloodthirsty warrior culture. Glancing away from the armband, she found herself the focus of at least twenty pairs of curious eyes. "We've got an audience again."

To her surprise, Galen frowned. "We don't need one—not in the condition you're in." Raising a hand, he made a sharp downward gesture.

A silver blue bullet dropped out of the sky, streaking toward the ground like lightning unleashed. Illium's landing was wildly showy, a hard, fast drive that left him grinning on one knee, his wings spread in blatant display. "Vain," she told him, figuring her heart would stop trying to leap out of her throat any minute now.

He rose to his feet. "It's not vanity if it's truth, Ellie."

Shaking her head, she looked to Galen. "What's Bluebell going to teach me?"

"Nothing. Illium is going to play butterfly."

Elena had no idea what the other angel meant until he ushered her inside the huge building that overlooked the ring of beaten earth they'd been using for the past weeks. An indoor training salle, she realized as Galen closed the doors, locking out their audience. "Impressive." The ceiling soared, reminding her of an amphitheatre stripped down to its very basics.

"*Voles-tu, mon petit papillon.*"

Illium laughed at Galen's instruction to "fly, little butterfly" and gave the other angel a desultory finger, replying in a language Elena thought might have been Greek.

She was shocked to see a grin crack Galen's face. That grin disappeared the instant he turned to her. "Good, you're wearing arm sheaths." He came closer, examined them with the quick, careful hands of a weapons expert. "Excellent quality."

"Deacon's the best."

Those pale green eyes locked on her. "You know Deacon personally?"

She tilted her head to the side. "He's married to my best friend."

Illium gasped. "Now you've got Galen by the short and curlies. He has wet dreams about getting into Deacon's . . . weapons shed."

Another rapid-fire exchange of Greek and French, Galen's French too fast for her to follow. She didn't need to understand—it was obvious the two were ribbing each other. Friends, she thought suddenly. For some reason, Illium, with his laughter and his heart, was friends with this cold-eyed angel who seemed hewn out of stone.

"I thought," she said when Galen turned back to her, "close-contact fighting was a no-no?"

"You won't be close. Illium."

Illium rose up into the air, not stopping until he was hovering at the very top of the salle, a bolt of blue against the dark grain of the wood.

"Hit him."

She took a step back, shook her head. "These knives are real."

"He's immortal. A minor knife wound won't hurt him. And if you can do it with a knife, you'll be unbeatable with a gun."

"He might be immortal, but he feels pain." And Illium had already hurt for her.

"I can take it, Ellie." A shout from the roof. "But you're not going to hit me."

"Oh yeah?" She played a knife in her hand.

"Yeah."

Still, she hesitated. "You sure?"

"I dare you."

Reassured by the playful goad, she tracked his lazy movements as he hovered . . . and threw. He was gone before the knife left her hand. And she understood why Galen had called him a butterfly. Illium could move incredibly fast in a contained space, seeming to need little to no room or time to turn, zip in another direction.

Sweat was pouring down her face by the time she ran out of knives—her own and the ones Galen had given her. Illium blew her a kiss from his perch on a rafter. "Poor Ellie. Want a nap?"

"Shut up." Wiping her face, she shook her head at Galen. "How the hell can he move like that?"

"They call his mother the Hummingbird." Galen caught a knife Illium threw down, one of several that had lodged in various parts of the salle. "You have some skill—it'll make it easier to get you to a point where you can consistently hit the neck."

She rubbed her own throat. "Most vulnerable spot?"

A nod. "But that's going to take time. For now, if you can pin or shoot an angel coming at you, you'll disorient him long enough to run."

A pause, and she realized he was waiting for a response. "I'm not too proud to run. My legs have kept me alive more times than you know."

Those ice green eyes seemed to gleam with subtle approval, but that was probably wishful thinking on her part. "If you're trapped in a situation where you have no choice but to fight, a good aim will give you a slight advantage."

"Emphasis on 'slight.' "

Galen pulled a knife out of the wall, his biceps flexing. "You're playing with archangels. Slight is an improvement on certain death."

25

Jason stood across from Raphael on the balcony off Raphael's office, the buildings of the Refuge spread out below.

"What have you learned?" Raphael asked his spymaster.

The tattoo on Jason's face appeared complete, but Raphael knew that while the chunk of flesh that had been ripped out by one of Lijuan's reborn had healed, the markings were only temporary, so as to betray no weakness. Jason was having the ink redone step by painful step. "She's keeping a secret."

Raphael waited. All archangels kept secrets, but for Jason to comment on it had to mean something.

"It's a secret she appears not to have shared with anyone, but I think the Shade knows," he said, referring to Phillip, the vampire who'd been with Lijuan longer than Raphael had been alive. "He's like a pet to her—she hasn't forbidden him from entering the sealed room as she has everyone else."

"Do you think you or one of the others can get a glimpse inside the room?"

Jason shook his head. "She has a ring of reborn around it

night and day." He touched his face. "I'm fairly certain they'd tear any intruder limb from limb."

Total dismemberment was one of the very few ways that *might* lead to the death of an angel Jason's age. However, if the head was left whole, there was a chance of regeneration. "Have you been able to confirm how many of Lijuan's reborn eat flesh?"

"It's no longer the old ones alone—I saw a pack of younger reborn feast on the bodies of the newly dead," the angel replied. "They did it out in the open."

"So, she crosses another boundary." It was one more indicator that her mind was no longer functioning as it should. "Tell me about this sealed room."

"It's in the center of her mountain hold, hidden deep within the core. The reborn roam all the corridors around it, and the ones that roam are the ones with eyes that shine—the ones who eat of flesh."

"Do you have any idea what she might be hiding?" It could be nothing good, that much was certain.

"Not yet. But I'll find out." Jason resettled his wings. "I did as you asked and had Maya work her way into Dahariel's domain. Something is going on, but whether it relates to the events at the Refuge, it's impossible to say. There are rumors that Dahariel killed several of his vampires recently, but that could've been a legitimate punishment."

"Have Maya remain where she is. I have people inside Nazarach's and Anoushka's homes."

"If it does prove to be Nazarach?"

"I'll execute him." Nazarach ruled Atlanta, but only under Raphael's grace. "Dahariel is the strongest of them all." And the most coldly intelligent. Leaving that decapitated head in Anoushka's bed was the kind of calculated threat Dahariel might make.

"If it is him," Jason said, "he's begun to strike close to home—one of Astaad's favorite concubines was found eviscerated yesterday. She was branded inside. All indications are that she was alive at the time."

"So . . ." It seemed nothing less than death—brutal, merciless—would satisfy this would-be archangel now. "Astaad hasn't informed the Cadre."

Jason didn't comment except to say, "Pride."

"Yes." The archangel who ruled the Pacific Isles had to be enraged that someone had managed to breach the walls of his harem. "One more archangel bested." In the most cowardly of ways, but drunk on vicious pleasure, the angel behind the assassination wouldn't see it that way. He, or she, would, Raphael was certain, view it as a true victory.

"Sire—there is more."

"Yes?"

"They found another Guild dagger in her chest cavity."

"Little hunter, little hunter, where aaaaaarre you?" Playful, singsong, horrifying.

Wrapping her arms around her raised knees, she ducked her head, making herself even smaller. The cupboard smelled of blood. Ari and Belle's blood. On her feet, in her hair, on her clothes.

Go away, she thought, please go away. Please, please, please, please . . . It was a litany in her head, her voice small and weak. Where was Daddy? Why didn't he come home? And why wasn't Mama in the kitchen like she was every morning? Why was there a monster there?

"Where are you hiding, little hunter?" The creeping footsteps stopped for a second. An instant later came an even more chilling sound—lips smacking together. "Your sisters are most delicious. Do excuse me while I go take another bite."

She didn't believe him, terror and a frustrated, clawing rage keeping her locked in position. The giggle came three seconds later.

"Smart little hunter." A deep breath, as if he was drawing in the freshest of air.

Her own nostrils burned with the pungent aroma of a

spice for which she had no name, mixed with ginger . . . and a golden, pure light. It nauseated her that this foul creature, this monster, smelled like summer days and a mother's warm embrace. He should smell like rot and pus. It was another affront, another pain to add to the ones he'd already carved across her heart.

Ari. Belle. Gone.

She blocked her sobs with a fist, knowing her sisters would never dance with her across the kitchen floor again. Belle's legs, those beautiful, long legs had been broken until they twisted in a way that was simply impossible. And Ari . . . the monster had nuzzled into the nightmare that was her neck before Elena found the courage to follow her sister's dying command to run. But the blood, the blood would give her away.

She waited, listened. He was moving around. She thought he might've gone upstairs, but her pulse was pounding too hard in her ears. She couldn't trust the sounds, couldn't run. Not when he could be standing in the corridor waiting for her. Then it was too late. His footsteps came back into the room.

"I've got a suuuuurprise for you." A sly, scraping sound, the knob of the cupboard where she was hiding being twisted away. She pushed back into the wood but there was nowhere to go, nowhere to run.

"Boo!" A single perfect brown eye stared mischievously through the hole made by removing the knob. "There you are."

She stabbed out with the knitting needle she'd picked up from her mother's basket in the living room, spearing that eye dead center. Liquid spurted onto her hand, but she didn't care. It was his scream—high, piercing, agonized—that mattered. Giving a savage little smile, she pushed out of the cupboard as he stumbled back, darting past him and up the stairs.

She should have gone outside, found help. But she wanted her mom, needed to see that she was alive, was breathing. Shoving through her parents' bedroom door, she slammed it shut behind her, turned the lock. "Mama!"

There was no answer.

But when she looked around, relief poured through her. Because Mama was just sleeping. Running over on feet that continued to leave fading red imprints on the carpet, she shook her mother's shoulder.

And saw the gag around her mouth, the knives that pinned her wrists and ankles to the sheets. "Mama." Her lower lip quivered, but she was already reaching to undo the gag. "I'll help you. I'll help you."

It was the terrified warning in her mother's eyes that made her turn.

"Bad little hunter." Shaking the bedroom key at her, the monster pulled the needle out, and looked at it with a single curious eye, the other a bloody ruin down his cheek. "Do you think Mommy would like a present?"

"Wake up, Elena!"

She jerked into a kneeling position in one go, reaching for the knife she'd slipped under the pillow out of habit. Raphael looked up at her as she stared down at him, knife held high, ready to go for his throat.

Red hazed her vision, her tendons quivering with the need to strike out.

Elena. The scent of the sea, of the wind. *You're safe.*

"I'll never be safe." It came out a withheld scream, so taut, so painful it was barely sound. "He hunts me in my dreams."

"Who?"

"You know." She tried to lower the knife. Her muscles refused.

"Say it. Make him real, not a phantom."

Her mouth filled with the taste of bitter rage. "Slater Patalis." The most infamous killer vampire in recent history. "We were his last snack stop."

"The records say the hunters were able to capture him because you disabled him."

"I remember stabbing him through the eye, but that

wouldn't have stopped him." Her fingers finally unclenched, dropping the knife. It would've sliced into her thigh had Raphael not caught it midfall.

Placing it on the small bedside table, he said, "Your memories are incomplete?"

"They're coming back more and more." She stared out at the wall, seeing nothing but blood. "I've always seen parts, but now I think they were jumbled up pieces of the whole. What I saw tonight . . ." Her eyes burned, her hands fisting on her thighs. "The monster broke my mother's legs, her arms, pinned her to the bed, made her listen as he killed Belle and Ari."

Raphael opened his arms. "Come here, hunter."

She shook her head, unwilling to surrender to weakness.

"Even an immortal," Raphael said quietly, "has nightmares."

She knew he wasn't talking about her. Somehow, that made it easier. She fell into his embrace, burying her face in the warm curve of his neck, the clean, bright scent of him filling her lungs. "Later, I saw the streaks on the carpet, realized she'd tried to come to us even after he hurt her so badly. But he came back upstairs, put her in that bed again."

"Your mother fought for you."

"She lost consciousness soon after I found her. I was so scared then, so afraid to be all alone with him, but now, I think her lack of consciousness was a mercy." Her stomach twisted because in the most secret depths of her mind, she knew Slater had hurt her mother in other ways, made Elena watch. "I stayed awake because I knew Beth was coming home from her sleepover soon. I knew I couldn't let the monster get her. But he was gone before that."

"So your youngest sister was saved from the horror."

"I don't know," Elena said, remembering the lack of comprehension on Beth's small face at the funeral ceremony for Ari and Belle. "It was her first ever sleepover, and I don't think she's spent a night away from home ever again. Somewhere deep inside, she's afraid of what she'll come home to."

"You, too, hold a hidden fear," Raphael murmured. "What is it that you're so scared to speak of?"

"I think," she said through the haze of tears she refused to let fall, "he did something to me." Then he'd left both her and Marguerite alive, while Ari and Belle lay dead on the kitchen tiles.

"Tell me." Raphael's voice was an icy breeze.

She welcomed the ice, wrapping it around herself like a safety blanket. "I haven't reached that part of the day yet." Her heart squeezed off panicked beats at the idea but she held on to Raphael, his body strong beneath hers, and confronted the nightmare head-on. "Whatever it was, it was so bad, I blanked it from my mind all these years."

"It may have been the transition that resurrected the memories." His arms were granite around her, possessive, protective, immoveable. "Your coma may have unlocked the same part of your mind as that which opens in immortals during *anshara*."

He'd fallen into the deep healing sleep during the hunt for Uram, had returned to his childhood, to the heartbreaking beauty of his mother's face looking down into his while he bled across a meadow floor. "It opens memories that have faded over time, until we believe that they are long gone."

"Nothing's ever gone." A warm breath across his neck, fingers curling into his chest. "We fool ourselves that things fade, but they never do."

Raphael brushed a hand over that brilliant near-white hair that had hung like a banner over his arm as they fell to earth in Manhattan. Some memories, he thought, were etched in stone.

"What do you dream of in *anshara*?"

"It's not something spoken of. Each angel's journey is his own."

Elena's fingers spread over his heart. "I guess it's about confronting your demons."

"Yes." And then he made a decision he'd never thought he'd make—not since the day he watched Caliane move across the dew-sparkling grass, her feet so light, her voice so clear as she hummed an old lullaby. "I dream of my mother."

Elena stilled. "Not your father?"

"My father was the monster who was known." His mother had been the horror in the dark, unknown, unknowable. "Caliane kissed me good-bye as I lay bleeding and bloody after a fight I knew I'd never win." But he'd had to try, had to stop the madness that had spread a dark stain across his mother's eyes. "That was the last time I saw her."

"Was she killed by the Cadre?"

"No one knows what happened to my mother." It was a mystery that had haunted him for hundreds of years, would probably continue to do so for thousands more. "She simply vanished. No trace of her was ever found after the day I watched her walk away." He hadn't been discovered for . . . a long time. So young, so damaged, he hadn't been able to summon help, had lain there a broken bird, his wings crushed.

"Do you think she knew?" Elena asked, sorrow in her voice. "That she took her own life to spare you the task?"

"Some say that." Raphael ran his fingers down her wings, fascinated as always by the blend of colors that marked his hunter as unique even among angelkind.

"What about you?"

"When angels have lived millennia, they sometimes choose to Sleep until such time as they feel compelled to wake." Secret places, hidden places, that was where angels slept when eternity became a burden.

"Do you think Caliane is Sleeping?"

"Until I see her body, see her burial place . . . yes, I think my mother Sleeps."

"Shh, my darling, shh."

26

The next six weeks passed in a fury of weapons and flight training—with Raphael when he was in the Refuge, and with Galen when Raphael had to return to the Tower. Her spare time, she spent inhaling as much information as she possibly could, and visiting Sam. To her delight, the boy was healing far faster than anyone had predicted. Noel, too, was well on the way to recovery.

There was no more overt violence at the Refuge . . . except for the bloodstained Guild daggers that kept showing up in places she frequented. The blood proved to be Noel's, so there could be no mistake about the origin of the threat. Unfortunately, the daggers had all been devoid of vampiric scents. And Elena's angel-tracking ability continued to be wildly erratic.

Frustrated at the lack of a solid lead—but determined to ensure she'd be no easy target—Elena had just dropped off another dagger at the forensic center one cool morning when she came face-to-face with Neha's daughter.

"Namaste." The greeting came from the mouth of an en-

chantingly beautiful woman with the sloe-eyed gaze of a born sybarite . . . if one didn't see the calculating intelligence behind it.

Elena kept her response calm, polite. So far, nothing pointed to Anoushka as being the angel they were looking for, and as Neha's daughter, she was a power—one Elena didn't need to piss off without reason. *"Namaste."*

Anoushka looked her up and down, making no effort to hide her appraisal. "I was curious about you." It was an almost girlish statement as she walked forward, graceful in a white sari embroidered in blush pink and powder blue. "So human you look, though you wear wings," she murmured. "Your skin must show every bruise, every wound." Such a casual comment. Such a quiet threat.

Elena answered with the truth. "Your skin is flawless."

A blink, as if she'd surprised the other angel. Then Anoushka inclined her head by the merest fraction. "I don't think I've heard a compliment from another female angel for at least a hundred years." A smile that should have been charming, and yet . . . "Will you walk with me?"

"I'm afraid I'm headed to training." She glimpsed Galen out of the corner of her eye, hoped he'd keep his distance. Right now, Anoushka did appear merely inquisitive. Any sign of aggression and things might get ugly.

"Of course." Anoushka waved her hand. "It must worry Raphael to have a mate who is so very weak."

Having the other angel at her back felt like beetles crawling over her skin. She was almost glad to fall into step beside Galen—right now, trying to protect herself from a weapons expert sounded like a far better bet than fencing with an angel who might be a true cobra. According to the rumors she'd heard, Anoushka had grown up drinking poison with her mother's milk.

A shiver skated across her body, and she was more than ready to throw herself into the gruelingly physical training. However, another one of Neha's creations—Venom—interrupted the hand-to-hand combat session midway. The vampire had on his ubiquitous shades, his body clothed in a black on black suit. But, for once, his expression held no hint of mockery. "Come. Sara is waiting for you on the phone."

She was already walking at a fast clip beside him. "Has something happened to Zoe?" Fear for her goddaughter caught her by the throat.

"You should speak to her directly."

Her wings brushed the steps as she walked up to Raphael's office. She pulled them up instinctively, the action second nature now—thanks to having been put on her ass by Galen more than once. He would give no quarter. Any mistake and she went down. She appreciated it—because Lijuan's reborn sure as hell wouldn't have mercy on her if the oldest of the archangels decided to set her pets on her guests.

Leading Elena to the corridor outside the office, Venom took a sentinel position by the door. She knew without asking that Illium was around somewhere—there were never less than two of the Seven with her when Raphael was away from the Refuge. It irritated her, more than irritated her. But facts were facts. She'd regained her strength, honed her skills, but she was no archangel, and the dagger threats aside, Michaela was still in the Refuge. Whatever softness the female archangel had in her heart for the young, she had none for Elena.

The last time Elena had spoken to Ransom, he'd told her the vampires were now laying bets on her living long enough to even attend Lijuan's ball, much less survive it.

"You know how your head was wanted on a silver platter? Well, the reward's been tripled for anyone who brings Michaela not only your head, but both your hands as well."

Grabbing the phone as soon as she reached the office, she said, "Sara?"

"Ellie." Sara's voice was strangely accented—a mix of worry and anger. "I've got your father waiting on another line."

Her hand tightened on the phone. Jeffrey Deveraux had pretty much called her a whore at their last meeting. "What does he want?"

"Something's happened." A pause. "I could tell you, but this time, I think he has the right."

Frowning, Elena nodded though Sara couldn't see her. "Transfer the call. Let's get it over with." She wouldn't let him hurt her, she vowed. The man who'd fought for her right to see her sisters, to say good-bye, was long gone, and she was through with being wounded by the bastard who'd taken his place.

Sara didn't waste any time. A hiss of air and then silence. "Yes?" Elena said, unable to call him father.

"You need to get back to New York. This is connected to your work." The last word was full of the same distaste that had flavored any mention of her skills as a hunter-born by her father as long as she could remember.

And now he thought her a vampire. It was a wonder he was deigning to speak to her at all. Her hand tightened impossibly further. "What?"

A pause that hummed with things long unsaid. "Your mother's grave was violated last night."

Lijuan. An icy anger uncurled in Elena's gut. "Did they take her?"

"No." A curt word. "The perpetrator was disturbed in the process by a vampire who appears to belong to Raphael."

Her knees threatened to crumple as relief tumbled through her. Of course Raphael had put guards on her family's graves after the gift Lijuan had sent her. Bracing herself against the desk, she fought to keep her tone even. "Maybe it's time you followed Mama's wishes to have her body cremated and her ashes scattered on the winds."

"So I can fly, chérie."

That had been Marguerite's response when Elena had questioned her after overhearing her talking to Jeffrey about what she'd want him to do if she died before him.

"There'll be no need for it if you can keep your friends away from her." Each word was hard, designed to cut, to bruise.

Flinching, she said, "There's every need—but then, you've

never known how to keep promises." She hung up before he could say anything else, her hand trembling as she lifted it to her mouth.

The door opened behind her the next instant, and she knew without turning that Raphael had come home for her. "They didn't touch her?"

"They didn't even get within touching distance of the headstone." Strong hands on her shoulders, pulling her back against a warm wall of a chest.

"My father made it sound like they'd dug her up." She closed her hands over his. "Why didn't you tell me?"

"I heard in transit." A kiss pressed to her cheek. "I wanted to tell you in person—I didn't expect that Jeffrey would have the resources to find out so quickly."

"My father knows everyone there is to know." Both legal and not, though he'd slap her for implying the latter. "The one who tried to get to my mother's grave. Were your men able to catch him?"

"Yes." A quiet acknowledgment that made the hairs on the back of her neck rise. "He was reborn."

She sucked in a breath. "He had enough of a mind to carry out the orders on his own?"

"It appears he was very newly reborn." Raphael slid his hands down her arms, then off, as he walked to open the balcony doors. "They do not speak, but Dmitri swears there was a plea for mercy in his eyes when he was caught."

"He wanted to live?"

"No." He held out a hand.

She took it and he led her out into the cool breeze of the balcony. They stood side by side, their wings touching in an intimacy she'd allow no one else. "Why didn't he run, commit suicide when he had the chance?"

"Lijuan has control over her puppets. I don't believe she has enough control to manipulate them over that distance, however, which makes me think she had someone else there whom Dmitri's men didn't find."

"Someone the reborn thought he had to follow." She blew

out a breath, wondering what kind of an evil could scare the dead. "What did Dmitri do to him?"

"Gave him what he wanted."

Elena's hand clenched on the railing. "Good." She'd want that same mercy if she was ever turned into the horror of one of Lijuan's reawakened dead.

"Her games," Raphael said, "they're escalating. The act against your mother's grave came on my territory, violating our implicit agreement not to enter each other's lands without permission."

"Plausible deniability. She can always say she knew nothing about the actions of her underlings."

"We would all know it for a lie, but yes, she's far enough removed from the act to do so credibly." Raphael's wings spread, one sliding over her back in a quiet caress. "It's time for us to make our own move."

She glanced at him, saw the pitiless angle of his jaw, remembered that this was the archangel who'd executed another. "You've already made it."

His lips curved in a smile no mortal would ever want to see. "Lijuan shows signs of believing that her status as the oldest among us makes her untouchable."

"Could you kill her if necessary?"

"I'm not sure Lijuan can truly die." He said the terrifying words with quiet power. "It's possible she's lived so long, she's become the truest of immortals, straddling the line between life and death."

"Except," Elena said, feeling a ghost walk across her grave, "it looks like she prefers the dead over the living."

"Yes."

27

"Fuck!" Illium dodged one knife, swiveled to find the tip of his opposite wing pinned to the wall. "Two knives is cheating!"

Something feral in Elena smiled in satisfaction—poor Illium was bearing the brunt of the turbulence incited by her father's call a day ago. "Strike one for the hunter."

The blue-winged angel reached over and pulled out the knife. Dropping to the earth, he handed it to her, hilt first. "Lucky hit."

"Sore loser."

"It was getting pathetic watching you fail."

"Look at that," she said with a mock gasp, "I think I nipped off a few feathers in the process. Poor, poor Bluebell."

He grinned, those golden eyes bright with mischief, with an ability to play that seemed to have been leached out of the other immortals. "Next time," he said, "I'm going to run you around so bad, they'll have to carry your whimpering body out of here."

Cleaning off the knife, she slid it back into her arm

sheath before bringing her hand up to hide an exaggerated yawn.

"If you two have finished," Galen said in that humorless way of his, "we still have an hour to go."

She glanced at Illium's wing—to see that it was already almost completely healed. "I guess it's time to put a few more holes in you."

"Tell you what," Illium said. "If you manage to hit me three times in a row, I'll give you a diamond necklace."

"Make it a diamond-studded decorative knife sheath and you've got a deal."

Illium raised an eyebrow. "Not very practical."

"It is if you're planning to wear it with a ball gown."

"Ah." A gleam of interest. "Fine. And if you don't hit me three times, you have to take me along with you on a hunt."

"Why?" she asked, perplexed. "They're hot, sweaty, often exhausting."

"I want to see how you hunt."

A pulse of memory: *Illium is fascinated by mortals.*

Maybe that was why she liked him so much. He saw her former status not as a weakness but as a gift. "Alright."

He stuck out a hand. "Done."

She shook it. "Now do your job, butterfly."

He left the ground in a sweep of wind, a single blue feather floating to her hand. She put it in a pocket, saving it for Zoe. So far, she had several of Raphael's golden-tipped ones, two of Illium's, and a few of her own.

"Go!"

Eyes on the target, she balanced her throwing knives in hand and set her feet. Her sight was sharper than when she'd been human, but not by much—not yet.

In the end, she hit Illium twice more, missing a third strike by the barest flicker of a feather. Illium swooped down. "I get to go on a hunt."

"See if you're smiling when we end up in some mosquito-infested swamp."

"I'm not scared of mosqui—"

She was swiveling on her heel before Illium stopped speaking, having picked up the scents of three unfamiliar vampires. But it was an angel she found in the doorway, his exotic cheekbones and near-black eyes nowhere near as unusual as the wings she glimpsed before he folded them inward.

Dark gray patterned with streaks of vivid, striking red.

Stunning wings.

But instead of admiration, it was fear, primal and deep, that stabbed her in the gut, sharpening her senses, her reflexes. "Who is he?" She could feel his power pressing down on her, a crushing weight.

The metallic slide of sword leaving scabbard. "Xi belongs to Lijuan." Illium stayed by her side as Galen walked forward to greet the other angel. "He's nine hundred years old."

"Why isn't he an archangel?" He could topple cities with that power, erase thousands.

"As long as Lijuan lives, Xi will continue to gain power. Without her, his body wouldn't be able to hold what it does."

"Can all archangels do that?" she asked, feeling her skin creep when Xi's eyes shifted to stroke over the exposed portion of her wings. "Share power?"

"Only Lijuan."

Galen appeared to be arguing with Xi and finally, several minutes later, the Chinese angel snapped his feet together in an almost military salute and passed over a gleaming wooden box. But his eyes, they lingered on Elena for a long, chilling second.

She began to walk toward Galen the instant Xi left. The red-haired angel remained standing with his back to her, his eyes on the entrance. "It would be better," he said in a very precise voice, "if you wait for Raphael to return before opening this."

"Raphael's gone to meet with Michaela and Elijah. It could be hours."

"I'll inform the sire—"

"No." She put her hand on the box, almost flinched at the inhuman coldness of it. "The meeting's important—it has something to do with Titus and Charisemnon."

Illium touched her shoulder, his expression grim. "Lijuan is playing games, Elena. Don't open the box without Raphael."

She'd accepted that she was physically weaker though it galled, but there was only so much a hunter could take. "Give me a reason."

"I don't know what's in there," Illium said, his eyes shadowed in a way that turned the gold to something razor-sharp, a reminder that for all his playfulness, Illium hid a core as ruthless as the man he called sire, "but I know it's meant to weaken Raphael."

"You think she'd hurt me?" Elena stared at the carvings on the box, stared until the complicated patterns shaped themselves into the horror they truly were. "Corpses. They're all corpses."

"I think," Illium said, placing both hands on her shoulders, his thumbs gentle against her nape, "there are many ways to hurt. Not all of them are physical."

Elena played with the latch, her lungs expanding as she took a deep breath. "I can smell them. Fresh grass crushed with ice, a warm woolen blanket sprinkled with rose petals, blood strained through silk." Her heart pounded in her chest, ready to hunt, to give chase. Under her fingertips, the box grew warm, as if sucking in her very life force.

Shoving away the unsettling thought, she swallowed. "There are pieces of vampire in here. Organs. They always smell the strongest."

"It's time for us to make our own move."

She took her hand off the latch. "I don't need to open it. I know what's inside." Lijuan had simply returned what Raphael had sent her. And if part of Elena was horrified by the form of his warning, another part—a raw, primal part born in a blood-soaked room almost twenty years ago—was viciously glad. "Do whatever you want with it." Shifting on her heel, she broke Illium's hold and walked out into the biting cold of a mountain afternoon.

Venom was waiting for her by a stony crag that had been left untouched by angelic hands, an incongruously untamed background for a vampire who looked as if he'd stepped out of the pages of some high-class men's magazine. Her sweaty, tense face reflected off the black lenses of his sunglasses, his own as untouched as always. "How much wax does it take to keep your hair that perfect?" she muttered as she tried to walk past.

He blocked her with a single smooth move. "It's a natural gift."

"Today is not the time to mess with me." She wasn't going to fall into the trap Lijuan had designed, wasn't going to see Raphael as a monster, but . . . each time he did something that pushed the boundaries, it slapped her in the face with her new reality. A reality in which archangels played with immortal and mortal lives as if they were nothing but the most disposable of chess pieces.

Venom smiled, and it was a sight that would've sent many women to their knees, full of an erotic promise that said he'd make even death feel good. "I've been trying to figure out what he sees in you."

Elena swiped out with a knife in her right hand, missing his arm by the barest fraction of a hair. His dodge was impossibly fast. When Venom moved, it reminded her only of the creature Neha had chosen as her avatar—as if he'd never been human. But today, even that wasn't enough to compel her curiosity. She kept on walking.

The vampire appeared beside her again a moment later. "Dmitri now," he murmured, "I can see why he'd want to play with you. He's into knives and pain."

"And you're not?" She remembered all too clearly that scene in the garage—Venom prowling with silky grace toward a woman stunned to silence by his dangerous brand of sex. There'd been male appreciation in his expression . . . but there'd also been the primordial hunger of the much colder creature that marked his eyes. "You're the one who secretes poison."

"So do you."

She halted, blinked, braced herself with her hands on her knees. "Shit." How could she have let that go? Not asked Raphael about the consequences of becoming an angel?

A coolly honest part of her answered with a single word.

Fear.

She was scared. Scared to accept the irreversible truth of her new life. Scared to know that she might one day look into eyes as worshipful as Geraldine's, and understand too late that she was creating a victim. Prey for the immortals circling like sharks.

Feeling her cheeks flare with a hot-cold burn, she said, "When?"

Venom gave her a slow smile. "When it's time."

"You know," she said, rising back to a standing position in spite of the sudden churning in her gut, "inscrutable doesn't work when you're smirking."

Venom's reply was abrogated by a tinny little beep. Holding up a finger, he took out a slick black cell phone, reading something on the screen. "What a pity, there's no more time to chat. You have to get ready for a meeting."

Elena didn't bother to ask who the meeting was with—the vampire would just take the chance to jerk her chain. Instead, she made quick work of the remaining distance to the stronghold, slammed the door to the private wing in Venom's face, and stripped, trying not to think about the box she'd touched, what lay beneath the macabre carvings.

There was a knock on the main door fifteen minutes later. Having rushed through a shower, Elena opened it to find an old vampire with eyes that twinkled. He had a measuring tape around his neck and pins in his pocket. His assistant carried tailor's chalk and what appeared to be a case containing a thousand swatches of material.

She was, it seemed, getting measured for clothing suitable for Lijuan's ball.

All of it in shades of blue.

Raphael returned from his meeting with Elijah and Michaela to discover Jason waiting for him. The black-winged angel kept his silence until they were in Raphael's office. "Maya's uncovered something disturbing about Dahariel." He handed over a file.

Opening it, Raphael found himself faced with the photographic image of a young male who'd only just crossed the threshold that separated man from boy. "Mortal?"

"No." Jason gripped the wrist of one hand with the other, the hold so tight, Raphael saw the blood flow stop to his hand. "He was Made half a millennium ago."

Before the Cadre decreed that no mortal below the age of twenty-five could be Made without lethal consequences for the Maker. Mortals today would judge the Making of this boy a crime, but five hundred years ago, humans had lived much shorter lives. At this age, the boy might've been a father already, would almost certainly have been expected to earn his own way in the world.

"He signed on to serve Dahariel for five decades, three years ago," Jason said, that grip ever tighter.

Raphael closed the file. "What is it you're not telling me, Jason?"

"The boy hasn't been seen for the past year."

Raphael felt a dark wave of anger. The Made were at the mercy of their Makers, and after the expiration of their original Contract, if they couldn't care for themselves—at the mercy of those to whom they chose to give their loyalty. Too many chose wrong. "Murder isn't a crime if a vampire is under contract." An inhuman law—but vampires weren't human. In many cases, they were predators barely leashed. But angels were predators, too. And this boy had delivered himself into the hands of one.

"The boy isn't dead," Jason said, to his surprise. "It appears that Dahariel is keeping him in a private cage for his . . . entertainment." The toneless way that word came out told Raphael more about Dahariel's idea of entertainment than anything else. "And because he signed on to serve Dahariel of his own free will, no one can do anything to help him."

"What did Dahariel promise in return for this vampire's allegiance?" Murder wasn't a crime, but there *were* certain unwritten laws that had to be followed, laws that kept the structure of the world from imploding on itself. One such law required that all service contracts be honored—on both sides.

"Protection against other angels." Jason's laugh was utterly without humor. "It seems the boy is still weak after all these years of existence. He's survived this long only by tying himself to those stronger than him."

"He chose his eternity, Jason." Harsh, but true. No one who'd lived for five hundred years could fail to understand the cruelty engendered by age, the darkness that lived in the heart of so many immortals. If this boy had signed with Dahariel without doing his homework as to the angel's proclivities, that was a mistake he'd have to live with—if he lived. "We can do nothing for him." Because Dahariel had only promised protection from *other* angels.

Jason's eyes met his, the pupils black against irises of almost the same austere shade. "According to those of his household who'd talk, Dahariel takes great pleasure in torturing the boy with such slowness that it ensures some part of him is always healed, able to bear more. They say he's already lost in madness." Raphael could see Jason fighting his rage, but his next words were icily rational. "The way Noel was beaten—it would fit Dahariel's methods."

"Astaad won't move against him for that alone." Especially since it would mean admitting he'd fostered a viper in his midst.

"Maya's continuing to keep watch. I've also got information coming out of Anoushka's court."

"Anything of note?"

"She emulates her mother, but she's stopped growing in power."

"So she knows she'll never be an archangel." It might be enough to push an already fractured personality over the edge. "Did she discover that recently?"

"No. A decade ago. And she displays no signs of disintegration."

Acceptance or a mask, there was no way to tell. "The Guild Director was able to track the theft of a crate of Guild daggers to a warehouse in Europe two days after Elena woke." It angered him to see Elena being stalked, but his hunter, he thought, could take care of herself. So, now that he was healing, so could Noel. It was the abuse suffered by Sam that drove them all. "Nazarach was embroiled in a hunt for one of his vampires at the time—a female who managed to cross over into Elijah's territory."

Jason nodded. "He'd have been distracted, unlikely to choose that time to orchestrate the theft."

That was what Raphael had concluded. "See if you can pin down Anoushka's and Dahariel's movements."

"Sire."

"Jason," Raphael said as the other angel turned to leave, "you can't rescue the boy, but I can buy out the remainder of his contract." Dahariel wouldn't say no to an archangel, especially not if he was the angel behind the *sekhem*-linked violence.

"Dahariel will only find another victim." Jason's eyes were bleak.

"But it won't be this boy."

As Jason left after a small nod, Raphael wondered if the scars on the angel's soul would ever heal. Most would have gone mad after a few years of Jason's "childhood." But the black-winged angel had endured. And when the time came, he'd given his loyalty to Raphael, harnessing his intelligence in service to an archangel.

If saving this boy would give him a measure of peace, then

Raphael would deal with Dahariel. And if the angel proved to be the one who'd hurt Sam, then Raphael would take even greater pleasure in tearing him apart one small piece at a time, keeping him alive so that he'd feel every burn, every break, every brutal slice.

Because while angels might be predators, it was the archangels who sat at the top of the food chain.

28

"*Have you come to play at last?*" A smile tinged red. "*You're late.*"

"*Run,*" a broken word. "*Run, Ellie.*"

The monster laughed. "*She won't run.*" A satisfied smile as he lowered his mouth to Ari's throat. "*She likes it, you see.*"

Something wrapped around her body, an invisible hand that touched her in her most private place. She went to scream. But her mouth didn't open, her throat didn't vibrate . . . because her body did like it. Horrified, she began to claw at her skin, trying to rip it off in a futile attempt to stop the insidious, terrifying pleasure. Warmth bloomed between her legs and her young mind couldn't take it. Whimpering, she scratched harder. Blossoms of blood appeared under her nails as welts rose on her arms.

The caress—the scent—stopped. "*What a pity you're too young for that. We would've had such fun.*" He wiped off a drop of blood from his mouth, held out his finger. "*Taste. You'll like it. You'll like everything.*"

* * *

Reaching home as night fell, Raphael saw Elena standing on the cliff edge below his stronghold, her eyes on the tiny lights that dotted the caves lining the gorge. The wind raised her unbound hair off her face as she turned back to the view after watching him land behind her, the white-gold silver under the moonlight.

"Did Galen tell you what Lijuan sent me?" she asked as he came to stand beside her.

"Of course." He'd heard Galen's report of her reaction, but now found himself watching her face. The line of her profile was clean, her lips the only hint of softness—his warrior, he thought, reaching out to brush a single strand of hair teasing her cheek.

Her lashes came down as she blew out a breath. "I understand the stakes. Part of me is violently glad you did what you did."

"Then?"

"Part of me wishes I'd never learned anything of this world."

He spread his wings, protecting her from the wind that had shifted direction, keeping his silence as she stared down at the river that crashed so far below.

"It was inevitable, wasn't it?" she said at last. "From the instant I was hunter-born, it was inevitable I'd know of blood and death."

"There are some for whom it's not inevitable." His wing brushed hers. "But for you, yes."

The moonlight caught the shine of her cheek and he realized his hunter was crying. "Elena." Enfolding her in his wings, he tugged her into his embrace, his hand on her hair. What would bring her to tears? "Did your father do something to hurt you?" If Raphael could have killed the man without destroying Elena, he would have long ago.

She shook her head. "He came for me." It was a raw whisper. "Slater Patalis was drawn to my family because of me."

"You can't know that."

"I *know*. I remembered." Her eyes were rain-coated diamonds when she looked up. " 'Pretty hunter,' " she said in an eerie singsong tune. " 'Pretty, pretty hunter. I've come to play with you.' " Giving a little scream, she fell to her knees.

He fell with her, enclosing her in the warmth of his wings as he pulled her stiff body into his embrace. "Are the memories coming to you outside of sleep?"

"I was reading one of Jessamy's texts, waiting for you to come home and my eyes closed for a second. It's like the memories are just waiting for a chance now." Her body jerked against him as she sobbed. "All this time I've hated my father because I *told* him the monster was coming and he wouldn't listen, when it's me Slater came for. Me! I drew him to our family."

"A child is not to be blamed for the actions of evil." Raphael wasn't used to feeling helpless, but there was nothing he could do as Elena's heart broke in front of him. Crushing her closer, he murmured wordless reassurances in her ear, fighting the urge to wipe her memories clean, to give her the peace she needed so desperately.

It was one of the hardest battles he'd ever fought. "You are not to blame," he repeated, his body glowing with an anger that had nowhere to go.

Elena didn't say a word, just cried so hard that her entire body shook. Pressing his lips to her temple, he rocked her as the stars got piercingly bright, as the lights went out in the ledges below, as the wind grew freezing with a touch of snow. He held her until her tears were long gone and the moon kissed her wings like a lover long denied. Then he rose with her to the sky.

Fly with me, Elena.

Her wings unfurled, though her voice remained silent.

Keeping an eye on her, he took her on a wild, exhilarating ride through mountain ridges and passes, the air cutting across their cheeks. She followed with grim determination, finding ways around obstacles when she couldn't move fast enough to slip in through the small gaps Raphael utilized.

It took concentration, which was exactly what he'd counted on.

By the time they landed, she was swaying on her feet. He all but carried her inside and put her to bed, nudging her into a dreamless sleep with a small mental push. She'd be angry with him for it, but she needed her rest. Because their time was nearly up.

Lijuan's ball was in a week.

29

Elena lay in bed as Raphael dressed the next morning, watching him pull on one of the specially designed shirts that flowed around his wings. She felt tender, bruised. He'd held her all night, she thought. He'd kept the nightmares at bay. For him, she'd find the strength to fight a guilt that threatened to choke her.

Sitting up, she took a sip of the coffee sitting beside Destiny's Rose. "How do your shirts seal at the bottom?" She'd never seen any buttons below the wing slots. That seemed to be what most of the powerful angels preferred, the closures small and discreet—all but invisible. The younger angels, in contrast, seemed to go for more intricately designed options, each as unique as the wearer.

Raphael raised an eyebrow. "I'm an archangel and you ask me how my shirts stay sealed?"

"I'm curious." Focusing on the distraction to keep her mind off the past, she put down the coffee and crooked a finger.

The archangel was apparently in the mood to obey, because he left his shirt unbuttoned to walk across, brace himself with his hands on either side of her, and bring his mouth down over hers. The kiss was a claiming, no two ways about it. Long and deep and slow, it curled her toes, brought her nerves to burning life, made her moan in the back of her throat. "Tease," she accused softly when he lifted his head.

"I must ensure you never lose interest."

"Even if I live a million years," she said, caught in endless blue, "I don't think I'll ever find any man as fascinating as you." Acute vulnerability hit a moment later. She pushed at the heat of his chest. "Show me the shirt."

A tipping up of her chin, a kiss that told her the archangel was in a tender kind of mood. "I do as my lady commands." He turned to give her his back.

Pushing off the sheets, she sat up on her knees. "There's no seam," she muttered, peering at the bottom of the slots. "No button, no zip. I half expected Velcro."

Raphael coughed. "If you were not mine, hunter, I'd have to punish you for that insult."

Her archangel was playing with her. It was an odd realization, and one that made the heavy weight on her heart lift a fraction. "Okay, I give. How do you seal the slots?"

He held out a hand, shifting to face her. "Watch."

It took real effort of will to turn her head from the gorgeous plane of his chest. If she wasn't careful, she thought, the archangel might yet make her his slave. Her eyes widened the instant she spied his hand. "Is that what I think it is?" Blue flame licked over his hand, making her heart kick.

"It's not angelfire." He closed his hand, ending the lightshow. "It's a physical manifestation of my power."

She blew out a breath. "You use that to seal the edges?"

"The edges aren't actually sealed. Look carefully."

She'd looked plenty carefully, but now, she lifted up the shirt almost to her eyes. And that was when she saw them. Strands of finest blue, so fine as to be almost invisible, threaded through the white of the linen. How much power, she thought, stunned, must he have to do something like this without thought? This man would never ever tell her she was too strong, too fast, too tough. "I'm guessing us peons can't do this?"

"It requires the ability to hold power outside the body." Turning, he rubbed a thumb over her lower lip. "As yet, you have very little power so the point is moot."

She caught his wrist, looked up. "Raphael, am I going to have to Make vampires?"

"You're an angel Made, not born." He caressed her with his thumb once more. "Even Keir doesn't know the answer to that question."

And Keir, she knew without asking, was an ancient. "But if I do—"

"It'll not be anytime soon." A rock-solid answer. "Your blood was free of the toxin when you woke. You'll be tested several times a year now that you're awake."

"Is it hard? To Make someone?"

Raphael nodded. "The choosing is difficult. It's to the Cadre's benefit not to select those who're weak, who'll break, but mistakes happen."

Hearing what he'd never enunciate, she pressed a kiss to his palm.

"However the act itself," he said, his voice dropping, "is as intimate as you choose to make it. For many, it's a clinical process akin to giving blood. The human is put into a medicated sleep during the transfer."

Relief made her shudder. "I thought it would be like when you kissed me." The intimacy of it had shaken her to the soul.

Cobalt flame. "Nothing will ever be like our kiss."

Heart thundering, she rose to stand on the bed, her hands on his shoulders. He looked up the naked sweep of her body. *"Elena."*

She kissed him. His response was an inferno, but she felt the tension beneath the surface. "We have to leave soon don't we?"

"Yes." His hands smoothing over her butt, slow and easy. "We'll take mortal means of transportation to Beijing."

"Wouldn't it be more impressive to fly in?"

"Endurance flying requires muscle strength you don't have yet." A practical answer, but his hands slid lower . . . lower. "It's to our benefit that she consider us weak going in. It'll make her careless. We'll need every advantage if she truly has crossed the line into irrevocable madness."

"Raphael . . ." She shuddered, thrust her hands into his hair. "Galen's right. I do make you vulnerable. And she knows my weaknesses."

So did I, Elena. And yet you hold my heart.

Two hours later found Elena back in the beaten earth ring that had become as familiar to her as her own face. Probably because she'd been up close and personal with it more than once.

"So," she said, staring into the slitted, inhuman eyes of her sparring partner, "you do occasionally lose the suit."

Venom smiled, displaying the canines she'd seen weep poison, his face at once starkly beautiful and unalterably alien. He'd not only lost the suit, he was dressed only in a pair of flowing black pants that shifted like liquid as he moved, his body as sinuous as the snake that looked at her out of those eyes.

And that body . . . yeah, it was definitely worth a second look. But she was more concerned at the ease with which he played with the foot-length curved knives in his hands. They reminded her almost of some short swords she'd seen, but they were a little *too* short, a little too curved. Not sickle-curved, but more of a soft, smooth flow. Blades meant for lethal grace.

Of course, identifying them didn't matter. It was what he could do with them that counted. She met his smirk with one of her own. "You didn't catch the knife I threw at you in New York."

He shrugged, gleaming dark gold skin over pure, lithe muscle. "I caught it."

"By the sharpest edge." She tested the long, slender blades Galen had handed her. Shorter than the rapier he'd started her on, they were weighted so she could throw them, too. If Venom's blades were made for grace, hers were made for power and maximum damage, both edges razor-sharp—she could gut someone with surgical precision if necessary. "Sloppy of you."

"I guess I'll have to make up for it today." Lowering his body into a semicrouch, he began to circle her, his movements almost painfully slow.

She moved in the opposite direction, wanting to get a handle on his style. Most people telegraphed their next move with some type of a tell. She was very aware of her own tell—her feet. It had taken years of training to ensure they never pointed in the same direction she intended to move. Venom didn't telegraph with his feet.

She shifted her attention to the next most common tell—the eyes. All the air rushed out of her lungs at the contact. Her brain continued to have trouble accepting what she saw when she looked into Venom's eyes. Just then, the slitted irises contracted and she took a startled step back.

A soft laugh.

Bastard was playing with her. Gritting her teeth, she kept her gaze locked to his as they continued to circle each other. It was on the second complete rotation that she felt herself blink, stagger a little.

Fuck!

She threw one of the blades without warning. He moved aside with snake swiftness but still ended up on his back on the ground with a nasty gash in his arm.

Galen was beside them in a single instant. "What was that?" he snapped, his jaw a hard line. "Throwing away your weapon before the fight starts isn't exactly going to keep you alive."

Elena didn't take her eyes from Venom. The vampire held a hand over his bleeding arm, but his smile . . . Slow. Taunting. Daring her to call him on it. Dropping her head, she lunged . . . and slammed the second blade right between his legs.

"Fuck!" He scrambled backward, flowing to his feet in a way that was simply not human. Normal bodies didn't move with that kind of liquid fluidity.

Galen was looking at Venom now. "Did you try to entrance her?"

"She should be prepared for the unexpected." Venom's eyes glittered bright green as he returned his gaze to Elena. "I would've had her in another half a turn."

"I could've also cut off your balls if I'd aimed a little higher," Elena said, retrieving her weapons. "You want to play more games or can we get to work? We're on a deadline."

"This'll take a few minutes to heal." He removed his hand to show that the wound was still gushing blood. "Now I can compare notes with Dmitri."

Ignoring his sly words, she set about practicing the moves Galen had drilled into her when she wasn't throwing knives at Illium. The terse angel watched her go through the entire set and gave a short nod at the end. Feeling unaccountably pleased, she pointed the tip of one blade at Venom. "Ready?"

He twirled both weapons in his hands. "I never did get a taste of you."

"Come here, little hunter. Taste."

Everything went cold, quiet. She was no longer aware of the taunting heat in Venom's eyes, the light layer of snow on the ground, Galen's watchful presence. All she knew was the hunt.

Venom struck without warning, moving with the swiftness of the snake that was patently a far bigger part of him than just his eyes. But Elena was already gone, her blades crossed in front of her as she moved, one hand slicing out to run a thin line of blood across the vampire's chest.

He said something as the blow landed. She didn't hear it, her mind set to kill.

This time, the monster wouldn't get in, wouldn't murder Ari and Belle, wouldn't break her mother's heart so badly that she never left that kitchen saturated with the screams of her children.

Her eye picked up the minute tensing of Venom's thigh muscles and she struck before he could. This time, he avoided her blades, but not the foot she swept out to trip him. But she'd made a mistake. A line of fire rippled up her side.

Stupid. She'd forgotten she had wings to worry about now.

Flicking a quick glance at the wing to ensure the damage wasn't serious, she twirled one blade, making it sing in the cold mountain air, and turned her attention to those eerie eyes again. Take those out and he'd go down. It was an utterly emotionless thought.

Venom's eyes contracted at that instant, his blades coming up in a defensive posture as he blocked her attempts to do him mortal harm. But Elena was past the point of thinking, moving with the speed and strength that made her hunter-born. Venom yelled something at her but all she heard was a cold hiss.

She went for his eyes.

A slam of black exploding in her head. Then nothing.

Raphael landed next to Elena's fallen form, his rage finely honed. "Did you incite this?" he asked as he picked her up in his arms, careful, so careful.

Venom wiped blood off his face. "Nothing worse than I've said to her before." The vampire's gaze lingered on Elena. "I think I made some quip about tasting her."

"You know I'd kill you for the attempt."

"Our task is to protect you from threats—especially those you might not recognize." Venom met his eyes. "Michaela, Astaad, Charisemnon, each will attempt to kill her at some stage, knowing it'll shake you. Better to get rid of the problem now."

Raphael spread his wings in preparation for flight. "She's more important to me than all of you. Don't ever forget."

"And you're an archangel. If you fall, millions will die."

Unsaid were the words—better for a once mortal, new angel to die in his stead. But that wasn't a bargain Raphael would ever make. "Choose your loyalty, Venom."

"I made my choice two centuries ago." Those slitted eyes flicked to Elena. "But if she courts death, it'll find her."

Well aware of what the vampire was speaking about, Raphael rose to the sky, holding Elena close to his heart. It was inevitable he'd remember the last time he'd held her so limp in his arms. Immortality hadn't made her safer, only more likely to survive the hurts sure to come her way. But he could do nothing to protect her from the memories that haunted her.

Galen's mental call had almost come too late. If Elena had managed to touch Venom's eyes, the cold-blooded creature that lived within the vampire would have struck out, sinking its fangs into her unprotected flesh.

It would've left her paralyzed, in agony.

And while in the grip of the cobra's hunger, it was quite possible Venom would have cut off Elena's head before Galen could intervene, causing true death.

Laying her on their bed, he reached into her mind. *Elena.*

Her head shifted from side to side as she moaned, as if fighting a savage internal battle. His promise to her—to keep his mental distance—warred with the protectiveness that clenched around his soul. The urge was even stronger today than it had been yesterday. It would be so very easy to reach in and erase what hurt her.

"I would rather die as Elena, than live as a shadow."

Brushing tangled strands of hair off her face, he repeated his command out loud. "Elena."

Her eyes flicked open and for a single instant, they weren't the silvery grey he'd become used to. Instead, they were almost midnight, filled with a thousand echoes of nightmare. Then she blinked and it was gone. Staring up at him with a confused expression on her face, she rubbed at her forehead. "I feel as if I've been hit by a two-by-four. What happened?"

"I had to intervene when you decided to turn training into mortal combat."

Her hand dropped from her face. "I remember." A whisper. "Is Venom alright?"

"Yes." But his concern was for her. "The memories are starting to seep into your waking life."

She pushed up into a sitting position. "It was like I was a different person. Not even that—like I was a machine focused on only one thing."

"It sounds like the Quiet."

Elena shivered at the memory of what he'd become in the Quiet, the soulless creature who'd treated human lives like so many effortlessly snuffed out flames. "Do you think it's the change—the immortality?"

"A factor." He nodded. "But it may be that it's just time."

Time she remembered all the things she'd rather forget. "I want to speak to my father."

30

"He has no right to your apologies."

Her head jerked up. "How did you know?"

"The guilt is a stain on your soul." Running his fingers down her face to close around her throat, he leaned in until their lips were a heartbeat apart. "You will not crawl for him."

Elena flinched. "But *I'm* the reason Slater chose our family." That, nothing could change.

"And your father's the reason that what remains of your family is broken in two."

She had no answer to that—because he was right. Jeffrey had splintered their family the day he threw her out, her things so much garbage on the manicured grass verge of the Big House. The neighbors on their tony street had been too well mannered to stare openly, but she'd felt their watching eyes. It hadn't mattered. All that had mattered was that he'd destroyed what little remained of the relationship between them when he tried to break her.

"Get on your knees and beg, and maybe I'll reconsider."

"It's a festering sore between us," she said, placing a hand over Raphael's heart. "I know now that he hates me because Slater was drawn to me." Like Dmitri, Slater had been able to entrance hunters with scent, but that hadn't been his only gift. "Can Dmitri track me?" she asked, something clicking into place inside her.

"Yes."

No mortal, she thought, no hunter knew that. "That's what Slater did. He scented me somewhere and changed course toward our neighborhood." Slater shouldn't have gained the scent ability—he'd been too young. But the vampire hadn't been normal in any way, shape, or form. "I could feel him getting closer, taste his scent on the wind." She'd tried so hard to convince her father, begging, pleading, screaming at the end.

"Enough, Elieanora." An angry command. "Marguerite, I think you need to stop with the fairy tales."

"But Daddy—"

"You are a Deveraux." A steely gaze. "No one in this family has ever been a common hunter. You're not going to be the first and telling me tall tales isn't going to help your case."

Later, her mother rocking her, telling her she'd talk to Jeffrey. "Give him time, azeeztee. *Your father was brought up with tradition—it takes a while for him to accept new ideas."*

"Mama, the monster—"

"Maybe you sense them, my darling. But they're simply living their lives." A mother's gentle teaching. "Being a vampire doesn't equal being evil."

At ten, Elena hadn't had the words to explain that she knew the difference, that what was coming *was* evil. By the time she found the words, it was too late.

The remaining days passed in a blur—most of it spent in flight training with Raphael. Any free time she had, she spent walking the Refuge, learning and listening. According to Jason's intel, both Anoushka and Dahariel were unac-

counted for during the time the Guild daggers were stolen, but
there was no way to narrow it down to either one. On the good
news side, the daggers had stopped turning up, and word was
that Anoushka and Dahariel—along with Nazarach—had left
for their territories, but she didn't drop her guard.

The constant vigilance, added to the rigorous flight training, was exhausting, but she welcomed it, unable to think about,
to accept, the truth of the part she'd played in her sisters'—
and ultimately, her mother's—deaths. So she focused on the
hunt, and on the upcoming ball, with regular visits to Sam. It
was as she was heading down the corridor after one such visit
that everything went wrong.

"Michaela." Her eyes widened as she saw the bodies strewn
behind the archangel. At least one was the angelic version of
a nurse, his hair matted with something slick, a line of red on
the wall where he lay slumped.

"Hunter." The archangel began to move forward, her body
clothed in a flowing burgundy dress that ran over her breasts
in a lush caress before parting a third of the way down her left
thigh to display a sleek length of flesh. No one would ever call
Michaela less than stunning.

But today . . . Elena swallowed. That dress wasn't burgundy. It had been white. It was blood that drenched it, parts
of it still wet enough to slick against Michaela's flesh. The
archangel's face was clean, her hair straight and gleaming
with health, but her fingernails, too, were encrusted with rust
red. Death clung to her.

"I've come to see the child."

Elena didn't make the mistake of thinking Michaela was
explaining herself. No, what she was hearing was a decree.
She should have let the archangel go, but—and quite aside
from the insanity of her dress—there was something supremely vicious about Michaela right now, something that
couldn't be allowed near a defenseless child. "Has the visit
been cleared?" Her hand closed around the butt of the gun
she'd slipped into the side pocket of her pants.

Michaela flicked a hand at Elena as she had once before.

But this time, Raphael wasn't there to stop her. A line of wet seared across Elena's cheek, her flesh parting as if it had been slit with a razor.

"I do not need anyone's permission." A slow smile. "Did you know there are ways to scar even an immortal?"

Elena thought she saw something alien in those eyes for a second, a flicker of red. But when she looked again, it was to see only that bright, blinding green. "You may," she said, taking out the gun, "have had nothing to do with Sam's injuries, but the boy is under Raphael's protection. You'll terrify him if you go in like this."

Michaela ignored the last part of Elena's statement. "Are you waiting for Raphael to rescue you?" A tinkling laugh. "He's with Elijah, flying over the opposite end of the Refuge. Apparently, there was word of an angelic body found there."

"Was there?" Consigning pride to Hades, she sent out a mental call for help, hoping her archangel wasn't out of range. *Raphael!*

A lithe shrug. "I will see the child now."

Elena found herself smashed against the wall, her teeth slamming down on her lower lip as her head snapped back, hitting the wall hard enough to make her vision blur. She struggled against the invisible bonds holding her to the stone, even as she tried to blink the dizziness from her eyes. The gun fell to the floor with a dull thud.

"Oh, you're bleeding." Michaela pressed her lips softly against Elena's, a macabre kiss flavored with malice . . . and something else.

Musk and orchids . . . touched by a jagged bite of acid.

Horror spread its wings inside her. Because that last note, the acid flavored by sunlight wasn't Michaela's scent. It belonged to an archangel who'd been executed above a pitch-black Manhattan. But Uram had had Michaela alone long enough to remove her heart. The question was—what had he put in her?

"I could kill you now," the female archangel murmured against Elena's mouth, "but I think it'll be rather amusing to watch you after Raphael tires of you." Another line carved into Elena's opposite cheek, the scent of iron filling the air as Michaela's words drew heart's-blood. "You'll just be meat then, easy prey for anyone who wants to taste an angel-Made. We'll have lots of time to play."

She was gone down the corridor in a swirl of rust-colored fabric an instant later, her words reverberating in Elena's skull. But it was Sam who was important at this moment—the female archangel might actually physically harm him in her current state of mind, one which seemed to hold nothing of sanity and everything of a sadistic kind of pleasure.

Beyond scared for the boy, she was fighting uselessly against her bonds when Galen and Venom swept past at preternatural speed. "Ugh!" It was an ungraceful cry as the power holding her to the wall evaporated at almost the same instant. Getting to her feet, she grabbed the gun, raced after the other two . . . and came to a screeching halt a few feet behind Michaela.

Galen stood in front of the archangel, bleeding from several cuts on his body and face. Venom was getting up from a corner where the stone itself had been shattered by the impact of his body. Blood dripped down his face, but his eyes were a hypnotic slitted gold-green, the cobra rising to the surface.

Michaela stared at Galen. "You think I would harm the child."

"You've already done violence in a place of healing."

Elena sucked in a breath at the faint glow around Michaela's wings. *Jesus.* "If you release that power here," she said through lips that were starting to swell, "you'll probably collapse the building, killing not only Sam but any other children inside."

Michaela turned to pin Elena with a gaze that was pure light, no pupils, no irises, no longer in any sense human. Of course, Michaela had never been that. But today the difference between angel and archangel was a heat that left Elena fighting to hold her gaze, her own eyes streaming with tears.

It was tempting, so tempting, to fire the gun, but if the

bullet went through Michaela's body, there was a chance it could ricochet off the walls and shatter the glass of the patient rooms a breath away. She put it away, dropped a knife into her hand, her eyes on Michaela's throat.

"I will not hurt the child." It was Michaela's voice, but so choked with power, it thundered with rage, a thousand voices contained.

Elena fought the urge to step back, knowing she was way out of her league, but also knowing she had to help delay Michaela long enough for more powerful help to arrive. "If you don't tamp it down, you will."

The female archangel continued to look at Elena, her head cocked in a way that was creepily inhuman. Elena had the feeling of fingers crawling across her mind, trying to pry their way in. Bile rose in her throat, but she held her position, realizing that if Michaela had to try to find a way in, it meant Raphael was protecting her. She wasn't stupid enough to rebuff that protection.

"So weak." A statement almost without malice—as if Elena was simply below her notice. That scared Elena even more. Because no matter what, Michaela had always been very human in her emotions. Right now, she could have been in the Quiet.

Turning back to Galen, Michaela raised a hand. Galen swayed as if hit by a blow, but stood his ground. Michaela laughed, made a hard slicing motion. This time, the big, heavily muscled angel slammed into the wall, saving his wings only by dint of twisting his body so he hit that wall face-first.

Blood smeared the stone, but Elena's attention was on Venom. The vampire had struck while Michaela's attention was on Galen, burying his fangs in the archangel's neck the moment after Galen hit the wall. Elena released her blade at the same instant. It hit home on the other side of Michaela's neck.

Screaming in rage, Michaela tore Venom off, throwing him so hard, he ended up motionless and twisted at the other end of the corridor. Then she reached up to pull the knife out as if it was nothing more than a toothpick, her arteries sealing up before Elena's eyes. The knife hit the floor with a metallic sound as she lifted a finger at Elena. "Which limb would you like to lose first?"

Jesus. Jesus. Elena knew there was no way she could stop Michaela when two much older immortals had failed—the archangel would crush her heart before she managed to get to the gun, much less pull the trigger. *Where are you, Raphael?*

The sea crashed into her mind, a violent storm. *I'm on my way. Keep her calm. If she releases her power, it'll destroy the Refuge itself.*

Making a split-second decision, Elena wiped the back of her hand across her mouth, the cuts on her lips still seeping blood. "I'll take you to Sam."

The female archangel waited.

The hairs on the back of her neck rising in primitive warning, Elena took the lead, hearing the whisper of Michaela's dress as she followed. *Galen and Venom are both down.* Galen's eyes had blinked open in the last few seconds, but Venom looked bad, really bad. *I think she broke his spine, maybe his neck.* And a vampire could die from a broken neck if enough other damage had been done.

He's not dead yet.

The last word was curt. A chill curled around her heart. She'd never thought she'd mourn his loss, but Venom had shown himself willing to lay down his life to protect a child. It made him better, far better, than an archangel who'd level the Refuge while enraged with power. It reminded her too much of another archangel—one bloated with toxin. Just how much of Uram did Michaela carry?

Heart thudding, Elena stopped in front of the glass enclosure where Sam lay in peaceful sleep. She saw Keir arrive out of the corner of her eye and tried to warn him off with a frantic movement of her hand, but Keir shook his head. "Sam's resting," he said in an easy tone, as if an archangel wasn't about to go nuclear beside them. "The healing is progressing extremely well."

"He won't be scarred?"

Elena found Michaela's question peculiar until she realized Michaela wasn't talking about the boy's superficial injuries.

"No, there'll be no permanent damage." Keir put an arm on Michaela's, braving the heat that blazed from her skin. "He'll grow up as he should."

Elena watched Michaela place her hand on the glass. "He's so fragile." The blaze faded in a slow wave. "So breakable."

"Children always are," Keir said, his tone gentle, his eyes ancient in that youthful face. "It's a risk we take."

"Too much," Michaela whispered. "The risk is too much."

The tableau froze in Elena's mind—an archangel of impossible beauty dressed in blood, her hand lying on the glass, her fingers trembling with emotions that brought tears to Elena's throat. What would Michaela have been, she wondered, if she hadn't lost her child? Would the selfishness that touched her every move have matured into something better? Or would she have become another Neha, creating her child as a poisonous mirror?

"Better to break their necks when they're born."

Elena slid out the gun. If Michaela made a single move, she'd empty the entire clip into the archangel's wings before Michaela could turn, use her powers to disarm Elena. Because given the choice of a possible ricochet versus certain death for Sam, she'd chance the ricochet.

"Don't you think so?" the archangel said to Keir in a voice that was jarring in its thoughtfulness.

"We do not kill our young."

Silence. When the archangel drew back from the glass, her face was as Elena had always seen it—perfection without mercy. Turning away with a nod to Keir, she left in a sweep of bronze wings and white silk stained dark red, her beauty imprinting an afterimage that was hard to ignore.

Elena let out a shuddering breath. *She's gone.*

Take Keir to Venom.

Elena was already moving in that direction, Keir at her side. They arrived to find Galen—his face a mess of blood and torn skin—kneeling beside the fallen vampire. "He's severely injured. Snapped spine, fractured skull, collapsed lung. His heart may have been pierced by a broken rib."

"He bit Michaela," Elena said, not sure if that made any difference.

"Then he likely discharged the poison in his fangs." Keir began to run featherlight fingers over Venom's body. "That'll make him easier to handle."

"Can his poison harm an angel?"

"Not in an enduring way," Galen responded, "but it causes violent pain in most."

"He's dying." Sitting back on his heels, his face white with strain, Keir nodded at Galen. "Will you carry him to the treatment room?"

Galen slid his arms beneath Venom's broken body. Elena bit back her negative response, born of the mortal knowledge that said the victim of a spinal cord injury shouldn't be moved. Keir surely knew a lot more about treating such injuries in vampires than she ever would. As they moved to the room, she felt the scent of the sea, the wind, fill her mind. Relief kicked her like a bucking horse. "Raphael's here."

But could even an archangel save a vampire so broken? What would it do to Raphael to lose one of his Seven?

31

Elena was wiping the blood off her cheeks when Raphael left Venom's room. "I have need of your gifts, Elena."

She put down the damp towel she'd found in one of the empty treatment rooms. Her face still hurt, but not as much as it would have if she'd still been human—healing had already begun on some level. "The dead angel?"

A nod.

"Venom—is he . . . ?"

"He's not easy to kill."

They didn't speak on the flight to the body. The site where it lay was a huge tumble of rocks. Making a quick appraisal of the dangerous, uneven area, she realized landing was going to be problematic. Pride might have led her to attempt it anyway, but she was supremely conscious that right now, Raphael needed her functional, capable of doing a task only she could. *A little help.*

Changing position so he flew above her, Raphael ordered her to fold her wings. It was surprisingly hard to go against her newborn instincts, but she managed to snap them shut.

Raphael caught her before she could even begin to fall, taking her down to a perfect landing on the nearest stable piece of rock.

"Thanks." Mind already on the body, she shifted closer. From above, it had appeared as if the angel had been thrown onto the rocks, his bones shattered, his limbs so damaged that not all were whole. Now, she saw that his head had been separated from his torso, his chest a gaping hole missing not just his heart, but all his internal organs.

"Someone wanted to make very sure he wouldn't rise." The angel's rib cage gleamed in the mountain sunlight, his blood no longer wet but holding a hard sheen that had her leaning forward in frowning concentration. "It's like his body's turning to stone." The carapace of dark red was strangely beautiful.

"It's an illusion," Raphael said. "His cells are trying to repair the damage."

She jerked back. "He's still alive?"

"No. But it takes a long time for an immortal to truly die."

"It's not immortality is it? If you can die?"

"Compared to a human life . . ."

Yes. "So cut off the head, remove the organs for extra insurance."

"His brain was also removed."

Elena stared at the head. "It looks whole." She reached forward, then drew back. "I really can't catch anything?" she asked, her fingers curling into her palms as she neared blood-matted hair that might've once been blond.

"No." But he was already crouching on the other side of the body, his hand lifting up what remained of the angel's head.

The back of it was gone. An empty husk. Feeling her face heat with a wave of disbelief, she nodded at him to put it back down. "Thorough job."

He placed it on the rock, face up. "His name was Aloysius. Four hundred and ten years old."

It was somehow harder, when you had a name. Taking a deep breath, she began to separate the scents. There were so many. "A lot of angels have been down here." And it looked as if her developing angel-sense was functioning just fine today.

"There was hope he might be able to be revived until his brain was discovered to be missing."

She stared at Raphael across the body that was nothing but the emptiest of shells. He had told her, but— "The victim honestly could've survived the rest of it?"

"Immortality isn't always pretty." An answer that left no room for ambiguity. "He was most likely conscious while his organs were being removed."

Swallowing, she shook her head. "I'm too young for that, right? If someone decides to fillet me, I'll lose consciousness?"

"Yes."

"Good." She wasn't the giving up kind, but neither did she want to know what it did to a person to survive this kind of torture. "Given the blood splatter, he was dropped from a fairly impressive height." She was trying not to think too hard about what might be sticking to the soles of her shoes— the M.E. would have had her behind bars for compromising a scene like this, but she salved her conscience with the fact that the scene was already so compromised it was worthless to anyone but a hunter-born.

"However," she continued, "it wasn't so high that it tore his body completely apart—do you have any way of knowing if he had his organs at that stage?" It was impossible to tell in all the gore.

"Yes." Raphael pointed to the open chest cavity. "Some of them left pieces behind." He reached in and picked up what appeared to be a hard pink stone, ragged at the edges. The stone gleamed a deep rose quartz in the sunlight. "A segment of his liver."

Goose bumps broke out over her skin. "Are you sure he can't feel that?"

"He's dead. What his body is doing, it's akin to a chicken running around after its head has been cut off."

"A nerve response." It made sense that it took longer for an older immortal to fade.

Returning the stone to the chest cavity, Raphael pointed at the head. "Parts of the brain were also found scattered on the rocks."

She was going to throw away these shoes the instant she got home. "That hard an impact would've turned his organs pretty much into soup," she said. "Wouldn't that make it more difficult to remove them?"

"Not if the 'surgeon' waited for him to heal enough for the organs to become viable again."

She'd been handling the gore fine, but ice filled her veins at the cold-blooded nature of the kill. "Jesus."

"Use your senses, hunter." It was a gentle reminder. "The wind is holding but it can change without warning."

Shaking off her horror, she began to filter out the scents she already knew—separating the good guys from the bad could come later. She was midway through the process when her angel-sense cut out without warning, leaving a single clean thread behind. "A vampire was here."

"Not with the rescue team," Raphael said, his expression intent.

"Means he was here before." Trying not to gag on the sickly sweet smell of the body in front of her—a body that didn't smell like death should—she arrowed her senses to that vampiric thread.

Cedar painted with ice, an unusual scent, full of elegance.

Her eyes snapped open. "Riker. Riker was here."

Raphael found Michaela hours later, high in the night sky above her home, her body clad in a catsuit that turned her into a sleek, dangerous predator. There was no hint of the insanity

Elena and Galen had both seen in her, her body as clean and as lushly graceful as always.

"Raphael," she said, coming to a vertical hover beside him. "Are you here to warn me off your hunter again?"

Elena, Raphael thought, might see in Michaela's past a hurt that had turned her bitter, but Raphael had known the young angel she'd been, her ambition a pyre on which she'd sacrifice anything. "You walked into the Medica with the intent to do harm."

A smile coated with the purest malice. "There was no intent until your pet hunter and her friends got in my way."

"You injured several healers on your way in. And you waited until after you knew Elena was inside."

"Does it not disgust you?" she whispered, her voice sliding from poison to purring sensuality in the blink of an eye. "That she's so weak?"

"Power without conscience rots the soul," he told her, watching her eyes harden even as her lips remained uptilted in a smile that promised the darkest of sins, the most excruciating of pleasures. He thought of Uram, falling into the trap of that smile, the selfish beauty of that mind—but then, the dead archangel had chosen his path long before Michaela was even born. "Why did you kill Aloysius?"

"Clever, Raphael." A small bow of her head, genuine delight in her eyes. "He was one of mine, became mine when I took over part of Uram's territory."

"What did he do to merit such an execution?" As the archangel who ruled his territory, Michaela had had the right to put Aloysius to death, but to have that death come at the hands of one of the Made—a vampire who'd likely been allowed to feed from the dying angel—was a ritual humiliation.

Michaela's green eyes turned into narrow slits of light. "He helped abduct Sam."

Any sympathy Raphael might've felt for Aloysius died a quick and permanent death. "Did you take his memories?"

"Useless." She slashed out a hand. "He was a bit player, a gullible sheep in this faceless would-be archangel's army."

"Were you able to discover anything that may lead to the identity of the one we seek?"

"No. Aloysius was but a pawn."

Raphael saw the truth in the small smile that flirted with her lips. It was cold, merciless, satisfied. "You lost your temper, killed him before taking all his memories."

"He laughed while he put Sam in that box." A thin line of red circled her irises. "I saw it when I looked into his mind."

"Is that when you dropped him?"

"Yes." A shrug. "I'd already broken his wings. Riker took care of the rest."

Raphael reined in his frustration. "How did you discover his involvement?"

"He was afraid his master had come to see him as expendable, couldn't keep from spilling his fears to his lover." A slow smile, that of a snake in the grass. "And loyalty is such a rare commodity when riches are involved."

Elena felt almost surreally calm as she stepped onto the plane the next day. They were flying to Beijing two days ahead of the ball itself, would arrive one day before the other archangels. "Venom?" she asked.

"He's safe." Raphael told her as they took flight. "I've moved all three—Sam, Noel, and Venom—to another location. Galen has gone with them."

"Good." She gripped the armrests. "I feel for Michaela, I do." Losing a child . . . she couldn't imagine the pain.

Her father had lost two daughters.

Because of Elena.

Swallowing the pain-lashed guilt that sat like a stone on her chest, she turned to look at the archangel she called her own. "But she was out of it at the hospital. All it would've taken was one conversation with you and there would've been no violence."

"You're expecting her to act human, Elena." An answer laced with cold. "Archangels aren't used to asking permission for anything."

She was no longer the same woman who'd woken from the coma, their relationship a complete mystery. She knew pieces of him now. Enough to ask, "What's wrong?"

Raphael glanced at her with eyes that had gone that metallic shade that never augured anything good. "What Michaela did to Aloysius? I wouldn't have been that merciful."

Her palms grew damp. "You call that mercy?"

"He died quickly." Frost in that gaze, a chill immortal winter. "I would've kept him alive for days while I tore his mind apart."

She blew out an unsteady breath. "Why are you telling me?"

You need to know who I am.

Elena thought of that, gave him her answer. "If Slater Patalis was standing in front of me, I'd do the same."

Raphael ran the back of his hand over her cheek. "No, Elena. I think your anger is a far hotter flame."

Reaching up, she tangled their fingers together. "I'll try to stop you if it ever comes to that."

"Why? Do you pity those who'd harm the innocent?"

"No." She brought their clasped hands to her lips. "I care about you."

Raphael felt the cold in him shift, begin to heat from within. "So you'll try to save me."

"I think it'll be mutual." A voice husky with shadowed memories. She'd woken on a scream again today, her mind locked inside a horror almost two decades in the past.

Mirroring her kiss, he raised her hand to his mouth. "We'll save each other."

There were no more words until his hunter shook her head. "What if this angel, the one who wants to become an archangel, tries something while we're gone?"

"Nazarach, Dahariel, and Anoushka have all been invited to the ball, as have others of comparable power."

Elena grew still. "That's when they'll make their move, isn't it? It'll be the perfect stage, especially with the Cadre meeting ahead of the ball."

"Yes." He looked at her, the pulse in her neck a fluttering, fragile thing. "Do not let them near. You remain the target who'll get this aspirant the most attention."

"Don't worry. They're not exactly people I want to spend time with." A shiver that he knew had nothing to do with the threat on her life even before she spoke. "Lijuan . . . have you heard anything?"

"She has brought her reborn to the Forbidden City. We will see the dead walk."

32

The Forbidden City took Elena's breath away. An intricate maze of delicate buildings and hidden pathways, the place really was a city within a city. And it was a city full of wonder—white marble bridges with dragons sleeping on the end-posts; paved courtyards replete with trees, each strung with twinkling silk lanterns in lieu of fruit; courtiers clothed in a myriad of jewel tones. It was like something out of a dream.

"Butterflies," she whispered, standing on the private balcony of the upper-level residence that was their own. "They remind me of butterflies."

Raphael's presence was a solid warmth behind her, his hands braced on the railing on either side of her. She savored the heat of him, feeling his chest vibrate against her wings as he spoke. "Neha and some of the others keep a court to a certain extent, but Lijuan's is the most extensive."

"She's truly a queen." Fans unfurled as she watched, coquettish smiles exchanged over their illusionary borders. All the women wore ankle-length dresses, most in styles that whispered of elegance rather than sex. "Do you think they know of the reborn?"

"Yes." His hands closed over her own, his voice an intimate darkness in her ear. "Jason's men tell him Lijuan has begun to bring some of her reborn to the inner court as entertainment."

Elena's hands, covered by the strength of Raphael's, clenched on the age-smoothed stone of the railing. "She'd debase them that way? I thought she considered them her creations?"

"Some, it seems, are more favored than others." He slid his hands up her arms, holding her to him. "Tomorrow morning, I meet with the Cadre. Take care when you walk the grounds—Lijuan may find it a game to pit one of them against you."

"Who's my bodyguard?"

"Aodhan." A pause. "You're not happy."

"I don't like the fact that I still have a babysitter."

"It's necessary."

"For now."

A dangerous quietness, and she knew this was one battle she'd have to fight again. She could handle that—and so, she thought, could Raphael. "You chose a warrior, remember?"

A kiss on the sensitive skin just below her ear. "As you chose an archangel."

She'd always known he'd be no easy lover. But then, neither was she. "I've never sparred with you." A playful invitation. "Do you like knives?"

The barest hint of a smile on the mouth he brushed against the same spot he'd tantalized before. "We'll dance with blades after the ball."

It was difficult to think with him so close, the Forbidden City humming with beauty below. "You didn't bring that many men with you." Jason had flown in with them, and with Aodhan, that made only two of the Seven in attendance.

"If it comes down to a fight, it'll be too late."

Elena finished putting her hair into the sleek French twist that Sara had taught her—the slithery strands anchored with what felt like five hundred pins—and examined herself in the mirror. The cap-sleeved ice blue dress was backless, didn't even come to midthigh—with slits up both sides—and, in spite of the shards of crystal embedded on the surface, slicked over her body like a second skin. She'd stared at the tailor when he'd first presented it to her, but the vamp was no idiot. Paired with thigh-high boots and tights, both in black, it turned her from arm candy to sleek assassin while leaving her plenty of freedom should she need to move.

Warm male hands on her hips. "Perfect." The raw hunger in that single word silvered over her body like a long, lazy stroke, her nipples beading against the soft fabric.

"Makeup," she gasped.

He relaxed his hold enough that she could brush some bronzer over her cheekbones, slap some mascara on her eyes. Opening the box included with the clothes, she found a tube of lipstick. It turned out to be an intense scarlet. "This isn't my style."

"Think of it as camouflage," Raphael said, pulling her back against his half-dressed body as she held the lipstick, his cock a brand against her back, her wings burning with the most erotic of sensations. "Allowing you to blend into enemy territory."

"I don't look much like the vampires and angels I saw out there." Her dress/tunic was in no way demure. Then there were the knives. Not to mention the gun. They were all concealed tonight, a courtesy that had gone against the grain after Lijuan's games. But she was learning to pick her battles. "I wouldn't know how to flutter a fan if you hit me over the head with one."

"No, you're too much the hunter." A glance so heated, she

half expected the mirror to melt. As it was, she had to clench her thighs to fight the urge to take him to the floor, to ride him to screaming ecstasy.

"But she won't see that," he murmured. "She'll see only a young, weak angel—intriguing because of the way she came to be, but otherwise not worthy of notice."

"Good." It'd give her the freedom to watch Lijuan un-awares. Elena had no illusions she could physically do anything to stop the oldest of the archangels, but maybe she could get an insight into her psyche, some small thing that might help Raphael.

Releasing her, Raphael walked to the side table. "Illium asked permission to give you a present."

Curious, she turned . . . to meet chrome blue. "What did he do to jerk your chain this time?"

A slow curve to his mouth, an archangel's dangerous humor. "Knives and sheaths," he murmured.

She touched the top of her right boot. "I've got mine—"

"Hmm." Taking something from a smooth wooden box, he moved to her. "But you have not got mine." His hand at her nape, a kiss so dark and full of possession it made her want to claim him in turn.

"We won't get to dinner if you keep that up." She held his gaze, held the beauty and cruelty of it, her palm on his bare chest.

His slid his hand up over the back of her thigh, his fingers brushing the oh-so-sensitive flesh between her legs. She sucked in a breath. "Teasing, Archangel?"

Teeth grazed over her lips. "Know this Elena—you'll never wear another man's knife."

She blinked. "He wanted to give me a blade? What's wrong with that?"

"Blades," he whispered, "and sheaths go together. And your sheath will only ever hold my blade."

It took her a second—desire had fogged up her mind. Her face flamed. "Raphael, that's—" She shook her head, unable to find the words. "Fighting is not sexual."

"Oh?" Eyes full of sea storms, violent and wild and exhilarating.

The heat turned to smoldering embers inside her, lush with the knowledge that his dangerous, beautiful man belonged to her. "Possession goes both ways, Archangel."

"Acknowledged, hunter." Stepping back, he opened his hand.

Her eye was dazzled, her mind entranced. "Are those stones real?" She was already taking it from him, already pulling the sweet, sweet blade out of the sheath that had been designed specifically for it. It gleamed razor-sharp in the light, warring with the brilliance of the jewels in the hilt, in the sheath, for dominance.

"Of course."

Of course. She played the knife in and over her hand, testing its heft, the balance. It was perfection in her grasp. "God, it's gorgeous." The jewels were breathtaking, but it was the blade that held her interest, the delicacy and strength of it. "Throw me that scarf."

Picking up the piece of gauzy, airy fabric, Raphael flicked it up. It came down in a mist . . . parting on either side of the blade as if it had broken flawlessly in half. "Oh, man." So sharp, so sweetly sharp. "You had this made for me?" Crossing the distance between them, she kissed him without waiting for an answer.

Raphael's eyes were glittering brightly enough to outshine the diamonds and blue sapphires on the hilt and sheath when she drew back. "You sound like you're having sex."

"A blade this sweet is as good as sex." She turned the sheath around, looking . . . admiring. She wasn't acquisitive by nature. Only with her apartment—a stabbing hurt—had she been different. But this blade, it spoke to that same part of her. *Mine*, she thought. "I need a—"

Raphael was already lifting a holster out of the box. Made of a soft, sleek black leather, it had a belt that slid into the slits on either side of the sheath, before fitting snugly over her upper arm. "Perfect." She slid the weapon into place. "The knife and sheath are light enough that it won't slip. And so pretty that they'll come across as decorative."

Raphael watched his hunter play with her gift, astounded by the pleasure he received from her joy. This gift meant something to her. He'd gotten it right.

He'd also almost killed Illium for daring to try to impinge on something that was his.

"Do you think I don't already have such a gift for my mate?"

"Sire, I meant no disrespect."

"Go, Illium. Before I forget she loves you."

It had been an irrational reaction, focused on an angel who'd long ago proven his loyalty, who'd bled for Elena. Raphael wasn't used to feeling so out of control, not for anyone.

"Then she will kill you. She will make you mortal."

He'd taken that to mean a physical weakening, but what if Lijuan had been warning against this—the slow warming of his heart, until it clouded the cold reason that had colored his rule for so long? "Reason or emotion," he said to Elena as she slid the knife back into its sheath after a complicated set of moves. "Which would you choose?"

She gave him a funny half smile over her shoulder. "It's not that simple. Reason without emotion is often a mask for cruelty; emotion without reason can allow people to excuse all sorts of excesses."

"Yes," he said, remembering the pitiless monster he'd become in the Quiet.

Turning, Elena walked over to him, her hips swaying in a way that was pure provocation, the spike heels of her boots bringing her height to just above his jaw. "Remember what I said about possession going both ways?"

"I will not betray you Elena." That she'd think to question that caused a ripple of anger in him.

"Don't get snarly on me, Archangel." Slipping past him, she opened one of the side zippers of the bag that had held her weapons and retrieved a small box. "I have a gift for you, too."

Surprised pleasure spread its wings inside him. He'd been given many, many things over the centuries. But most had meant nothing, mortals and immortals alike courting him for power, for prestige, for gain large and small. "Did you purchase it in the Refuge?"

"No."

"Then how did you get it?"

"I have my ways." Coming to stand before him, she opened the small box to retrieve a ring.

A ring set with amber.

"You," she said, sliding the ring onto the appropriate finger of his left hand, "are well and truly entangled."

His heart tight in a way that he had no experience with, he brought the ring up to his eyes. The band was platinum, thick and solid, the amber a square polished chunk. But it was dark, the darkest amber he'd ever seen . . . with a heart of pure white fire. Intrigued, he slid off the ring to bring it up to the light. The colors changed constantly, now dark, now light.

It was then that he saw it, the inscription on the inside. *Knhebek.*

He had lived in the Maghreb for a while, traveled through Morocco before he became an archangel, had heard that word whispered by eager youths to dark-eyed, blushing beauties.

I love you.

The tightness in his chest grew ever more powerful. Sliding the ring back onto his finger, he said, *"Shokran."*

Her face broke out into a delighted smile. "You're welcome."

"Do you speak the language of your grandmother?" He closed his fingers into his palm, possessive about an object for the first time in centuries.

"I only know a few words my mom used to say." A smile filled with memories—happy ones. "She'd mix up the Moroccan Arabic with Parisian French and English all the time. But we grew up with her, so we all understood." Even Jeffrey.

He'd laughed then, she thought, remembering. Her father

had laughed at her mother's mishmash of languages—laughed at himself, not her.

"Have pity." Holding his head in his hands. *"I'm a poor country boy. I don't know no fancy languages."*

"Girls." Sparkling eyes, pale silver and bright with mischief. *"Don't believe a word your papa says. He speaks French like a native."*

"Ma chérie, you wound me." Dramatic hands slapping over his heart.

"Where do you go, Elena?" Fingers tipped up her chin, until she met eyes so blue she could drown in them forever.

"Home," she whispered. "Home before it was all taken away."

"We'll build our own home."

The promise curled around her heart, a vivid ray of sunlight. "In Manhattan."

"Of course." A slow, slow smile. "What kind of mansion would you like?"

Damn, but the archangel was playing with her again. The sunshine grew, filled her veins. "Actually, I kind of like yours." She slid her arms around his neck. "Can I have it? Oh, and can I have Jeeves, too? I've always wanted a butler."

"Yes."

She blinked. "Just like that?"

"It's only a place."

"We'll make it more," she promised, her mouth to his. "We'll make it ours."

But first, she thought as a knock came on the door, they had to survive Lijuan's madness.

33

Raphael in formal clothes made Elena drool, his profile etched with perfect clarity against the night sky as they walked along the curving pathways of the Forbidden City—following their escort to dinner. Her archangel was wearing a white shirt with black pants, but that shirt was a work of art, the fabric on either side of the wing slots embroidered in a black design that curved and flowed—without ever losing the edge that said this was the Archangel of New York.

"Sexy" was too tame a word to describe him.

And it was obvious the silken-maned vampire beauties around them thought the same. She pinned her eyes on one who had the temerity to flutter her fan in his direction. The fan drooped.

Satisfied, she turned back to Raphael. "Jason and Aodhan?"

"They have their tasks."

Doesn't she know about Jason?

Yes.

And then they were being ushered through intricately

painted doors—into a room that seemed to absorb all light, all air, crushing her ribs into her organs. Shifting the barest fraction, Raphael caught her gaze, giving her a focus, a way to fight the feeling of suffocation. It felt like hours passed, but it couldn't have been more than two seconds at most. When she turned her attention back to the room, her heart scrabbling to regain its rhythm, she found her gaze drawn to a grouping of chairs below a wall filled with butterflies, their wings forever unfurled, a single sharp pin spearing each.

"Raphael." Lijuan whispered across the room to greet them, her pupils a strange pearlescent shade, her gown a disconcertingly girlish concoction created from layers of floating gauze that swirled around her body in a haunting gray and white mist, her hair blowing off her face in a wind that Elena couldn't feel, a wind that touched neither the heavy brocade curtains, nor the exquisite tapestries on the walls.

Elena's skin pricked in primitive warning, millions of years of evolution telling her she should never, ever let herself come to the attention of the creature in front of her. Because it wasn't the room that absorbed all light. It was Lijuan. Elena's primitive hindbrain sent a bolt of panic through her when she stayed in place, telling her to run, to hide.

But, of course, it was already too late.

She watched as Raphael took Lijuan's hands in his, as he bent his head to brush his lips across that pale, perfect skin. Lijuan's eyes met hers over Raphael's shoulder, and there was nothing remotely human in them, nothing Elena could even attempt to read.

As the delicate angel drew back, those unearthly eyes returned to Raphael. "You are different."

"And you never change."

A tinkling laugh, one that shouldn't have felt so cutting against Elena's skin, as if it was made of razors crushed into glass. "Why did I not meet you when I was younger?"

"I wouldn't have held your interest then," Raphael said, turning to put one hand on Elena's lower back. "This is Elena."

"Your hunter." Lijuan's pale eyes settled on Elena, and it took every ounce of will she had not to step back, not to hide.

Because Lijuan was the horror in the closet. The one mothers scared their children with. The one you were never actually supposed to see.

"Lady Lijuan." The formal title, learned from Jessamy, came out, sounded normal. How, Elena wasn't sure.

Lijuan's eyes went to Elena's neck. "You wear no necklace."

Elena didn't drop her gaze, though her stomach was a knot of fury. "I prefer Raphael's gift."

"A knife—such ornamentation was popular in another age." Lijuan's attention shifted, as if the necklace that had caused Elena so much pain no longer mattered. "Such beautiful wings. Will you show them to me?"

Elena didn't want to show this creature anything, but the request had been polite. She wasn't going to cause a political incident simply because Lijuan was so inhuman it defied understanding. Moving to give herself space, she spread out the wings her archangel had given her even as he gave her life. But when Lijuan raised a hand as if to touch, she snapped them back.

Raphael was already speaking. "It's not like you to break protocol."

"My apologies." Lijuan's hand dropped, but her eyes remained on the parts of Elena's wings visible around her body. "My only defense is that they're quite extraordinary."

Elena wished she could tighten her wings even further. "Thank you."

Lijuan took the acknowledgment as if it was her right. "My own, as you can see, are so very plain." She spread her wings.

They were a soft dove gray. Gentle. Utterly exquisite in their silky perfection. "Plain perhaps," Elena found herself saying, "but all the more beautiful for it."

Lijuan refolded her wings. "So honest. Is that why she intrigues you?"

Raphael answered with an implied question. "You care little for such earthly emotions."

"Ah, but *you* intrigue me." Touching his hand, Lijuan gestured to her left. "I thought we could eat informally."

Elena about swallowed her tongue at that. This room might not be a dining room, but it was sumptuous beyond description, the back wall lined with mirrored panels bordered in ornate gold, the right wall hung with tapestries that surely cost in the hundreds of thousands, the front wall full of windows that looked out into the sparkling—and always elegant—revelry of the courtiers below. The left wall, the wall below which they were to sit, was where the butterflies lingered.

Moving reluctantly to stand beside a chair upholstered in a stunning jade, she couldn't help but look up at the creatures frozen forever in stasis. "There's no glass," she said almost to herself. "How do you keep them from decaying?"

Another tinkle of laughter. Her heart chilled as she realized what she'd said.

"Have you not told her my secret, Raphael?" Eyes that sparkled with girlish mischief.

Creepy.

Raphael touched his hand briefly to Elena's back. "It isn't such a secret any longer. Favashi spoke to me about it yesterday."

"But you knew before them all." Lijuan took a seat on a chair that had been made to accommodate wings, having a central column for support, with the sides curving gracefully away. "How is the black-winged angel?"

Raphael waited for Elena to take a seat before taking one beside her. "Jason's looking forward to the ball."

The civilized conversation masked an undercurrent of danger that licked at Elena's ankles like a sentient fire. Raphael had told her that Jason had been injured by Lijuan's reborn. Now she wondered if the attack had been on purpose. A warning?

Lijuan lifted a hand and the corpse of a bright blue butterfly fell from the wall into her hand, the pin dropping soundlessly to the carpet. "And the young one? The pretty one?"

"I decided it would be best if Illium didn't join us," Raphael said without missing a beat. "He might have proved too much of a temptation."

Dropping the butterfly onto the table, Lijuan laughed, and this time, it was darker, full of—if you could call it that—true humor. "Hmm, yes, those wings are rather magnificent." Her eyes tracked to Elena's. "As unusual as yours."

"Unfortunately," Elena said, knowing she had to stand her ground, no matter if this archangel could crush her with a single thought, "I'm not a collectable, either."

"Oh, I don't want to have your wings mounted," Lijuan said, her hair continuing to dance softly in that eerie breeze that touched nothing else. "I find you far too interesting alive."

"Lucky for me." Except she didn't think so. Leaning back in her chair, she let Raphael and Lijuan carry on the conversation. As they talked, she watched, she listened . . . and she tried to figure out why Lijuan seemed so very *wrong*.

Yes, her power was one that made Elena's skin crawl, but Raphael had once broken every bone in a vampire's body and left him as a caution to others. And their conversation on the plane had made it clear he was as capable of that kind of brutality today as he'd been the day she first met him.

Yet she took Raphael to her bed night after night, clung to his embrace when the nightmares got too bad. Trust, there was trust between them. But even before, when he'd only been the Archangel of New York—hard, cruel, certainly without mercy—she'd never felt this creep across her skin, this sense that she was in the presence of something that simply *should not be*.

"Ah, here is the meal."

Elena had already turned her head toward the door, having scented the approaching vampires.

Jasmine and honey.

Sweet balsam wood dusted in cinnamon.

A kiss of sunshine touched with paint.

Odd combinations, strange scents, but vampires were like

that. She'd asked Dmitri what they smelled like to each other. The vampire had given her that taunting smile he kept just for her. "Nothing. We save our senses for the mortals—for the food."

The three who came into the room were all male, but one alone bore the oil-slick black hair and almond-shaped eyes of Lijuan's homeland. He was the balsam wood. Beside him was a Eurasian man with the solid shoulders of a boxer and the sky blue eyes of some boy from Kansas, his face not quite put together right, but arresting all the same despite, or perhaps because of, his unusual features. He was the jasmine. And the sunshine—her stomach twisted at the memories evoked by that scent, memories of blood and death, putrid flesh lying on every side as Uram squeezed her shattered ankle.

The sunshine shifted closer, laid a delicate setting of hand-painted porcelain on the low, carved table that was the only barrier between her and Raphael, and Lijuan. His hand was the lustrous darkness found at the heart of the *mpingo* tree, so rich, so pure that furniture made from the heartwood went for thousands upon thousands of dollars.

His skin was so beautiful, so evocative of the months she'd once spent in Africa, that it took her a moment to look into his eyes, to realize that he was dead.

Raphael knew the instant Elena realized the vampire standing before her, pouring honey-colored oolong tea into a tiny cup, was one of the reborn. Her entire frame went still, so very still, the quiet of a hunter who'd sighted prey.

He could've spoken to her mentally, warned her not to betray fear, but with Lijuan's growing abilities, it was possible she might hear the warning—and Raphael would not do anything that would paint Elena as weaker. Instead, he trusted his hunter, and she didn't let him down.

"Thank you," she said politely as the reborn finished pouring.

A small nod from the vampire who was so fresh, so new,

he couldn't have been reborn long. His eyes—yes, there was something there, knowledge of who he'd been, what he was now. But there was no panic in them. Perhaps the man didn't yet understand what he'd become. Raphael waited as the reborn moved around to pour for him, even as the blue-eyed one poured for Lijuan.

"A toast," Lijuan said, lifting the cup as the men began to transfer the food onto the table from a serving cart made of wood and gilded with gold. "To new beginnings." Her eyes were on Elena.

Raphael fought the primal urge to step in between, to protect Elena from a threat she had no hope of surviving . . . but then, he thought, his hunter had survived him. "To change," he said.

Lijuan's gaze moved to him, but she didn't challenge the subtle difference in his toast. "That will do." She waved a hand at the three men, and they left as silently as they'd arrived.

"No audience?" Raphael passed Elena a small platter that held a sweet red bean cake he knew she'd like.

"Not today." She watched Elena eat the cake he'd given her. "Does food continue to hold pleasure for you, Raphael?"

"Yes." It was a simple answer. He was still rooted to this earth, to the world. "You no longer eat." It was a guess, but he wasn't expecting her nod.

"It's become unnecessary." She sipped from the cup in her hand. "With friends, I make an effort, but . . ."

He understood what she was saying. No archangel would ever starve to death, even if he or she stopped eating altogether. However, lack of sustenance would eventually begin to leach power. It might take years, perhaps decades, but the loss might well be permanent. An archangel couldn't afford to take that chance.

Lijuan was telling him she'd gone beyond that. Which brought up the question of how she was now gaining her power.

"Blood and flesh?" he asked, conscious of Elena remaining uncharacteristically quiet beside him. Some would've said she'd been cowed into silence. He knew very well that she was listening, honing her knowledge, making note of any possible weakness.

"That would be a devolution," Lijuan said, her hair feathering as if caressed by ghostly fingers, "and I am evolving."

Elena waited until they were behind the closed doors of their bedroom before giving in to the shivers. "She's . . . what is she?"

"Power in its purest form." Walking to the painted wooden doors that led to their private courtyard and balcony, he spread them open. "Come. The air will cleanse."

She took the hand he held out, let him lead her into the crisp winter air. The Forbidden City spread out like a sea of multicolored stars before her, dancers still swirling gracefully in the main courtyard as music played, haunting, evocative, beautiful enough to bring tears to the eye.

Standing in the circle of Raphael's arms, her head against his shoulder, her arms around him, she took her first real breath in hours. Her lungs sucked in the air as if parched, her throat seeming to unlock with a quiver of relief. "That music—what is it?"

"The *ehru*."

For long, quiet moments, they just stood there, letting the music soak into their bones. Elena was the one who spoke first. "You don't think she steals power from others?"

"No." Raphael stroked his hands over her wings, and the rush of sensation was welcome, a reminder that she was real, nothing like the creature who'd sat across from them in that room full of silence. "If she could do that, her courtiers wouldn't be so healthy. Lijuan has always first played in her own territory."

"Like with the reborn." She shivered again, slipped her hand under his shirt to touch the uncompromising masculine heat of his skin. "That vampire—he smelled of sunshine and paint. He was new . . . fresh."

"He thinks he's been given a second chance," Raphael said, remembering the loyalty in that dark gaze as it had swung to Lijuan.

"When do they start to rot?" she forced herself to ask.

"Jason is almost here." He could sense his spymaster getting ever closer. "He'll have the most recent information—but from what we know, it depends not only on the amount of power she expends, but on what she feeds them."

"Flesh," she whispered. "Human?"

"Or vampire. It seems to have little significance." There'd been no reports of angels being sacrificed for Lijuan's pets, but Raphael wouldn't put that depravity past the oldest of the archangels.

Elena's head lifted up at that instant. "Storms," she whispered. "Jason smells of the wildest of rainstorms, lightning and fire."

"Has the new aspect of your ability stabilized?"

"No." Her eyes followed Jason's descent from the sky, though the black-winged angel was but a shadow. "It switches on and off. Mostly off." She pressed her lips to Raphael's jaw. "But you, you've always been the rain, the wind, inside my mind. I taste you when I sleep, when I wake, when I breathe."

If Jason hadn't landed then, Raphael would have drawn Elena inside, taken his fill of her own unique scent. As it was, he ran his hand to close over her nape, brushing his mouth over the sweet curve of her ear. *I will taste you tonight, Elena. Be ready for me—I won't stop until you scream your pleasure.*

He heard her heart hitch, her breath catch. But his hunter had never yet backed down from a challenge. *Anytime, angel boy.*

34

"Sire." Jason folded his wings behind him and waited for permission to speak.

Raising his head, Raphael nodded in greeting. "Come, we'll talk inside." Lijuan's strange sense of honor would ensure their living space was free of spies—real and technological. She'd consider it beyond the pale to intrude upon her guests' privacy.

Inside, Elena leaned up against the dresser as Raphael and Jason stood in front of it. The angel's tattoo was almost totally re-inked, a piece of living art that covered the left-hand side of a face and spoke of ancestry from lands far distant from one another. The story of Jason's parents was considered one of the great angelic romances. And for a while, it had been.

"Were your men able to discover anything else?" he asked his spymaster.

"Whatever it is that she kept in that room in her stronghold," the black-winged angel told him, his voice crystal clear, perfectly pitched, "it has been shifted here."

"One of the reborn?"

"Yes, but a special one—extreme care has been taken to protect it on the way here." That perfect pitch altered just enough to telegraph Jason's revulsion. "There are reports of young women missing along the caravan route."

"She's feeding her reborn with the living?" Killing humans was no taboo, but for this, in this way . . . it might disgust even Charisemnon.

"We haven't been able to find any remains to confirm," Jason said. "But the disappearances match the caravan route—and had they wanted the dead, bodies had recently been interred in all the villages."

"Lijuan is considered a goddess," Raphael said, remembering another time, another angel turned god. "The villagers would've raised no complaint."

"No." Jason's jet-black hair, unbound, caught the light as he bent his head, took a deep breath. "That isn't the worst of it."

"There's more?" Elena's voice was openly shocked.

Jason raised his head. "There are rumors, strong rumors, that those mortals in her inner court who weren't chosen to be Made . . ."

"Dear God," Elena whispered. "They're asking to be reborn?"

"It seems they are being seduced by the newer reborn," Jason confirmed. "The ones who're being kept long-term in a physical state akin to life by being fed flesh."

"The young or the old?" Raphael asked.

"Older—but I don't think that'll last." Jason shook his head.

"Why?" Elena looked at Raphael, her eyes uncomprehending. "They must know or guess that they'll likely have much shorter lifespans than if they'd allowed nature to take its course."

Jason answered before Raphael could. "It's the promise of immortality, the hope that Lijuan will find a way to keep them alive for eternity. Some would give up everything for that."

Elena heard something in that statement, an undercurrent that held a wealth of meaning. She looked at the angel who was always a shadow, his exotically handsome face inscrutable, his wings a sooty charcoal that let him blend seamlessly into the night. "For the promise?" She shook her head. "I just can't understand when the reality is that they'd become less than slaves."

"You've never chased immortality," Raphael answered. "You don't comprehend the hunger of those that do."

That made her pause. "Maybe I do," she said, and wished she didn't. "My brother-in-law loves my sister . . . but he didn't wait for her to be accepted as a Candidate. He wanted to live forever more than he wanted my sister beside him." And now Beth would grow old while Harry remained forever young.

Harry had vowed to stay beside Beth, and for some reason, Elena believed him. But she wondered if *Beth* would accept his devotion. Would her sister's love survive the knowledge that she'd been second best to immortality, that one day she'd die, leaving Harry to meet someone else, love someone else?

Her gaze locked with Raphael's, her heart a painful fist in her chest. Because she, too, would have to watch her sister die.

I won't apologize, Elena. It would be a lie—I couldn't let you leave me.

The raw honesty of the answer, of the emotion behind it, rocked her. *I forget, and then I remember and it hurts all the more.*

Beth will turn to dust when her time comes, but she'll die knowing her children will be watched over by an angel.

She gave a jerky nod, met Jason's gaze, realizing for the first time that his eyes were black, so black it was almost impossible to distinguish pupil from iris. "Will the courtiers turn against Lijuan if we prove to them that there's no immortality in being reborn?"

Jason's wings rustled as he resettled them, but even here,

in this room full of light, he'd managed to find a shadow, until she had to concentrate to see their outline. "We may turn a few, but most are too used to seeing her as their goddess. They'll follow blindly where she leads."

Giving Lijuan an endless supply of bodies for her army of the dead.

35

Elena lay in Raphael's arms, her body exhausted in the most sexual of ways. The archangel had kept his promise. He'd made her scream. Her heart was still thumping with the echo of searing pleasure when she fell into the warm darkness of a peaceful sleep. So peaceful that it took her a while to understand what it was she was hearing.

Drip.
Drip.
Drip.

"Come here, little hunter, taste." A finger pressing to her mouth.

She clamped her lips tight, but the taste, it seeped inside anyway, an insidious, unspeakable thing. No! Her mind refused to realize what it was, refused to understand.

But the monster wouldn't let her escape. "Isn't Belle delicious?" His eyes were darkest brown, ringed with a thin circle of bloodred. "I saved some for you. Here." Hands brushing away her sister's golden blonde hair from her neck, revealing the raw meat that was her throat. "I think it might still be warm." His face nuzzling into Belle's neck, his hand on breasts that had just begun to bud.

The scream tore out of her. "No!" She was on him, fists and hands like claws, teeth and kicks and fury.

But even a hunter-born wasn't as strong as a vampire full grown. A vampire glutted with blood. He played with her, made her believe she'd hurt him. And when her guard was down, when she was gasping from the fight . . . he kissed her.

Elena woke choking.

Black spots hazed her vision, threatening to tip her into unconsciousness until the scent of the rain, of the sea, infiltrated her mind. Fresh and wild and far from the horror she could feel in her mouth, it wrenched her out of the loop of nightmare and had her sucking in air as she turned desperately into Raphael's arms.

They locked around her, an absolute, unbreakable haven. "Shh, I have you."

"Oh God, oh God, oh God."

Raphael held Elena tight, so tight he had to be putting bruises on her. But still she trembled, her words garbled, her fear so thick he could taste it. "Elena." He kept saying her name, kept brushing his mind across hers until she seemed to see him, to know him. Continuing to hold her, he swept his hand down her wings over and over, soothing her, reminding her that she was here, with him, not locked in a past she couldn't escape.

He kept his own anger, his rage, contained behind iron shields. Archangels could do many things, but not even he could turn back the clock and erase the evil that had ravaged Elena before she'd had a chance to grow.

"He fed me Belle's blood." It was a husky whisper, as if her throat was torn from screaming.

"Tell me."

"My sister's blood. He kissed me, feeding me Belle's blood." Rage and horror and a bewildered kind of pain. "I tried to spit it out but he covered my mouth, my nose, and I drank it. Oh God, I drank it."

Sensing the hysteria beginning to retake hold of her, he tugged her head from his chest, taking her mouth in a kiss that was pure, untrammeled demand. She froze for a fractured instant before her hands thrust into his hair, before her body twisted until she slid beneath him, her legs wrapping around his waist.

There was a wild kind of desperation in her kiss, a kiss flavored with the salt of her tears. She wanted to forget. He'd do anything in his power to help her find what peace she could. He took her as hard as she wanted, pinning her wrists to the sheets with one hand, shoving her thigh aside with the other, and sliding into her welcoming sheath in a single thrust.

Her scream echoed into his mouth. He kissed her through the taking, through the raw, almost painful emotion of their joining. He kissed her until she gasped for breath, until her eyes went blank with pleasure, with passion, with ecstasy. And then he kissed her as she came down from the peak.

"Again," he whispered into her mouth.

She met him stroke for stroke, her hips rising in welcome, in demand. Tugging her hands free, she held him to her, trailing her mouth over his cheek, his jaw, his neck. At the end, she buried her head in his neck and simply held on . . . let him hold her, let him protect her.

It was her trust that brought him to his knees, that shoved him over the edge and into her arms.

"Thank you." Elena refused to let Raphael move off her body, her lips brushing his ear as she spoke, the dark silk of his hair cool against her flesh. "Thank you."

"I would take your nightmares, Elena."

"I know." And that he hadn't forced them from her when she could feel the savage need he had to wipe away her pain, it made her heart expand impossibly more. "But they're a part of the package."

She hadn't voiced the question, but he knew.

"It's a package that belongs to me." No hesitation, no sense of him pulling away.

"I'm so messed up. Doesn't that bother you?"

"You have lived." Untangling his arms, he used them to brace himself above her, his forearms forming a bracket around her head. "As have I. Would you throw me back?"

The idea of losing him was a violent pain in her heart. "I told you—you're mine. No getting away now."

Lips on her own, a slow, so slow, kiss that curled her toes, made the nightmare seem a lifetime away. Her breasts rubbed against his chest as she drew in deep, trembling breaths. "Something in this place . . ." Shaking her head, she pushed damp strands of hair off her face. "The death, all this death. It's fertile ground for my imagination."

"You don't believe it was a true memory?"

"I don't want it to be." A whisper, because deep inside she knew it wasn't just a figment of her mind. "If it's true . . ." Her eyes burned. "He came for me and he left a piece of himself inside me."

"No." Raphael forced her to meet his gaze, the cobalt having overtaken his irises until it was all that remained. "If he made you drink your sister's blood"—he spoke through the cry she couldn't hold back—"then you carry a piece of her."

"How is that any better? I can taste her." Her hand went to her own throat. "It was thick, rich, full of *life*." The horror of it was a noose around her neck.

"Even my mother," Raphael said, one hand cupping her face, "no matter what she became at the end, never blamed me for that which couldn't be changed. Your sister, I think, was a far gentler creature—one who loved you."

"Yes. Belle loved me." She needed to say that, to hear it out loud. "She used to tell me all the time. She would've never called me a monster." It had been her father who'd done that.

"I will not have a child of mine become an abomination!" Hands shaking her, shaking her so hard she couldn't speak. "Don't ever bring up that scent nonsense again. Understood?"

"Tell me something about your mother," she blurted out, her soul too brittle to handle the memories of the night her father had first hurt her with his words.

It had been a month after they buried her mother. Awash in a black wall of anguish, she'd brought up something she hadn't even whispered about for three long years. Her hunter sense had been the only constant in her life by then, and she'd thought Jeffrey would understand her need to cling to it. But his anger that night . . . "Something good," she added. "Tell me a good memory about your mother."

"Caliane had a voice like the heavens," he said. "Not even Jason can sing as beautifully as my mother."

"Jason—he sings?"

"His is perhaps the most magnificent voice in all angel-kind, but he has not sung for centuries." He shook his head when she glanced up. "Those are his secrets, Elena. They're not mine to tell."

It was easy to accept that—she understood about loyalty, about friendship. "Did he learn from your mother?"

"No. Caliane was long gone by the time Jason was born." He dropped his forehead to hers, their breaths mingling in the most tender of intimacies. "She used to sing to me when I was but a babe, a child who could barely walk. And her songs would bring the Refuge to a standstill as every heart ached, every soul soared. They all listened . . . but it was me she sang to.

"I was," he said, falling into memory, "so proud to know that I had that right, the right to her song. Not even my father fought me for it." Nadiel had already been losing pieces of himself by then, but there were a few joyful memories of the time before the madness stole him from Raphael, from his mate. "He used to say that my mother's song was so beautiful because it was formed of the purest love—the kind of love only a mother can feel for her child."

"I wish I could've heard her."

"One day," he said, "when our minds are able to truly merge, when you're old enough to hold your own, I will share

my memories of her song." They were his most precious treasures, the biggest gift he had to give.

Her eyes shone even in the darkness, and he knew his
hunter understood. *One day.*

They stayed that way, entangled in each other for the rest
of the night. She turned to him more than once, and he will-
ingly gave her the oblivion she sought.

The next morning found Elena glancing again and again
at the angel who walked beside her, half certain he couldn't be
real. His hair was the color of the mist, of the blinding heart
of the sun. It was the most fair blond hair she'd ever seen,
whiter than her own. If she had to, she'd label it white-gold,
but even that spoke of color. This angel's hair had no color but
it shimmered in the sunlight, as if each strand was coated with
crushed diamonds.

His skin matched the hair. Pale, so, so pale—but with a
golden sheen that turned him from stone to a living, breathing man. Alabaster touched with sunshine, she thought, that
might possibly describe the color of his skin.

Then there were the eyes.

A black pupil, shattered outward in spikes of crystalline
green and blue. You could look endlessly into those eyes and
see nothing but your own image reflected back at you a thousand times over. They were beyond clear, beyond translucent,
and yet they were impenetrable.

His wings were white. Absolute and with the same diamond shine as his hair. They glittered in the bright winter
sunlight, until she almost wanted to look away. He should
have been beautiful. And he was. An astonishing being, one
who would never in a thousand years pass for human. But
there was something so remote about him that it felt akin to
admiring a statue or a great work of art.

As it was, this angel was the last member of Raphael's
Seven. His name was Aodhan, and he wore two swords side
by side in a vertical sheath on his back, their hilts unadorned

except for a symbol similar to a Gaelic knot, but unique in a subtle fashion. She'd have asked him about it, but he spoke so rarely, she hadn't yet learned the timbre of his voice. His silence felt strange after Illium's humor, Venom's barbs, even Dmitri's sensual taunts. But it did allow her to focus uninterrupted on their surroundings.

Her eye fell on a particular carving at the bottom of a small flight of steps. Walking down, she found herself on the same level as the main courtyard, a winter-bare tree to her left, the carved panel to her right. Ignoring the courtiers who were pretending to ignore *her*, she turned her attention to the carving.

One touch and she knew it was old. She'd always been able to estimate the age of things, especially buildings. And this panel was at least a few centuries old. It had been carved with painstaking care, the scene one of a day in court life. Lijuan sat on a throne, while below her, courtiers danced and acrobats played. Nothing extraordinary . . . and yet. She frowned, examined it again.

There.

"It's Uram." It shouldn't have been a shock to find an image of the dead archangel, but— "I never saw him this way." So compelling, his presence darkly beautiful beside Lijuan's elegance. "All I saw was the monster he became."

It surprised her when Aodhan spoke, his voice holding the music of a land of green hills and faerie mounds. "He was a monster even then."

"Yes," she said, knowing such depravity couldn't have come into being overnight. "He just hid it better I suppose."

She was about to head down a narrow pathway when her instincts jerked awake. Shifting on her heel, she saw an angel walking toward her. His eyes were amber, his wings the same shade, his skin darker than Naasir's.

She'd never met him, but she knew him. *Nazarach.*

Ashwini's voice had been full of whispered horror when she'd spoken of him.

"The screams in that place, Ellie." A shiver, rich brown

eyes darkening to black. "He enjoys pain, enjoys it more than anyone I've ever met."

"Raphael's hunter." The angel inclined his head in a slight nod.

"Elena." She slid her hand into a pocket, closed it around the gun. The short sword she and Galen had decided on as best fitting her style hung from her waist, along her right thigh. But even Galen had agreed it was to be a last choice weapon—she simply wasn't fast enough to take on most other angels.

"I am Nazarach." Those distinctive amber eyes went to Aodhan. "I haven't seen you in public for decades."

Aodhan didn't reply, but Nazarach didn't seem to need one, his attention returning to Elena. "I look forward to dancing with you, Elena."

Elena was very sure she wanted those hands nowhere near her. She might not have been born with the extra senses that haunted Ashwini, but the way Nazarach looked at her . . . as if he was imagining her scream. "Sorry, but Raphael's claimed them all."

A smile that made her female instincts scream in warning. "I'm not one to give up so easily."

"Then I guess I'll see you tonight."

"Yes." His eyes flicked to their right. "I must speak to my men."

Glancing at Aodhan after Nazarach walked off, she realized the angel's spine was rigid. "Are you alright?"

He gave her a look of surprise. Then, a slight inclination of his head.

Figuring Nazarach was enough to give even one of the Seven the creeps, she pointed to a narrow passageway that would take them away from Nazarach's current position. "Let's go this way."

Aodhan followed her without a word, their wings touching as they turned. "Sorry," she said, stepping away in a quick movement.

A jerky nod, his wings held tight to his back.

It looked like Aodhan *really* didn't like having his wings

touched. His wings . . . or anything else. She belatedly realized he'd made no contact with anyone in the time since Raphael had introduced him to her. Making a mental note to keep her distance, she blinked as her eyes adjusted to the brighter light on the other side of the passageway.

They'd exited into a small, empty square surrounded by intricately painted wooden walls, each panel showcasing a scene from outside the Forbidden City, from farmers in their fields, to young girls running through a market, to an old man sitting in the sun. There was peace here, a number of small evergreen trees placed strategically to create a soothing mix of shade and sunlight. Color dappled the paving stones and when she glanced up to find the source, her eye was caught by the bubbled glass of an old stained glass window.

Pretty. And distracting.

That was why it took her a fraction too long to realize the scents she was picking up were too close, that the small object she glimpsed buried in the trunk of a nearby tree was a Guild dagger . . . and that the sound she barely caught was that of a crossbow being cocked.

36

"Get down!" she screamed even as the bolts fired.

Not one. *Two* crossbows.

Aodhan moved to protect her, and that was his mistake. He took a bolt through his wing, the force of it pinning him to the wall even as she went facedown on the paving stones, feeling a bolt pass overhead. Raising her head, she saw Aodhan reach over to pull the projectile out of his wing. Another bolt pinned his opposite shoulder to the wall before he could succeed.

Rolling sideways—something it had been damn difficult to re-teach herself now that she had wings—she got herself into the shadow of one of the trees not far from Aodhan. Her first instinct was to go for the gun, but the bullets were meant to shred angelic wings. She didn't know what effect they'd have on vamps, but if they worked like normal bullets, there was a slight chance she'd hit a vulnerable spot, killing their attackers—and they needed them alive to get to the bottom of this.

Having made up her mind, she dropped the knives in her

arm sheaths down into her palms, ignored the bolts thudding into the trunk at her back . . . and focused.

Everything went still, until it was as if the world was moving in slow motion, the sun's haze a blinding mist. Once again, she heard the crossbow being pulled back, the bolt being notched into place. But hearing had never been her primary sense.

Elderberries with sugar.

Taking aim, she threw.

The stained glass shattered, littering the ground in a thousand fractures of color. Her second knife was already traveling—to hit the vampire behind the glass in the neck. She saw the blood geyser up, but her attention was on tracking the second shooter. He remained in position, hidden behind a small, solid wall. Safe. But also unable to shoot without exposing himself.

Scrambling up from her hiding position, she ran to Aodhan, ripping out the bolt in his wing while he took care of the one in his shoulder. "Behind the wa—" Her head jerked up as the scent of elderberries began to move. An instant later, it was joined by a rich burst of bitter coffee.

Swearing, she dropped the blood-slick bolt and ran for the stairs cut into one side of the square, cursing the fact that she couldn't manage a vertical takeoff. Aodhan rose into the air behind her, the draft of his ascent hitting her in the back as she reached the upper-level pavilion the vampires had used as their hide. The scent of coffee was thick, the elderberries stained with blood.

They'd gone down the steps on the other side.

Walking backward, she took a running start, and was airborne. Exhilaration burst into life inside her, a rush that accompanied each and every fight. Fighting the urge to simply follow the air currents, she looked down. From above, the Forbidden City was even bigger than it appeared from the ground, a sprawling warren of upper and lower courtyards connected by delicate bridges, and lanes that split off in several different directions—leading to elegantly shaped buildings and the privacy of closed doors.

Aodhan, bleeding from the shoulder, one of his wings damaged but still functional, met her above the main courtyard. "They lost themselves in the courtiers below."

"Guess it's time to go hunting. Cover me." Narrowing her senses, she decided to focus on the one who'd been injured. He'd be slower, easier to run to ground.

Scents swirled like a thousand strands of color.

Violets. Lush. Sweet. Intoxicating.

Wood. Freshly cut.

Rain on a sunny day. Bright. New.

Tangled sheets and champagne. Heavy. Feminine.

Elderberries dripping darkest red.

The thrill of the hunt in her blood, she swooped to the area where she'd tracked the elderberries. It was almost too easy. Dressed in a coat of peacock blue, the vampire stood with a group of others of his kind, a silk scarf knotted around his neck. The scarf was wet, drenched with the pulse of his life's fluid.

She was about to point him out to Aodhan when the vampire jerked and fell to the ground, his body twisting as if in the throes of a grand mal seizure. Cries of dismay, the other courtiers scattering like the butterflies they were. Landing on the ground beside the vampire's jerking body, she rolled him to the side, conscious of the blood foaming around his mouth. "Keep his jaw open!" she said to Aodhan as he landed. "If he chokes on his own tongue—"

The body went silent under her hands.

Vampires could survive a lot, but she knew this one was dead, a tool that had become a liability. "What a fucking waste." He was so young. Likely not even a decade into his vampirism. Going by his face, he'd been Made in his late twenties. "Some kind of immortality."

Aodhan's eyes were glacial when he looked up. "Track the other. I'll be right behind you."

"We need the body."

A curt nod.

Elena stood, gun in hand, angling her head into the wind. The scents had changed now, become charged with fear and a nauseating undertone of arousal. Violence as a drug— it seemed to be an inevitable side effect of immortality for some. Shaking off the extraneous thought, she began to walk through the square, tracking the second shooter on the ground.

He'd gone a fair distance, crossing the entire length of the courtyard, down a long, winding passageway filled with carvings that exited into a sunny plaza, up a flight of stairs and across three curved bridges, then down into what was obviously a very private section of the city. No lanterns swung from the sole tree she could see. No beautifully clad women peered flirtatiously from behind deftly lowered fans. No music played.

Instead, there was only an angel sitting on a marble bench beneath that tree with its winter-green leaves, a vampire at her feet. Elena didn't see it coming. One moment the vampire was kneeling, his chest heaving. And the next, his head rolled to a stop at Elena's feet, having been cut off with ruthless ease.

"Stupid," Anoushka murmured, putting the wickedly curved blade on the bench beside her and brushing at her flowing white skirt as if unaware of the blood that spotted it, covering the tiny mirrors worked into the embroidery. "Leading you straight to me."

Elena couldn't ignore the head touching her foot, strands of hair drifting across the black leather of her boot. She saw Anoushka's lips tilt upward as she took a step to the side. "You won't have many men left if you kill so indiscriminately," Elena said, gauging if she could shoot and hit Anoushka's wing, given the way the other angel was sitting.

Conclusion: Uncertain.

Running wasn't an option either. Not unless she wanted a blade buried in her back.

"If you're waiting for the broken one," Anoushka said, "he's been detained. Unfortunately, before he could call for reinforcements." The angel rose to her feet. "Do you hear that?"

It was eerie, how silence could weigh so much. "Why target me?"

"You know already, but you're trying to stall me. Shall I humor you?" Anoushka kept her wings tight to her back as she picked up her weapon, continuing to deprive Elena of a clear target. Hitting an angel in the body with a bullet, even one of Vivek's special bullets, was a no go—you might as well be defending yourself with a flyswatter. Only the wings were vulnerable.

Her eyes went to the knife. She recognized it from her weapons class at Guild Academy. It was called a *kukri*, the curved blade consisting of a single sharp edge. Perfect if you were looking for something with which to efficiently separate a head from its body.

Anoushka's next words proved as much. "It's really very practical—walking into the Cadre's current meeting with your head as my trophy will, as the humans say, make a splash no one will be able to ignore. I planned to do it at the ball itself, but one must adapt." A sigh. "It's a pity we have so little time. I actually might have liked you had things been different." The *kukri* turned into a blur in her hand.

And Elena realized the Princess knew exactly what she was doing with that blade.

She didn't hesitate, firing her gun at Anoushka the instant the angel moved, her wings spreading just a fraction. But Neha's daughter, moving with that reptilian speed, snapped her wings to her back before the bullet reached her. It lodged harmlessly in the opposite wall in a shower of plaster. *Fuck!* Elena shot again, had the satisfaction of seeing blood bloom on Anoushka's leg, but the angel ignored that, reaching for what Elena had taken to be a belt.

It wasn't.

The whip wrapped around Elena's wrist with the quickness of a snake's tongue, threatening to snap her bones. Shooting as she fell, she managed to distract Anoushka enough to pull her hand free. But the gun was out of bullets, and, as Galen had once warned her, she didn't have the luxury of reloading, not with an opponent who needed a scant instant to kill.

Dropping the useless metal, she rolled to her feet, a knife falling into her hand.

"So," Anoushka said, the top of her left wing bearing a burn mark that had her hissing in pain. "That ruffian Raphael insists on keeping in his Seven managed to teach you something after all."

"I'm hunter-born," she said, shifting to keep Anoushka off balance as the angel played with the blade in her hand.

Anoushka moved with her, sinuous, graceful.

Recalling Venom's little trick, she kept her own gaze slightly to the left. Anoushka laughed. "Oh, you *are* smart. Such a shame you were too young to save your family."

Elena jerked as if kicked, her guard dropping for a fragment of a second. Anoushka struck, slicing deep into Elena's arm before she managed to get out of the way. Ignoring the burn, ignoring the heart-pain caused by the angel's words, Elena caught a second knife in her free hand. "To the death, then?"

"Did you really think otherwise?" Anoushka swept out with the *kukri*, her movements blindingly fast.

Elena threw both knives, heard Anoushka deflect one with the blade as she twisted out of the way of the other. And still the angel managed to cut a line into Elena's unmarked arm.

The bitch was playing with her.

It was, Elena realized, Anoushka's sole weakness. That and an ego that made her believe herself fit to be an archangel. "They say your blood is poison."

"Thomas drank from me before he went to scare you." A piece of swift bladework that had Elena falling to the earth, only just managing to roll out of the way before Anoushka sliced off a piece of her wing. "Impressive." A mocking bow, as if they were sparring in the most civilized of fashions.

She could feel the blood loss from the deep cuts on her arms beginning to have an effect. Not disabling. Not yet. But it was going to slow her down soon. "Thomas's death was a delayed response to the poison?"

"He thought he'd been honored above all others, allowed to sip from my veins."

"So he was dead no matter what happened, even if he didn't find me?"

"He was getting a little too possessive, the sweet dear." A sigh. "Such fools are men. Even Raphael—he should've killed you the first time he met you. Now you are his weakness."

Elena saw something in Anoushka's expression change at that instant, and knew death was looking her in the face. She threw a blade. It went harmlessly to the ground as Anoushka moved . . . but that move put her in direct sunlight, blinding her for a split second. Elena's next two knives slammed home in her eye sockets, driving her backward.

Anoushka screamed, dropped the *kukri*. Ignoring it, Elena retrieved the short sword hanging from her belt and—without giving herself a chance to think—slammed the blade down into the angel's heart, pinning her to the earth. Blood bloomed across the white of Anoushka's top as Elena opened up her mind and screamed. *Raphael!* She didn't care who the fuck else heard her, as long as he did.

Hissing in open fury, Anoushka ripped the knives from her eyes, throwing them to the side. As she jerked upward, in spite of the blade that anchored her to the earth, her nails clawed, Elena remembered that Anoushka was her mother's daughter. Moving out of the way in the nick of time, she twisted the blade while it remained in the angel's body. Anoushka's scream was a thin, bloodcurdling cry as she fell back to the ground, her poisonous fingers dropping to flutter on the paving stones. Fighting the nausea in her stomach, Elena twisted the blade again, turning Anoushka's heart into so much mush.

It would regenerate, but right now, Anoushka lay twitching on the ground, her mutilated eyes bleeding red on her cheeks.

Her mother's eyes, so beautiful, so like her own, sightless and distorted, the veins scarlet against the white.

Elena wrenched herself out of the memory, fighting the abyss that threatened to suck her in, leave her helpless.

"I'm not strong enough. Forgive me, my babies."

Elena had tried not to hear those whispered words. She'd been half asleep that night, Beth still so small, tucked in beside her. Her baby sister had always been afraid of her new room in the Big House. But she'd slept soundlessly that night, as if sure Elena would keep her safe. Only Elena had heard their mother enter their bedroom, only Elena had tried not to understand.

Elena.

She shuddered at the scent of the wind, of the rain. Relief made her careless, her body completely unprotected as Anoushka rose in a screaming rush, kicking Elena to the stones and clawing out with her hand.

Agony blazed down Elena's thigh. She fell to the ground, hearing Anoushka's body hit the stone wall with an audible snap at almost the same instant. Raphael touched her thigh a moment later . . . and she realized she couldn't feel anything in that leg.

"Raphael," she whispered, panicked. The numbness was spreading, crawling up her body, making her heart shudder.

His wings covered her from view as he leaned close. "A bare scratch."

She knew it had been more than that. She'd felt her flesh being gouged out, but she understood the message. Nodding, she bit her lower lip and tried to stay calm. When she glanced down, she saw his hands on either side of the wound. They were glowing blue.

Fear rose, but she knew that couldn't be angelfire. It wasn't hurting her. In fact, she could feel a soft warmth at the site. As she watched, her eyes wide, an umber-colored liquid seeped out of the wound to discolor the paving stones. "Dear God." It was an almost soundless whisper. The stuff was eroding the stone.

"You're fine, Elena. It was simple shock." *Betray no weakness.*

Elena let him pull her to her feet, sliding her foot over the discolored part of the paving as she did so. As Raphael folded away his wings, she realized two things. One, both the claw marks and the cuts on her arms had stopped bleeding, and two, the entire Cadre had come with Raphael. Neha knelt by her daughter's slumped body, the sword flung aside, a spray of red marking its path on the stones. Her daughter's blood was scarlet against the archangel's dusky skin, her eyes ice when she glanced back. "She will die."

Elena didn't think Neha was talking about Anoushka.

37

Raphael's face was expressionless. "Elena isn't the one who orchestrated the brutalization of a child."

Someone sucked in a breath and Elena realized it was Michaela, the female archangel's body angled toward Anoushka though she stood to Raphael's left.

"Lies," Anoushka said, her breath coming easier as her body healed. "The hunter sought to make her name by killing an angel."

It just came out. "I helped kill an archangel. I have no need to prove myself."

Neha rose, her movement as sinuous, as silky as that of the pythons she kept as pets. "Give me your mind."

Elena was suddenly drowning in the scent of rain, of the sea, as Raphael lifted a hand filled with angelfire. "No one will touch Elena. It's Anoushka's mind you should search."

There was a blur of movement overhead and then Aodhan was landing beside Elena, though, given his angle of descent, it would have been far easier for him to land between Michaela and Raphael. The angel was covered in so much blood, it had turned his diamond-bright wings to rust. But that wasn't what chilled the whole courtyard to silence. Aodhan had a vampire in his arms. That vampire was missing all his limbs. But he was still alive.

Elena fought not to show her horror. The last time she'd seen a vampire in that condition, the man had been a victim, tortured for days by a hate group.

"Sire." Aodhan placed his burden on the stones. "I was detained by Anoushka's Master of the Guard. His mind holds the truth."

From the look on Anoushka's face, there was no denying the vampire's identity. Elena saw it only because she was looking directly at the Princess—a spark of pain, of loss. The angel actually felt something for this vampire. But not enough. Rising, she picked up the *kukri* in one of those reptilian snaps of movement, and threw it at the vampire's neck.

Raphael caught it by the blade, his blood dripping onto the vampire's ravaged chest. "Favashi, Titus, take his mind."

The quiet Persian archangel closed her eyes. The big, black archangel did the same. It took less than a second.

"Guilty," Favashi whispered, speaking to Neha. "Even if Astaad forgives the murder of his concubine, even if Titus forgives the killing of the female from his lands, even if Raphael forgives the torture of his man, the attempt on his mate's life, you cannot save her."

"She broke our supreme law." Titus's voice was incongruously soft for such a big man, the slabs of muscle on his chest gleaming around the steel gray of his breastplate.

"The abuse of a child," Astaad murmured in an almost academic tone, stroking two fingers over his small, neat black beard, "may be the only true remaining taboo we have. Cross that line, and we may as well surrender to the darkness that stalks us all."

"The boy isn't dead," Neha responded.

"Murder or vicious assault, the penalty is the same—and the child was so close to death as to make little difference." An archangel with iron in his voice and eyes of golden brown.

Elijah. "The worst is that she didn't do it alone. She taught others to savor the pain of an innocent."

"She planned to take other angelic children once she became Cadre," Favashi said, her tone sorrowful but unbending, "to rule her angels by keeping their young hostage."

"Witnessed." Titus's soft voice.

"Even I," Lijuan murmured, a hint of surprise in her tone, "did not go that far." Her eyes almost disappeared in daylight. "What have you birthed, Neha?"

What happened next was a blur. Michaela moved her hand in a brutally hard gesture. It took a second for Anoushka's head to fall off her body, her blood fountaining in an arterial spray. Wet hit Elena's face, her clothes, but she forced herself to stand her ground as Neha rose with a scream, her nails elongating and turning black even as Michaela continued to make those lethal slashing motions.

Sweet mercy. Anoushka was being cut apart piece by piece.

Moving at a speed no mortal would ever reach, Neha clawed Michaela's face, leaving a spread of black. Michaela slammed her hand to Neha's chest, shoving her back. The black marks on her face turned a noxious, putrid green. . . . then drew back, as if the poison was being rejected. By the time Neha got to her feet, Michaela's face was whole again, the poison dripping to scar the square-cut pavings of the courtyard.

Neha twisted toward her daughter, anguish in her eyes. "She's old enough to—"

Angelfire, cold and blue, engulfed what remained of Anoushka. Elena stared at the hard line of Raphael's face, without mercy, an archangel passing judgment. It shook her to the core, the speed of the execution, but she didn't disagree with it—the image of Sam's crumpled and bloody body would be with her forever.

Neha's scream rent the air, so piercing it was something *other*, something beyond comprehension. The Queen of Snakes, of Poisons, went to her knees in the courtyard, tearing at her hair with the clawed tips of her hands. Raphael stepped

back and met Elena's gaze. It was time to go. They left on foot,
all of them, even Lijuan. A silent show of respect.

No one spoke even when they reached the blinding light
of the main courtyard. It was empty, the first time Elena
had seen it that way in all her time here. Shadows blotted
out the sunlight an instant later, a heavy cloudbank rolling
in from the east. Looking up, she felt a chill crawl down
her spine.

It wasn't over.

Elena entered their rooms behind Raphael, with Aodhan
bringing up the rear. Jason had made a rare daylight appearance to take Anoushka's Master of the Guard to healers, leaving Aodhan free to return with them. "Sire," the angel said
after they were behind the closed doors. "I'm injured." It was
a calm statement.

Elena watched as he peeled off his bloody shirt to reveal
a gash so deep he'd been all but been cut in half. "Jesus. How
the hell did you fly to us?"

Aodhan didn't reply, speaking to Raphael as he came to
stand in front of him. "I may be a little slow tonight."

"Stay," Raphael said, raising his hand, that warm blue fire
ringing his palm.

Aodhan's face showed emotion for the first time. Panic,
rage, fear, it was a twisting viciousness in his eyes. But he
stood in place, let Raphael touch him, his flinch not noticeable
unless you were looking very carefully. Raphael removed his
hand a few moments later. The gash no longer looked as raw,
as red.

Relief flooded Aodhan's expression but Elena wasn't sure
it had anything to do with the fact that his wound was well on
the way to being healed. She didn't speak until after he'd left
to return to his own room. "He doesn't like being touched."

"No," Raphael confirmed, pulling off his own shirt and
wiping his bloody hands on it.

Wondering what—or *who*—could have damaged an immortal so much that he flinched from even the most casual of touches, Elena began to remove what weapons she had left. "Good thing I brought spares." Checking her thigh, she saw that while the wound was still pink, it didn't need a dressing. "Shower?"

"Yes."

It wasn't until they'd both showered and were sinking into the wet heat of a desperately needed bath that she said, "You're the reason Sam is recovering faster than anyone expected." Her heart overflowed with a fierce kind of pride.

"I've evolved," he said, his eyes holding an almost lost look. Blue fire ringed the hand he lifted out of the water. "The gift is new, weak—I couldn't heal Sam fully, though I returned many times."

"But you sped up the process." Moving to cup his face in her hands, she touched her forehead to his. "The scales are balanced, Raphael."

"No," he said. "They will never be balanced. I must never forget what I became in the Quiet."

She thought of the swiftness of the justice meted out tonight, thought too of the thin line between power and cruelty, and knew he was right. "Well, one thing's for sure—if you hadn't been there tonight, I'd be dead."

His eyes turned that forever, endless blue that made it seem as if she was falling into another universe. "You must never let Neha touch you," he said, gripping her nape, pulling her even closer. "I was only able to stop Anoushka's poison because it was on the surface. Neha's is a thousand times more venomous."

She didn't resist his touch, sensing a fear the archangel would never admit aloud. It did something to her to know that her life mattered that much to him. Part of her, a part that was still that scared young teenager standing on the doorstep to the Big House, was so afraid that he'd tire of her, that her love wouldn't be enough.

"So many nightmares," he whispered, stroking his hand up her back as she straddled him.

"She left me," Elena whispered. "She loved me, but she left me."

"I'll never leave you, Elena." A glimpse of the archangel he was, used to power, to control. "And I'll never let you go."

Other women might've rebelled against such a claim, but Elena had never belonged to anyone. Now she did, and the knowledge began to fix something broken inside of her. "Two-way street, Archangel," she reminded him.

"I think I enjoy being claimed by a hunter." Hands on her hips, strong, demanding. "Come, take me inside. Make us one."

The words were gentle, the hard thrust of his cock anything but. Spreading her hands on his shoulders, she slid down the dark heat of him, shuddering as her flesh stretched to accommodate that unforgiving length. "Raphael." Whispered against his mouth as her body closed around him.

He gasped, dropping his head for an instant. His lips brushed the pulse in her neck and she felt teeth. A bite. Not gentle. A hiss of air escaped her as he licked over the small hurt, as he moved his mouth up her neck, across her jaw. *You didn't call me when Anoushka attacked.*

She weaved her fingers through his hair, biting at his lower lip when he lifted his head. *I called you when I needed you.*

A frozen moment, their eyes locked into each other.

It felt as if he was looking through her heart, through her soul, through to the very core of who she was. But she saw him, too, this magnificent being full of power and secrets so deep and old, she wondered that she'd ever learn them all.

The kiss stole her breath, her thoughts, her everything. Moaning, she ran her fingers over the arch of his wings, felt him grow impossibly harder inside her. It was almost too much. She rose, her body releasing his with tortuous slowness, his mouth taking hers until she was a creature of the flesh, her senses awash in pleasure.

Tightening his grip on her waist, he pulled her back down. She went, needing the intimate friction, the earthy pleasure. *"Raphael."* He broke the kiss to move one hand up to cup her breast, running his thumb over the part of her nipple that peeked above the waterline.

There was something unbelievably erotic about watching him touch her, his eyes a brand, his fingers so long and sure. Clenching her own hand on the slope of his wing, she moved impatiently against him. His head jerked up, eyes glittering like gemstones. The hand on her back shifted, fingers stroking the oh-so-sensitive inner curve of her wings.

"Stop that," she said against his lips, unable to halt the slow, hot caress of her flesh on his, a tight release and sheathing that made her heart thunder.

So sensitive, hbeebti.

She didn't understand it, and yet she did. He'd said something beautiful to her in a language that she only ever heard in hazy dreams now, a language that—no matter the associated memories of pain and loss—had always meant love.

Taking his hand, she brought it to her lips. The kiss she pressed to his palm was soft, his response a blaze of cobalt. And then there were no more words. Only pleasure. Searing, bone-deep pleasure. She broke apart, held in the arms of an archangel who would never let her fall.

"Mama?" Why was her mother's high-heeled shoe lying on the tile of the foyer? Where was the other one? Mama hadn't worn high heels for . . . a long time. She'd probably just gotten sick of it and kicked it off. Yeah, that must be it. But if she'd started to wear them again . . . maybe things would get better, maybe she'd smile and it would be real.

Her chest hurt with a painful kind of hope.

Stepping inside the cool wealth of the Big House, the house that had turned her daddy into a man she didn't know, she went to reach for the shoe lying abandoned on its side. That was when she saw the shadow. So thin, swinging so gently.

She knew.

She knew.

She didn't want to know.

*Her heart a savage knot of barbed wire, she looked up.
"Mama." She didn't scream. Because she knew.*

*The sound of tires on gravel, Beth being driven home
from elementary school. Elena dropped her bag and ran. She
knew. But Beth must never know. Beth must never see. Grabbing her sister's small body in her arms, she pushed past the
man who'd once been her father and out into the bright sunshine of a cloudless summer day.*

And wished she didn't know.

Elena dressed with quiet determination the night of the
ball. But the past, it lay like a thick black blanket over her,
heavy, suffocating. She wanted to claw at her neck, to gasp in
desperately needed air, but that would betray weakness. And
here, any weakness would be blood to the sharks that circled
below the music that permeated the city.

Turning, she spied the sweep of blue the tailor had designed
for the ball. It was a dress. But it was a dress for a warrior.
Already wearing panties and the spike-heeled black boots that
came up to her thighs, her weapons strapped to her body, she
picked up the dress, the fabric like water against her fingertips.

"You tempt a man into mortal sin."

She sucked in a breath as she saw her archangel, his chest
bare, his legs clad in formal black pants. "Look who's talking." He was beauty cut by time, a lethal blade honed through
the ages.

Lifting the dress, she stepped into it. The material slid
against her legs as she drew it up, the top half pooling at her
hips. Raphael prowled to her, his eyes skating over the naked
flesh of her breasts. Possession glittered in those eyes, and
that was all the warning she got before the storm of his kiss,
the touch of his fingers . . . the angel dust that filtered into her
very pores.

She held the kiss when he would have broken it. "Not yet."
Then she took her archangel, drinking in the taste of him until
it suffused her veins, infiltrated her cells.

"You," Raphael said against her mouth when she finally set him free, "will kiss me like that tonight."

It was an order she could live with. "Deal."

Stroking both hands down over her breasts, Raphael lifted the two pieces of fabric that made up the top to her shoulders—after crisscrossing them below the neck—and began to tie a knot at her nape.

"I guess," she said, licking her lips, feeling her thighs clench, "I don't need makeup now." Angel dust shimmered like diamonds on her skin.

Placing one hand on the naked plane of her stomach after ensuring the knot was secure, Raphael pressed a kiss to her nape, bared since she'd put her hair up in a tight bun. She'd considered spearing that knot with chopsticks, but her hair was too slippery to hold the ornamentation. Instead, she'd tucked in a small hairpin detailed with the image of a wildflower.

Simple. Perfectly adapted. Hard to kill.

It had been a gift from Sara, tucked beside the ring Elena had asked her best friend to order. The amber had come from a dealer who'd owed Elena a favor, the specific piece one she'd seen in his private collection. Balli had paid up the favor because it had been a matter of honor, but she knew it had to have hurt. Of course, once he saw where his amber had gone . . . The thought of his round face wreathed in smiles made her heart lighten.

Raphael played his fingers over her abdomen, his ring catching the light. "Your injuries?"

"Nothing to worry about." Her thigh ached enough to remind her of Anoushka's attack, but the cuts on her arms had scabbed over.

"Can you move?"

She spun out, reaching for the blades hidden in the butter-soft black leather arm sheaths she was wearing openly tonight, protocol be damned. The skirts of the dress parted like liquid, as if attuned to her every move. She lobbed a knife toward the archangel who watched her.

Catching it with lethal ease, he threw it back. She tucked it into the arm sheath, before testing how difficult it would be to get to the gun strapped to her left thigh. Not hard at all. "No problems."

As she rose, the dress fell seamlessly around her body, all the slits elegantly concealed. "What are the chances I won't need to use my weapons tonight?"

Raphael's answer was terrifying in its starkness. "Lijuan's reborn walk the halls."

38

The ball was held outdoors in a massive courtyard framed by low buildings full of light, food, and musicians, the hypnotic strains of the *ehru* lingering in the air. Looking around, Elena couldn't do anything but admire the stunning simplicity of it all—the thin, rectangular paving stones beneath the revelers' feet had been washed until they gleamed a creamy white, the entire area lit with delicate lanterns in a thousand different hues, their light reflecting off the star-studded night sky.

Cherry blossom trees in full bloom—*impossible*—spread their lush pink arms over the courtiers, their limbs twined with lights that twinkled like diamonds. Elena picked a single perfect blossom from her hair. "I can feel the truth whispering beneath," she said, scenting the barest hint of rot, of death, "but on the surface, it's magical."

"A queen keeps a court that is spoken about. A goddess keeps a court that is never forgotten."

Wings filled her vision as angel after angel flew down for a graceful landing, all of them dressed in clothing that accentuated loveliness beyond mortal ken. Even the vampires, their own faces a study in the most sensual symmetry, stood enthralled. The few mortals who'd been invited or brought as dates fought not to stare, but it was a losing battle.

Elena might have had the same reaction—had she not been standing next to the most compelling man in the room. Raphael had chosen to wear black tonight, the severe color throwing his eyes into vivid focus. He was at once a being of unearthly beauty and a warrior king who wouldn't hesitate to spill blood.

"I didn't expect her to attend."

Following his gaze, she saw Neha, a queen dressed in a silk sari of unembellished white, her hair pulled off her face in an austere bun. Those dark eyes burned with hatred as she stared at Michaela.

Michaela appeared unconcerned, her body caressed by an exquisite ankle-length gown in the colors of sunset, her fingers curled around Dahariel's forearm. The male angel wasn't smiling, his expression as detached as that of the predator brought to mind by his wings. But there was no mistaking the sexual heat between the two.

Elena looked away, her eyes colliding with Neha's as the Archangel of India glimpsed her and Raphael. Elena froze at the contact. What lived in Neha was older than civilization, a cold, cold creature without soul or sentience. She watched, her blood turning to ice as Neha began to move toward them with jerky footsteps quite unlike her usual sensual grace.

Wings rustled as Aodhan and Jason emerged out of the night to flank them.

Neha ignored everyone but Raphael. "I will forgive you, Raphael." Flat, toneless words. "Anoushka broke our greatest law. For that, she died."

Raphael stayed silent as Neha turned and left without another word, heading toward a circle of vampires with brown eyes and skin that spoke of an ancient land of heat and a sleek, hidden violence, much like the tigers that prowled its forests.

"How much," Elena said, withdrawing her hand from its

position over the butt of her gun, "of that did she actually mean?"

"None and all." *Neha will act as an archangel, but hate is a poison in her soul.*

Releasing the breath she hadn't been aware of holding, Elena let her gaze drift forward, to the steps that led up to what was, without question, a throne. Lijuan sat on a masterfully carved chair of what was almost certainly ivory. Three men stood beside her—Xi, with his wings of red on gray; a Chinese vampire with a flawless face; and the reborn who'd served Elena and Raphael that first night. But he was no longer the sole one of his kind.

They stood on the edges of the crowd, a silent army with eyes that tracked all movement. There was an odd sheen to their gaze, a hunger that made her instincts rise in warning. Flesh, she thought, remembering the report she'd read sitting in Jessamy's sunny classroom, they lived on flesh. "Her reborn surround us," she said, wondering how the other guests couldn't smell the rot, the musty smell of a grave desecrated.

Raphael didn't shift his gaze off Lijuan, but his words told her he was conscious of everything around them. "An angel without wings is a creature maimed, prey brought to ground."

She took a deep breath, mind awash with the images of that sunset in the wildflower garden, Illium's sword a silver blur as he amputated the wings of Michaela's guard. It was instinct to tighten her own wings even further before turning her attention toward the throne once more.

To find Lijuan looking straight at her.

Even from this far away, Elena felt the bone-crushing impact of that gaze. She wasn't surprised when the archangel rose, and the gathering fell silent.

"Tonight," Lijuan said, her voice carrying effortlessly on the eerily warm air currents, "we celebrate a new beginning for our race, the Making of an angel."

Heads turned, following Lijuan's gaze, until Elena felt the weight of stares from every side. Some were curious, some angry, others malevolent. And one . . . Her nape prickled. *Evil.* It stroked over her, a malignant kiss she wanted to reject with every breath in her. But she stayed silent, unmoving. Let them think her unaware, let them believe her an easy target.

"Elena," Lijuan continued, beginning to move down the steps and toward them, "is a unique creation, an immortal with a mortal heart." The crowd parted in front of her, watching her progress . . . except for an awestruck human/vampire couple who didn't get out of the way fast enough. "Adrian." It was less than a whisper.

The reborn male—the one with skin that spoke of the savannah—tore out the human woman's heart, sinking his fangs into her neck at almost the same instant to tear open her jugular. She was still standing when Adrian reached over to rip out the male's throat, wrenching the vampire's body apart with his hands until the unfortunate male was nothing but a pile of discarded meat. The dead human female lay beside the lumps of flesh, steam rising from the viscera as Adrian— hesitating for a second, as if tempted to lick up the blood that had soaked into his skin—took out a handkerchief and began to wipe off the mess.

Moving past the butchered couple as if nothing had happened, Lijuan came to stand in front of Elena. "That mortal heart, some would say, is a weakness that will steal the gift Raphael has given you."

"Better a mortal heart," Elena said in a quiet voice, "than a heart that feels nothing at all."

A smile, almost girlish, and all the more terrible for it. "Well said, Elena. Well said." A single clap of her hands, an unspoken command. "To mark this occasion, this meeting between the ancient and the barely born, I'd like to present you with a remembrance—a gift from the old to the new, one so special, so unique, that I have kept it hidden even from my own court."

The pain caused by Lijuan's last gift was still a burn on her soul, but Elena steeled her spine, held her place, knowing this was a test she had to pass—or she'd be discounted for the rest of her existence as nothing but Raphael's once-mortal toy.

"Phillip." A glance at the Chinese vampire with that heart-breakingly beautiful face.

Phillip melted away into the crowd.

"It will be but a moment." Lijuan turned her attention to Raphael. "How is Keir? I haven't seen him in centuries."

It was an attempt at small talk but it fell oddly flat, as if Lijuan was putting on a mask that didn't quite fit. Elena heard Raphael respond, but her eyes were locked on the shadows where Phillip had disappeared, her heart pounding one sluggish beat at a time as a single drop of sweat rolled down her back.

The evil whispered nearer with every beat that passed, until she could almost taste it on her tongue.

Dirt, that sweet rot that accompanied all of the reborn.

A spice for which she had no name, a hint of ginger, warm golden sunlight.

She knew what the horror would be before Phillip reappeared with a handsome mahogany-haired man who'd been blessed with eyes of darkest brown, eyes that invited a woman into temptation. He'd been a movie star before being Made. Young girls had put posters of him on their bedroom walls, giggled as they whispered his name.

His eyes locked with hers.

"Come here, little hunter. Taste."

The words were a husky whisper inside her head, a thousand screams rolled into one. She knew Lijuan was speaking to her, but all she heard was that singsong voice that had haunted her for almost two decades.

"Run, run, run." A giggling parody of Ari's dying attempt to help Elena. "She won't run. She likes it, you see."

Elena felt the nightmare spiraling out beneath her, a bottomless pit from which she might never escape. It sucked at her, tinged with the laughter in the monster's eyes, the nauseating joy in his expression—*as if they were bound, as if he had a claim on her.* She felt her legs begin to tremble, her

heart jerk as she found herself back on that floor, scrabbling
back on bloody tiles with hands that kept slipping, kept holding her prisoner. It was wet, cold, but Ari's eyes—

A rush of rain in her head, untainted and strong, a scent
that thundered of the sea, of the wind. *Elena, I stand with
you.*

It was a sudden, sharp realization flavored with the relentless strength of the tide—she wasn't alone in that room. Not
anymore. Buoyed by that truth, she stepped back from the
abyss, walked into the present, and saw the repugnance that
was Slater Patalis standing beside Lijuan.

The vee of his shirt revealed smooth, unblemished skin,
free of the ugly scar created by the *Y* incision cut into his flesh
during the autopsy performed by a Guild pathologist. Elena
had watched the video over and over, until she'd convinced
herself that he was dead. It had been too little justice for what
he'd stolen from her, but it *had* been justice. Lijuan had no
right to erase that, no right to use Belle's and Ari's deaths as
part of a game that would hold Lijuan's interest for no more
than a flicker of time.

Her entire body filled with anger, clean and bright. It sang
with a kind of purity she'd never before known. *The monster
was smiling while her sisters lay dead in their graves, while
her mother's body hung forever in the wall of her mind, creating a shadow she'd never forget.*

Her spine turned to iron forged in the fires of grief. "Aodhan," she said, knowing Lijuan wouldn't guess her intent—
wouldn't imagine she'd dare, "would you mind kneeling for
a second?"

The angel went down in a graceful kneeling position an
instant later, his head bowed . . . to allow her to reach the
swords that lay flush against the center of his back. Sliding
one lethally sharp blade from its sheath, she sliced off Slater
Patalis's grinning head with a single clean stroke, her strength
fueled by decades-old anguish.

Blood fountained in an arterial spray that wet her face,
turned the cherry blossoms black, but she was already shov-

ing the blade into his heart and twisting it into so much pulp.
His twitching body fell to the ground with a thud as she removed the red-slick blade. "Will she be able to make him rise
from this?" she asked Raphael, her voice without inflection,
without mercy. Slater didn't deserve her emotions, didn't deserve anything but the cold hand of a long-delayed justice.

"Perhaps." Blue fire ringed Raphael's hand. "But this
should ensure a permanent death."

A dark gray ash replaced what had remained of the worst
killer vampire in living memory.

The entire thing had only taken a few seconds. Still holding the sword, she met Lijuan's eyes. "My apologies," she said
through the heavy blanket of silence, "but the gift wasn't to
my taste."

The Chinese archangel's hair whipped back in that ghostly
breeze as she walked to stand opposite Elena, the ashes of
Slater's body between them. "You cut my amusement short."

"If death is truly the only thing that amuses you any
longer"—Raphael's knife-edged voice—"perhaps it's time
you stopped interfering in the world of the living."

Lijuan met his eyes, her own so pale that there were no
irises, no pupils, just an endless spread of pearlescent white.
"No, it is not my time to Sleep." Raising a hand, she ran the
back of it along the face of the dark-skinned reborn who'd
come to stand beside her. "Adrian is not ready to die, either."

Power filled the air, until the electricity of it sparked along
Elena's skin. She felt Raphael begin to glow, heard Aodhan
rise, unsheathe his remaining sword as Jason moved out of
the shadows, and she knew this battle might end them all.
Death will be an easy price to pay to stop her, she thought
to Raphael.

So brave, my hunter. It was a kiss.

As she handed his sword back to Aodhan, taking out the
gun that wouldn't stop a vampire, but might just slow down
an archangel if only for a fraction of an instant, she saw a
flare of power on Raphael's right, a power she'd tasted before.
Michaela. Standing beside Raphael.

Another flare of power. Then another, and another, and another.

Elijah, Titus, Charisemnon, Favashi, Astaad.

Whatever drove the other archangels to unite against Lijuan, their combined power was a blast of heat, one that would have shoved her out of the circle had she not been pinioned between Raphael and Aodhan.

A cool, cool wind. Power, such *power*. All of it touched with death.

Lijuan laughed. "So, you would all stand against me." Amusement in every syllable. "You cannot imagine what I am."

Lijuan's power was cold, frigid against the heat of the others. Raphael had been right, Elena realized with horror, the oldest of the archangels might just have become the truest of immortals, going beyond the hand of death. It was as that thought passed through her head that her eyes met Adrian's.

Liquid dark, those eyes were so calm, so patient, and . . . so full of pain. He knew, she thought, he understood now what he was. Yet in spite of it all, his devotion burned a steady flame, until it hurt to witness it. As she watched, he shifted behind Lijuan, lifting her hair away from her neck. The archangel seemed not to notice—or maybe it was that he was so much her creature, she simply accepted him.

So when Adrian bent his head and placed his mouth on Lijuan's skin, Elena thought it only a macabre kiss, a prayer to his goddess. Then she glimpsed the single, bright tear sliding down Adrian's midnight skin—he loved Lijuan, she thought with an ache in her own heart, but trapped inside the silent shell that had been the Chinese archangel's gift to him, he also saw her for the horror she was. Lijuan began to bleed before that tear reached his jaw, two thin trails of red snaking down her body to sink into the diaphanous fabric of her gown, a stark wash of color in the white heat of power.

Lijuan staggered. "Adrian?" She sounded almost mortal in her surprise. "What are you doing?"

"He's killing you," Raphael said. "You've created your own death."

Lijuan shoved with a single hand. Adrian's body flew to hit Favashi, taking them both down. The Persian archangel rose to her feet after bare seconds, but the reborn stayed down.

"I *am* death," Lijuan said, her voice regaining its strength even as blood continued to seep into her gown. "You have no claim to this land. Leave and I will spare you."

Elijah shook his head. "Your reborn are infectious."

Elena followed his gaze, her own widening in horror as she realized the human female Adrian had killed was now struggling to get to her feet, her fingers scrabbling on the tiles as the people around her watched in disbelief.

Dear God.

39

"I will not allow the plague to spread to my lands." Neha, Lijuan's closest neighbor, stepped into the circle at last, her rage finding a target.

Lijuan whipped out a hand and every single archangel in the circle began to bleed from cuts on their faces, their chests. "Perhaps it's time the world had only one archangel."

Elena wondered if anyone realized that Lijuan herself was still bleeding. And that her blood was turning dark, almost black. Elena's eyes went to Adrian's lifeless body. A vampire was Made by being pumped full of a toxin noxious to angels. In the normal scheme of things, that toxin turned human into vampire, then became harmless to all. But— *What happens to the toxin if a vampire is brought back from the dead? If he is reborn?*

Raphael's wing brushed hers in silent acknowledgement. *It seems the toxin, too, was reborn. And it was reborn in a stronger, more deadly form.*

Will it kill her?

No. But it may make her easier to defeat. A touch against

her mind. *You won't survive this fight. Get out of the blast zone and take the others with you.*

Elena's heart threatened to break. *You die, I'll make her bring you back.*

You would not do that to me, Elena. A brush of the sea, of the wind, across her senses. *But I have no intention of dying— we have not yet danced as angels dance.*

Then he was gone from her mind. Blinking back her worry, her pain, she jerked her head at Aodhan, ready to do what her archangel had asked of her. Working with Jason and incredibly, Nazarach and Dahariel, they managed to light a fire under the courtiers. Most left. The reborn lingered.

"Kill them," Elena ordered, slamming her pity into a dark corner. "If she thinks enough to call them . . ."

"She could disable Raphael and the rest of the Cadre." Jason looked at the gun in her hand. "The quickest method is beheading." He slid out a gleaming black sword from a sheath she hadn't seen until that moment, hidden as it was in the curve of his back. "Take out their hearts, Elena. We'll do the rest, ensure full death."

"Works for me." She began shooting. Turned out that the gun meant to shred angelic wings wasn't as effective as a normal gun would have been on reborn hearts—vampiric and human—but it did the job. When she ran out of bullets, she switched to knives.

The task was grim . . . and sad. Without Lijuan's active guidance, the reborn didn't know what to do. So they mostly just stood there. A few tried to run but even that was a weak effort. Elena didn't feel good about doing what she was doing, but it had to be done. Because if the reborn began to feed, if they left their victims dead, but whole, those victims would rise. And the reborn would creep a murderous tide across the world.

If even one of them realized that . . .

A pair of tired blue eyes met hers as her arm lifted. There was only gratitude in them as her knife hit home. Jason's sword cut off his head an instant later, the black blade rippling with a fire that reduced the reborn to embers in less than ten seconds. Elena stared at that blade, at the angel who seemed kin to the dark.

"It is done." Aodhan sheathed his swords, having cut those Jason hadn't burned, into several neat pieces.

Nazarach and Dahariel had used their own methods, but the end result was a courtyard empty of life but for the Cadre, and their small group.

"I believe it's time to leave." Nazarach offered her his hand. "A dance at last."

"I can fly myself out." She'd slit her own throat before going anywhere with him.

The amber-eyed angel bowed his head. "Then I hope you'll save me a dance the next time we meet." He lifted off.

Dahariel waited until Nazarach had gone to say, "If Raphael survives, tell him he can have the vampire he wished to buy into his service. The boy's too broken to be of much use to me any longer." He rose into the sky even as the last word left his lips.

"We must go," Jason said, his voice so tight, she could hardly understand him.

Elena glanced back, saw nothing but a blaze of white heat, a wall of static blocking her attempts to reach Raphael with her mind. Her heart clenched. But she left. Because her archangel had asked her to. And he'd be pissed to survive—and he *would* survive—only to find her dead. Power began to increase behind them at an exponential rate as they ran, an inferno that shoved at them with waves of searing fire.

Jason and Aodhan ran beside her as she climbed up a small flight of stairs. "It's too low!" she yelled, knowing she'd never make it up.

One hand gripped her under her left arm, the other under her right. She snapped her wings together in the nick of time. Jason and Aodhan took off even as a massive *lack of sound* filled the air—power being sucked into a vacuum before expanding outward. It threatened to crush, but somehow, the two angels managed to get airborne.

"Go!"

But Jason and Aodhan waited three more seconds before releasing her. Her wings spread instinctively, the tips curling away from the death racing toward them. Heat waves licked across the air, each more dangerous than the last. She saw vampires fall even as they ran, heard screams as human homes went up in flames, saw angels flying ever higher in an attempt to escape. But Jason and Aodhan stayed stubbornly by her side, though she was weaker, far slower.

Fire singed her nape. Glancing over her shoulder, she saw the edge of the inferno mere seconds behind them. "Drop!" she screamed. "Drop!"

The blast hit with the force of a two-ton truck, crumpling their wings and slamming them to earth like pieces of glass.

Killing Lijuan was impossible. Raphael realized that with the first wave of her power. She tasted of death and life intertwined, a being who straddled worlds.

Blood continued to streak down her shoulder, black and viscous, but still her power grew, her wings backlit by the glow until they ceased to exist. The rest of the Cadre rose with her, holding back the blinding wave that might destroy the world itself. Already, thousands had likely died. If they stopped, if they let her release the unmitigated fury of her strength, that death toll would reach millions. Billions.

But that wasn't why his fellow archangels fought. Human life meant little to most. They fought for their own lives, and because Lijuan had made a mistake. He'd felt their shock as Adrian tore apart the vampire who'd had the ill fortune to be enthralled by Lijuan. The blood, the death, was nothing new. But the control she had over her reborn, the strength of those reborn against the vampires . . . no archangel wanted to face that kind of an army. The fact that that army was a plague that held the potential to end them all was the final nail in the coffin.

I will not be contained. I cannot be contained.

Lijuan's voice in their heads, the seeming sanity of it more disturbing than Uram's viciousness had been in those last minutes above New York. Now Beijing burned below them and in that rubble lay Elena. The primal core of him raged to go to her. But he held his position. Because his warrior with her mortal heart would expect nothing less.

He felt one of the tendons in his left wing snap against the wake of a power that slapped into him over and over. Only Favashi, younger than him, was showing signs of similar damage.

"Then she will kill you. She will make you mortal."

He was weaker than he should have been, but he was also stronger. Looking up into Lijuan's face, the human mask stripped away to reveal the screaming darkness, he said, "Now," speaking to the archangels ringing Lijuan, knowing she was far beyond hearing. *Now!*

A savage cascade of power, all of it focused on one central target. Lijuan's body bowed as the power hit her, the sky turning to daylight for a single startling second. When night returned, Zhou Lijuan was simply gone, the Forbidden City nothing but a black crater, Beijing a memory in immortal and mortal minds.

The agony of the dying was drowned out only by the silence of the dead.

He found Elena buried under the wings of two of his Seven. Jason and Aodhan were unconscious, the bones in their legs twisted. But those injuries were nothing to immortals of their age. They'd survive. Elena was far, far younger.

But she had the will of a hunter-born.

He felt the stubborn flicker of her life even as he picked her crumpled body up from the hard earth where she'd been thrown. Her hands were torn open, her face bruised, but her body . . . Stroking his hand down it, he realized he felt only a few fractures. Minor. Even for such a young angel. He should have let her rest, but he couldn't bear the silence.

Elena.

Her lashes fluttered.

He couldn't hasten her healing, having burned out his power in the fight to hold Lijuan. It would take time to recover.

Hunter mine.

Pale silver eyes looking into his.

Love, he thought as he held her to his heart, was an agony beyond compare.

Epilogue

Raphael wasn't surprised to see Lijuan's image form in the clear waters of a rain-filled pool just beyond the Refuge. He knelt by its side as Elena sat swaddled in a blanket, her face uplifted to the warm rays of the rising sun. But he felt her look his way the instant Lijuan appeared, though the sending would be invisible to her.

"I live, Raphael." Lijuan's voice was a million screams and endless silence. "Are you not afraid?"

"You've evolved," he said, seeing her hand fade into mist, her face half disappear before it returned. "You no longer need the flesh. Our concerns are not yours."

A laugh, whispers, and something more, something that spoke of caresses under the cover of dark as blood flowed warm and rich. "I have killed the last of my reborn." Her form solidified, until it appeared almost normal. "Sometimes, I have need of the flesh."

"Why tell me?" he asked. "They are your weakness."

"I like you, Raphael." A smile that froze the water in the pond, her visage framed in frost. "And your hunter, yes, she intrigues me still."

He met those eyes that were beyond immortal and wondered at the truth. "Did you need to die to evolve?"

"Ask me that question when we next meet. Perhaps I will answer."

"You walk between life and death," he said. "What do you see?"

"Mysteries, answers, yesterdays, and tomorrows." An enigmatic smile. "We'll speak again. I do so like you, Raphael."

The words echoed in the air as her image faded. Rising, he took the hand Elena held out, brought her gently to her feet. Her eyes were troubled as she looked to him. "Lijuan?"

"She isn't a threat." He drew her deeper into his arms. "I think, for now, Lijuan has little interest in the concerns of the world." Her face had held an eerily childish joy in her new life, her new sphere of existence.

"That's good enough for me." A long breath, Elena's arms snaking out of the blanket to wrap around him. "I want to go home, Archangel."

Stroking his hand over the warm curve of her hip, he wondered if New York was ready for a hunter turned angel. "We leave with the next sunrise."

Turn the page for a special preview of
Nalini Singh's next book in the
Psy-Changeling series

Bonds of Justice

Coming July 2010 from Berkley Sensation!

Justice

When the Psy first chose Silence, first chose to bury their emotions and turn into ice-cold individuals who cared nothing for love or hate, they tried to isolate their race from the humans and changelings. Constant contact with the races who continued to embrace emotion made it much harder to hold onto their own conditioning.

It was a logical thought.

However it proved impossible in practice. Economics alone made isolation an unfeasible goal—Psy might have all been linked into the PsyNet, the sprawling psychic network that anchored their minds, but they were not all equal. Some were rich, some were poor, and some were just getting by.

They needed jobs, needed money, needed food. And the Psy Council, for all its brutal power, could not provide enough internal positions for millions. The Psy had to remain part of the world, a world filled with chaos on every side, bursting at the seams with the extremes of joy and sadness, fear and despair. Those Psy who fractured under the pressure were quietly "rehabilitated," their minds wiped, their personalities erased. But others thrived.

The M-Psy, gifted with the ability to look inside the body and diagnose illnesses, had never really withdrawn from the world. Their skills were prized by all three races, and they brought in a good income.

The less powerful members of the Psy populace returned to their ordinary, everyday jobs as accountants and engineers, shop owners and businessmen. Except that what they had once enjoyed, despised, or merely tolerated, they now simply *did*.

The most powerful, in contrast, *were* absorbed into the Council superstructure wherever possible. The Council did not want to chance losing its strongest.

Then there were the Js.

Telepaths born with a quirk that allowed them to slip into minds and retrieve memories, then share those memories with others, the Js had been part of the world's justice system since the world first had one. There weren't enough J-Psy to shed light on the guilt or innocence of every accused—they were brought in on only the most heinous of cases, the kinds of cases that made veteran detectives throw up and long-jaded reporters take a horrified step backward.

Realizing how advantageous it would be to have an entrée into a system that processed both humans and, at times, the secretive and pack-natured changelings as well, the Council allowed the Js to not just continue, but expand their work. Now, in the dawn of the year 2081, the Js are so much a part of the justice system that their presence raises no eyebrows, causes no ripples.

And, as for the unexpected mental consequences of long-term work as a J . . . well, the benefits outweigh the occasional murderous problem.

1

Circumstance doesn't make a man. If it did, I'd have committed my first burglary at twelve, my first robbery at fifteen, and my first murder at seventeen.

—*From the private case notes of Detective Max Shannon*

It was as she was sitting, staring into the face of a sociopath that Sophia Russo realized three irrefutable truths.

One: In all likelihood, she had less than a year left before she was sentenced to comprehensive rehabilitation. Unlike normal rehabilitation, the process wouldn't only wipe out her personality, leave her a drooling vegetable. Comprehensives had ninety-nine percent of their psychic senses fried as well. All for their own good of course.

Two: Not a single individual on this earth would remember her name after she disappeared from active duty.

Three: If she wasn't careful, she would soon end up as empty and as inhuman as the man on the other side of the table . . . because the *otherness* in her wanted to squeeze his mind until he whimpered, until he bled, until he begged for mercy.

"Evil is hard to define, but it's sitting in that room."

The echo of Detective Max Shannon's words pulled her back from the whispering temptation of the abyss. For some reason, the idea of being labeled evil by him was . . . not acceptable. He had looked at her in a different way from other human males, his eyes noting her scars, but only as part of the package that was her body. The response had been extraordinary enough to make her pause, meet his gaze, attempt to divine what he was thinking.

That had proved impossible. But she knew what Max Shannon wanted.

"Bonner alone knows where he buried the bodies—we need that information."

Shutting the door on the darkness inside of her, she opened her psychic eye and reaching out with her telepathic senses, began to walk the twisted pathways of Gerard Bonner's mind. She had touched many, many depraved minds over the course of her career, but this one was utterly and absolutely unique. Many who committed crimes of this caliber had a mental illness of some kind. She understood how to work with their sometimes disjointed and fragmented memories.

Bonner's mind, in contrast, was neat, organized, each memory in its proper place. Except those places and the memories they contained made no sense, having been filtered through the cold lens of his sociopathic desires. He saw things as he wished to see them, the reality distorted until it was impossible to pinpoint the truth among the spiderweb of lies.

Ending the telepathic sweep, she took three discreet seconds to center herself before opening her physical eyes to stare into the rich blue irises of the man the media found so compelling. According to them, he was handsome, intelligent, magnetic. What she knew for fact was that he held an MBA from a highly regarded institution and came from one of the premier human families in Boston—there was a prevailing sense of disbelief that he was also the Butcher of Newark, the moniker coined after the discovery of Carissa Starling's body, the only one of his victims to have ever been found.

"I got much more careful after that," Bonner said, wearing the faint smile that made people think they were being invited to share a secret joke. "Everyone's a little clumsy the first time."

Sophia betrayed no reaction to the fact that the human

across from her had just "read her mind," having expected the trick. According to his file, Gerard Bonner was a master manipulator, able to read body language cues and minute facial expressions to genius-level accuracy. Even Silence, it seemed, was not protection enough against his abilities—having reviewed the visual transcripts of his trial, she'd seen him do the same thing to other Psy.

"That's why we're here, Mr. Bonner," she said with a calm that was growing ever colder, ever more remote—a survival mechanism that would soon chill the few remaining splinters of her soul. "You agreed to give up the locations of your later victims' bodies in return for more privileges during your incarceration." Bonner's sentence meant he'd be spending the rest of his natural life in D2, a maximum security facility located deep in the mountainous interior of Wyoming.

"I like your eyes," Bonner said, his smile widening as he traced the network of fine lines on her face with a gaze the media had labeled "murderously sensual." "They remind me of pansies."

Sophia simply waited, letting him speak, knowing his words would be of interest to the profilers who stood in the room on the other side of the wall at her back—observing her meeting with Bonner on a large comm screen. Unusually for a human criminal, there were Psy observers in that group, Bonner's mental patterns so aberrant as to incite their interest.

But no matter the credentials of those Psy profilers, Max Shannon's conclusions were the ones that interested Sophia. The enforcement detective had no Psy abilities, and unlike the butcher sitting across from her, his body was whipcord lean. Sleek, she thought, akin to a lithely muscled puma. Yet, when it came down to it, it was the puma who'd won—both over the bulging strength that strained at Bonner's prison overalls *and* over the mental abilities of the Psy detectives who'd been enlisted into the task force once Bonner's perversions began to have a serious economic impact.

"They were my pansies, you know." A small sigh. "So

pretty, so sweet. So easily bruised. Like you." His eyes lingered on a scar that ran a ragged line over her cheekbone.

Ignoring the blatant attempt at provocation, she said, "What did you do to bruise them?" Bonner had ultimately been convicted on the basis of the evidence he'd left on the battered and broken body of his first victim. He hadn't left a trace at the scenes of the other abductions, been connected to them only by the most circumstantial of evidence—and Max Shannon's relentless persistence.

"So delicate and so damaged you are, Sophia," he murmured, moving his gaze across her cheek, down to her lips. "I've always been drawn to damaged women."

"A lie, Mr. Bonner." It was extraordinary to her that people found him handsome—when she could all but smell the rot. "Every one of your victims was remarkably beautiful."

"*Alleged* victims," he said, eyes sparkling. "I was only convicted of poor Carissa's murder. Though I'm innocent, of course."

"You agreed to cooperate," she reminded him. And she needed that cooperation to do her job. Because—"It's obvious you've learned to control your thought patterns to a certain degree." It was something the telepaths in the J-Corps had noted in a number of human sociopaths—they seemed to develop an almost Psy ability to consciously manipulate their own memories. Bonner had learned to do it well enough that she couldn't get what she needed from a surface scan—to go deeper, dig harder might cause permanent damage, erasing the very impressions she needed to access.

But, the *otherness* in her murmured, he only had to remain alive until they located his victims. After that . . .

"I'm human." Exaggerated surprise. "I'm sure they told you—my memory's not what it used to be. That's why I need a J to go in and dig up my pansies."

It was a game. She was certain he knew the exact position of each discarded body down to the last centimeter of dirt on a shallow grave. But he'd played the game well enough that the authorities had pulled her in, giving Bonner the chance to sate his urges once again. By making her go into his mind, he was attempting to violate her—the solitary way he had to hurt a woman now.

"Since it's obvious I'm ineffective," she said, rising to her feet, "I'll get Justice to send in my colleague, Bryan Ames. He's an—"

"No." The first trace of a crack in his polished veneer, covered over almost as soon as it appeared. "I'm sure you'll get what you need."

She tugged at the thin black leather-synth of her left glove, smoothing it over her wrist so it sat neatly below the cuff of her crisp white shirt. "I'm too expensive a resource to waste. My skills will be better utilized in other cases." Then she walked out, ignoring his order—and it *was* an order—that she stay.

Once out in the observation chamber, she turned to Max Shannon. "Make sure any replacements you send him are male."

A professional nod, but his hand clenched on the top of the chairback beside him, his skin having the warm golden-brown tone of someone whose ancestry appeared to be a mix of Asian and Caucasian. While the Asian side of his genetic structure had made itself known in the shape of his eyes, the Caucasian side had won in the height department—he was six feet one according to her visual estimate.

All that was fact.

But the impact was more than the sum of its parts. He had, she realized, that strange something the humans called charisma. Psy professed not to accept that such a thing existed, but they all knew it did. Even among their Silent race, there were those who could walk into a room and hold it with nothing but their presence.

As she watched, Max's tendons turned white against his skin from the force of his grip. "He got his rocks off making you trawl through his memories." He didn't say anything about her scars, but Sophia knew as well as he did that they played a large part in what made her so very attractive to Bonner.

Those scars had long ago become a part of her, a thin tracery of lines that spoke of a history, a past. Without them, she'd
have no past at all. Max Shannon, she thought, had a past as
well. But he didn't wear it on that beautiful—not handsome,
beautiful—face. "I have shields." However, those shields were
beginning to fail, an inevitable side effect of her occupation.
If she'd had the option, she wouldn't have become a J. But at
eight years of age, she'd been given a single choice—become
a J or die.

"I heard J-Psy have eidetic memories," Max said, his eyes
intent.

"Yes—but only when it comes to the images we take during the course of our work." She'd forgotten parts of her "real
life," but she'd never forget even an instant of the things she'd
seen over the years she'd spent in the Justice Corps.

Max had opened his mouth to reply when Bartholomew
Reuben, the prosecutor who'd worked side by side with him to
capture Gerard Bonner, finished his conversation with two of
the profilers and walked over. "That's a good idea about male
Js. It'll give Bonner time to stew—we can bring you in again
when he's in a more cooperative frame of mind."

Max's jaw set at a brutal angle as he responded. "He'll
draw this out as long as possible—those girls are nothing but
pawns to him."

Reuben was pulled away by another profiler before he
could reply, leaving Sophia alone with Max again. She found
herself staying in place though she should've joined those of
her race, her task complete. But being perfect hadn't kept her
safe—she'd be dead within the year, one way or another—so
why not indulge her desire for further conversation with this
human detective whose mind worked in a fashion that fascinated her? "His ego won't let him hide his secrets forever,"
she said, having dealt with that kind of a narcissistic personality before. "He wants to share his cleverness."

"And will you continue to listen if the first body he gives
up is that of Daria Xiu?" His tone was abrasive, gritty with
lack of sleep.

Daria Xiu, Sophia knew, was the reason a J had been pulled into this situation. The daughter of a powerful human businessman, she was theorized to have been Bonner's final victim. "Yes," she said, telling him one truth. "Bonner is deviant enough that our psychologists find him a worthwhile study subject." Perhaps because the kind of deviancy exhibited by the Butcher of Newark had once been exhibited by Psy in statistically high numbers . . . and was no longer being fully contained by Silence.

The Council thought the populace didn't know, and perhaps they didn't. But to Sophia, a J who'd spent her life steeped in the miasma of evil, the new shadows in the PsyNet had a texture she could almost feel—thick, oily, and beginning to riddle the fabric of the sprawling neural network with insidious efficiency.

"And you?" Max asked, watching her with a piercing focus that made her feel as if that quicksilver mind might penetrate secrets she'd kept concealed for over two decades. "What about you?"

The otherness in her stirred, wanting to give him the unvarnished, deadly truth, but that was something she could never ever share with a man who'd made Justice his life. "I'll do my job." Then she said something a perfect Psy never would have said. "We'll bring them home. No one should have to spend eternity in the cold dark."

Max watched Sophia Russo walk away with the civilian observers, unable to take his attention off her. It had been the eyes that had first slammed into him. *River's* eyes, he'd thought as she walked in, she had River's eyes. But he'd been wrong. Sophia's eyes were darker, more dramatically blue-violet, so vivid he'd almost missed the lush softness of her mouth. Except he hadn't.

And that was one hell of a kick to the teeth.

Because for all her curves and the tracery of scars that spoke of a violent past, she was Psy. Ice-cold and tied to a

Council that had far more blood on its hands than Gerard Bonner ever would. Except . . . Her final words circled in his mind.

"We'll bring them home."

It had held the weight of a vow. Or maybe that was what he'd wanted to hear.

Wrenching back his attention when she disappeared from view, he turned to Bart Reuben, the only other person who remained. "She wear the gloves all the time?" Thin black leather-synth, they'd covered everything below the cuffs of her shirt and suit jacket. It might have been because she had more serious scars on the backs of her hands—but Sophia Russo didn't strike him as the kind of woman who'd hide behind such a shield.

"Yes. Every time I've seen her." Frown lines marred the prosecutor's forehead for a second, before he seemed to shake off whatever was bothering him. "She's got an excellent record—never fumbled a retraction yet."

"We saw at the trial that Bonner's smart enough to fuck with his own memories," Max said, watching as the prisoner was led from the interrogation room. The blue-eyed butcher, the media's murderous darling, stared out at the cameras until the door closed, his smile a silent taunt. "Even if his mind wasn't twisted at the core, he knows his pharmaceuticals—could've got his hands on something, deliberately dosed himself."

"Wouldn't put it past the bastard," Bart said, the grooves around his mouth carved deep. "I'll line up a couple of male Js for Bonner's next little show."

"Xiu have that much clout?" The case of Gerard Bonner, scion of a blue-blooded Boston family and the most sadistic killer the state had seen in decades, would've qualified for a J at the trial stage but for the fact that his memories were close to impenetrable.

"Sociopaths," one J had said to Max after testifying that he couldn't retrieve anything usable from the accused's mind, "don't see the truth as others see it."

"Give me an example," Max had said, frustrated that the killer who'd snuffed out so many young lives had managed to slither through another net.

"According to the memories in Bonner's surface mind, Carissa Starling orgasmed as he stabbed her."

Shaking off that sickening evidence of Bonner's warped reality, he glanced at Bart, who'd paused to check an e-mail on his cell phone. "Xiu?" he prompted.

"Yeah, looks like he has some 'friends' in high level Psy ranks. His company does a lot of business with them." Putting away the phone, Bart began to gather up his papers. "But in this, he's just a shattered father. Daria was his only child."

"I know." The face of each and every victim was imprinted on Max's mind. Twenty-one-year old Daria's was a gap-toothed smile, masses of curly black hair, and skin the color of polished mahogany. She didn't look anything like the other victims—unlike most killers of his pathology, Bonner hadn't differentiated between white, black, Hispanic, Asian. It had only been age and a certain kind of beauty that drew him.

Which turned his thoughts back to the woman who'd stared unblinking into the face of a killer while Max forced himself to stand back, to watch. "She fits his victim profile—Ms. Russo." Sophia Russo's eyes, her scars, made her strikingly unique—a critical aspect of Bonner's pathology. He'd targeted women who would never blend into a crowd—the violence spoken of by Sophia's scars would, for him, be the icing on the cake. "Did you arrange that?" His hand tightened on a pen as he helped Bart clear the table.

"Stroke of luck." The prosecutor put the file in his briefcase. "When Bonner said he'd cooperate to a scan, we requested the closest J. Russo had just completed a job here. She's on her way to the airport now—heading to our neck of the woods as a matter of fact."

"Liberty?" Max asked, mentioning the maximum-security penitentiary located on an artificial island off the New York coast.

Bart nodded as they walked out and toward the first security door. "She's scheduled to meet a prisoner who claims another prisoner confessed to the currently unsolved mutilation murder of a high-profile victim."

Max thought of what Bonner had done to the only one of his victims they'd ever found, the bloody ruin that had been the once-gamine beauty of Carissa Starling. And he wondered what Sophia Russo saw when she closed her eyes at night.

Don't miss Nalini Singh's next
Guild Hunter Novel
Coming in 2011 from Berkley Sensation!

Book seven in the *New York Times* bestselling
Psy-Changeling series from

NALINI SINGH

Dev Santos finds a woman with amnesia—all she can
remember is that she's dangerous. Stripped of her memories by a shadowy oppressor and programmed to kill,
Katya's only hope for sanity is Dev. But how can he trust
her when he could very well be her next target?

penguin.com

It's the time of year when dreams come true,
miracles happen every day,
and love is the greatest gift of all . . .

An anthology from *New York Times* bestselling authors

NALINI SINGH
MAGGIE SHAYNE

And national bestselling authors

ERIN McCARTHY
JEAN JOHNSON

Four paranormal romances celebrating the holidays
as never before. From a shape-shifting leopardess who
wants a packmate to be her soul mate to a snowstorm
that brings a surprise gift, these tales will stir your spirit
in all the right places.

M512T0609

First in the Guild Hunters series from
New York Times bestselling author

Nalini Singh

ANGELS' BLOOD

Vampire hunter Elena Deveraux
is hired by the dangerously beautiful
archangel Raphael. But this time, it's
not a wayward vamp she has to track.
It's an archangel gone bad.

**"NALINI SINGH IS A
MAJOR NEW TALENT."**
—Christine Feehan

penguin.com

Penguin Group (USA) Online

What will you be reading tomorrow?

Tom Clancy, Patricia Cornwell, W.E.B. Griffin,
Nora Roberts, William Gibson, Robin Cook,
Brian Jacques, Catherine Coulter, Stephen King,
Dean Koontz, Ken Follett, Clive Cussler,
Eric Jerome Dickey, John Sandford,
Terry McMillan, Sue Monk Kidd, Amy Tan,
John Berendt…

You'll find them all at
penguin.com

*Read excerpts and newsletters,
find tour schedules and reading group guides,
and enter contests.*

Subscribe to Penguin Group (USA) newsletters
and get an exclusive inside look
at exciting new titles and the authors you love
long before everyone else does.

PENGUIN GROUP (USA)
us.penguingroup.com

Photo by Ashwini Singh

Nalini Singh is passionate about writing. Though she's traveled as far afield as the deserts of China and the temples of Japan, it is the journey of the imagination that fascinates her the most. She's beyond delighted to be able to follow her dream as a writer.

Nalini lives and works in beautiful New Zealand. For contact details and to find out more about the Psy-Changeling and Guild Hunter series, please visit her website at www.nalinisingh.com.

ISBN 978-0-425-23336-8

...selling author Nalini Singh
...l of angelic rulers, vampiric
...man thrust into their darkly
seductive world...

Vampire hunter Elena Deveraux wakes from a year-long coma to find
herself changed—an angel with wings the colors of midnight and dawn—
but her fragile body needs time to heal before she can take flight. Her
lover, the stunningly dangerous archangel Raphael, is used to being in
control—especially when it comes to the woman he considers his own.
But Elena has never done well with authority...

They've barely begun to understand each other when Raphael receives
an invitation to a ball from the archangel Lijuan. To refuse would be a
sign of fatal weakness, so Raphael must ready Elena for the flight to
Beijing—and to the nightmare that awaits them there. Ancient and without
conscience, Lijuan holds a power that lies with the dead. And she has
organized the most perfect and most vicious of welcomes for Elena...

Praise for *Angels' Blood*

"I loved every word, could picture every scene, and
cannot recommend this book highly enough."
—*New York Times* bestselling author Gena Showalter

"Amazing. Fantastic...Simmering with both violence
and sexual tension...that blew my socks off."
—National bestselling author Meljean Brook

ISBN 978-0-425-23336-8

www.penguin.com

$7.99 U.S.
$9.99 CAN